EVIL
IS AS
EVIL DOES

Joseph Anthony

ISBN 978-1-955156-30-1 (paperback)
ISBN 978-1-955156-31-8 (digital)

Rushmore Press LLC
1 800 460 9188
www.rushmorepress.com

Printed in the United States of America

Dedication

To Susan, My favorite muse.

CHAPTER 1

Michael Edward Woodman was a nice, decent man. He loved to be helpful and would go out of his way on a daily basis to be obliging, helpful and almost subservient to family, friends, co-workers, students and virtually everyone that he ever ran into. But then Michael would often bemoan the fact that far from receiving accolades, everyone tended to treat him like dog poop. Sadly, he had never read Molière's comment that: "The friend of all the world is not to my taste." The world did not care what Michael Edward Woodman did or didn't do and his constant efforts to try to please anyone and everyone was the recipe for disaster.

Oh don't get me wrong, Michael had his faults just like the rest of us but it was mysterious if not inconceivable to him that being nice, helpful, etc. would be an open invitation for all and sundry to take advantage of him and his good nature. The trouble with Michael was that it never occurred to him to say "no", "get lost" or even "you have to be kidding!" but that was the way he was raised. On the other hand, when he took a stand and drew the proverbial line in the sand, he tended to lose "his cool" as they say and everyone would head for the hills muttering something along the lines of, "So what set him off?" Domineering, bossy and almost congenitally lazy parents and older siblings had, as the saying goes, done a "number" on him. It was second nature to him to do almost anything in order to justify his existence and he had done so all his life

Michael's parents had emigrated to the United States shortly after he had graduated from one of the minor and anachronistically named "public schools" in England. These bastions of privilege and outstanding education were far from "public" in that they charged high fees, maintained exclusivity and had stiff entrance requirements. But, as Michael's parents said, "We'll make sure he gets a good education in England before we expose him to the uncouth and largely ineffective American system". So, after Michael had acquired a great education and an upper crust accent, the Woodman family settled in America and Michael went off to an Ivy League college. As his parents also said, "Harvard, Yale and Princeton and the rest of those places are quite good but, of course, they're not Oxford or Cambridge but they'll have to do, won't they?"

Michael Edward Woodman graduated with a decent GPA but, as someone once said, what was he going to do with a degree in Economics and Fine Arts? In a society that had no idea what the fine arts were let alone actually employed someone with that sort of education, Michael ended up as he almost always did – lost and forlorn, and with nowhere to turn. Economics should have been a good career pathway but the Enron scandal and the near-collapse of the entire Western economy because of Wall Street put paid to that possibility.

Michael parents had no idea of what he should have majored in at college and really did not care. As long as he was a Harvard man, that was all that counted. As for a career, they had no clue but they were most vocal in their comments regarding what he should have, could have or might have done in his life to date. But rather than actually encourage him, it was easier, and probably safer, for them to tell him what he could not do or was incapable of doing. Thus, with most careers that might have opened up for a man of Michael's intelligence, medicine, the law, science, engineering, dentistry, veterinary science and virtually every other avenue with a clear career pathway was shut down for him before he had even set foot at Harvard.

Throughout most of his working career at a medium-sized University in Western Pennsylvania, Michael had a safe and secure job and slowly but surely worked his way up the ladder. The trouble he faced, however, was that he was a sort-of scientist with an uncommon skill-set that made him valuable to the Department in the small college that employed his talents. He did quite well at first;

he had been promoted and made a progressively increasing salary but, to his chagrin and bemusement, somehow or other he was always passed-over for the accolades, recognition and general praise that were showered on his cohorts. He did achieve tenure as an associate professor but stopped there on the academic ladder, never becoming a full professor. Departmental chairman, deanship and every other senior administrative position was as likely for him as scaling Mount Everest unaided on a Sunday afternoon in the dead of winter.

As he grew older and retirement was starting to loom on the horizon, it became obvious that to him that the Department had hung an invisible but still tangible sign that stated, "And here is Michael Edward Woodman…now, moving right along, let's go meet…."

Michael's wife, Linda, alternated between commiseration and downright condemnation of her husband and her attitude had rubbed off on their two children. Consequently, the Woodman' offspring barely acknowledged that their father was the household bread winner and that he was the sole source of the generous allowances they spent so freely. If dad/hubby wanted to talk about something at the dinner table or discuss something with friends, Linda, Damon and Rebecca made it clear that not only were they not interested in anything that Michael had to say but, in their opinion, nothing he said was worth listening to anyway. If they had guests at dinner and Michael started to say something, mother and two children pointedly looked away and made it manifestly obvious to all and sundry that he was incapable of saying anything significant or noteworthy that deserved any sort of attention from them. After this happened a few times, friends and colleagues avoided the Woodman' household and not only refused to join them even for hot dogs or hamburgers in the backyard, they avoided him at work too.

Michael soldiered on, dogged as ever, but life was miserable for him, and he knew it. As Linda was wont to say, "Michael, you went to a good private school in England, graduated Magna cum Laude from an Ivy League College and you are still a lowly and poorly paid associate professor in a minor college in the middle of nowhere! What's wrong with you? Can't you cut it? You know, do what you're supposed to do and do it well? Or is it because you have that funny

British accent and they don't like you, is that it? I'll bet it's because you upset someone and that settled it for your career, didn't it?"

"But Linda, my dear, I am reasonably well-paid, have a safe and secure job and I actually like what I do. What difference does it make that I was born and raised in England? I'm an American citizen now and it shouldn't make any difference."

"So what?" she would snap, "It does make a difference. Lots of people started at that college of yours and some of them even in the same department at the same time you did but they have all shot up the ladder, but not you. Those people are far less educated and are nowhere near intelligent as you but you…you're still slaving away in the trenches. Besides that, who in their right minds would want to stay in this rinky-dink town. It sucks. Someone with your education should be in a far more prestigious place than here."

"Prejudice is everywhere, so why should it be any different for me? Besides, you're from here yourself."

"Oh you make me sick. You put up with everything and, frankly, I'm sick of not hearing an American accent in this house, that's what. Even Rebecca and Damon sound like you although, heaven knows, I can't understand why because they never talk to you. Must be in the genes because they didn't learn to speak that way from talking to you."

"I'm sorry to hear that."

"Oh shut up…just shut up. I'm going out…and you can get your own supper and feed the kids. I've had enough."

Linda, as she often did, stormed out to leave a stunned and saddened Michael staring at the door that slammed behind her. Miserable, Michael wondered whether this was what life was all about? Would anything ever change? Was this how the rest of his life was to be lived out? Shrugging, he got to his feet and headed towards the kitchen to see about dinner for himself and the brats, as he thought of them but never said out loud. Just then, there was a clatter of feet coming downstairs and Rebecca stopped on the bottom step and stared at him before saying, "So, you're making dinner, are you? Did you piss mom off again and did she storm off, just like she always does?"

Michael stared back at his daughter, silently waiting for the first jibe which he knew would be coming from his 14-year old going on 30 daughter.

"Well, I don't want whatever it is that you're thinking of cooking. I'm going to go over to Sarah's house where I'll get something decent to eat…and the company's better too." With a contemptuous twitch of nose, Rebecca headed out the door, slamming it behind her just like her mother had a few minutes earlier.

Almost on cue, Damion appeared from his bedroom upstairs, looked around and saw that it was just him and his father in the house. "So they've gone out, have they? Well, I might as well join them…no point in hanging around here. If anyone wants me, I'll be at Mark's house although I doubt that anyone here cares."

He sauntered out the door with all the insouciance of a 16 year old youth with raging hormones, an acne-covered face and an attitude that barely fit into their home.

Michael shrugged yet again and started to rummage in the freezer. Perhaps there was a TV dinner or pizza lurking somewhere amidst the detritus of meals-past that Linda had frozen on the off-chance that they would eat them sometime or other. As he dug deeper into the depths of the freezer drawer, Michael saw the mass of frost and freezer burn that surrounded each and every bag dumped in there. As his depression deepened, Michael suddenly spotted a solitary frozen chicken pot-pie carton that looked to be edible. Success! He pulled it out, brushed off the hoar frost coating the container and was astonished to see that it was still in date…at least he would not get food poisoning from eating it although he wondered whether anyone would care if he did. Looking at the ingredients on the package, he wondered whether his cardiac system would survive the salt content let alone the strangely arcane ingredients listed in small print.

As he sat at the kitchen table slowly chumping down on the microwaved pot-pie, he understood how that singular item had managed to avoid being eaten by anyone else. It was truly dreadful and he could feel his blood pressure starting to rise and his arteries clogging with each and every mouthful. Idly, he picked up the container and looked again at the ingredients listed on the outside and wondered how commercial foodstuffs could contain such a disparate list of chemicals and still be considered food. Out loud, he muttered, "They talk about the hazards of cholesterol from dairy products but I still have more faith in Mother Nature than I do in DuPont or Dow Chemical!" and then laughed. It was really quite comical. Here he was, slaving away and trying to provide for his family and then they had all abandoned him, as they did on a distressingly regular basis. Shades of working at College, "Leave him be," they would often say and that is exactly what everyone seemed to do. He wondered why that was the case.

Wryly he thought about the new Dean's attempts to modernize the faculty by forcing attendance at sensitivity-training seminars. The seminars were always presented by young graduates barely out of MBA programs and knowing nothing about the real world other than the management theories propounded in the assigned texts by faculty who likewise had never worked in a real job. Sensitivity training? What a hoot. Most University administrators had elevated insensitivity to an art form, had had minimal teaching experience or real world experience and yet they felt the need to educate their highly experienced faculty in the art of effective communication.

Then Michael stopped. Did anyone actually listen to what he was saying in his lectures? Did anyone care what he said? A few former students would stop by his office when visiting their alma mater and mutter that they wished they had paid closer attention to what he had said because they now realized that what they had blown off was actually important. Realization that his instruction would help their careers had come late but these grateful individuals were few and far between. The rest did not care and never would.

Yet Michael cared. He kept plugging away, doing his best but was it enough? A few cynical colleagues over the years had told him just to do his job. "Let's face it Mike, your best is never good enough, so why bother?" Shrugging off his irritation at the bastardization of his name, Michael thought about what others had said over and over again throughout the years. Had he wasted his time? Should he get out now? Get out while he could? Linda, Damon and Rebecca could care less about him...he stopped and smiled. "Could care less?" What a dreadful expression. Surely "could not care less" was the grammatically correct expression not that pathetic approach to cuteness practiced by the younger generation and which was actually an oxymoron.

Suddenly deciding, Michael jumped to his feet. He swept the remains of his dinner into the trash can. He walked purposefully upstairs and pulled a couple of pieces of luggage out of the storage room. Throwing a few items of clothing and a few essentials like his razor and deodorant into them, he wheeled the bags downstairs and stood looking around his home. With a silent nod of farewell, he opened the front door and wheeled the suitcases to his car and loaded them into the trunk. He looked back at the house, smiled and said quietly, "Well, you've all done what you set out to do. I'm out of here. No more nagging by a dissatisfied wife, no more bratty, disrespectful and obnoxious kids and goodbye to that miserable college that I hate and which, in turn, apparently hates me".

Starting the car, he backed out of the driveway and put the car into drive. As he pressed down on the accelerator and drove off, a tremendous sense of well-being, if not happiness, swept through him. He was headed towards freedom...not freedom to sin, as the bible so quaintly put it, but freedom to do what he could to right the woes of the world. Freedom to help others, people who were truly deserving and really wanted to make a difference in their own lives and in the lives of others.

Just before heading out of town, Michael stopped at an ATM and withdrew as much cash as he could. Climbing back into the car, he snapped the seatbelt in place and accelerated away from his old life. Where was he going? What was he going to do? He didn't know and certainly didn't care. For a moment he thought about how people who committed suicide apparently had the attitude that their actions would "show them", the ones they left behind. But Michael didn't care. He didn't care whether he had "showed" his wife and children anything. He was gone...goodbye!

CHAPTER 2

Michael sat in his car and watched the man swagger out of the bar. What was it about the man that he disliked so much? He was noisy, belligerent, uncouth, slightly drunk and simply spoiling for a fight but he was no different from most of the other men in the bar. In fact, despite small variations in their features, they all looked like cooker-cutter replicas of some quasi-Neanderthal species brought back from a bygone age. Amused, Michael watched as the man fumbled for his keys, struggled for a few moments and then eventually got the key in the door lock before opening the car door and levering himself inside. The engine whirled for a second or two and then fired, finally settling down and ticking over noisily but steadily.

The man slid the car in gear and started to pull out of the parking slot when he sensed that all was not well. Cursing, the man shut down the engine and climbed back out of the car, slamming the door shut. He walked around the car and spotted the two flat tires on the passenger side. This time his curses were not muffled by being inside the car and he gave vent to his anger at the top of his voice. "What the fuck happened here?" he asked the moon, barely peeking out from behind the clouds. "Which motherfucker did this to my car? I'll kill him when I find out, that's what." He kicked one tire and then gave it a second kick. "How am I going to get this fixed at this time of night, that's what I'd like to know?" He gave a third and final kick at the tire and slowly walked back to the bar, fumbling for his cell phone before realizing he'd left it in the car. Retracing his steps, he opened the car door, leaned inside and grabbed for the phone. He had it in hand and was pulling back out of the car when he felt the sickening blow of something very hard and wielded with great force hitting the trapezius muscle running from his neck towards the shoulder, paralyzing his right arm. "What the fuck?" he shouted and tried to turn his head to see what had happened when another blow hit the other side of his neck so that both arms were effectively paralyzed. "What..." but said nothing more as a thick plastic bag was slipped over his head and tightened with a nylon cord. His eyes bulged as the air inside the bag was quickly exhausted and his efforts to tear the bag became weaker and more futile. It was over in a few more seconds and all movement of his limbs stopped.

Michael looked down at the man, nodded in satisfaction and then slid the body fully into the car before softly closing the door. As he walked away, he felt both a sudden release and a surge of happiness. This time things had gone very well, far better than in the small town a hundred or so miles away and in a different state. How had he picked his victim? It had been quite simple really. He had parked over near the trees in one corner of the bar's parking lot and simply watched and waited. Then the man had pulled into the parking lot, spewing gravel as he roared in and spun the car around, taking up two spaces. After the man had got out and locked the car door, he had sauntered over to the bar, idly kicking the sides of one or two cars on the way, obviously taking satisfaction from scratching up the paintwork.

After he was safely inside the building, Michael quietly climbed out of his car and, with box cutter in hand, he walked over to the offside of the man's car and slashed the tires. Then he walked slowly back to his own vehicle and waited. A thermos of strong black coffee, a bottle to pee in and patience served him well, as did the intermittent moonlight, the fact that the bar had not been busy that night as well as his visceral dislike of his intended victim.

Leaving his lights off, Michael slowly drove out of the parking lot, using the far exit, well away from the bar itself, and only pulled into the street when it was completely clear. A few hundred yards down the road, he turned off into a side street, turned on his lights and then drove towards the freeway at a moderate speed. In an hour or two he would be in another state and, with luck, would find a discreet motel where he could spend the rest of the night before moving on. As he drove through the late evening along the Interstate, Michael laughed aloud as he tossed the box cutter out of the window. A few miles down the road, he threw out his gloves one at a time as well as the bail of nylon cord. Finally, he looked at the heavy wrench he had purchased several hundred miles away. It was a wrench indistinguishable from thousands like it in hardware stores across the country but, as a precaution, Michael peeled off the UPC code and flicked the balled-up strip of paper out of the window. Finally, after a fond glance at the wrench, it too joined the other items scattered alongside the roadway over a couple of dozen miles. Unless the local authorities were clairvoyant or someone had actually seen him or his very nondescript car, he would be untraceable… unknown, unacknowledged, unidentified and invisible…just like at College.

For a moment, he wondered about the victim. Who was he? Was he single or married? Did he have children? Was he employed and did he have a good job or was he simply some sort of day laborer out for a drink in the evening after a hard day's work? What was his name and where did he live? Dozens of questions buzzed around in Michael's brain before he laughed and had to admit to himself that he really didn't care a whit about the fellow. He was history now and, for all he knew, it might be several hours before his body was even found or perhaps not until the next day.

'So what?' Michael had shrugged. 'He served his purpose and now I can move on and find someone else. This time I'll try something different. Suffocating the man was interesting but it did lack immediacy. In fact, it wasn't as satisfying as I'd hoped. Hmm, how should I do it next time? Guns are noisy and these days ballistics are way too sophisticated and can easily identify the weapon. A knife? Crude but effective although there often is a lot of blood involved in stabbing someone. Poison? Could work but how do I get something that is untraceable? Actually I don't care if the cause of death is determined, what I don't want is to leave some sort of trail behind me so that the police can track me down. Besides, dosing someone's drink surreptitiously might be more challenging than I realize. Hey ho, this is something I'll have to think about. Besides, I don't know whether the next one should be a man or a woman. Oh, there's so much to think about.'

As his thought processes slowed down, Michael leaned over and turned on the radio, looking for some music. He fumbled in the glove compartment, found the cigarette pack and lit one up with pleasure and satisfaction. Yet another success. It was proving to be remarkably easy, almost too easy and that worried him slightly. Nothing had ever been that easy for him in his life, so why was this going so well? It didn't seem right.

Sheriff's Deputy Greg Gaston pulled into the parking lot of the Lonesome Ranch Bar and turned off the flashing light bar. As he climbed heavily out of the cruiser, he could see a small crowd surrounding a vaguely familiar automobile. As far as he was concerned, he had been called out on a 911 call to deal with yet another comatose drunk, and he was not amused. Shoes lightly crunching on the gravel, he approached the six or seven people gawking at the car and its contents, and even from a few yards away, he could smell alcohol fumes. 'Just what I need,' he thought. 'A bunch of drunk do-gooders and looky-loos calling the cops to take care of one of their own that's passed out in his car. Still I wonder why the car looks familiar.'

As he reached the small crowd, he asked loudly, "Okay, who called this in?"

One man looked up and answered, "I did, officer."

"And what makes this a police emergency?" Greg asked, barely resisting the impulse to wave away the beer fumes emanating from the man.

"It looks as though he's dead, that's why."

Greg shrugged and then asked, "You a doctor or something? What makes you think he's dead?"

"The plastic bag wrapped over his head, that's what," snapped the man and moved away from the car so that the Deputy could see what he was talking about."

Looking in, Greg confirmed the man's impression and then took another look at the victim. Muttering "Holy shit!", he quickly walked back to his cruiser and called dispatch. "Hey, this is Deputy

Gaston. You asked me to respond to a 911 call at Lonesome Ranch Bar on East 3rd Street and Forsythe."

"Yes?" came the laconic response.

"You'd better send me some back-up ASAP and also tell the Sheriff to get his butt over here as soon as he can. Both the Sheriff and homicide too for that matter."

"What? What's going on?"

"Well, not only do I have a dead person, one who looks as though he's been murdered but the vic' is one of ours."

"Shit! I'll get right on it. Are you securing the scene?"

"I was just about to do so when I realized who had been killed, so I called it in immediately. Anyway, I'll get the names and addresses of these people and try to keep them here until the Sheriff, Homicide and everyone else arrives. Oh yes, you'd better call the Medical Examiner in too."

"Ten-four Greg, I'll take care of it." The dispatcher paused and then added, "Have a nice night, Greg."

"Fuck you, Jim."

Within 15 minutes or so of the call from the dispatcher, Sherriff Archie Mitchell arrived on the scene. The Sherriff was a large, bluff, no-nonsense man who was very competent. He knew his men and when one of his deputies said that a man had been murdered and, worse, the victim was one of their own, he took it very seriously. As he looked around and carefully but surreptitiously studied the onlookers, he could hear the Homicide Squad pulling into the parking lot. Fred and Mark were competent enough and he knew that he could leave them to it but, he wondered, what had Lance Reynolds been doing here that got him murdered, and in such an odd way? Sure Lance was undercover and is, rather was, a good narcotics detective but surely Lonesome Ranch Bar was an unlikely drug haven? The onlookers looked like office workers and a couple of workmen out for an evening's drinking and chatting. None of them looked like coke heads and if they used weed, well he couldn't smell any marijuana so they all might be inebriated but not stoned.

Clearing his throat, Archie raised his voice, "Okay now, did any of you see the victim leave the bar or see what happened to him after he left?"

No-one said anything and most just shook their heads. Seeing the lack of response, Archie tried again. "Sorry, I wasn't very specific. Did any of you see him leave the bar?"

Two men muttered yes. "Right then, do you have any idea when that might have been?"

"Oh about 9 or 9.30, or so."

"How was it that you saw him leave?"

"Our table was near the door and he bumped it on the way out. Knocked the bottles over, spilling our beers."

"Yeah," said the other man. "Looked sort of deliberate but he's a big guy and we didn't want any trouble…you know how it is."

Archie nodded. He did know how it was and he also knew that the victim, Lance Reynolds, was a bully and loved to jam people up just for the fun of it. It came as no surprise that he had jogged the table just to spill the men's beers. He hesitated for a moment. Was Lance's death a drug deal that had gone wrong or was it something else? Perhaps he had slept with the wrong woman, perhaps someone's wife and a vengeful husband had taken him out? He looked at the two men narrowly, "Did anyone follow him out of the bar?"

"Nah, nobody came in or out either before or after he left."

He was about to question them further when Fred tapped him lightly on the arm to let him know they were at the scene and had quickly looked at the body. Turning, Archie nodded and said, "Okay, I'll leave things to you guys. I'll get back to the Department and check with Lance's lieutenant as to what Lance had been working on. If you learn anything, make sure you keep me informed, will you?" With a nod, he turned to leave.

Mark and Fred looked at each other in surprise. The victim was Lance Reynolds? Wow, how did that happen? Lance could certainly take care of himself, so how did this happen? "Hey Sheriff, how could someone do that to Lance? He must have been surprised otherwise how else did it happen? Lance was a bit of a bruiser and, besides, this don't look like the usual drug-related killing. Plastic bags ain't their style…more like a bullet in the back of the head, that sort of thing. We might know more when the Medical Examiner gets here and checks the body over. Once he gets the…er…victim back to the morgue, the autopsy may reveal something that isn't obvious right now."

Archie nodded in agreement. "Mark, you may be right. There's something hinky here. Anyway, see what you can find out from these guys," with a wave at the onlookers. "One of them may have seen something although I doubt it." He nodded again and with a curt, "Keep me informed of progress," he walked back to his official vehicle. It was going to be a long night.

"So Bill, what was Lance working on?" Sherriff Archie Mitchel asked his senior Lieutenant, Bill Sykes.

"Nothing in particular."

"What does nothing in particular mean?"

"Well, there's no big Mexican drug cartel operation going on here. In fact, Lance was telling me just the other day that he was heartily sick of busting high schoolers and college kids for weed, ecstasy and prescription drug abuse. I suspect he was wondering whether a move to the State Capital might lead to more action. Oh there's coke and some heroin going around but not enough to get excited about. He knew most of the dealers around town and would bust them regularly but nothing too bad is happening here. We're probably too small to be worth it for the big boys to move in.

"Hm. So you don't think this homicide is drug-related?"

"Chief, based on what you've told me and what I know about drug cartels, this particular killing doesn't look like one of their actions. Besides, drug cartels probably know better than to kill a cop, even an undercover one and don't think they don't know the narcs that operate around here. I think it's gotta be something else."

"Was Lance a cocksman, you know, apt to screw anything in a skirt?"

"Not really, no. He has…had…a semi-live-in girlfriend….."

"What's a semi-live-in girlfriend?"

"She ….Belinda…lives up state and either she'd come down to him on a Friday and stay through the weekend or he'd go up there.

I gather it is a pretty solid relationship and they are planning to get married."

"So while it's possible that he was screwing around, you don't think it's likely because he's about to get engaged?"

"Yes, Chief, that's exactly what I think."

"Hm. So that possibly rules out a jealous spouse and a drug cartel. So, why was he murdered and in such a weird way?"

"No idea but something's not right, is it?"

"No, Bill, there's something very amiss. Why do you think he'd gone to that bar anyway?"

"Perhaps he just wanted to get out of the house and have a drink….his place is just around the corner from there."

"It is? Then this particular murder is even weirder. If someone was going to kill him, why not go to his house and shoot him there rather than in this hinky way? Nothing adds up, does it?"

"No sir, it doesn't. Perhaps the Homicide guys will learn something."

"They might but I somehow doubt it. Whoever did this was very careful and pretty smart too. Okay, get me the information on Lance's girlfriend and I'll get in touch with her to break the bad news and, you never know, she might know something." Archie paused and stared at the ceiling. "Hey, while you're at it, get onto the FBI's State Capital Office and touch base with them. It's always possible that something like this happened somewhere else within the State and they've got a whole lot more and better resources than we have."

"I'll get on it first thing in the morning, Chief."

"Do that…and if anything turns up, let me know ASAP. Okay?"

"Yessir."

After Bill Sykes left his office, Archie Mitchell resumed his study of the ceiling. One of his officers was killed for no apparent reason and in a way that was unusual to say the least. Maybe it was just coincidence that some maniacal killer had picked Lance Reynolds at random as a murder target and it was pure coincidence that his selected and random victim was a cop? Nah, that didn't fly… coincidences like that were as common as hen's teeth and Archie had a visceral distrust if not total disbelief in coincidences, especially ones like this. So why was Lance murdered and who by? He got to his feet and went in search of coffee. There was no point in going home…he'd never sleep or even relax until he heard back from his Homicide Detectives. Coffee…strong, black and very hot…was what he needed, and also to find some way to get his thoughts in order and on paper. A clear summary and a brief press release would be needed for the Mayor and Town Council as well as the local newspaper once the news broke. As he had decided earlier, it was going to be a long night and he could feel the waves of exhaustion starting up already.

The two homicide detectives, Mark and Fred, eventually finished processing the scene. They had found nothing other than the slashed tires. The gravel top to the parking lot had been so scuffed by all the on-lookers that even finding any clear footprints was impossible. There were fingerprints on the car door but they both were prepared to bet their pensions that the prints belonged only to the victim – forensics would later confirm their impressions. The gravel on the passenger side of the car had been carefully scuffed by the person who had slashed the tires, so nothing there. As for the plastic bag and nylon cord – both were generic items available in perhaps a thousand convenient stores, Dollar Generals, handyman shops, Lowes and Home Depots within a radius of 50 miles. They would go through the motions but both knew it would be pointless. Eventually Mark broke the silence and asked the question that had been hanging over them, almost palpable in its pertinence, "So, Fred, whaddaya think?"

"Man, I have no idea, none at all. Who the hell would've killed Lance anyway, let alone in this way? It just doesn't add up, does it?"

"I agree…nothing makes sense. Lance could be a pain but he was a good cop. If it was drug-related, this sure doesn't have the feel of it here."

"Could it be the work of a jealous husband or boyfriend?"

"Perhaps but in most cases, that sort of perp wants revenge and usually goes out of his way to cause lots of damage and pain before doing the deed. Nah, I don't buy it. It doesn't fit."

"I don't buy it either. This killing has an almost surgical feel about it. Whoever did it obviously planned well but how did he know Lance would be here this evening? I didn't think Lance was a big drinker…or was he?"

"He isn't…I mean, he wasn't. Oh he'd hoist a couple of brews with the guys after work but that was about it. We'll check inside but I'll bet he didn't come in here that often and certainly not on a regular basis."

"Why'd you say that?"

"Oh, just a hunch, that's all."

"Hmm, so you think that this could just be a random act? You know, someone passing by, saw Lance and decided to off him, that's it?"

"Makes as much sense as anything else."

"Well, nothing makes sense here and that's a fact. The boss ain't going to like it, not at all. I can't see the State Police being too happy either.

"That you can bet on. Well, let's go chat to the bar tender, for all the good it'll do."

Later in the day, Sheriff Mitchell slammed his coffee mug on his desk, marring the surface and shattering his mug. "Whaddaya mean, you've got nothing?" he shouted at his two homicide detectives. "Nothing at all?"

"No sir, we've got zip. No motive, no suspects, no evidence… nothing. A big fat zero."

"D'you mean to tell me that someone can off one of ours and get clean away with it? Are you sure about this?"

"'Fraid so, boss. The autopsy indicates that Lance had received a couple of heavy blows to the trapezius muscles which would have effectively paralyzed his arms and made it easy to slip the bag over his head. He had a couple of beers in his stomach but certainly wasn't drunk. No drugs either. Whoever banged him up seemed to know what they were doing."

"Man—o—man, the mayor ain't gonna like this." Sheriff Mitchell paused for a moment and then added, "Did you contact the Staties and/or the FBI?"

"Yup, nothing there either," said Mark. "Nothing like this within the State and certainly nothing like it in recent years other than a weird accidental death of child playing with a plastic bag – careless parents, that's all."

"Shit, shit, shit…and more shit!"

"I hear you, boss," said Fred. "We've never seen anything like this before and, hopefully, never will again."

"Okay, okay, I hear you. Look, there's got to be a reason someone killed Lance. Go and talk to everyone, you know, friends, neighbors, colleagues on the force, everyone! Someone has got to know something, so go find out what. Okay?"

"Yessir," chorused Mark and Fred but they, and the sheriff, knew it would be a futile exercise. Whoever had done this was either long gone, perhaps out of the State or had simply vanished into the woodwork. The Interstate just a few miles away could allow the killer, if he was an outsider, to go east or west and, within a few miles, also go north or south. There was a very large rabbit hole down which the perp could disappear. How the hell would anyone even know where to start? As for a local? Who knows? It could be anyone…or no-one. They would go through the motions but this particular killing had the unmistakable signs of a cold case written all over it and it was less than twenty-four hours old. Still and all, it was weird. If it was someone from out-of-town and it was drug-related, why not just shoot the guy? If it was someone else, why would a homicidal maniac pick this particular town and this particular place to kill an off-duty narcotics detective – and in such a weird way? Nothing made sense but then, as Fred said philosophically, nothing much did these days.

CHAPTER 3

Linda Woodman stared at the detective in exasperation. "Look, my husband has disappeared and no-one has seen neither hide nor hair of him in over two weeks. We've heard nothing from him and the College keeps calling to find out when he's coming back to finish the course he's teaching. Just what are you doing about it?"

Detective Dick Schmidt sighed and tried once again to get through to the woman. "Look Mrs. Woodman, your husband has taken off somewhere for reasons best known to himself. There's no crime in that and the fact that he's withdrawn money from various ATMs in a number of different places and using the correct passwords as well as using his credit cards on a regular basis tells me that whereas he might have gone off, he certainly hasn't disappeared. You might not like it but I'm afraid you have to accept that people go off on their own for all sorts of reasons."

"Oh rubbish…that's not like Michael, not at all."

"You did check that he hadn't been in accident or had been taken to hospital, didn't you?"

"Why would I do that? Michael has always been healthy and I don't see any reason for me to traipse around visiting hospitals to see if he's there. Surely I'd have heard by now if that were the case?"

"Possibly, possibly not…it would depend on what might have happened to him." Changing tactics but somewhat surprised at the woman's cavalier attitude, Dick Schmidt asked, "Has your husband ever been in trouble with the law?"

"Absolutely not!"

"Well…er…has there been any history of…er…drug abuse or heavy drinking….anything like that?"

"Certainly not."

"I assume that he hasn't done anything like this before, you know, just taken off for a few days on his own…that sort of thing?"

"Over the years he has gone to various conferences in different cities but only for two or three days at most. When he did that, I always made sure that he called me to let me know that he had arrived and to keep me informed on what was happening. And, for that matter, to tell me when he expected to return home."

"I see. So, he kept you informed of his whereabouts and what he was doing – that sort of thing?"

"Always."

"He never went off to see relations or his parents, that sort of thing?"

"No, never – besides, his parents are both dead and he has no other relations. Besides, he's been gone for more than just a few days!" Linda snapped.

"I see, What about friends at work? Was he particularly close to anyone at the College? Did he go out for a drink or something after work?"

"No, never. He was very much a homebody and rarely met up with anyone outside of work unless there was a special Faculty meeting, a Christmas party or the like…and they were few and far between in recent years. In fact, I can't remember the last time he attended anything like that. For some reason, he was never invited and certainly I was never included."

Privately, Detective Schmidt could understand why. Aloud, he continued, "I see. So you kept pretty close tabs on him, did you?"

"Detective, I resent the implication underlying your question. If Michael wanted to spend his free time with us at home, that was his choice and there was no coercion involved, none at all!"

Dick Schmidt nodded although he felt a growing sense of pity for the poor schmuck who seemed to have just taken off. Despite being attractive in a hard-sort of way and certainly she had a good figure which she obviously kept in trim with regular exercise, there was an unpleasant edge to the woman. Mrs. Woodman gave every appearance of being a domineering bitch and he could well see how someone might simply decide he'd had enough. Before closing his notebook, he posed another question, "I assume that there is no history of…ah…extra-marital affairs? You know, a girlfriend or mistress anywhere in the background?"

"Absolutely not! What a horrible suggestion. I cannot believe you even dared to ask that of him. Michael wouldn't dare have a girlfriend or the like – there was no need."

Detective Schmidt blinked and thought about the woman's comment. His immediate thought was that he'd be prepared to bet a month's salary that any sort of love or affection from Linda Woodman would be a rare commodity indeed and especially not any form of sexual intimacy. Stifling his feelings and an almost irresistible urge to make a tart comment, he simply said, "Mrs. Woodman, we have to check everything when a person is reported missing. As I said, people do go off on their own without explanation – it happens all the time. Before we can do anything, we have to check out every possibility. If, as you say, there's no history of drugs or alcohol abuse, no mistress in the background and certainly no evidence of any sort of criminal activity, then there's not a whole lot anyone can do when it looks as though his leaving home was wholly voluntary. I take it that you didn't…er…have a big blow-up or row, anything like that?"

"Certainly not!" she snapped. "We were very happy together – just ask anyone. That's nonsense. Something happened and it's up to you to find him."

Dick Schmidt was silent for a few seconds and then a thought struck him. "Your husband, did he have a bad temper, you know, any tendencies towards violence or possibly a habit of blowing up for any reason?"

"No, certainly not – I wouldn't have allowed it."

Detective Schmidt blinked again. If nothing else, this woman probably had the same affect that the fictional Madame Defarge adopted while watching the French aristocrats being beheaded by the guillotine. Linda Woodman was definitely something else and another wave of sympathy for the missing man passed through him.

"Mrs. Woodman, there's no indication that your husband has been abducted…I assume that there's been no ransom demands or the like?"

"No, of course not! Besides, we're hardly wealthy so why would anyone kidnap a lowly college professor and demand money? We don't have any, at least nothing to speak of. We existed on Michael's salary and that is our sole source of income. Let me tell you, him going off like that and taking money on a regular basis from ATM machines all over the place has left us in a dreadful state." Linda Woodman screwed up her face as she took a deep breath. "Let me tell you," she said again but with more venom in her voice. "The children are complaining bitterly about not getting their allowances and all sorts of bills are coming due. I mean, how can I show my face at the gym or the country club when I can't pay the monthly membership dues? It's so selfish of him to leave me to do everything. I mean, Damon wants a new play station or whatever that thing is and Rebecca needs new clothes for all the parties she's going to these days. I tell you, it just isn't right, is it? Good thing the three of us got new cellular phones a couple of months back or we'd be in a sorry state. Of course, money being tight, Michael had to make do with his old one but then he never calls anyone anyway."

Looking up from his notes, Dick said, "I take it that you don't work, or do you?"

"Certainly not - at least not outside the home. That's why I got married in the first place. It's a husband's job to take care of his wife and family and there's no reason why I should have to take on that responsibility. If finances are tight, that's his fault – he should go out and earn more….you know, get a second job or something. There's no need for us to suffer, is there?"

"I see," breathed Dick. So she really was a bitch, this Linda Woodman. No wonder the guy took off – can't say I blame him. I wonder where the kids are? They don't seem to care that their father's gone except that they weren't getting their allowances. A thought struck him. "Did your husband take his cell phone with him, or a lap-top?"

"No. They were left in the hallway, just like always."

"He doesn't have an office at home or somewhere special that he puts his things?"

"He didn't have any *special* things, as you put it. I didn't let him bring work home so he didn't have an office here, or need one. Besides, if Michael took up space with an office, where would Rebecca and Damion put their things, you know the things that wouldn't fit in their rooms. No, there was no need for him having anything like that here."

'Ouch' thought Dick. 'I was right, that poor schmuck took off because he'd had enough and I can't say I blame him. What a life!' Looking at the wife again, he added, "I take it that because he left his lap-top and phone here, you couldn't contact him even if you wanted to, is that right?"

"Yes," said Linda flatly.

As the wife lapsed into silence, presumably gathering strength for the next diatribe, Dick thought about the missing man leaving his cell phone and lap-top at home. In his experience, most people only let loose of their cell phones and lap-tops under dire circumstances. Evidently this Michael Woodman seemed to be only too willing to leave everything behind. Strange. Still and all, he'd go through the motions and check whether he had made or received any unusual calls in the past days or weeks – he'd have to check 'phone records at the college too for that matter.

As she watched the detective mulling things over in his mind, Linda wondered for a moment why Michael had taken off so suddenly but then decided that it really was typical of him. He was always selfish like that and didn't seem to care that she and their two children might have to go without because of him. After all, he didn't have to put up with Damon's whining about not getting the new tablet he wanted or that Rebecca's new and very fancy sneakers were going to cost over $200…didn't he *want* his daughter to look nice and be one of the in-crowd at school or his son to be hip like the other boys in his class? Just how selfish and inconsiderate could he be? No, she decided, he is just selfish and that's all there was to say. As the silence stretched between her and the detective, Linda added, "But why would I get to get in touch with him?"

"But Mrs. Woodman, on one hand you're complaining that your husband has disappeared and on the other you're telling me that you don't want to get in touch with him…so which is it?"

"Oh you're impossible. I suppose I should have known better than to expect the police to do anything."

"Well ma'am, I'm sorry you feel that way. We'll do what we can but I don't see that we really have a crime here but if something does change, please call us and we'll do what we can. Okay?"

"Oh, just go away – you're useless," snapped Linda and got up to show the detective out, muttering, "Good riddance to you! And good riddance to that worthless husband of mine too!" Of course it did not occur to her that if Michael didn't come back anytime soon, she'd have to do something herself about the household finances such as finding a job…an unthinkable situation. She tut-tutted at the thought that she'd have to take on all the cooking too – just how selfish could Michael be?

As Dick Schmidt drove away, he thought about the report he'd have to file. Despite a strong urge to do so, he knew he couldn't put down on paper, or into the computer actually, that the missing man's wife was a domineering, self-centered bitch and apparently the children weren't much better. It was clear that Michael Edward Woodman had taken off to parts unknown…and good luck to him. With no evidence of a crime being committed, no outstanding arrest warrants and certainly no indication that he had been abducted or severely injured, there was nothing that anyone could do. He smiled for a moment at the thought of that stuck-up bitch having to eat humble-pie and actually do something for herself such as get a job, but that was her problem. As far as he was concerned, and the police as a whole, there was nothing they had to do other pass on the word to the State Police that one Michael Edward Woodman had left home and was reported missing by his wife. That brief report would be accompanied by the comment that there were no outstanding warrants or any other criminal activities connected with the man, not even unpaid parking tickets.

As Michael lay on the lumpy bed in the No-Tell motel somewhere in Nebraska and stared at the ceiling, he thought about what had happened since he'd left home so abruptly. All in all, he was pretty satisfied with the way things were going but he was aware that sooner or later, probably sooner, the meager Woodman bank accounts would be depleted and money could become a problem.

"So," he muttered out loud. "I'll have to settle somewhere and get a job, at least temporarily until I can accumulate enough cash to get back on the road." He smiled. Doing that would spare the lives of a few people who didn't even know that their lives might have been in danger. Thinking aloud again, he muttered, "I'll have to find a reasonably large town with good Interstate access so that I can go off in different directions and find suitable victims while avoiding obvious patterns of behavior. Perhaps one that's located in a tri-state area? Now, just how am I going to take care of the next one? Hmm, I'll have to think about that – got to be inventive or at least unpredictable. Funny how it's easy to find my targets but deciding on the best method of killing them is problematical."

He lapsed into silence and thought about the fact that unlike the fictional TV serial killer, Dexter Morgan, Michael didn't have a base of operations or a boat to conveniently take the bodies out to sea to dump them. Perhaps he should get a boat and then ruled that out because there was no way he could afford one and he knew nothing about boats anyway. He did have a car but driving around with a dead body in the back seat or in the trunk might be a recipe for disaster. No, he'd have to find another method of killing people and preferably one that he could use more than once without it being obvious that he was doing so. He wondered why TV shows and the movies always made killing someone look so easy. Perhaps he should write to the producers or screen-writers to tell them that it was a lot more difficult to kill someone than they thought. He laughed and muttered, "Hey, writing a letter like that would ruffle a few feathers if not create a panic. What a hoot but I think not. No point in attracting attention even if no-one has a clue who I am or what I'm doing. So where should I go next?" He decided that he would buy a map of the country when he had breakfast the next morning. It was so much easier to plan things when he had some idea of where he might go next. Having made that decision, Michael turned on his side and promptly slipped into a deep, dreamless sleep.

After he had had breakfast in the motel coffee shop, Michael sipped at his coffee and pored over the large scale map that he had purchased at the front desk. The West Coast loomed large but the common advice "Go West, young man!" didn't apply to him – he was much too old for anyone, other than an octogenarian, to call him young. Heading East might be a good option. There were plenty of moderate to large cities that he could visit and lots of Interstates with easy access that he could get around on. Not only that, bumping off one or two people in each of the cities he visited or passed through might go unnoticed for some time if he was careful to avoid any set pattern. He smiled to himself, 'There we go again, just how *do* I kill someone easily without being detected or raising too many red flags? I really will have to write to those television people …. I need help here!' He laughed silently and went back to perusing the map. Where to go next? 'Maybe I should select someone here? I don't like Nebraska and if one or two people are taken out of the gene pool, so what?" He laughed again and decided that maybe he did need to retrace his steps to some degree. A bigger town or city would provide him with more opportunities and, by and large, people living in larger locales were less concerned with other people than in smaller places. 'Okay" he said to himself firmly, 'Get on with it and make a decision.' He looked at the map more closely and spotted what appeared to be a prime location. "Yes," he muttered aloud, "This is it! Now do I pick a man or a woman? Perhaps a female this time…they're generally not as strong as men and, besides, it is time for me to stop being sexist. No, I've got to be catholic in whom I kill."

He signaled to the waitress and got a refill on his coffee and thought about how he would do it. Slowly a plan formed in his brain. As the details firmed up, Michael got to his feet and walked over to the cash register to settle his bill. He was about to ask the cashier where the nearest hardware store was located and then thought better of it. No point in giving anyone any indication of what he might, or might not, be doing.

Climbing into his car, he pulled away from the motel and set off to explore the town and there, almost on cue, he spotted a Home Depot about 100 yards further up the road. Swinging into the parking lot, Michael carefully parked away from the entrance. No point in putting his car anywhere that his out-of-town plates might be obvious. As he got out of the car, he mentally reviewed what he might need…mineral spirits, a spray bottle, some nylon clothes line, a couple of plastic bags – wait, he'd get those at the check-out – but what else did he need? A sharp box cutter or linoleum knife in case he cut to cut the woman's throat? Might be messy but at least it was fast and effective. No, too much blood. Better to spray her with mineral spirits to stifle her as he slipped a plastic bag over her head, then a quick placement of the noose over her head and around the throat and it would be over. As he packed his items in the shopping cart, it occurred to Michael that he had made a decision. It would be a woman this time but where would he meet her? Perhaps outside a bar again…always a good meeting place and if it was dark and not crowded, the parking lot could be ideal.

After leaving the Home Depot, Michael filled his car and headed East on the Interstate and then stopped. He didn't want to drive too far because that would mean driving back late at night and his movements might be more obvious. He pulled over and thought about it. No, best go back and check out of the motel. Then drive a hundred or so miles down the Interstate, find a suitable lodging for the night, get a decent lunch and then take a long nap. After that, he could go out on the prowl at least 50 or more miles down the Interstate to the next large town. He nodded in affirmation – it was a workable plan.

Linda Woodman set down at the dinner table and looked at her two children. "Well darlings, it seems your father has taken off for parts unknown and no-one knows where he's gone."

"He's gone?" asked Rebecca. "Where'd he go?"

"I just told you, no-one knows where he's gone!" snapped Linda, exasperated with her daughter and her whiny tone. The last thing she needed was any sort of attitude from her precious daughter.

"So he's gone, has he?" said Damion. "So what? We don't need him anyway."

"Well, actually we do," sighed his mother.

"How so?" demanded Damion. "Just what did he do around here?"

"Actually he paid all the bills, that's what he did," replied Linda. "Without him, we've no money."

"So what?" persisted Damion.

"So what? Did you say *So What*" said Linda, her voice rising to a screech. "That fancy new tablet you keep whining about and those expensive sneakers both you and Rebecca want – well, guess what, you can't have them now. In fact, we can't afford those smart phones of yours and even I have to stop going to the gym and the country club. Those days are over!"

"But that's not fair," cried both of her children in unison. "Why should we suffer because of him?"

"Life's not fair, that's why," snapped Linda.

There was silence in the dining room while all three mulled over what Linda had just said. Finally Damion broke the silence, saying "So, just how long will this last? When will he come back and we can get what we need? All the people at school have new phones, tablets, game boys and that sort of thing – I'll look stupid….it's just not fair. Why must I suffer?"

"Well," sighed Linda. "Guess what? You're going to just have to suck it up. Besides, if your father doesn't come back – well, you'll just have to go to the local school."

"What?" cried Rebecca and Damion in unison. "Why do we have to do that?"

"Because we can't afford those expensive private school fees after this semester, that's why."

"But Mom, we'll lose all our friends and we won't know anyone if we have to go to another school," shouted Damion.

"Well, it's either that or we don't eat, have electricity or anything."

"But that's not…." protested Damion.

"I don't care what you think is fair or unfair," snapped Linda. "If your father doesn't come back soon, very soon, I'll have to go out and get a job just to pay the bills and keep everything up. So, frankly, I don't give a flying fuck what you two want or don't want because what I am going to have to go through matters more to me than you two whining about the expensive things you think you need just to keep up with your friends. Now, if you have finished moaning and groaning, I'll prepare dinner although it won't be anything like what you've had in the past. As I said, from now on, money is tight. So there."

Damion and Rebecca sat in stunned and sullen silence. This was the first time they had ever heard their mother swear. In fact, truth be told, neither would have believed that she even knew the "f word" let alone might actually use it. The seriousness of their collective situation was now becoming very apparent and when they looked at each other, they could see emotions like anger, fear, worry, unhappiness and a whole host of other things pass over each other's face. For a moment, both wondered whether it might have been their fault that their father had taken off so suddenly but then, selfish brats that they were, they decided by mutual but unspoken agreement that it was all their father's fault with perhaps, just perhaps, some contribution from their mother.

As they sat and watched their mother flap about the kitchen, both Damion and Rebecca started wondering what they should put on their Facebook pages and perhaps Twitter to their closest friends regarding what had happened. It was all so irritating and unfair…. what did they ever do to deserve this?

Several hundred miles away, their errant father pulled into a medium-sized motel a mile or so off the busy Interstate. Scanning the parking lot, Michael was pleased to see that a dozen or more vehicles were parked outside various rooms even at mid-afternoon and, he surmised, many more might still pull in off the highway over the next few hours. "This looks perfect," he muttered. "Just what I want…I wonder whether they'll take cash…I'll make some excuse about having mislaid my credit card…best to remain anonymous if I can. Okay, here goes…let's find a room for a night or two."

He was given a key to Room No. 4 – a good omen, he thought, because tonight would be his fourth target. The fact that the receptionist was a pimply, overweight, gum-chewing, slovenly-dressed woman of indeterminate age only confirmed that he had made the right choice for his next victim. 'Pity,' he thought. 'It might have been nice to take care of this person but that would have been far too risky, however much she probably deserved it. Oh well, perhaps on my way out tomorrow or the day after when I leave…we'll see.'

CHAPTER 4

Michael Woodman sat in his car and stared out through the windshield into the parking lot. He wondered why the parking area behind virtually every bar in urban America was always so poorly lit. "Talk about inviting trouble," he muttered aloud. There were several cars scattered about, usually in clusters of two or three but there was also a large number of empty spaces. The place was not busy, which was surprising for a Friday night, so he wondered why parking spots were outlined so carefully. 'Perhaps,' he wondered. 'They were thinking about installing flood lights. After tonight, that intention might just become a high priority item.' He smiled and settled back to wait for his next victim.

The cool night air was starting to slip into the car through the open driver's window and it was curiously peaceful, disturbed only by the occasional passing car on the adjoining street but that was all. Just as Michael started to wonder whether he had picked a poor location, the backdoor of the bar opened and two men stepped out. Within seconds, both had lit up cigarettes and they puffed companionably and exchanged small talk.

"Nice night," said one of them, the tall man standing on the left.

"Yeah it is," agreed the other. "But it won't be long before winter gets here and stepping out for a quick smoke will become a lot more unpleasant."

"Yeah, I tell you, this banning of smoking in bars is a royal pain."

"Bunch of do-gooders," snarled the shorter man. "I don't see why they can't mind their own business. If we want to smoke, why can't we? It doesn't affect them, does it? What do they care what we do to our bodies?"

"Oh they claim it's all to do with second-hand smoke and they are protecting the non-smokers among us, that's what."

"That may be part of it but I'll bet it has more to do with stopping people having fun. The next thing you'll see is the banning of cigarettes altogether – can you imagine the mess that will cause?"

"You think tobacco might become something like drinking booze during the prohibition years?"

"Wouldn't surprise me if it did. Let's face it, a well-organized bunch of do-gooders got those gut-less idiots in Congress to amend the Constitution back then and look what happened to the country. Crime suddenly became organized and developed into big, and I mean BIG, business. No-one had even heard of the Mafia before prohibition. Now that sort of criminal element, especially the drug cartels, have so much money they can buy any politician, police officer or bureaucrat any day of the week. If they ban cigarettes, it'll be even worse."

"Yeah," agreed his companion. "Not only that, no-one seems to give a damn if they do. Bunch of greedy crooks, all of them."

"Do what? Ban cigarettes?"

"No, buy politicians."

"You're probably right there. We keep electing those bozos to Congress and everyone knows that they are all corrupt. I tell you, man, what is happening to America?"

"Search me. Hey, let's get back inside. By the way, I think Lucy might turn up tonight."

"She will? Cool!"

"Yeah, cool is right with her. I've never met anyone one who likes to screw as much and as often as she does. I tell you, she's one of the wonders of the world. What an appetite."

"Have you had any?"

"Many times and it was great. What about you?"

"Yes indeed. So, if she does turn up, who has first dibs?"

"Let's flip a coin and we'll go from there. Okay?"

"Sure thing, buddy You never know, we might both get lucky."

With that settled, the two men returned inside.

Michael sat digesting what he had just heard. In short order, a mental image of this Lucy woman started to form in his mind: 'Around the late thirties or early forties, somewhat plump and probably heavily made up – something along the lines of mutton dressed up as lamb, as the Brits used to say. Probably a bit blousy and working class but she'll have a pleasant-enough manner and is likely to be attractive in a slightly well-worn way. So,' he decided. 'She might be a good choice – let's wait and see.'

Almost on cue, a small, slightly older model, red sports car pulled into the parking lot. As Michael watched, a youngish older woman climbed out and then stretched. She looked around and seeing what apparently was a familiar vehicle, she nodded and started to straighten her clothes. She dug into her purse and withdrew a small mirror, placed the purse on the front fender and applied yet more lipstick to her slightly pouting lips. Even from several yards away, Michael could see that the woman had subjected herself to a fair amount of plastic surgery which went along with bleached-blonde hair and very tight clothing. After the finishing touches of make-up were applied, the woman replaced the mirror, powder compact and lipstick, and picked up her purse. Just as she was pushing out her prominent and severely upholstered breasts, Michael exited his car and walked over quickly., his shoes crunching on the gravel.

"Excuse me," he said, making the woman jump slightly.

"Yes?" she said uncertainly.

"I'm sorry that I startled you but my cell phone's almost dead and it seems the car battery might be dead too. I've been trying to call someone to get help but can't get through. Either there's a dead zone here or my phone is acting up."

"Oh dear, that's unfortunate. Did you ask inside?"

"Not yet – it's only just happened. Besides, they never seem to have working phones in bars. Not only that, bars are always so noisy that it's hard to hear anything anyway."

"You're right there. Want to try with my phone?" and without waiting for a reply, she started to dig in her purse. "Oh shit, it's not here – I'll bet it dropped out onto the floorboard when I had to brake suddenly on the way here. My purse fell over and things went everywhere, you know what I mean?"

Michael nodded and thought, 'This is going to be even easier than I thought.' He stepped to one side as Lucy turned back and leaned into her car. As she fumbled around under the passenger seat, Michael stepped forward and quickly slipped the plastic bag over her head. Before Lucy even realized what was happening, the nylon cord went over her head and was looped tightly around her neck. Within a few seconds, Lucy stopped twitching and the plastic bag slowly pulled away from her mouth and nostrils as she stopped breathing. Michael waited a few more seconds to make sure that she had indeed stopped breathing and fingers gently placed on the carotid artery confirmed that she was dead. Quickly he loosened the noose and pulled off the plastic bag. After a final check that Lucy was not breathing and that there was no pulse, Michael gathered up the bag and nylon cord and stuffed them into his pocket. He walked quietly but quickly back to his car, carefully looking around the parking lot to make sure that it was empty.

Once inside the car, he again scanned the parking lot and started the engine. After taking off his gloves and checking that both bag and nylon were securely placed in his coat pocket, he carefully pulled out of the parking lot, making sure that his lights were off and that he didn't apply the brakes and accidently illuminate his rear number plate. A few hundred yards down the road and well out of the range of view of the bar or its parking lot, he flipped on the lights and stepped on the accelerator. He was back on the Interstate in a matter of minutes.

As he reached cruising speed, Michael finally relaxed and reviewed the evening. "Yes," he told the car. "We did it, didn't we? It all went pretty well. In an hour or so, we'll stop at McDonalds or a Burger King and get some coffee and toss the rope and bag into a trash can."

After a few miles, Michael thought about the two men who had been chatting outside the bar. One or other was going to be disappointed not to get laid this evening but, as someone once said, "Life's hard and then you die!" He laughed aloud, feeling on top of the world. As he drove back to the motel, Michael again spoke aloud, "Wilma, it's so easy to kill someone, isn't it?" He stopped talking for a moment, and then said to himself, "Wilma? Why am I calling my car Wilma? I never give things names and here I am calling the car Wilma – how odd is that? On the other, the car looks like a Wilma although I'm not sure what a Wilma actually looks like. Oh well, you're now Wilma to me." He lapsed into silence and then thought about his friend Chuck. He remembered Chuck telling him how a cat had walked into his apartment one day and took up residence.

"He just walked in – really?" he asked.

"Yup!"

"Is it a male or female?"

"No idea – I never looked."

"Oh! What color is it?"

"It's sort of grey – you know, a tabby or whatever they're called."

"So what do you call it?"

"Cat."

"Cat?"

"Why not? That's what it is."

"I suppose." After that, the two men went on to chat about other things. So, as Michael reasoned, why not call the car Wilma – it was as good a name as any and it conjured up images of a comfortable if slightly old-fashioned and somewhat motherly lady who took great pleasure in taking care of other people. He leaned forward and gently patted the front console, saying, "So Wilma, are we having fun yet?" and laughed. In the distance he saw a signpost indicating the availability of food and gas at the next exit, and decided to pull off to fill Wilma up and get coffee.

Back at the bar, the tall man looked at his watch and the shorter man followed suit. "I thought you said Lucy was coming," said one of them, to which the other replied, "So did I. Seems she stood us up, don't it Jack?"

"Evidently," muttered the taller man. "Not like her, not at all." He glanced at his watch again and said, "Oh well, it's getting late. One more drink and I'll call it a night. What about you, Rick?"

The other also looked at his watch, shrugged and responded, "Not a bad idea, to call it a night I mean. I think I'll pass on the drink – I don't like to drink and drive….you know how it is."

"Yeah, you're right. No point in inviting trouble."

The pair of them headed out the rear door and stood for a moment, lighting up cigarettes. Almost simultaneously, they both saw the familiar small red sports car with the driver's door open and looking forlorn almost all alone in the parking lot.

"Hey," said Jack. "Isn't that Lucy's car?" and the pair of them walked towards it.

"It sure is but where's Lucy?" asked Rick, and then they saw her legs projecting from inside the car. Because it was dark and the car was in the shadows cast by a large tree, they weren't certain what they were seeing until they got closer. Then both stopped abruptly and Jack, the taller man, said almost as a shout, "What the hell?"

They ran to the car and stopped abruptly when they saw a very dead-looking Lucy laid out across the front seats.

"Oh shit," said Rick. "What the hell happened to her?"

"I don't know buddy, but it sure don't look good. We'd better call the police."

Sheriff's deputy Arthur "Willie" Wilson snapped shut his notebook and reached into his cruiser for the radio. After calling in and summoning back-up, he turned back to the two men. "So, gentlemen, let's start with your names and addresses and we'll go from there. The homicide boys will probably ask you the same questions but I've got to get the details down so my report's complete. I hate to say it, but it might take a bit of time. Do you need to call anyone to let them know that you'll be delayed a bit?" thinking to himself that "delayed a bit" was a gross understatement of how long it would take.

As Willie took down the details on the two men and noted the fact that they had been expecting Lucy to come to the bar that evening, the two Homicide detectives, Fred and Butch, arrived. They were closely followed by the watch commander, the supervisory Lieutenant, and several patrol cars, all of whom were agog to see a real dead body, especially a woman who might or might not have been murdered. Murders were a rare occurrence in their neck of the woods and everyone wanted to take a look. Eventually the Medical Examiner on call, a local family doctor arrived and proceeded to examine the body. Noting the blue lips and odd placement of the body, Dr. Prentice turned to the Homicide detectives and said matter-of-factly, "I think this is one for you guys. She didn't die from natural causes."

"Why'd you say that, doc?" asked one of them.

"Well, the placement of the body is odd, to say the least, but the tell-tale sign is petechial hemorrhaging in the eyes. Besides, she's got ligature marks around the neck. I'm afraid that someone choked this poor woman to death. We'll know for certain once we get an autopsy but that's my first impression."

"Ouch," said Fred, and stared down at the body. "Who the hell did this and, for that matter, why?"

"Who is she? Do we know?" asked Butch, turning to Willie and the two men standing there beside Lucy's car. He stared hard at Jack and Rick, paused and then asked, "So, who is this lady and how do you know her?"

Jack and Rick looked at each other for a moment or two and then Jack said, "She's Lucy."

"Lucy who?" asked Butch.

Jack and Rick looked at each other again and both Fred and Butch caught the uncertainty and embarrassment that flitted across the two men's faces. 'Okay,' thought Fred. 'There's something going on here but somehow I don't get the feeling that either of these clowns had anything to do with her murder. Besides, they've got a concrete alibi for the whole evening but, nevertheless, there's something that's going on between them and this Lucy…no, correction, that had been going on between them and Lucy before someone offed her. But why was she killed? Was a jealous boyfriend or husband involved? Somehow I get the feeling that this murder ain't going to be simple.' Out of the corner of his eye, Fred could see the CSI truck turn into the parking lot and he said to the two men standing there, "Look, let's get down to the station and we'll take statements." Tongue firmly in cheek, he added, "Shouldn't take long."

Again Jack and Rick exchanged glances and guilty looks appeared to flit across their faces. 'Uh oh,' thought Fred. 'These guys are probably married but I'll bet there's been some hanky-panky going on between them and this lady, whoever she is.'

While this was going on, Butch had been busy going through Lucy's purse and whistled slightly. Fred stopped talking to the two men and looked at Butch questioningly. "This lady, one Lucy Manning, is, or rather was, a parole officer."

"Uh, oh," muttered Fred. So he had been right, this was not going to be a simple murder and the field of suspects had suddenly expanded. It was going to be a long night and both he and Butch knew that the "brass", let alone the press, would be all over this like white on rice. Once any sort of law enforcement officer was involved, murder investigations suddenly took on a whole new significance.

Fred sat opposite Jack in Interview Room No. 1 with Butch and the other guy in Interview Room No. 2. He stared at Jack for a few minutes, sighed and pulled a notepad towards himself and clicked his pen, "So, Jack is it?, let's get down some particulars."

Within a few minutes it was established that Jack was divorced, had a steady job as a warehouse manager, was financially secure but not affluent, had no criminal record and had an off-and-on relationship with a young lady across the other side of town. Gentle probing revealed that Jack and Lucy had "got it on" a few times but only as friends with no commitments on either side. Jack knew that a similar situation existed between Lucy and his friend Rick and, apparently, neither of them cared about the other's relationship with Lucy. They were long-time friends and "share-and-share alike" was okay with both of them. Apparently Jack's lady friend did not consider their relationship to be exclusive and had no idea of what Jack did or did not do when they were not together. She had not even gone to that bar with Jack or on her own to meet up with him there. As far as Jack knew, his girlfriend had no idea where the bar was or ever had any reason to go there. It seemed that Jack's personal life had nothing to do with her and that was the way she liked it to be.

Curiously, neither Jack nor Rick knew or even cared what Lucy's surname was and he, Jack, was surprised to learn that Lucy was a parole officer. "She is…or, rather, was a parole officer? I did not know that. Funny, that's not something that I would have suspected although I'm not too sure what a parole officer is like when they're not working." Fred grunted but he could understand that the vast majority of law-abiding citizens were probably equally ignorant of what parole officers did.

He was about to ask a question when that was a polite tap on the door and the head CSI man poked his head in, "Hey Fred, can I have a minute?"

Fred joined the man outside and, after exchanging glances with Butch who had likewise exited the adjoining interview room, looked expectantly at the CSI, "What've you got, Bob?"

"Nothing."

"What," cried Butch and Fred almost in unison. "Whaddaya mean, nothing?"

"Nothing, zip, zilch, nada….nothing."

"Are you sure?" asked Butch.

"Abso-bloody-lutely. That crime scene was pristine. The only prints I got were those of the victim and nothing else. Not even the parking lot gravel was disturbed. Whoever did this was either extremely lucky, very careful or he, maybe she, knows something about crime scene investigation. Of course, with all those television series, most people have some idea of what we look for but this seems to be above and beyond. Go figure!"

Butch shook his head in exasperation before saying, "Sorry Bob, I didn't mean to imply that you didn't know what you were doing."

"That's alright, no offense taken. Did I hear that the victim was a parole officer?"

"That's right but from what we can tell, she's based over in Pleasantville, not here. Checking up on her parolees is going to be a bear. The Sheriff over there is a real asshole."

"I hear you," muttered Fred in agreement. "Mind you," he added. "It's pretty unusual for a parolee to "off" his or her parole officer – it's far too easy to check up on them and they probably know it, not that most parolees are Einsteins, not even close."

Butch nodded in agreement. As Fred had already said, this investigation was going to be a bear in every respect. In his head, he could already hear the Sheriff screaming at him for results. He knew that he and Fred were in for another all-nighter and his wife was not going to be happy when she heard. He sighed and said, "Well, thanks Bob. It's a pity you didn't find anything and I'll bet the medical examiner is probably also going to come up empty. Shit!"

"Shit is right," agreed his partner. "Somehow I don't get the impression that this was the work of a jealous wife or girlfriend and, unless I'm much mistaken, I'll bet there's nobody on Lucy's side that was involved either. We'll soon find out but I'm not holding my breath."

"Yeah," sighed Butch. "Those are my thoughts too. I don't hold out much hope that one of Lucy's clients did this either."

CSI Bob nodded. "I'm afraid I must agree with you both. This attack was far too well-planned to be a random act of jealousy or even revenge by an angry parolee. Anyway, be that as it may, I'll get on back to the 'lab. Let me know if there's anything I can do to help. Sorry not to be of more help."

"Yeah, thanks," muttered Butch, his mind already moved on.

Fred and Butch sat across the desk from Sheriff Hensley Burke, known to one and all police officers in his department as "The Hen". A short, fussy and slightly rotund man, The Hen was a good cop – very experienced and in contrast to his appearance and general demeanor, he was very efficient and took good care of his men and the department. On this occasion, however, he was not happy.

"Let me get this straight. There was no evidence, none at all, at the crime scene – yes?" he barked.

"No sir, nothing."

"And you're telling me that that the medical examiner found nothing other than that the victim was strangled in some way?"

"Yessir."

"Those two men, whatever their names are, both had sexual relations with this woman on various occasions but know, or rather knew, nothing about her, not even what she did for a living?"

"That's right," agreed Butch and Fred nodded in affirmation.

"How can that be?" muttered The Hen.

"'Fraid that's the case, sir," said Fred. "Seems that they both had a "wham, bam, thank you, ma'am" relationship with her without too many questions being asked or answered."

"Hmm. What about an ex-husband or lover? Anything like that?"

"There is an ex-husband but he's living up in Montana and his new wife wasn't too pleased with being wakened in the middle of the night by police officers inquiring about her husband's ex-wife."

"So there's nothing there? What about any boyfriends or the like here?"

"We checked her apartment and there's nothing. We'll check her telephone and cell phone records but a quick look showed nothing," said Fred apologetically.

The Hen grunted and thought about what he'd heard. Finally he straightened and said, "What about her active clients? Anything there?"

"They all seem to be fairly innocuous, based on the case files on her desk at home. There may be more in her office in Pleasantville but I don't imagine that there'll be any hard core cases that she's been handling. Let's face it, we'd have heard if there had been any drug cartel activity over there and I can't remember the last serious crime that happened there, or here for that matter, in the last couple of years."

The Hen nodded and thought some more. Eventually he said, "You know, this case is coming to look like a random and spontaneous homicide but why here? I can't remember the last murder, other than some stupid jerk getting tanked up and killing his wife or girlfriend in a drunken rage. That sort of thing just doesn't happen here. So why now and why this particular woman?"

"Perhaps it's just a coincidence?" ventured Butch.

"Come on, man," snapped The Hen. "You know how I feel about coincidences. They are feasibly possible but not in my experience. No, there has to be a connection somehow, somewhere - so get searching. Something will turn up and better sooner than later." He paused before continuing, "Check with the State Police and the FBI for anything similar. I tell you guys, this case don't feel right to me. Random acts of murder are like random acts of kindness – they're both about as common as hen's teeth! Dig deeper. There's got to be something." and then he glared at Butch and Fred when he realized what he'd just said combined with the nickname assigned to him by his staff. The last thing he needed or wanted was any levity from his homicide detectives.

40

As they left the Sheriff's office, Butch and Fred barely stifled their sniggers. Despite the humor about the Hen's teeth, they both knew that they were about to hit a brick wall, if they hadn't done so already. In their collective but albeit limited experience, there had not been a serial killer in the tri-county area for years if not decades. Besides, as they both knew, serial killers usually selected prostitutes or young women as their targets, not older and more mature ladies. It was obvious that robbery was not an issue here but there was nothing to indicate why this particular woman had been targeted. They would check up on the lady's history but they both instinctively felt, better knew, that however deep they delved, nothing was going to come to light. As The Hen had said, the case didn't feel right, not at all.

Butch, turning to Fred, "Okay, let's call it a night and we'll get started again first thing. You call the State Police and I'll contact the FBI. Then we can both have a go at Pleasantville."

"Sounds like a plan" agreed Fred. "Besides, you never know, we might even turn something up in her office."

"Fat chance, buddy," snarled Butch. "Dream on. As The Hen said, this case don't feel right but I'm damned if I know why it doesn't. I'm getting too old for this shit."

"You are indeed," agreed Fred. "In fact, you're getting too old for most things these days…at least that's what I've heard." And he laughed.

"Oh piss off," snarled Butch. "I'll see you in the morning."

CHAPTER 5

Sheriff Hensley Burke looked askance at his two homicide detectives, sighed loudly and shook his head in disbelief. He could not believe that anything like this could have happened in his quiet little town in Eastern Iowa. It just did not seem possible.

"Look guys," he said eventually. "I cannot believe that after all this time that you have found nothing, no clues, no traces, nothing – is that right?"

"No, nothing."

"And you checked that there are no old lovers or boyfriends hidden out there in the woods and you positively ruled out her ex? No jealous wives or girlfriends either?"

"Yessir we did, and there is nothing."

"No indications of resentful parolees here or wherever she was before moving down here?"

"None at all. It seems that Ms. Lucy was pretty well-liked by all her…er…clients and she was widely known as someone who went out of her way to help them, being accommodating almost to a fault."

"Damn – so even digging around gave us nothing?"

"Hmm. So, what do you guys think?"

Burch and Fred looked at each other and shrugged. Eventually Fred said, "Well, as Sherlock Holmes once famously said, once you eliminate every possibility, what you're left with, however implausible or unlikely, is likely the answer."

"Gave me a break," snarled The Hen. "Sherlock Holmes isn't a real person – he's a fictional character, just like Miss Marple and Hercule Poirot, and don't ask me who they are either."

Both Butch and Fred smiled slightly and then caught the angry glare of their chief. However much The Hen liked to cluck, he could be pretty mean when he got upset and he was now clearly very upset. The three men sat in silence for a few moments before Fred piped up again.

"Boss, much as neither of us wants to admit it, this homicide looks like a random act by a person or persons unknown." Watching the red wave of anger climbing the Sheriff's face, he hurriedly added, "I know it don't make no sense but neither of us can explain this murder in any other way. As far as we can tell, and we really did work hard on this, there don't seem to be any reason why anyone should have "offed" the lady, none at all."

"Shit!" growled The Hen. He sighed again and thought for a few minutes. "Okay, let's file this one for a while and wait to see if anything comes up. I hate to settle for listing it as a cold case but I see your point. Send copies of the paperwork to the State Police and the FBI – maybe something will shake loose with them."

He paused and slammed his desk. "So it looks as though this *was* the act of a random killer here? That's your conclusion?"

"But boss, what other explanation do we have?" ventured Fred.

"If, and I repeat *if,* that's the case, I wonder why he picked here of all places and how did he focus on Lucy Manning? Nothing makes sense about any of this." The Hen sighed again. "Okay, file it for now but if anything, *anything*, turns up, let me know at once."

He glared at his two detectives and added, "Just keep this quiet, will you? I don't want panic to set in. There's enough craziness going around already without adding to it. The last thing we need is for the papers to start going on about a random killer on the loose. Got it?"

Fred and Butch nodded and beat a hasty retreat from their angry boss. Murders were rare in their town and those that did occur were quickly solved, but this one? This one was different but both accepted that they could do nothing about it.

Linda Woodman had lost it with her two children yet again and screamed at them, "I don't care what your friends say at school – I just don't care."

"But mom," Rebecca started to say.

"But nothing," snapped her mother. "We have no money and even if we did, the last thing I'd do is buy you yet another pair of sneakers, however trendy they are." She turned to Damion and added, "And you can stop that pouting too. I cannot afford to get that Play Station, Gameboy or whatever it is that you think you can't live without."

She paused and said more quietly, "I'd have thought that all those issues about what's trendy and that sort of thing would not be a problem in a public school. I guess I'm wrong but there's nothing I can do about it anyway. You'll just have to deal with it and that's that."

Her two children looked at each in horror. What was happening to them? Their lives were getting ever more ruined each and every day. Rebecca still smarted from the remark made by her so-called best friend Ashley about her sneakers. "Those are so past it, Becky. When are you getting some new ones? I can't believe you'd be seen dead wearing those."

Damion didn't fare much better, with his friends snidely commenting on how all his games were months if not years out-of-date. Slowly but surely he was being excluded from the activities of his friends and he now felt the sting of rejection. Neither he nor Rebecca got invitations to hang out with their friends and visits to their homes was long past. They were pariahs and their mother was doing nothing about it and didn't seem to care.

Linda slammed the dishes on the table and snarled at her children that they'd better eat what she'd put in front of them or they'd simply go hungry. Damion and Rebecca stared at the reheated hamburger-helper and canned vegetables and grimaced. What had happened to them?

Seeing their looks, Linda nearly burst into tears. It was all so unfair. Why did Michael take off like that? What was he thinking? How could he have been that selfish? Didn't he care what happened to her? Seeing Rebecca start pouting again, she almost shouted, "Look, I know it's not much but it's all we can afford these days." As tears filled Rebecca's eyes, Linda softened her tone slightly and added, "Look Sweetie, I know things are tough right now but we'll get through it. Lots of people have far worse things happen to them and they survived – so will we."

"But mom," Damion started to say in an unconscious imitation of his sister.

"But nothing, Damion," snapped Linda. "You two think you've got it bad but what about me? I cannot go to the country club or the gym and if I see any of my friends on the street or in the supermarket, they turn their backs or hurry off as if I've got some dreadful disease…which I suppose I have in their eyes. As far as they're concerned, being poor is about as bad as having the plague. Some friends they are!"

She scooped some of the slop from her plate into her mouth and nearly gagged. It looked awful and tasted worse. No wonder Damion and Rebecca were unhappy. Unhappy? She almost smiled. Unhappy was hardly the word for what any of them were feeling. Her former friends were so patronizing and usually smirked when they went into the boutique where she worked at a salary barely above minimum wage. They seemed to take delight in asking her about this or that ridiculously expensive item on display and then would pull out a credit card to buy something that cost ten times what the same thing might be in Target or Walmart. Their unfeeling demands and unpleasant comments about poor service were designed to hurt, and they did. Linda now knew the effect that her unthinking comments and superior attitude had had on other people and a pang of guilt passed through her.

Later that evening, after the children had gone to their rooms, Linda treated herself to a rare glass of wine and an even rarer cigarette while sitting out on the back porch. At first she felt sorry for herself and furious with Michael but slowly she started to think about the past few years of her marriage. She sat up straight, stubbed out the cigarette and then went to refill her glass and find another smoke.

Returning to her seat, she slowly, reluctantly and painfully started to think about things. She really had been a bitch to Michael and their children had been spoiled rotten. She had never taken an interest in anything he did and, truth be told, she had taken a great deal of pleasure in putting him down to everyone. Michael had his faults but he had been a loyal, dutiful husband, and a great father, not that the children would ever have said so. Then she thought about her so-called friends. How she had thought nothing of spending hours at the beauty salon or the gym, dissing anyone who had less money than they did and the snide, cruel remarks she had made to the less-affluent parents of children at that private school. How she had made mock-sympathetic comments about the cost of clothes and toys and other things that were so important to she and her friends but way out of the reach of these hard-working people. Fate had stepped in and now she had even less money than they did! As for her friends, that was another unkind blow from fickle fate. None of them wanted anything to do with her and even the less-affluent parents, the very ones that she had disdained, ridiculed and put down at every opportunity, now treated her exactly the same way. When she had been a race horse, she had ignored them and now that she was a cart horse, they in turn ignored her. Now she could not even afford to pay those school fees let alone do anything else. "What goes round, comes round" Linda muttered aloud, "and I deserve it – every bit of it." A painful, almost palpable wave of regret passed through her.

She sniffed and wiped her suddenly wet eyes. 'There's no point in moaning about things,' she thought. 'Nothing is going to change unless I change and do something about it.' Suddenly an irresistible urge to pray swept over her. She had not prayed in years but now she did. She could not remember when she had last thought of God and prayer was something she would have disdained, just like talking to the less affluent parents at school. Slowly she recited the now-unfamiliar Lord's Prayer and sobbed her apologies to Michael, God and everyone else for her past actions. She vowed to change, and change she would.

Deciding, Linda climbed to her feet and went back into the house. She called out to her children, "Damion, Rebecca – would you come down here. We need to talk. Right now please."

Both children stopped whatever they had been doing and emerged from their rooms. They looked at each other, silently asking "What's going on?" It was the first time in weeks if not months that their mother had spoken softly, almost pleadingly to them. Curious, they walked downstairs side by side and went into the living room where their mother was sitting, the room lit only by a small table lamp and stray light coming in from street lamps.

Linda looked and smiled slightly. They were good-looking children but their looks were marred by their sulky expressions. She shrugged. They could sulk all they want but that changed nothing. It was time to talk, *really talk*, to them and start to assess the present and plan the future.

"Damion and Rebecca, I have something to say to you. So, please sit down and listen carefully."

Michael Woodman stared at the map, willing it to tell him where to head next. He knew it was time to move on, what with the store owner starting to making comments about giving him so much money under the table. No, he'd got away with being evasive for long enough and the income had certainly boosted his meagre resources but it was time. The decision to move on was the right one but where to next? Michael realized that he had unconsciously stayed in the Mid-West but perhaps he should go south. All those Southern States beckoned him and given that they were all gun-happy and probably incestuous as all get out, one or two more killings there would probably go unnoticed for a while. "Okay," he asked himself. "Where do I go? What looks appealing? Hmm, Alabama looks nice and with the coming of Fall, it might even be quite pretty. But first, perhaps just one more while I'm here – sort of one for the road, as they say." He smiled.

Maybe this time he'd head a little north on the expressway, a change in scenery would be good. Then Michael thought about how he'd do it. The bag over the head and garrote was getting to be a bit passé despite its effectiveness and low cost. As he had thought before, a knife would be pretty effective too and silent but stabbing tended to be messy, and cleaning up any spatter from himself would take a lot of effort, and would probably leave traces everywhere. No, stabbing was out of the question. He wished he had a gun but buying one would present problems because of all the gun laws and identification that most states seemed to require these days. Damn the students at Columbine and those other schools. They made things difficult for everyone – typical kids, completely thoughtless and with no regard for anyone else. Then he laughed. How ironic that he, a now hardened killer, was complaining about the actions of deranged kids taking revenge on their cruel schoolmates. It also occurred to him that he himself was doing something similar.

Eventually he made a decision. He would use his tried and true method one more time and then head south. He'd put getting a gun on the back burner for the moment. Something would turn up, as it usually did, and then the problem would be solved.

It was early evening when Michael climbed into Wilma and headed north on the expressway. Every few miles there was yet another road sign indicating this place or that a few miles off the Interstate but none of the town names appealed to him. For a moment he thought nostalgically of the quaint names of towns and villages back in England and each and every one had some historical significance. Well, not all of them, but certainly most did. 'Funny,' he reflected. 'This is the first time I've thought about England in years. If I went back, would I even recognize the place? All those foreigners and darkies coming in and the Russian Mafia and Arab oil millionaires buying up all the property in London. No, no point in even thinking about going back. It would be even worse than going back home and living with Linda and the brats. Not a good idea.'

Then a road sign almost leaped out at him. *London, next exit, 2 miles.* 'That's it,' he thought. 'Perfect. No need to cross the ocean, it's right here. Of course It's not really London, England but it's a good omen.' He laughed silently and watched carefully as he approached the town, passing two or three gas stations and the obligatory McDonalds on the side of the road. A few scattered houses, a small store or two and then he saw it, set back from the road and barely visible through the large trees and overgrown bushes that separated the parking lot from the road. *The Wayside Hang-out* proclaimed the sign and he could see a few cars scattered near to the front door. Obviously not a local hang-out but it had a few customers. He wondered whether they were regulars or just people stopping in for a quick drink or snack before heading home after work.

Michael pulled slowly into the parking lot and stopped beneath a large oak with heavy branches hanging down, almost touching the ground. "Needs some tree surgery," he muttered and then turned off the engine. The widely spaced street lights cast a few shadows and there was a small splash of light from the bar itself. Almost an ideal spot for him to wait - yet again, luck was with him.

He sipped on the coffee that he had brought with him and fingered the plastic bag and nylon noose in his pocket, preparing himself for a long wait. A few cars roared past on the road but nothing turned into the parking lot for at least 30 minutes. Then he heard the rumble of a large diesel engine followed by the scrunch of tires on the loose gravel surface. 'Funny how these out-of-the-way places almost always have gravel parking lots.' he thought. 'It must be some sort of cultural thing or simply a matter of expediency.' He watched the truck come to a stop a few yards away and then the lights were switched off. Fortunately it was not one of those street monsters jacked up high on their suspensions – that might have complicated matters. He watched with interest as a youngish man climbed out and proceeded to walk around the truck, kicking at the tires. Making a decision, Michael got out of his car and strolled over to the man. As he got closer, he could see that the other driver was barely in his twenties, scarcely of drinking age but already seemed to have had a few judging by the beer fumes that wafted towards him.

"Got trouble?" he asked politely.

"Dunno – it seems to be pulling to one side when I drive," said the other man. "I wonder if I've got a flat tire or something."

"Let's have look," offered Michael. "Maybe nothing or..." and he left the sentence hanging.

The other man nodded and started to walk around the truck again. As he got around to the passenger side, Michael moved ahead of him and appeared to look down at the wheel. "Hey what's that?" he said, pointing down at the tire.

In an almost Pavlovian response, the younger man pushed Michael out of the way and crouched down, peering at the tire. Immediately Michael slipped the bag over his head and as the man struggled to get upright, he looped the nylon cord around his head and pulled it tight. The young man threshed about for a few seconds, trying desperately to tear the bag off and/or loosen the noose and also fumbling in his jacket pocket. Then it was all over. The bag loosened on its own, pulling away from his face as the man stopped breathing.

Michael nodded, satisfied with his work and pulled off the plastic bag and noose. He started to walk back to his car and then stopped. 'What was he trying to get from his pocket?' he asked himself and hurried over to the prostrate man. Quickly he patted the right hand coat pocket and felt the hard outline of a gun. Checking that the plastic gloves were still in place, he slid one hand into the pocket and quickly retrieved a small Ruger. Happily he slipped it into his pocket and walked quickly back to his car. Then he hesitated and returned again to the truck. He opened the driver's side door and bundled the younger man's body inside, muttering "No point in letting anyone know what happened too soon. The truck's far enough away from the entrance that nobody will see the body for hours, and hopefully longer." Nodding in satisfaction, he walked back to his car and thought 'So things do work out sometimes. What a bit of luck. I knew seeing that sign to London was a good omen, and so it was.'

After checking around carefully yet again and winding down the car window to listen for cars on the road, Michael started the engine and pulled slowly out of the parking lot. Nothing on the road and no-one coming out of *The Wayside Hang-out* - it was safe to go, and he did. Switching on his lights and accelerating carefully once he was a few hundred yards away from the bar.

As he drove, he patted the dashboard, "Nice going Wilma, we did it again. Easy as pie and we got a gun too. Now that's what I call a successful venture." Carefully keeping below the speed limit, he reached the Interstate entrance ramp and sped up until he was safely on the roadway, pleased that there was so little traffic. "Less chance of anyone seeing me get on the Interstate from the London entrance ramp," he muttered. As he drove, he wondered how the town got its name and whether there were any English people living in the place. Maybe London was situated in the County of Middlesex and then he sniggered. Not hardly likely but one never knew in America. Places and locales sometimes were given the weirdest names here.

Several miles down the road, he disposed of the bag and then the noose and finally the gloves. Feeling relaxed, Michael sat back and enjoyed the drive. He was about to lower the window to enjoy the night air when he saw the first heavy drops of rain spatter against the windshield. 'Better and better,' he thought. 'Everything, including the weather, is helping tonight. It's almost as if the fates are working hard to help me.' And he laughed again. Then it struck him, killing people with a gun was fast and efficient but those forensics people can match bullets to any gun in the world because the rifling or somesuch in the barrel left marks on the bullet as it was fired. He thought about the problem for several miles and then it struck him. Michael cleared his throat and spoke to his car again.

"Hey Wilma, I think I've got a solution. What if I get a sharp round file and run it down the barrel after each time I shoot the gun? That should mess up the rifling and make it hard to identify which gun was used to fire the bullet. If I do it all the time, then eventually all the rifling should be thoroughly messed up. Doing that will reduce the gun's accuracy but who cares? I'm not going to use it on any firing range for target practice and I'm certainly never going to get to be a marksman. No point. Wilma, old girl, this little thing is always going to be a close-up and personal weapon. Now, got any ideas on a silencer? That's not something I'm going to able to buy in a hardware store or at a gun-meet, so what am I to do?"

He drove in silence and mulled the problem. The trouble with guns is that they're inherently noisy and gunshots in the middle of the night inevitably generate interest. Then another half-remembered thought hit him. Was it on CSI or one of those TV shows that he heard that someone had used a potato as a crude but effective silencer? What did he care if some mashed potato was driven into the victim's head? He was dead and wouldn't care anyway. As he approached the motel, Michael made a mental note that he'd have to buy a couple of very sharp circular files – were they called rat-tails? – and some large potatoes. He could always try to fashion a silencer himself using steel wool or somesuch but why bother if a potato works well? He'd try the idea out when he was on the road tomorrow, pulling off into a secluded rest area and fire the gun with and without the potato. Then he reminded himself that he'd have to buy some ammunition too, but certainly well away from where he would eventually wind up on his journey south.

James "Big Jim" Cunningham slammed and locked the front door of *The Wayside Hang-out* behind him and glanced through the windows to check that only the security lights were on. In this day and age, he didn't want to waste electricity but leaving the place completely dark was simply inviting trouble. He turned on the alarm system by the remote control on his key chain and headed towards his car parked well off to one side of the parking lot. He spotted the truck parked several hundred feet from his own vehicle and wondered who it belonged to. He shrugged and decided he was simply too tired to walk over and have a look. If it was a customer sleeping off too many beers, he didn't care as long as whomever it was had got them at *The Wayside Hang-out*. He stretched, yawned and climbed into his car. The wife probably had been in bed for hours by now and he was anxious to join her there. All too soon it would be morning and the daily grind would start all over again.

As he drove home, Big Jim idly wondered what it was all about. "Is this all there is to life?" he asked his car. When he had retired from the police force those many years ago, it had seemed a great idea to buy a bar where his old colleagues could hang out and swap cop stories but somehow it hadn't happened the way he'd hoped. At first, a few of his old friends and colleagues would stop by and down a few but the intervals between their visits lengthened until weeks might go by before he saw any of them. In the 20/20 hindsight of most investors who had made bad or unwise investments, he could see that he had made a poor decision. Cops, like most people, loved and sought out the familiar and the fact that they would have to drive an extra 10 or 15 miles to go to *The Wayside Hang-out* was reason enough not to go there. And, Big Jim admitted sadly to himself, a retired cop was just that, an ex-cop. Gossiping about ongoing cases, shoptalk, stationhouse gossip and the myriad other things that cops discussed regularly were now topics from which Big Jim was excluded either because of potential legal issues or simply because he was no longer "one of them". Of course if anything happened to him, then the Blue Line would reform rapidly but otherwise he was just another guy behind the bar who served beers and liquor with a welcoming smile.

He pulled into his driveway, switched off the car lights and slowly plodded into the house. The cat got up from the couch, walked over and sniffed his pants and then went back to the warm place she had just vacated. "Dad" was home to her and that was enough disruption for one night. Rufus, the bone-idle and less than gifted German shepherd, padded out of the kitchen to check that it indeed was Big Jim that had come in the front door and then he too retreated back to his bed, toe-nails clicking on the hardwood floor. As Big Jim watched the dog go back to the kitchen, he wondered whether Rufus would actually do anything if a stranger had come in. He got the impression that as long as the intruder did not make too much noise or interfere with his food bowl, Rufus probably would not care less that someone had come into the house. "What's it all about?' he asked himself out loud. "Did the wife and I make a really bad mistake or was this what retirement was like for everyone, not just ex-cops?'

Looking around to make sure that no lights were on and that the security system was reset, he slowly climbed the stairs, his steps being serenaded by his wife's gentle snores. "Oh screw it," he muttered. "Things could be a whole lot worse."

Michael Woodman settled into bed, satisfied with his evening's work and especially pleased that he had acquired a much-needed weapon. He breathed a sigh of contentment when, to his surprise, he suddenly thought of Linda and the children. For a moment or two he wondered how they were coping with all the changes in their lives. He felt a momentary pang of guilt and then reflected that he had once read that someone somewhere had said that *Guilt makes cowards of us all* and yet another had commented that *Guilt is the best friend she has.* Michael snorted in derision. His children had treated him like crap and their actions were aided and abetted by his wife. "Serves them all right," he muttered and thought some more. 'If money is tight, then Linda is going to have to go out and get a job and the whiny brats would just have to do without all those expensive things, whatever they were, that they felt not only entitled to but without which life for them was not worth living.' He snorted again and muttered aloud, "For the life of me I cannot see why Rebecca has to have, just *has* to have, a pair of sneakers that cost almost as much as the last suit I bought. The damn things last less than 6 months, either because she's outgrown them, they've gone out of fashion or they've simply fallen apart. Why the hell we insist of buying crap from

China or wherever at greatly inflated prices and which just fall apart in a few weeks is beyond me. All in the name of profit, I suppose. Well guess what America, I'm redressing the balance. This little man is fighting back!" and Michael almost cheered but thought better of it. No point waking the neighbors and drawing attention to himself. Tomorrow he'd head south and some more consumers of junk and overpriced foreign goods would be gone from the world. His last thoughts before slipping into sleep were that he might actually be doing the world a service.

CHAPTER 6

Big Jim Cunningham pulled into the parking lot of *The Wayside Hang-out* and climbed out of his car. At 6 feet 3 inches and close to 300 pounds, his appellation was justified and Big Jim thought, not for the first time, that he really should think about getting a big SUV or even a truck. His small sedan car was cheap to run and very reliable but it was pain for him to get in and out of it. He sighed and wondered when, or even if, he would ever be able to trade it in for something more befitting his size.

He looked up at the clear blue sky. It was starting to shape up to be a beautiful day and, for a change, he felt light-hearted. Maybe things would work out with the bar. As he walked towards the front door, he glanced to his right and noted that the truck was still there from the previous evening. He was about to walk over and take a look and then thought better of it – he had things to do inside and satisfying his curiosity could wait for a bit.

As he turned on the lights and set up glasses behind the bar, he glanced out of the window again at the truck. Idly he wondered who it belonged to and then dismissed the thought as his rather dimwitted but ever obliging helper Duane turned up closely followed by Daisy who worked the kitchen. Big Jim nodded at both of them and then told Duane to help Daisy bring in the bread, meat and other things that had been delivered a short while previously. When Duane eventually returned, he told Big Jim that Daisy was preparing the meat patties for the lunch time burgers and that she was getting the deep fryer ready for the inevitable orders of French Fries.

"I'm glad you told me that, Duane," said Big Jim sarcastically. "I'd have been worried that she wasn't doing her job otherwise."

Duane nodded, apparently thinking he'd received a compliment. Big Jim shook his head. Was Duane really that dumb or was it all an act? Duane had been working for him the past six months and he still wasn't sure about the man. Sometimes he could be incredibly obtuse and then every so often Duane would come out with a really astonishingly perceptive comment. Big Jim shrugged. No point in wasting time on that question. Duane was Duane and since he was a willing worker, what did it matter? "Okay," he said eventually. "Let's get the floor swept and the tables cleaned off. We've got about an hour before anyone is likely to turn up."

The two men busied themselves getting *The Wayside Hang-out* tidied up and the bar restocked although Big Jim kept peering out at the truck in the parking lot, looking very still and forlorn in the early sunshine. Eventually curiosity got the better of him and he said, "Hey Duane, go out and look at that truck, will you?"

"Sure thing Big Jim," said Duane and moved slowly to the door and then across the parking lot. Several minutes later, he returned and Big Jim looked at him expectantly. Duane, oblivious to Big Jim's questioning look, went back to wiping down the tables. Eventually Big Jim broke the silence, "Well?"

"Well what boss?" asked Duane.

"Oh give me a break, Duane! What about the truck?"

"Well it's there in the parking lot."

"I can see that but who does it belong to?"

"I dunno."

"You didn't open the door and take a look?"

"No – there was someone inside and I didn't want to disturb him."

"There's someone there? What's he look like."

"I dunno. He's sort of lying across the seats and I couldn't see his face."

"Didn't you open the door and ask him who he was and what he was doing?"

"You didn't tell me to, did you?"

"Oh for crying out loud!," snapped Big Jim. "I'll go and look for myself." He stormed out of *The Wayside Hang-out* muttering "Stupid of me to send a boy to do a man's job."

As he walked towards the truck, Big Jim's police training clicked in and he approached it cautiously and slightly to one side of the driver's door. When he reached the door he looked in and saw the man lying across the front seats. He noted that contrary to what he might have expected, the man was sprawled across the seats from the passenger side, not the driver's side. He lightly tapped on the window and was about to open the door when he looked again. "Uh oh," he muttered. "This don't look good." He took another careful look and hurried back to *The Wayside Hang-out*. Immediately he called 911 and told the dispatcher that he thought there might be a dead body in a truck that was in his parking lot.

It didn't take too long for the circus to get started. Police cruisers with sirens blaring and lights flashing descended from all directions and uniformed police were suddenly all over his parking lot. Each and every police officer went over and peered into the truck and one young officer was foolish or incautious enough to actually open the truck door to get a better look. Amidst all the chaos, the duty sergeant turned up closely followed by the watch commander, Lieutenant Alfred Symes.

Lt. Symes was a nice man but officious to a fault. Despite never having been a street cop, he had the attitude that he, and only he, knew how to process a crime scene and his men would sigh in exasperation if he turned up at any incident. True to form, Symes snapped at the duty sergeant, one Albert Finney, no relation to the actor,

"Did you call homicide?"

"Yes sir. They're on their way."

"What about the medical examiner?"

"He's on his way too."

"Huh! I don't suppose you called the CSI team."

"Yes sir, I did that too. They are on their way also."

"Huh! Well sergeant, it looks as though you've got things under control here."

"Yes sir, I think I have."

"Good, good…" and Lt. Symes paused when he saw the open truck door. He glared at his sergeant and said, "I suppose you opened the truck door or was it the guy who called this in?"

"Neither of us, sir. It was Officer Storey, over there."

"He did? What was he thinking?" Looking over at the young police officer, he shouted, "Hey you, come over here." And then, scanning all the police officers standing idly around, he bellowed, "You all, get back on patrol and earn your pay for a change" As all the uniforms retreated to their cruisers, he snapped at the young officer, "No, not you – I want a word with you." Lt. Symes was about to dress down the young policeman when he saw Sgt. Finney talking to a civilian. He turned to the young officer and said emphatically, "You stay right here." He walked over to his sergeant and the civilian, bristling with misplaced and unwarranted anger.

"So, why did you call this in? Why'd you think it was a homicide?"

Sgt. Finney was about to answer when Lt. Symes snapped at him that he was talking to the civilian, not him. Sgt. Finney shrugged and lapsed into silence, knowing full-well that once his lieutenant had got the bit between his teeth, nothing was going to stop him, and certainly not anything he might say.

"Well, what have you got to say for yourself?" demanded Lt. Symes of Big Jim.

"About what LT?" replied Big Jim calmly.

"About all this, that's what?"

Puzzled by the lieutenant's attitude, Big Jim simply said, "Well, I saw this truck in the parking lot last night when I closed up shop. When I saw it was still here this morning, I decided to investigate."

"Did you touch anything?" asked Symes belligerently.

"No. I was on the force for far too long to do anything like that. No, I simply called it in once I realized that the man was dead."

Oblivious to Big Jim's reference to being a police officer, or simply ignoring it, Symes continued, "What made you think he was dead?"

"Several things, the first being that he was positioned in a strange way for someone just sleeping off a heavy night of drinking, if that was what it was."

"Had he been drinking?" asked Symes.

"That I don't know but if he had, it certainly wasn't in my bar."

"So you've never seen him before?"

"Not that I recall, no."

"And you didn't touch anything? You didn't open the truck door?"

"No, that was one of your officers."

"Huh! Well, what else?"

"What else what?" asked Big Jim.

"What else made you think he was dead?"

"I rapped lightly on the window and the guy didn't stir."

"So you did touch something," said Lt. Symes triumphantly. "I knew it."

"Look lieutenant, I don't know what you're getting at but I was a police officer for a great many years and I'm sufficiently experienced to know not to interfere with a potential crime scene."

Lt. Symes snorted and turned back to his sergeant, "Do you know this man?"

"Yes sir, of course. He's Big Jim Cunningham and he was on the force when I became a sergeant. He was a good cop and, knowing him, he would have followed protocol to the letter."

"So you say," sneered Symes. "Well, you'd best secure the scene until the medical examiner and CSI team arrive."

"I already did, LT and both the medical examiner and CSI boys are already on the job. They're talking to Homicide as we speak."

"About time too," snapped Lt. Symes. "Well, I'd best get back to work – I've got things to do and I cannot waste my time making sure that you do your job properly." With that, Lt Symes stalked back to his car, studiously ignoring the muttered "What a dickhead" from Big Jim. Possibly because of the dickhead comment from Big Jim, Symes took off in a hurry and completely forgot to say anything to Officer Storey.

Seeing him leave, Finney nodded briefly at Storey and said, "You'd best get out of here before the LT remembers about you and comes back. And next time, keep your damn hands to yourself. You were lucky this time but if it happens again, I'll write you up, okay?" He watched as the embarrassed officer climbed in his cruiser and sped off, blessing a kind fate for his lucky escape and vowing never to go near a crime scene again if he could help it.

"So, Jim," said Finney. "Who is this guy?"

"I don't know…not sure I've seen him before. Whoever he is, he's certainly not a regular."

"Really? What's he doing here then?"

"No idea. Who is he? Or, rather, who was he?"

Sgt. Finney was about to respond when one of the homicide detectives, Rich Butler, appeared at his elbow, saying, "His name's Clyde Wilkins. Sound familiar to either of you?" Both Sgt. Finney and Big Jim shook their heads and Finney asked, "Where's he from?"

"Seems like he lived the other side of town."

"So what's he doing here? And how did he die?"

"The ME says he was strangled with some sort of rope judging by the ligature marks. He'll know for sure once he's done an autopsy but that's his initial impression. Not only that, he was killed sometime last evening, around about 9 or 9.30."

"He was garroted?" asked an incredulous Sgt. Finney. "That's weird. Not heard of anything like that around here and I've been on the job a long time." He turned to Big Jim, "What about you Jim?"

"Like you, that's a new one on me. That of course raises the question of what he was doing here and how did he get killed in my parking lot, assuming of course that somebody didn't just drive his truck over here with him in it and dump it."

"Hey, don't ask me," said Butler. "Nothing makes any sense at this stage and I've a nasty feeling that it never will. Let's face it, if someone was going to do this guy in, why strangle or garrote him, put him on the passenger side of the truck and drive the body over here? And if he did do that, how'd he get home after he dumped the truck and body here?" He looked hard at Big Jim and added, "I don't suppose you saw or heard anything last evening?"

"Nada. It was a quiet evening with a few regulars coming in and staying for a while but nothing out of the ordinary."

The homicide detective looked at him for a long moment and then asked, "Can you identify the regulars? You know, give me their names and addresses?"

"Names – yes, addresses – no. But as they come in all the time, I can ask them to contact you."

"Fine, thanks. So, coming back to last evening, do you remember anyone coming in, or leaving for that matter, between 8.30 say and 9.30?"

"Not that I recall. You can always ask Duane if he saw anything."

"Who's Duane?" asked Sgt. Finney.

"He helps me behind the bar and with the cleaning up etc. You can also ask Daisy if she saw anything too." Anticipating the question, Big Jim added, "Daisy works in the kitchen but she sometimes steps out back for a quick smoke. Daisy is pretty reliable but Duane…well, Duane is a good guy but not too bright so he might not be much of a help but you never know. Anyway, if you need me for anything else, I'll be inside."

He started to walk back to the bar and then stopped and returned, "Hey, I assume that I can open up now?"

"The homicide cop and Finney looked at each and shrugged, with Butler finally saying, "Sure why not? Maybe some of the regulars will come in and we can talk to them. Call me if you remember anything, okay?"

Big Jim nodded and walked back to his bar, puzzling over what had happened but also secretly pleased about the possible business that a good murder might generate. With luck, they'd be swamped by curious and downright nosy people, and not just the regulars, all wanting to experience a murder even if only viscerally. He laughed and remembered the old saying that *it's a bad wind that blows no-one any good* and with luck, at least his business would benefit from the murder. Then he thought about the victim, muttering, "What on earth was he doing in my parking lot? And why did someone kill him anyway and why here?" Then he dismissed the questions rattling around in his brain. He was no longer on the force and investigating murders was something that he had not dealt while on the force so why should he bother now? Besides, Finney was an ok-guy but Symes looked as though he'd burst a blood vessel if he, Big Jim Cunningham so much as asked a question let alone try to get involved in the investigation.

Going back inside, he called out for Duane and Daisy. And when they appeared, he quickly filled them in on what had happened, forestalling their questions by adding that they now knew as much as he did about who the victim was, why he was in their parking lot and why he had been killed there. Then he called his wife – he didn't want her to hear anything from a nosy neighbor.

Michael and Wilma headed south and he enjoyed the drive although, like most Interstates, I49 was a boring roadway. Still he was headed for new territories and now that he was carrying a weapon, Michael was enjoying the thought that he had new opportunities and greater latitude to carry out his mission as he liked to call it. But, before he got anywhere near his final destination, wherever that might be, he decided he'd best pull off somewhere and get some ammunition. If he loaded up in a town on his progress south, he should be reasonably safe from detection or easy identification.

Again, unbidden thoughts of Linda and the brats crept into his mind but he quickly dismissed them. He would not be going back to Western Pennsylvania any time soon, if at all, and he wished them luck in getting themselves sorted out. He smiled. He could just imagine all the moaning, groaning and lamentations from Damion and Rebecca over not getting every single thing they demanded. As for Linda, no more country club, gym sessions or anything else. Now she'd have to get a job and actually earn the money that she freely spent in the past. "Turn about's fair play, isn't it Wilma?" he said to the car and then spotted a promising exit. It was time to get some extra rounds for the gun and this might be a great opportunity to do just that. That evening he would start to work on roughing up the riffling in the barrel and, hopefully, add confusion to everything else that he had been doing for some months now. He tried to remember just how many he had killed and wondered whether he should have taken some identification from his victims – it would have made remembering each one that much easier. Then he dismissed the notion. Did he really need to keep that sort of score of his activities? As he drove, Michael wondered what distinguished his victims. Was it just happenstance or was there something about each of them that triggered the desire to kill them? He decided he would think about that on the drive tomorrow. Perhaps there was a visceral emotion to which he subconsciously responded? Some Pavlovian urge that drove him on or was it simply a desire to kill? Was he that unbalanced or was something else going on? He shrugged mentally and continued driving, looking for somewhere to stop for the night.

The next day, Lt. Symes looked at the two homicide detectives balefully. He was not pleased at the lack of progress they had made and made his annoyance very clear to them before telling them to get to work. When he had reported the latest information, or lack thereof, the captain and other higher-ups had been even less pleased and they had chewed him out over the killing of Clyde Wilkins, almost blaming him for the fact that someone had been killed on his watch in their town. Almost echoing the comments made by other law enforcement officers in several places across the Mid-west, the collective attitude was that this sort of crime did not happen there. It did not help that no-one knew why the victim had stopped in the parking lot of *The Wayside Hang-out* or that he apparently had never visited the place before.

"Look Alfie," said his captain. "He must have stopped there for a reason. He wasn't too far from home and nothing appears to be wrong with his truck, so why'd he stop there if he wasn't meeting up with someone? Answer me that."

"Captain, we just don't know. It's early days but it seems that Clyde was a bit of a loner, you know, no girlfriend or any other relationships that we could find."

"No jealous boyfriend or husband, anything like that?"

"Not that we could discover, no."

"He wasn't gay or anything?"

"Apparently not. He had a few girlie magazines in his apartment and a couple X-rated videos but nothing suggestive of homosexual interests. In fact the place was pretty stark with almost no furniture other than recliner placed in front of the TV and a queen-size bed. Typical low income bachelor pad, according to the detectives who went through his place. His parents live a couple of towns over and he worked in the local supermarket at barely above minimum wage. The manager said that Clyde was a good worker and got on reasonably well with everyone although he wasn't close to any of them."

"Hmm. Any signs of drug abuse or buying and selling of narcotics? Could he have got into debt over gambling and someone took action to get the debt settled. Anything like that?"

"No, nothing. Besides, drug cartels tend to be much more direct when they kill someone, you know, put out a strong message. This killing looked to be very discreet, if that's the right term? Likewise with bookies who are owed money. They usually just beat someone up or smash their knee caps. This one looks like a plain and ordinary killing."

The captain thought about what Symes had said and eventually concluded, "I suppose you could be right. Well, tell them to keep looking. There's got to be a reason why he was killed. You did say that he still had his wallet in his back pocket, didn't you?"

"Yes sir. And his cell phone was in the truck too."

"So robbery wasn't the motive and you say there's no apparent revenge motive either, right?"

"No."

"Anything from the parents?"

"Nothing. According to them, Clyde was a good boy who was working hard to save up for college. He had a good GPA in high school but his parents are far from rich, so he had to take care of college on his own. Apparently, he's never been in any trouble, not even a speeding ticket. Saw them regularly and talked on the telephone to them all the time."

"Well, keep me informed if anything turns up," and the captain returned to the papers on his desk. He personally didn't care for Alfred Symes but accepted the fact that he was a good police officer and if he said his detectives had turned up nothing, then that was probably true. As he picked up the latest budget report, he sighed and wondered why anyone would kill a nonentity like Clyde Wilkins.

After an hour or so of trying to get his head around the big disparity between department expenditures and the limited town budget, a thought struck him. Opening his office door, he called out to Symes, "Hey Alfie, do you know if the vic' ever carried a weapon?"

Lt. Symes shook his head but promised to look into that question. After the captain retreated to his office, Symes thought, 'If Wilkins *did* own a gun, where was it? If he had been carrying it when he was killed, why hadn't he gone for it instead of letting himself be garroted without putting up any sort of fight? The guy might have been a bit of a wimp but not too many people let themselves be killed if they did have a gun. I'll mention this to the homicide guys. Trouble is, if Wilkins was armed and didn't shoot whoever attacked him, what the hell happened?' Eventually he decided he would ask the homicide detectives to look into whether the victim did indeed own a gun and if he did, where it might be. There had been no mention of a concealed weapon permit but if he did have one and the gun to go with it, and the gun was not in his truck or in his home, then where was it? As he walked out of his office, it suddenly struck him that if Wilkins had possessed a weapon that had disappeared, then it was possible that his killer had taken it, and that was a worrying thought because it opened up a number of possibilities, none of them good.

The next morning when Big Jim got out of bed, his wife poured him a mug of coffee and said delightedly, "Randy's coming home this weekend."

Big Jim blinked and stared at her. "I thought he was off on assignment somewhere up North."

"He was," said his wife triumphantly. "However, his supervisory special agent decided that he was doing so well, he should be transferred back here to Kansas. Our boy's coming home – well not here, but at least closer to home than before."

Big Jim grunted. Their son, Randolph, was an honest, hard-working but far too serious young man. He was what his friends had called a nerd with a tendency to memorize chunks of information from books and encyclopedias and then spout them at the first opportunity. The boy was decidedly bright but lacking in social skills. After college and a degree in criminology, he had joined the FBI and done well, at least that was what he had told his mother. Big Jim suspected that Randy's supervisory special agent had got fed up with the endless recitation of facts and simply had him transferred as far away as possible. As a retired cop, Big Jim did not need an endless stream of forensic matter thrust at him by his son but then the thought struck him. Perhaps he could push Randy into looking at the killing of Clyde Wilkins? That might keep him occupied and out his hair for a while. Besides, taking on an apparently insoluble murder might be good for him. Nothing like failure to keep you humble.

For the first time since everything had gone down at *The Wayside Hang-out*, Big Jim smiled. He loved his son but the boy could be a pain. Even as a child, Randy had talked at you rather than to you and seemed to have no interests, certainly not sports and he had been close to dreadful in everything athletic that he tried to get involved with. Of course, he decided, Randy is pretty smart and perhaps he might solve the case. What a hoot! That would be one in the eye for that a-hole police lieutenant Symes, pompous ass that he was.

As he drove to the office, as he called *The Wayside Hang-out*, Big Jim thought about the murder again. Sure enough, lots of people had come in to take a look around and business was booming for the first time in months. But nevertheless, it *was* a most unlikely killing – who ever garroted a complete stranger? It made no sense and in all the years he had been on the force, he yet to come across a completely random killing. His old friend Bert Finney, now Sergeant Albert Finney, had quietly told him that everyone was at a total loss as to the why of the killing but no-one wanted to acknowledge that it was a totally random act by an unknown killer. Apparently everyone would file the case in due course and hope that nothing like it would happen again, which was quite likely.

Pulling into the parking lot, Big Jim said aloud, "Yes Randy, this is one for you. Time for you to cut your teeth on a real mystery instead of wasting time on all those classroom exercises, and good luck on it!"

CHAPTER 7

Linda Woodman hesitated before speaking as Damion and Rebecca stared at her expectantly. She cleared her throat but continued to look at her children in silence. She loved them but they were such a trial. She knew from conversations with other parents that this was quite common with teenagers these days. But that sort of exchange between mothers was back in the days when they were still speaking to her and before her two children had to be switched to a public school. Now she had no-one with whom to discuss parenting problems and she missed Michael. Parents of children at the public school knew, either from gossip or from chance remarks by her own children to classmates that her husband had abandoned her and Linda had been relegated to the status of an untouchable in the Indian subcontinent. It wasn't because she had once been affluent and now was even more hard-up than they were, or because Linda had been nasty to them in the past. There was no reason for Linda to have been nasty to them in the old, pre-Michael departure days because she had never come into contact with them. No, it was because Linda was still a very attractive, near-beautiful woman and most of them, slightly dowdy and care-worn, were scared stiff of their husbands going after what would be immensely appealing to their men-folk. The fact that Linda had little or no interest in men and certainly none for the uncouth, beer-swilling male counterparts of the mothers she sometimes saw at school was irrelevant. Linda was a threat to them and a potential predator, and they treated her accordingly.

The women at the boutique were single, very young or childless so conversations with them, infrequent as they were, rarely addressed anything other than the latest fashions, gossip about celebrities on TV or in films, or the rare current event. Linda had tried to go to the local church but despite claims by the minister that first-time visitors to the church were guests but after that they were family, she had been isolated and ignored. Attempts at conversation were rebuffed and no overtures of friendship were offered or received. After similar treatment at several different churches, Linda gave up on organized religion and tried to reach God by reading the bible and watching religious programs on television. Slowly but surely her spirituality increased and she became aware that she was being tested. Nothing like to the degree that Job had experienced but that was what was happening to her although she was keenly aware that, unlike Job, her problems were of her own doing and she did not have "friends" like those of Job to tell her about them.

Snapping out of her reverie, Linda looked directly at her children and said softly, "Damion and Rebecca, I know that things have been hard lately and you must be wondering what is going on, tight?"

The two young teenagers looked at each other and then at their mother, mystified expressions on their faces. The soft tone of voice, the distracted manner and the sympathetic expression were all very atypical of their mother. Finally Linda broke the silence again,

"As you know, your father took off some time ago and left us on our own. This has been hard for all of us and we've all suffered. At this stage, I don't think we need to compete with each other over who has suffered the most. The bottom line is that as far as anyone knows, your father is not coming back. In fact, no-one seems to know where he is although, if we are honest with ourselves, I think we all know why he left, don't we?"

Damion and Rebecca looked at each other and both shook their heads in confusion, asking themselves what had *they* done wrong?

"Oh don't look like that," snapped Linda. "All three of us were awful to your father and while I don't like the outcome, we have nobody to blame but ourselves."

Silence and then Damion protested, "But mom, what did I do wrong? Why blame me for dad taking off like that?"

"Look, Damion, we are all to blame, not just you," said Linda, and paused. "If we are honest with ourselves, we treated daddy badly and did so for years." As her children started to protest, Linda held up her hand in the age-old "stop" signal. "Let's face it, when was the last time any of us, and I mean *any* of us actually spent time with him? Frankly, we were all too busy to even bother saying "hello" let alone talk to him."

Silence.

Looking from one to the other, Linda continued, "You two, and me for that matter, simply ignored him. Daddy was someone who came home every day, changed and then, more often than not, cooked dinner for us all and then cleaned up afterwards while none of us even bothered to thank him. All those expensive clothes, games and computers that you demanded almost weekly as well as my country club and gym membership were paid for by your father. Not by you, not by me but by your father."

Looking at them again, Linda added sadly, "None of us ever expressed any gratitude or appreciation for what he did for us….we just took it all for granted. I know your father was not happy at the University; in fact, he probably hated it because he was treated so unfairly but none of us cared in the slightest, none of us!"

The last said almost in a shout and Linda nearly sobbed. She knew that she had blamed Michael for everything that was happening but she had had to accept the fact that she had been more than culpable. It was her blithely contemptuous attitude towards her husband that had created the two near-monsters that were her children – thoughtless, selfish, self-centered brats who did nothing but complain about any and everything. Helping around the house? Tidying up their rooms? Clearing the table or washing the dishes after dinner? Fat chance! Cut the grass or help clear snow in winter? Not likely! Their allowances were given on a weekly basis regardless of the fact that helping their parents do anything, *anything*, was beneath their dignity. But, as Linda thought ruefully, she had encouraged them to do nothing. She had tidied up occasionally and made the beds, even ran the washing machine once a week but that was the extent of her domestic chores. As she often said to her "friends" at the country club, the gym or the coffee shop where they all gathered to gossip, she Linda Woodman did not do housework! If the house was dirty and Michael didn't take care of it, then the house stayed dirty unless and until he arranged for a cleaning service to come in.

Damion and Rebeccas were confused. Their unspoken thoughts were remarkably similar: 'Their mother had largely ignored them for the past few years and, when pressed, had given in to every demand, however unreasonable. Now, suddenly, she was blaming them for what had happened. It was so unfair when all they had ever done was what all their school friends did…and why was it now so wrong?' Anger and resentment boiled up inside but one look at their mother's face dissuaded them from saying anything.

"Anyway, your father has gone…left us for whatever reason." Seeing Damion about to speak, Linda hurried on. "The police have been no help in finding him because, as they said, he's committed no crimes, has no criminal record, hasn't stolen anything and doesn't owe anyone money or anything like that. As that stupid police detective said, people leave home all the time and unless there is a very good reason, such as a crime, they can't do anything. Oh yes, they did check all the hospitals and shelters, that sort of thing, but no-one even remotely answering to your father's description has been seen and he's not dead either. He's just gone."

The three of them sat in silence for a few moments and then Damion piped up, "So mom, what do we do? Are things really that bad? What can we do to help?"

Linda was astonished. This was the first time that Damion showed any awareness of anything other than himself. Almost before her eyes he was starting to mature from a self-centered little boy into a young man and she could almost see what sort of man he might develop into.

"Well my darlings, we'll have to tighten our belts. I know things have not been good but I'm afraid that they might get worse. I am trying to find a better-paid job but it is hard to do so these days, the economy being what it is. The long and short of it is that money is tight and might get tighter and we'll all have to pull together until things get better."

A sad and thoughtful silence descended on the room. "So," said Linda, breaking the silence, "we're going to have to have to watch our pennies. No leaving the lights on when we're not in a room, no long hot showers that use up lots of water and burn up electricity, no fancy clothes or computer games – we all will have to make do with what we've got. Okay? In fact, let's have a yard sale. We've all got lots of *stuff* and we certainly don't need all those things that just clutter up the house. If we get rid of things that we don't want or haven't touched in months or years, let's get rid of them and make some much-needed money." Linda hesitated for a moment before adding, "It would be nice if we could sell this place and find somewhere smaller but I can't sell the house without your father being here, so that's not possible."

Damion and Rebecca nodded. Reality had sunk in although they knew from the progressive downward spiral of household expenditures, at least those that they were aware of, that things were no longer what they had been. Now it was "official" – the three of them were poor and that was that.

"Okay, mom," said Damion. "We'll do what we can." He hesitated and then asked, "Would it help if I got a newspaper delivery job or worked somewhere like in a store? You know, packing groceries, that sort of thing?"

"I don't know about that, Damion, but it is wonderful that you would even ask."

"Hey, maybe I can babysit," said Rebecca. "If Damion's got to get a job, then so must I. We'll do what we can to help, won't we Damion?"

Linda burst into tears and help out her arms for her children, hugging them close until all three were crying. Suddenly they were a family and they would survive no matter what.

Michael dumped his few belongings on the motel bed and surveyed the room. It was pretty shabby with worn carpets, stained walls and he didn't want to think about what might be buried inside the mattress or lurking in the bathroom. "It's not much, old boy," he said aloud, "but it's home and cheap. I'll probably have to share the place with cockroaches and sundry other bugs but at least I've got a roof over my head. Now, where's that map? Might as well see where we are."

He decided he'd find somewhere to eat that evening, a place that was cheap but nourishing, and then he'd look around the town, such as it appeared to be, to see if he could find some employment. No point in depleting his meager resources unless absolutely necessary. Besides, he needed to scout out alternative routes to freeways and safe ways to come and go from the motel and remain unobserved. This was always a problem with small towns – lots of prying eyes and bored residents who had nothing better to do than to observe comings and goings. Even if he operated, as he liked to refer to his arcane homicidal activities, in towns well away from this one, it was always possible that someone might see him leaving the motel and returning later, and mention it to the police or even volunteer the information. No, he needed to be as discreet as possible.

Later, after dinner in a greasy spoon – literally in this case – he settled back in his room and studied the map. There were several larger towns to the north, east and west of his location, all of which looked likely prospects. The last thing he wanted to do was pick a victim in a town to the south because that was where he was still headed and there was no point in announcing his intentions. He paused and thought about that decision. What if he did take someone out south of where he was and then only got there some time after the killing? Wouldn't that eliminate him as a suspect? After all, if he wasn't staying in the place where a murder was committed and only arrived there some days or weeks later, why would anyone even think that he might have been involved? Hmm, that was an interesting thought – an iron-clad alibi, always an useful thing, when all else failed. He smiled. Thinking of every possibility was so satisfying. Then he looked at the map again.

If he went far enough south, he could get on I10 and drive over to Florida., Florida is the armpit of America and with all those retirees, there should be good pickings for him. Perhaps that's where he should go within the next year – yes, Florida would be good.

Big Jim Cunningham sat back in his recliner and stared at his son. Eventually he said, "It's good to have you home Randy, even if it's only for a few days."

"Thanks, Dad," replied Randy Cunningham. "It is good to be home but I have to say I'm looking forward to getting started in my new assignment in the big city."

"Oh? I thought that you were enjoying yourself up north?"

"It was okay but not really challenging. Not much ever happened and my boss…well…er…he and I didn't see eye-to-eye on many things."

'I'll bet you didn't' thought Big Jim. 'No senior FBI agent takes kindly to some young whipper-snapper thinking he knows all the answers while he's still wet behind the ears – actually that's true in most cases, not just the FBI. Well, now Randy's here, I'll find an opportunity to tell him about Clyde Wilkins. If nothing else, if he tackles a local case that the police have given up on, then he'll come visiting a lot more and that'll keep the wife happy. Cooking lots of meals for him and taking care of his laundry will occupy many happy hours for her and that's a good thing. It'll also keep her off my back and stop her worrying about the bar.'

He took another pull at his coffee mug. After serving booze all day, the last thing Big Jim wanted to do is have a drink at night or on the weekends – ironic that he made his living, such as it was, serving drinks and didn't even care that much for alcohol himself. While on the job, he had enjoyed a beer or two with his colleagues after work but that was more about the company and a chance to vent rather than the beer itself. He thought about all the confidences that were exchanged between friends after a beer or two. The trouble was that being a cop tended to separate the average police officer from the rest of the population and even wives and girlfriends got excluded. It was hard to carry a badge and a gun during the day and to be always on the look-out for trouble and then go home and shed the uniform like an old skin. Even off duty, a cop was a cop, and that was that. He sighed.

Randy looked at him, and asked, "What was that sigh for Dad? Something wrong?"

"There's always something wrong but, no, nothing in particular. I was just thinking how one can never completely stop being a cop even when off duty or, as in my case, retired from the force. I suppose it gets into the blood like one of those nasty diseases that crop up all the time."

"What diseases are those, Dad?" asked the ever-literal Randy.

"Oh it doesn't matter…I was just trying to make a point."

"I see…and the point is?" Randy persisted.

"Forget it, Randy. It wasn't that important." Seeing his son about to make another comment, Big Jim forestalled him with "What I was saying is that once a cop, always a cop" but before Randy could say anything else, he went on, "We had a weird murder here quite recently."

"Really? Who did it?"

"That's just it, no-one knows and it made no sense back then or, in hind-sight, now when one thinks about it."

"That's odd. What happened?"

Given the opportunity, Big Jim seized it and related the sequence of events to his son. He concluded with the comment, "So there you have it. Someone killed a man for no apparent reason and no-one knows whether it was the work of a local, someone from a neighboring town or simply that some random serial killer just happened upon Clyde and offed him for fun."

"You're joking!" said Randy.

"Far from it son – that's the last thing I'm doing. Random killings just don't happen here but then one did, and in the parking lot of *The Wayside Hang-out* of all places. Of course no-one saw a thing but that's nothing new, is it?"

Randy was silent, slowly digesting what he had just heard. He was aware that his father had been a good police officer and had served for many, many years. He rarely made snap decisions and if he commented on a subject, then more often than not, he was right. 'But was he right in assuming that a random killer had simply swept into town and killed a nobody like Clyde Wilkins just for fun?' he asked himself. He vaguely remembered Clyde when he was growing up and, as far as he Randy was concerned, Clyde was a spotty-faced kid who visited his grandmother on occasions but had lived with his parents in another town a few miles away. That raised the question of what Clyde was doing in the parking lot of *The Wayside Hang-out* at night when, according to his father, he lived the other side of town. Randy sat silent and thought about the incident, using FBI jargon for criminal acts. Then he started to ask his father for as many details as Big Jim could remember, vowing to look into this case on the following Monday when he went into the Bureau and also to see if there had been any other similar incidents. Although relatively new to the FBI, Randy was well aware that seldom did murders like this come out of the blue. There might well be similar incidents, maybe not here or even in the same state but there logically had to be others, all he had to do was start digging. For all he knew, this could be a career-making path for him to follow but first he needed to do some research.

Michael pulled into the car parking area, noting with satisfaction that it too had a gravel surface. He picked a quiet spot close to the entrance and turned his car around so that he could take off in a hurry if needs be. As he sat in Wilma, waiting for the ticking of the hot engine to die down, he pulled out his gun and checked that there was a round in the barrel and then he cocked it. Next he pulled on plastic gloves and after taking one of the large potatoes out of his pocket, he carefully wiped the surface. Then he wiped it over again with a Kleenex to make sure that there were no prints on the tuber. Finally he settled back to wait.

It wasn't long before an expensive late-model BMW sedan roared into the parking lot and five college-age students climbed out, shouting loudly. Judging by their sizes and the fact that they were all wearing lettered zip-up jackets, Michael deduced that they were football players from the local college and probably in their early twenties and all exuded arrogance and privilege. As they walked towards the bar entrance, one of them, the largest with a pronounced swagger to his gait, held back.

"Hey Matt, what're you doing?" called one of them. "Are you coming or what?"

"Oh I'm just going to have a little fun before I get a drink."

"Not again, Matt," said another man. "Don't you get tired of doing that?"

"Nah, not me," said Matt. He pointed at the various parked vehicles and said, "Just look at those cars, all clean and polished. I think I'll just mess up the paintwork a little - how about you guys keeping watch for me?"

"Not this time, Matt," said one of his companions. "It's no longer funny to mess up someone else's car. In fact it never was and if you do it, then you're on your own as far as I am concerned." The young man turned on his heel and walked towards the bar. He didn't particularly care for Matt but he was a team mate, so he just kept his mouth shut about what the quarterback was doing. As he heard the footsteps of the others following, he knew that sooner or later, Matt's actions would catch up with him and he, for one, wanted to be far away from what was likely to happen.

Watching them go into the bar, Michael shifted his attention to Matt and watched as he pulled a box cutter out of his pocket and systematically sliced through the paintwork on several new and not-so-new cars, giggling as he did so. As Matt leaned down to carve some letters into the side of a shiny Mercedes, Michael quietly stole up behind him, pressed the potato and gun against the left side of his back and pulled the trigger. There was a muffled thump and Matt keeled over, shot through the heart. Michael crouched down and felt the man's carotid artery – he was dead. Straightening up, he walked quickly back to Wilma, tossing the blown potato as far as he could into the undergrowth off to one side of the parking lot.

He started the engine and, again without switching on his lights, he pulled out onto the road and headed back to the Interstate, only turning on his lights when he was about half a mile from the bar. As he drove, Michael hummed to himself and then said to his car, "Well, Wilma, we've done it again. That little shit – actually not so little but still a shit – won't be carving up cars again, will he? Damn college kids – those football players think they can get away with anything because they're sports heroes. Well, not this time, Wilma, not this time," and he drove on, humming happily and feeling as though he had performed yet another beneficial service to humanity.

Several miles down the Interstate, Michael spoke aloud, "I wonder what position that guy Matt played? Judging by his size and general arrogance, he was probably a quarterback or some sort of defensive player. Well, whatever he was, that team'll have to find someone else to replace him. Perhaps now the coach will teach his team to respect other people's property although I doubt it. Coaches seem to be all-forgiving of any and all antics of their star players and I'll bet this one's no different."

He lapsed into silence and, carefully keeping to the speed limit, he drove on back to his motel. It had been a long drive but worthwhile. As the miles passed, Michael was pleased that this time he had used a gun. A person that size might not have succumbed easily to the now familiar plastic bag and garrote method, and the last thing that Michael wanted to have happen was a large intended victim suddenly turning on him.

Just as he reached his motel, another thought struck him. Forensics experts could easily detect GSR – gunshot residue – and that could be dangerous. He decided he'd buy a couple of throw-away plastic raincoats to use the next time and also get some liquid paraffin to wash off any residue from his hands, not that there be much since always wore plastic gloves. Still, one never knew and a few precautions would not go amiss. Satisfied, he pulled up outside his motel room and, from habit, made sure that no-one was about. As far as he knew, he hadn't been seen leaving the place and now, hopefully, no-one had seen him return. Again he envied Dexter Morgan who had a safe haven to return to unobserved but that was television and this was real-life and not everything was perfect.

Later, after he had carefully showered and stored his potentially soiled clothes in a large plastic bag to be disposed of later, Michael settled down to sleep. For a few moments he tried to remember how many victims he had taken care of and, after losing count, slipped into a deep, dreamless sleep. Then he woke up with a start. What had he done with the spent cartridge? His gun was an automatic, not a revolver and spent cartridges were shot out the side of the weapon, and he had forgotten to pick it up. He was slightly sick for a moment because he had left behind trace evidence that could cause problems. Then he relaxed. When he had bought extra ammunition, he had also purchased a spare magazine and had loaded and used those new rounds when he had been practicing. Fortunately he had inserted the old magazine in the gun before going out so if there were any fingerprints on the brass casings, they were those of his previous victim. He smiled to himself. If the police found the spent cartridge, which they probably would, then they would find someone else's fingerprints on it, not his. That was a stroke of luck but he'd have to be more careful in the future. Satisfied, Michael lay back and dropped off to sleep.

The four college football players were just starting noisily on their second pitcher of beer when one of them asked, "Hey, where's Matt?"

They all looked at each other somewhat blearily before another said, "Didn't he stay outside to do something?' Then he lowered his voice before saying, "You know how he likes to mess up cars. It's a weird hobby of his but….er…that's what he seems to get off on."

"That may be," said the first player. "But he's been out there for a long time and there weren't *that* many cars in the parking lot. Surely he'd have finished his *business* by now?"

"Knowing him," said another. "He's a quick slice and dice artist and doesn't hang around too long afterwards, does he?"

"Yeah, that's true…so where is he?"

"Not here, that's for sure. Okay, I'll check the bathroom and one of you go and look around outside. He's probably out there drunk or something, knowing Matt."

A few minutes later, the young man who had gone outside came rushing back, face ashen and a frightened look on his face.

"Hey, what's going on, Jim?" asked one of the others. "You look as if you've seen a ghost. Did the boogeyman out there scare you?" and the other three laughed.

"It's Matt," Jim gasped.

"What about him? Did he get lost or something?" and the three now slightly drunk footballers all laughed again.

"No, he didn't get lost – he's dead!"

"He's what?" cried one of them. "Get real!"

"Oh it's real – as real as a heart attack. Go see for yourself but I'm calling the police. I'd better let the bar tender know too. Oh shit, shit, shit…what happened to Matt?"

It did not take long for a police cruiser to arrive on the scene or for the officer, Ed Marcum, to call for back-up once he saw the gaping exit wound in the young man's chest. Being an experienced policeman, Ed Marcum started to take down the names of the four young men gathered around him and alternated this with shouting at the bar patrons to stay away from the crime scene. As he noted down the names, it struck him that they were familiar and he took another careful look at them as it dawned on him that they were members of the college football team. Without missing a beat, he turned and stared hard at the dead man a few yards away. "Holy crap," he muttered. "That's Matt Levine. Oh man, this is not going to be good!"

As soon as one of the slightly drunk patrons heard his muttering, the word spread like wildfire and cell phone cameras started to click like mad as everyone tried to photograph the dead man. One very inebriated man was almost on top of the prone Matt before Ed screamed at him to back off. Before the situation got completely out of hand, reinforcements arrived and the crowd was moved back and crime scene tape was placed around the body.

At this point the duty sergeant and the watch commander arrived and some semblance of order was established although the on-lookers whispered excitedly to each other. Murder was uncommon in this town and when a local hero was killed, then this was big news. By the time the homicide detectives arrived, together with the medical examiner and crime scene investigators, the media hawks, print and television, turned up, obviously in response to the "bush telegraph" that existed in every town whenever something newsworthy happened and this *was* newsworthy.

CHAPTER 8

"Okay, hotshots," said the no-nonsense Captain Sid Rogers of the Oklahoma State Police. "What've you got?"

"You mean the killing of that football player at the *Sunset Tavern*?" said Rich Armstrong, the lead homicide detective.

"No, I'm talking about Santa Claus offing one of his reindeer. What the hell do you think I'm asking about?"

"Well Captain, we don't have much."

"Just how much is *not much*?"

"Ah….er…well, there's not much that we can say."

"Spare me, Armstrong, just spare me. So what *have* you got?"

"Frankly there are no clues to speak of although CSI did find a spent cartridge near the stiff…"

"For crying out loud, Armstrong, show some respect for the dead. The victim was a young man in the prime of his life who's now dead. Referring to him as a stiff is enough to get you written up, okay?"

"Sorry Captain."

"So you should be. Okay, CSI found a shell casing near the deceased. Did it match the round that killed the victim?"

"We're not sure. The round that killed him was a through-and-through and try as we might, we couldn't find it. CSI searched the whole parking lot and either the killer picked it up or it bounced off somewhere and was picked up by someone."

"Great, just great!" sighed Capt. Rogers. "I cannot believe that the perp picked up the bullet but left the cartridge behind. That doesn't make a lot of sense to me or is there something that I'm missing?"

"Not really, no."

"So, what else have you got?"

"The ME found traces of what looked like potato imbedded in the victim's clothing and inside the wound."

"Potato? Damn, so the killer used a crude but effective silencer and that's presumably why no-one heard a gun-shot, right?"

"We think so., yes."

"Okay then, did you get anything from the victim's friends, the guys he'd been drinking with that evening? What about his family... anything there?"

"The kid was a good and possibly great quarterback and, by all accounts, was likely to be recruited to the NFL in his senior year. So he was pretty popular with the townsfolk. You know, he was a local hero who was putting the place on the map, so to speak."

"Hmm...what about his team-mates?" asked Captain Rogers, sensing something unsaid by his lead detective.

"That's interesting Captain. As far as we can tell, he wasn't that popular with the rest of the team...apparently he was pretty arrogant and belittled the rest of the team but everyone accepts that he was the primary reason for the team's successes over the past couple of years. They had no choice really because he made the plays."

"I see," said Captain Rogers. "So, the townsfolk and presumably the College loved the guy but it was a different story with his teammates, that what you're saying?"

"That about sums it up," said Brian Henderson, the junior homicide detective. "On the other hand, there wasn't any notable animosity towards the guy other than frequent references to him being an asshole."

"What about girlfriends or involvement with married women – you know, the sort of thing that can get people riled up?"

"Apparently he and a co-ed have been dating for the past two or three years and theirs was an exclusive relationship. No hint of either of them straying and if Matt Levine was screwing around with someone else, he was unbelievably discreet about it because no-one, not even his few friends or close team-mates had caught even a whisper of anything like that."

"You said *his few friends*. What's that all about?" asked Capt. Rogers.

"Apparently Matt's time was carefully controlled, for want of a better term." said Rich. "He was pretty studious and, surprisingly for a jock, he maintained good grades. So when he wasn't studying, training or playing, he spent all his free time, such as it was, with his girlfriend."

"In that case, what was he doing at that bar with the other guys on that particular evening?"

"Apparently his girlfriend had gone home for the weekend and the team didn't have a game the next day, so five of them went out for a drink together that night."

"Okay, I'll buy that but why were the other four inside while Matt was hanging around outside in the parking lot? What in heaven's name was he doing out there on his own?"

The two homicide detectives looked at each other and grimaced.

Catching their looks, Captain Rogers pounced, "Okay, what gives?"

Both men hesitated and then Rich Armstrong said, "Apparently, on the infrequent occasions that those five got together, Levine would like to carve his initials or the like into the sides of parked vehicles."

"What?" screamed Sid Rogers. "He did what?"

"This was some sort of hobby for the guy…the others didn't want anything to do with it but it was something that Levine enjoyed doing. Apparently he did that whenever they went out drinking."

"These guys, they didn't report him to the coach?"

"Get real, Captain," said Brian, immediately regretting his words. But he had spoken out and now he had to continue. "The coach is old school, as I know from when I was playing for him in college. His players could do no wrong and a star quarterback like Levine walked on water as far as he was concerned. Any player that blew the whistle on him would be in deep doo-doos and probably get dropped from the team, that's assuming the coach even bothered to hear what he had to say."

"So you're saying a star player like Levine could get away with misdemeanors like vandalism?"

"A whole lot more than just vandalism," said Rich. "Football coaches everywhere, not just at the College, run their programs like fiefdoms and no-one, not even the College President wants to get in the way of success. The alumni, benefactors and the whole town for that matter would probably lynch him if he tried."

"Great," snarled Rogers. "Alright then, we have a victim who's apparently as clean and pure as the driven snow as far as the team, the coach and the whole damn college is concerned. No sex, outside of his long-term relationship that is, no drugs and good grades – the kid sounds like a model citizen apart from his tendency to vandalize parked cars…that right?"

"I'm afraid so, Captain," agreed Rich.

"When you talked to the patrons of the bar, did anyone come in, or leave, while Matt Levine was out in the parking lot?"

The two detectives shook their heads. When they heard about Levine's car carving proclivities, both immediately wondered whether a customer had happened upon him vandalizing their vehicle, but that apparently was not the case. Likewise, if someone had driven into the parking lot and seen Levine at work, it was more likely that they would have called the police rather than shoot the fellow. People often got upset over damaged property but that usually only applied to their own possessions.

"No," said Rich eventually. "Nothing there either."

"From his name, I gather that Matt Levine was Jewish…was he?"

"I believe so," said Brian. "But I don't think he was strict Orthodox or anything like that. Apparently he rarely attended Temple."

"So an anti-Semitic angle is unlikely?" asked Rogers.

""I would say so," agreed Rich. "People here are pretty tolerant when it comes to religion and, as I say, not only was Matt Levine the star quarterback and one of the few Jews in town and at the College; I gather he was regarded as *their* Jew. I honestly don't think anti-Semitism had any part in his murder…it just seems too far-fetched."

"Far-fetched?" snapped Rogers. "You're telling me that you cannot come up with a reason, *any reason*, why the guy was killed, right?" He sighed and looked at his two homicide detectives and then stared up at the ceiling, saying softly, almost to himself, "Occam's Razor!"

He looked at the detectives and smiled at their puzzled expressions, and added, "What Occam's razor tells us is that when there are several possible explanations, take the one with the fewest assumptions. In other words, when all else fails, take the simplest explanation."

"So what *is* the simplest explanation?" asked Brian, still mystified.

"The simplest explanation, in fact the only one, is that some random killer happened upon Matt Levine and killed him. Why he did so is beyond me and in that particular locale but why else is that young man dead?"

The two detectives looked at each other and then at their captain in astonishment. There was silence for a few beats and then Rich asked, "Captain, do you really think some random killer just turned up here, killed that football player and then simply took off again? Man, that just doesn't seem possible."

"What other explanation can there be? The kid might not have been popular with his team-mates but everyone else seemed to love him. There's no hint of a jealous boyfriend or husband lurking out there. No drugs, no gambling debts….nothing…so why should anyone have killed him?"

Rich and Brian looked at each other again and nodded, perhaps the Captain was right, however unlikely that scenario was. "Okay," said Rich eventually. "What do we do?"

"Frankly you've exhausted every possibility. Credit where credit's due and you guys are pretty good detectives. Your clearance rate is excellent and that CSI team is very efficient, so if you can't find anything, then it's not there to be found. Pass the file over to the Cold Case Squad and move on…that's what I suggest. Okay?"

The detectives nodded and got to their feet. It wasn't satisfactory but there was no alternative. As they were leaving the captain's office, Rogers called out to them, "Hey, while you're at it, send a copy of the file over to the FBI Field Office. You never know but they might come up with something - it's not unknown."

Linda sat on the bench across the road from *La Petite Patisserie* and stared at the coffee shop longingly. It had been literally months since she had frequented the place with her friends but she could no longer afford to drop $10-20 for cakes and coffee let alone spend one or two hours sitting around gossiping with them. She missed that unofficial routine but if she could not afford it, then that was that. She sighed loudly and felt very sad.

"My word," came a soft voice from the other end of the bench. "That's a sad sigh from such a pretty woman."

Linda was startled. She had not even been aware that someone else had sat down on the bench and certainly did not welcome unwanted overtures from strangers. She turned towards the end of the bench and saw that an older man was sitting there and looking at her quizzically. It was difficult to judge his age but, Linda surmised, he was probably in his late 50s or early 60s with a full head of salt-and-pepper hair and a neatly trimmed moustache and goatee. He had slightly irregular features, was well-dressed and spoke with an educated accent. Definitely attractive but so what? The last thing she needed was a man in her life what with Michael still out there somewhere. Life was pretty bad already and she had no need of any complications right now, if ever.

Deciding, Linda turned to the man and said with some asperity, "That's a very poor pick-up line."

"It wasn't meant to be one." said the man. And he smiled slightly. As Linda continued to regard him with a slightly hostile expression, he added, "When a beautiful woman sighs so sadly, it's not unreasonable to assume that something is troubling her and all I was doing was offering a friendly ear. A shoulder to cry on, if you will."

"I don't will," snapped Linda. "I don't know you and the last thing I would ever do is talk to a stranger about any problems that I do or don't have, thank you very much."

"Well, that's interesting but not necessarily an issue. We can easily resolve the stranger part – quick introductions take care of that. But I do believe that you have some problems, which might not be so easily resolved."

Linda stared at him and smiled slightly. Whatever else the man might be, he certainly appeared to be charming and he exuded an aura of calm competence. After hesitating a few seconds, she held out her hand and said, "I'm Linda Woodman."

The man took her hand and shook it firmly without exerting any pressure. "My name is Victor Bascombe." He smiled at Linda, adding, "There, now we're not strangers any longer. That wasn't too difficult, was it?"

Linda nodded, smiled slightly again and then glanced down at her watch. "Oops," she said. "I've got to go. My lunch break is up."

Victor looked at his own watch and raised an eyebrow, "Your lunch break is up at 11.30 in the morning?"

"In retail, you have to take breaks in between times that customers come into the store, and they start to flood in around noon…you know, during *their* lunch breaks."

"I see," said Victor. "So where do you work that they have such Dickensian rules regarding lunch breaks?"

"I work at Bennet's Department Store and I'm not sure that their rules are Dickensian, as you put it. Irregular break times are simply a part of being in retail, as is the need to work late and on weekends and holidays. That's just the way it is." She got to her feet.

"You don't seem to be too upset about it," said Victor.

"I'm not….as I said, that's just the way it is. They pay me quite well and I have good benefits as Bennet's treat their employees well. So if you'll excuse, I need to get back to work. I don't want to get in trouble and lose my job. It's the only one I've got."

Annoyed with herself for possibly revealing too much, Linda started to walk away. As she did so, Victor called after her, "I enjoyed meeting you, Linda. Next time we'll talk about what's troubling you."

Linda nodded and walked on. She doubted that there would be a next time and the last thing she wanted was to talk about her problems with a near stranger, however attractive and sympathetic that person appeared to be. As she made her way back to Bennet's, Linda mulled over the encounter with Victor Bascombe. The name was somehow familiar to her but she could not place it or in what context. However, by the time she reached the staff entrance to the department store, she had dismissed the matter from her mind, sharing her thoughts between what she would cook for dinner that evening and how busy she might be that afternoon after the lunchtime time rush was over.

The rest of her afternoon went quite quickly and, being busy, Linda thought no more about her chance encounter earlier that day. Although there had been an unusually high number of returns, the majority of customers still had their receipts and one or two even exchanged their purchases for more expensive items so that, overall, Linda's commission probably increased slightly, to her delight. At the end of her shift Linda was astonished to find that her register actually balanced so she was feeling quite relaxed if not pleased with herself for the day. Collecting her belongings, she made her way down to the staff entrance and turned towards the employees' parking lot. It had been a long day and her feet and legs ached. For a moment she wondered whether she was developing varicose veins, the bane of all retail workers, and she made a mental note to get some support hose as well as better footwear to help ease the stress of standing for hours on end.

As she was about to turn into the parking lot, a vaguely familiar voice behind her said, "Linda, we meet again."

She whirled around and there stood Victor Bascombe with a smile on his face. Surprised, Linda said, "Victor? What are you doing here?"

"Oh I was just passing Bennet's and saw you, so I followed."

"I see. Why did you do that?"

"Well, it's the end of the day and I wondered whether you might like to go and have a coffee or even a drink."

"Thanks but no thanks," responded Linda. "I have to get home. I need to shower and change and then get dinner ready for my kids. Then I suppose I'll have to help them with their homework, so…"

"Ah the never-ending chores of the working mother," commented Victor. "So, if you can't have a coffee or drink with me, can I at least give you a lift home?"

"Again no thanks," said Linda. "My car's right here." She turned away but was brought to an abrupt stop by Victor's next words: "Alright then, why don't I take you and your children out to dinner tonight?"

"What?"

"Just as I said, why not come to dinner with me."

"Er...."

"It's alright, there's no obligation or strings attached. I'll follow you home and while you are showering and changing, I'll talk to your offspring and then we'll all go to dinner. Steak suit you?"

"Look Victor, this is very strange. I hardly know you – in fact I don't know you at all and here you are inviting us out to dinner. It's crazy. Besides, my children have probably made arrangements to meet up with their friends, so that I doubt that they would want to come to dinner. They may think they have better things to do than spend time with their mother and some strange man that she's just met."

"Probably," agreed Victor. "But then again, what could be a better way of getting to know each other than over a good meal? That way we'll no longer be such strangers. Just say yes, okay?"

Linda shook her head in bemusement. The man was either a lunatic, a strong possibility in this day and age, or he was genuine. 'What the hell,' she thought. 'A steak dinner sounds divine and what have I got to lose?' Deciding, she nodded and said, "Okay then, just follow me. It's a little bit of a trek to get to my house but not too bad. Where are you parked?"

Victor simply smiled and held up his hand. Within seconds, a large chauffeur-driven car pulled up and Victor got in but not before saying, "We'll follow you, Linda."

As Linda got into her car and pulled out of the parking lot, she muttered, "This is all very strange. I don't have any idea who this man is or why he wants to have dinner with me but then again, having dinner in a good restaurant with an attractive man is really appealing after all the dreadful meals we've been having of late. Rebecca and Damion might be delighted although I suspect that they'd rather spend time with their friends. If nothing else, I'll give them some money and they can go off and get pizza or whatever it is they like to eat when they are with their friends."

As she drove, noting that Victor's car stayed quite close, her thoughts turned towards the man. 'I wonder who he is. Not too many people in this city have chauffeurs or have the time to sit on street benches chatting to strange women or to hang around waiting for them to leave work. I wonder what on earth is going on…well, we'll soon find out. For that matter, why is his name familiar to me?'

When she arrived at her house, Linda drove up the driveway and as the garage door opened remotely, she deftly guided her car inside, noting that Victor's car had pulled up in front of her house.

Quickly going into the house, Linda reached the front door and opened it just as Victor was about to ring the bell. "Please come in," she said. "Look, I'll sit you in the living room while I quickly shower and change. My children, Damion and Rebecca, may or may not look in to see who's here but I wouldn't bank on it. In fact, they've probably already gone off to see their friends, this being a Friday and not a school night." She paused, "Anyway, there are a couple of magazines in there – they might be out-of-date but they should give you something to look at while I'm getting ready." She smiled at Victor and added, "Hopefully I won't be too long. Is there anything I can get you in the meantime?"

Victor said, "Thank you, no…and take your time, we are in no hurry."

Randy Cunningham looked at the pile of file folders n his In Box and smiled to himself. As the low man on the totem pole, this was not unexpected. What did surprise him, however, was that they had appeared in the short time span between his arrival at the office and settling of all the necessary and inevitable paperwork with Human Resources and then his taking up "residence" at his assigned desk. He could not remember the last time that any Government agency had operated that speedily. Equally amusing and expected was the positioning of his desk in the "bull pen" – in a corner as far removed as possible from the action near to the senior agent's office. He was the new man and he had to prove himself before anyone would accept him as a real member of the team. Still and all, the SAC Steve Wellington seemed to be pleasant enough and with his new position and office location, Randy could at least visit his parents on a fairly regular basis.

He pulled the pile of files out of his In-box and laid them out on his desk. As was his custom, he scanned each document in turn just to make sure that there were no bombshells or files requiring urgent attention tucked in amidst the many items of dross and inter-office memoranda. SACs liked to play tricks on new staff members and slipping high priority items in among a whole lot of unimportant verbiage was a favorite.

As he had expected, the majority of items in the In Box were routine memoranda together with a few reports regarding on-going cases. Randy felt himself being slowly pulled into the routine of the large and fairly busy Regional FBI Center and then one file gave him pause for thought and he placed the file to one side. Then to his surprise, he found another file that, like the other one, had been forwarded by the State Police but from a different state. Whistling softly to himself, he cleared the dross and re-read both files very carefully.

Randy sat back and stared into space. Like all law enforcement people the world over, he disliked and distrusted coincidences. As he was digesting what he had just read, Steve Wellington appeared at his desk and held out his hand, "Randy," he said. "I'm Steve Wellington and I just wanted to welcome you to our office." He paused and added, "Look it's lunchtime, so let's go and get a bite to eat. This'll give us a chance to get to know each other, okay?"

Nodding his agreement, Randy got to his feet and Steve added that it would be nothing fancy, just burgers and fries but at least it would get them both out of the office.

Michael had found one more cheap motel on the outskirts of yet another look-alike small town but this time in Arkansas. After unpacking his few things, he sauntered out and drove the trusty Wilma around town, getting a feel for the place and the relative locations of the various businesses, stores and housing scattered around the town but he was especially interested in where he could eat on a fairly regular basis without attracting unwanted attention. As he found in other towns, he was surprised by the number of establishments and businesses with Help Wanted notices and, not for the first time, he wondered why there was such a high unemployment rate when so many enterprises seemed to be desperate for workers. Then he remembered that regular and full-time employment required workers to satisfy background checks and a whole lot of things could result in negative reviews and, consequently, unemployability. So far he had been lucky that no-one seemed interested in his background but sooner or later, a prospective employer would look into it and that might cause problems. Well, he decided, we'll worry about that when the time comes.

Finding a small diner, he entered and found a table where someone had left a copy of the local newspaper. A waitress came up and without asking, placed a glass of water in front of him together with a brimming cup of hot coffee. These were quickly followed by cutlery and a napkin together with the comment, "Today's special is meatloaf. It's pretty good but you can have anything on the menu", and she ceremoniously held out a small, plastic coated and very battered menu to him.

"Meatloaf sounds good to me," said Michael and then turned his attention to the Help Wanted columns in the newspaper. As he looked at the relatively large number of available opportunities, he wondered what he wanted to do this time. Retail had begun to pall with him although cash payments and an almost total disinterest in his background or where he had been prior to taking the position had a certain appeal. A couple of openings caught his eye but then he realized that he would not be staying here, wherever "here" might be, for long enough to be of any real help to any business other than a retail operation. Given what he had been doing for the past several months, Michael realized that any concern that he had for satisfying the needs of a potential employer was almost inappropriate. He smiled and looked again, this time concentrating on small retail operations. Flipping burgers on the like had a certain appeal in its near mindlessness and that occupation did have the advantage of free food. As he circled a couple of likely openings, the waitress re-appeared and laid a large plate loaded with food next to his right hand where it held the newspaper.

Seeing what he was reading, the waitress asked, "Are you looking for work?"

"Actually, I am," said Michael. "Why do you ask?"

"We need help back in the kitchen, that's why. Can you cook?"

"Oh yes – nothing too fancy mind you, but I can cook."

"Okay then when can you start?"

Michael looked at her in surprise. "You're offering me a job?" Since when did waitresses offer jobs to customers?

The waitress, seeing the surprised look on Michael's face, added, "My brother and I own this place and we can get so busy at times, we can't keep up with everything."

Michael nodded.

"So we need help but we can't find anyone suitable. Either they're spotty-faced kids just out of high school, street people, druggies or ex-military with a big chip on their shoulders and none of them, repeat none of them, want to work and certainly not at the pace we need in here."

"What makes you think I'm not like them?" asked Michael curiously.

"For a start you're clean, especially your fingernails, you're obviously looking for a job and, judging by the plates on your car, you're not from around here."

"That matters?" asked Michael. "Being not from around here, I mean."

"Yes. Most locals are lazy and cleanliness isn't big around here, at least not with those that are looking for work." She stared at him for a moment. "You don't do drugs or anything, do you?"

"No ma'am, I don't and as for working hard and fast, try me."

"Okay," she nodded. "You're on." She held out a hand, saying, "I'm Bella and my brother, who'll you meet when you're finished eating, is Andrew. We've had *The Second Street Cafe* for about five years now – we inherited the place from our father when he died and we've done quite well. The customers are nice and we try to give them good food at a reasonable price." Bella looked at him again, "When can you start?"

"How about tomorrow?" asked Michael.

"Don't you want to know what we'll pay you?" asked Bella in surprise.

"Oh I know it'll be fair and I doubt that it's up for negotiation, so surprise me."

Bella laughed. "You're crazy but I like you. Okay you're on. When you're finished…and by the way, the meal's on us…come and meet Andrew and we'll sort out the details later. As I said, Andrew is my brother and the co-owner of this fine eating establishment. Okay?"

Michael nodded, and said, "Okay. That sounds like a plan and thank you for dinner but how do you know that I'm not just angling for a free meal?"

"You don't look the type…you've got an honest face…besides, a plate of meatloaf isn't much to lose if you want to stiff us."

Michael smiled. Fate had stepped in once again so he shrugged and tucked into his dinner, thinking 'Maybe I do have an honest face which, given what I've been doing for the past few months, has a real touch of irony. Still, I've never wittingly cheated or stolen from anyone, so what's a murder or two in the grand scheme of things? Hey, who knows, I might just like it here and stay for a while. Bella is very attractive and, as far as I can see, she's single, so who knows?'

As Randy and Steve munched on their burgers and fries, the SAC looked at the younger man and said, "You were really deep in thought, you know the 1000 yard stare, when I got to your desk. You don't strike me as someone who tends to daydream, so what were you thinking about? I assume it was one of those case files littering your desk, right?"

Randy hesitated for a few moments as he gathered his thoughts. This was an important moment and he didn't want to come across as a conspiracy nut and he certainly did not want to chase the wind by wasting his time on something his boss thought unimportant. Taking a sip of coffee, he cleared his throat and said, "There was something in that stack of files, in fact two somethings and they may or may not be related to something I heard about this past weekend when I went home."

"Really?" said Steve. "Now you've got my attention, so what gives?"

CHAPTER 9

Victor sat in Linda's living room and idly flipped through a couple of magazines which were, as Linda had said, somewhat out-of-date. He could hear her children pounding down the stairs and out the front door accompanied by muffled shouts to their mother to the effect that they were going out with their friends. He was amused by this because Linda had hurried home to get dinner ready for them but, obviously, they had other plans and those plans did not include spending time with their mother. Typical teenagers.

After about 20 minutes, he heard Linda coming downstairs and there she was, standing in the doorway. Wearing a simple black dress that fitted her slim figure well and Victor could see and appreciate the lightly applied make-up and the slight sheen of dampness on her dark hair. He got to his feet and bowed slightly, saying "You look lovely, Linda."

Linda smiled and barely resisted the urge to twirl around. It had been a long time since anyone, let alone a man, had complimented her on how she looked and she was delighted. Victor then ceremoniously escorted her out to his waiting car.

Sitting in the back of the large car, sinking into the plush leather, Linda started to relax and then looked at Victor to ask, "Do you always have a car and driver to carry you around?"

"Actually, yes," said Victor. When Linda raised an eyebrow, he continued, "I get so distracted when I am driving that I decided I was a danger to myself and to everyone else on the road."

"Oh!"

"My accountant tells me that the expense is tax-deductible but I actually cover it myself. No point in inviting an audit, is there?"

Linda shrugged. Tax deductions were foreign territory to her but she felt a twinge of envy that someone could afford to have a car and driver at his personal beck and call. The she asked, "What do you do, Victor?"

"I'm a businessman." He said vaguely. "I own a couple of businesses and they take up a lot of time."

"You must be good at running them if you can afford a car and chauffeur," said Linda, and silently asked herself what she was doing with this man.

When they arrived at the restaurant, she and Victor were ushered by an obsequious maître d' to a secluded table and within seconds a waiter appeared.

"Good evening, Mr. Bascombe. Always a pleasure to see you."

"Thank you Edward. While we are perusing the menu, perhaps you would be kind enough to bring us a bottle of Margaux?" Then Victor paused and looked at Linda, "Is red wine okay with you…or would you prefer a white?"

"No, I like red wine…and Margaux sounds delightful."

Victor turned back to the waiter, "Well, you heard the lady, Edward. A bottle of Margaux will be good, thank you."

As Linda sat across the table from Victor and slowly ate her perfectly prepared filet mignon, she felt warm and relaxed from the food and the excellent, and ridiculously expensive wine. It had been a long time since she had eaten steak of any kind let alone one as perfectly prepared as this. It was also a major departure from her life to be able to go out with a man, albeit a relative stranger, for a meal without the children being present. For a moment she wondered whether Victor Bascombe might have the same attitude to children as the great W. C. Fields which was that any person who hated kids couldn't be all bad. Following this thought pattern, she reflected that 'It's funny how none of my friends, when they were still talking to me, were particularly happy that they had children although every single one of them looked down on women who had no children. Talk about hypocrisy!' Then she glanced at Victor and asked herself, 'Why am I here with him? Whatever reason prompted him to invite me to dinner? What is someone with a chauffeur-driven Mercedes and clearly very rich doing with me?'

Watching the various emotions flitting across Linda's face and amused at her valiant efforts to stifle them, he asked mildly, "So, Linda, tell me about yourself."

Startled, Linda's eyes snapped back into focus and she smiled before taking a sip of wine but thinking, 'What can I say that's not trite or so self-condemnatory that it would turn him off completely? On the other hand, I hardly know the man and do I really care what he thinks?' After a second or so, she said, "Actually there's not much to say."

"Really?" said Victor. "I find that hard to believe."

"How so?"

"Well you have two beautiful children and a nice house but no husband in sight, not even in photographs…and you are not wearing a wedding band. So, assuming that your children were not immaculate conceptions, I can only surmise that you were once married but now you are not. Besides, the two of them look so alike that they must have had the same father."

Linda nodded. "Well," and hesitated, immediately regretting having started a sentence the same way that Victor had although that one word was a great way of skirting around a difficult subject. "It's a long story."

"These things often are," said Victor sympathetically. "But Linda, we are in no hurry to go anywhere and we have yet to eat desert, so talk to me. Tell me about your early life."

Linda looked at the man curiously. In her experience most men only wanted to talk about themselves and she could not believe that someone, other than Michael, had the slightest interest in how she grew up or where she went to school. If Victor Bascombe was simply angling to get into her panties, he really was taking a long and circuitous route to do so. Deciding that he was genuine, she decided to open up a little just as Victor signaled the waiter to bring over the desert menu.

After they had decided what they wanted, there was small talk until the deserts arrived. Then Victor looked at Linda and said, "You were saying?"

"I actually grew here in Pittsburg, believe it or not. My father was a pharmacist and my mother was a librarian so we had a reasonably comfortable existence but certainly nothing lavish. I went to college here and, well, things happened…" and she tailed off.

"I thought only the British talked about children being hatched, matched and dispatched. You are glossing over a lot, aren't you?"

"Perhaps," said Linda vaguely, reluctant to say too much.

"Go on," said Victor calmly but thinking, 'This lady is carrying around a lot of guilt and it is paralyzing her. I know she doesn't want to say too much but if I don't seize the moment, we might never have another opportunity to talk like this. What was that hackneyed phrase popularized by Robin Williams? Ah yes, *Carpe diem*…yes this is a *Carpe diem* moment.'

Linda blinked and thought for a moment or two. "As I said, I grew up here in a solid middle class family. I had an older brother and sister who are respectively ten and eight years older than me…" and her voice tailed off.

"And?" said Victor.

"So I was an afterthought or perhaps I was an accident."

"That happens, I suppose but I think you could be wrong on that," said Victor doubtfully.

"Trouble is, I was the ugly duckling. You know, not particularly attractive as a child and I did nowhere near as well as Blake and Amanda at school. They were both Valedictorians with 4.0 GPAs, good at sports – Blake was the star quarterback and Amanda captained the swimming and tennis teams, you know how that goes. They went off to Harvard and did well, getting all sorts of scholarships and things. My grades were never that good so there was no way I could get into a top-tier college. So I went to Hathaway College. Not the greatest college in the world but at least it was affordable and not difficult to be accepted there."

Victor nodded, silently encouraging Linda to speak. He probed gently, "Your parents?"

"They died years ago, basking in the successes of Blake and Amanda, and probably lamenting my lack of academic success."

"What was your major?"

"Art History although my parents wondered why I chose that particular field. My mother often asked whether I was just going to college to find a husband, which wasn't the case actually. Thinking back, I really don't know why I picked art history but probably because I could draw quite well and art history looked interesting."

"So, did you find a husband and settle down with a brood of kids?"

"Not exactly."

"Oh?" asked Victor.

Linda hesitated and glanced down at her desert. Deciding, she continued, "As I inferred, I had a major self-confidence problem and would do anything to get attention and…uh…be accepted."

Victor just looked at Linda and waited for her to continue, which she did eventually after a spoonful or two of desert.

"Inevitably I got into trouble. Oh not in that sort of trouble, you know getting pregnant or anything, but I spent a lot of time partying and hanging out with the wrong sort of people – you know what it's like when you go to college after a strict upbringing. Anyway, my grades plummeted and I nearly got thrown out of college. It was all so stupid. Fortunately I did not do what so many of the other girls did, you know, get involved with a faculty member or anything trite like that but I did do lots of drugs and, to be honest, I was high a lot of the time.

"Of course my parents, strict Baptists that they were, were furious." She shrugged and added, "After that, I was basically rejected and disowned by them and my siblings, if they even knew what I'd been up to, paid no mind. What happened to their kid sister in dear old Pittsburg was irrelevant to their lives." She shrugged.

Victor nodded, beginning to understand what this enchanting woman had experienced during her late-teens and early twenties. "What happened after that, if I might ask? You know, college and all that?"

"After everything got smoothed over, I became somewhat of a recluse, concentrating on my studies and basically having no social life. Not surprising really. Eventually I graduated and had to go out and get a job. My parents were comfortable but certainly not rich so I had fairly large student loans to pay off. There were no scholarships for me. Anyway, living at home was not an option and I could not afford to go anywhere else. So I found a very small place and just stayed here in town."

"You got a job?"

"Ah, there's the rub. What career can anyone expect with a degree in art history? There are some art galleries here in town and of course the museum and the University, but they certainly didn't need an inexperienced curator. Let's face it, most of my fellow students in art history were rich kids with nothing better to do or artsy-fartsy types who loved pontificating on old and modern masters at great length but without ever saying anything new or insightful. College for them was one continuous party with their parents happily footing the bill." Linda stopped for a moment or two before continuing. "Don't get me wrong, art history was no walk in the park and we did have to work quite hard but there were still lots of time for partying – at least for the others. I was too busy keeping my nose clean and staying out of trouble."

Victor nodded and waited for Linda to continue but she stole a glance at him and flushed slightly, saying, "I am running my mouth off like a leaky faucet. I can't believe that I'm telling you all this – you must be dreadfully bored and I shudder to even think what *you* must be thinking."

"I'm not thinking anything," said Victor blandly. "I'm just listening."

Linda nodded and then quickly looked at her watch. "Oh my, look at the time."

"Is something wrong?" asked Victor sympathetically.

"Not really but I know my children. They tend to be somewhat scatterbrained and while they would never go anywhere without their cell phones, it is quite common for them to leave home without their keys and they have even lost them on the odd occasion."

Victor looked at her curiously before saying, "I'm not sure I understand."

"I forgot to bring *my* cell phone with me and without it, Damion and Rebecca have no way of contacting me and if they forgot their keys, they can't get in the house. I hate to say it but we really should leave, if you don't mind?"

"Not at all," said Victor affably. "These things happen….don't worry about it." He signaled for the waiter and said to Linda, "Since home seems to be calling, I don't suppose coffee is on the menu for us, is it?"

Linda reddened slightly and hurriedly said, "Let's get home so I can check on things and I'll make us coffee. At one time I earned a living in a coffee shop and if nothing else, I make good coffee…I've had lots of practice. I think I've got some brandy at home, so…."

"That will be delightful," said Victor and said to the waiter that he'd waved to the table, "Just put tonight on my account, would you Edward?"

"Thank you, Mr. Bascombe. I trust that everything was satisfactory this evening?"

"It was indeed, Edward, as always."

With that he got to his feet, waited for Linda to get up and then headed towards the door, clicking on his cell phone as he did so. As they emerged from the restaurant, there stood his chauffeur holding the car door open.

"Thank you, Brian," said Victor and ushered Linda into the limousine for the drive back to her house.

The journey did not take long, which was fortunate as Linda was embarrassed at feeling compelled to cut the evening short because she needed to check on her children. Victor smiled to himself, thinking, 'These two children look like angels in their photographs but what are they really like? Somehow I get the impression that they are very demanding. Poor Linda, I wonder how she copes?' Aloud, he tapped on the partition between driver and passengers and asked, "Brian, I trust that you got something to eat, this evening. You did, didn't you?"

"I did, sir, thank you. I went to a burger place just down the road."

"Good, good," said Victor absently and then he chuckled. "I wonder what the expressions were like on the faces of the other patrons at that place when you pulled up in this car, you being in uniform and all that."

"They were a little surprised but no-one said anything. Not quite an everyday occurrence here I gather, you know, a chauffeur-driven Mercedes pulling up outside but nothing too strange." He paused and added, "They were probably furiously checking their calendars to make sure that they hadn't somehow missed prom night or something."

Victor laughed. Just then they pulled up outside Linda's home. As he and Linda got out of the vehicle, Victor leaned in and said to Brian, "I'm not sure how long I'll be."

"That's alright, Mr. Bascombe. I always carry a book with me and I already took care of nature's call earlier. Just take your time… I'll be here when you need me."

As soon as they arrived at her house, Linda checked that there were no messages on either the home or her cell phone and then gestured to the living room, "Victor, please make yourself comfortable while I go make some coffee."

Victor nodded and then said, "Let me help you. I might need a driver to make sure I don't run anyone over but I can help in the kitchen. Like you, at one time I had some practice," and he laughed before following Linda into the kitchen.

Seated at the kitchen table, he enjoyed watching Linda bustle around and was pleased to see that she prepared coffee using a French press.

After pouring two mugs of coffee and sitting at the table, Linda suddenly jumped up, saying, "I'm sorry, I promised you brandy. Let me go look for it."

"That's alright, Linda, just sit down. I really don't need any but I appreciate the offer."

Linda nodded and sipped her coffee. Victor followed suit and then said, "Yes, you really do make good coffee, don't you?"

"Thank you, kind sir," said Linda, and smiled.

"So how did you come to work in a coffee shop?"

Linda collected her thoughts for a second or two. "I had to get a job after graduating and like most unemployable college graduates with a totally useless college degree, I got a job in a coffee shop." She stopped and smiled ruefully. "I actually got to be quite good at serving up expressos, lattes and plain old Americano coffee - a great career for a would-be art historian. At least I could pay off my student loans and even could afford to have something of a life."

"What happened then? How did you meet your husband…or did you know him while at college?"

"No, he came later."

Linda cleared her throat and, seeing that the coffee mugs were empty, she jumped to her feet, saying, "Your mug is empty - let me make some more coffee. You would like another cup?"

"Heavens no," laughed Victor. "After another cup of your excellent coffee, I'll never get to sleep tonight." He glanced at his watch and added, "No, it is time for me to go. Thank you for a lovely evening."

As Linda walked with him to the front door, Victor suddenly turned and kissed her gently on the cheek, "Thank you for a delightful evening. We must do it again, and soon."

Watching Victor climb into the car and then turning to wave at her, Linda muttered, "Sure we'll do it again. What does a rich and obviously successful businessman like you want with me, a failed housewife and lowly sales associate in a department store?" As she walked back to the kitchen and rinsed out the mugs and coffee press, she thought, 'Victor Bascombe – that name really does ring a bell. I don't think you are a drug lord and you certainly aren't Italian, which rules out the mafia, so who and what are you? Tomorrow, I'll Google you and find out all I can about you. Most successful business men cannot afford a chauffeur, at least not in my limited experience, so who are you and, more to the point, what do you want with me? Well I might find something out tomorrow. Ah well, time for bed. Should I wait up for the children? Probably not ….I'll only worry about them being out late and that will cause more ructions.'

Back home and safely ensconced in a well-padded leather armchair, Victor sipped at a snifter of vintage VSOP brandy and thought about the evening. For a moment he wondered whether he wanted to indulge in an as-yet illegally imported Havana cigar and then decided against it. The brandy would suffice to round off the evening's pleasures.

He asked himself what it was about Linda Woodman that interested him. Undeniably attractive and intelligent, she presented a very favorable image but so did a lot of other women. Perhaps it was because she reminded him of his late wife Elizabeth and, to some degree, of his daughter. Both Linda and Elizabeth had the same bearing - what was called deportment back in the old days, but now a term sadly fallen into disuse. In the end, he decided, it did not matter what the appeal might be, it was there and decision-maker that he was, he decided he would explore possibilities.

He had to admit to himself that he had no idea of where things were going with the lady or even why but, he reasoned, some things are best not analyzed and he closed down his mental dialogue by draining his brandy snifter. He still had things to attend to before going to bed and musing over someone he had just met was the behavior of an adolescent, not someone like him. With a sigh, he left his comfortable armchair and migrated into his study to review the monthly returns of his various enterprises. Although his accountant and highly paid financial advisors did this on a regular basis, he still liked to keep a finger on the company pulse. He knew of too many people who lost money by leaving running of a business in the hands of others.

Victor was a very successful businessman and although urban legend liked to refer to him as a self-made man, the reality was quite different. He and his twin brother Reginald had been born to affluent parents, his father Royce Bascombe having inherited Bennet's from *his* father who in turn, had inherited the department store from his father-in-law, Nathan Bennet.

From an early age Victor had shown an aptitude for business whereas Reggie was a scientist almost from birth. Because Royce and his wife Juanita strongly believed in education, Victor went to Harvard University while Reggie went to MIT, both boys graduating *Magna cum Laude* from their respective universities. Victor went on to Harvard Business School to get his MBA whereas Reggie devoted his time and energy to obtaining a Master's degree and then a PhD in the then burgeoning field of information technology and computer science.

After graduate school, Royce Bascombe called his two sons into his office and handed them each a check for $500,000, saying, "This is your inheritance. I shall be interested to see what you do with it. You can invest it, gamble it away or spend it on wine, women and song – what you do is up to you."

Victor invested carefully in radio and television as well as in the growing field of information technology and computers, the latter on Reggie's advice. Within a few years, both brothers were multi-millionaires and both men had married their childhood sweethearts, and fathered families. Victor had two sons and a daughter whereas Reggie had two daughters and a son. The two men had been close while growing up and maintained this closeness over the years. Unlike the situation in many families, the two brothers were never competitive and gave each other every possible support.

Eventually, Royce Bascombe called a family conference and once every one was seated around the huge family table, he spoke slowly and carefully, "I am getting old and it is time to relinquish control of Bennet's as well as all of my other business ventures." As his sons and daughters-in-law started to protest, he held up a hand, saying, "This is reality. Running Bennet's is almost a full-time occupation let alone managing everything else." He paused and then continued. "Reggie has been extremely successful in information technology and though he has a good business brain, I am well aware that his calling is in computers and information technology. Because of him, Bennet's was one of the first department stores in the country, if not the world, to be almost wholly served by computers. This has done wonders for our bottom line and much of our financial success has been due to his innovations. And for that, we must all thank Reggie. But I know that Reggie has little interest in commerce. That is not a criticism, just reality." He paused before continuing.

"Victor, on the other hand, loves commerce and his wealth has grown in leaps and bounds over the years through shrewd money management and investments. Further, he has been managing Bennet's for the past few years, very successfully too. So, in accepting the reality of my age and my declining health and mental acuity, I have a proposal for you all to consider." Again Royce paused and looked fondly at his wife and his two sons and their wives, all of whom looked at him expectantly. He cleared his throat and continued, "Bennet's will be jointly owned by Victor and Reggie but, and here is the big *but*, Victor and only Victor will have sole financial and managerial control of the store. It is in his blood and I think we all agree that he is the person to continue to run Bennet's. So, Victor will be the CEO and the interim CFO; he will be paid an appropriate salary but all profits will be shared equally between Victor and Reggie. As for all my other assets, I will set-up trust funds for all the grandchildren and after your mother and I pass on, the estate will be divided equally between Victor and Reginald."

Silence greeted his words as everyone digested what he had said, all except for Juanita with whom her beloved husband had discussed everything over the past few weeks. Eventually everyone agreed that Royce's proposal was in the best interests of the family as well as those of the hundreds of employees of Bennet's. Reggie summed up for everyone when he said, "Well dad, I for one am glad that Bennet's is to remain in the family. When you first started to talk about this, I was afraid that you might want to sell Bennet's - thank goodness that is not on the table. As for Victor running the place, I cannot think of a better man to do so. So, if you want my agreement or blessing or whatever might be the appropriate word, you have it."

Victor assumed complete control of Bennet's and with the expert technological input from Reggie, the department store went from strength to strength, modern technology contributing in no small part to its continuing success.

Then, sadly, his wife Elizabeth contracted an inoperable and very aggressive breast cancer and died very quickly. The loss of his wife and closest friend, the light of his life, devastated Victor. Grief propelled him to devote his time and energy to running his businesses, especially Bennet's, and other than a few obligatory business and social functions in the evenings, Victor became almost a recluse. He divided his time between work, his children and grandchildren, and taking himself out to his favorite restaurant on a fairly regular basis, always dining alone.

Despite the best efforts of his children and the numerous overtures from a variety of attractive and available women, Victor shut himself off from everything. As far as he was concerned, no-one could replace Elizabeth and he cherished her memory.

Closing down his computer and yawning, Victor decided it was time for bed when, unbidden, Linda Woodman slipped into his mind and he thought about her with a small smile. Again he asked himself what had interested him about the lady. He had first noticed her on one of his periodic and discreet strolls through the Bennet's. He had seen her serving a customer in the household linens department and even though it was close to the end of her shift and she was likely quite tired, Linda had been unfailingly polite and helpful to her customers. She had even gone so far as to advise a young couple on which sheets, pillow cases and bed pillows would be best for them at a price they could afford. Victor had been impressed and whenever he walked through the store, he routinely swung past that particular department to see how she was doing. Just from his idle inspection of Linda, albeit discreet and at a distance, he could see that she was different from the other sales people and surmised that she was someone who had fallen on hard times and needed this sales position to pay her bills. Nevertheless, it was also apparent that regardless of being a simple sales associate, Linda took her job seriously and did her best for the store and for her customers. Not only that, it did not seem to matter whether the customer was buying very expensive items or simply the best they could afford, with Linda everyone received the same care and attention.

As a good CEO, Victor liked to check on what was going on in his store. Although he had the greatest regard and respect for the various buyers in his employ, he still liked to make sure that the merchandise they offered for sale did in fact sell. Non-selling inventory was a drain on capital and that was not something he liked to see or approved of although the surplus did go on sale at regular intervals allowing their customers to snare the odd bargain. Victor also maintained a careful watch on the operations of his other major investments but he did so to a lesser hands-on degree than with Bennet's. Likewise, he liked to stroll periodically through downtown to check on the customer traffic in his major rivals. Only a select few could match the variety of goods sold in Bennet's but he still liked to see what appealed to customers and then check that his store carried the same or similar merchandise. As his father had often said, running a department store required careful attention to detail and a good understanding of what people want to buy, and Victor took pains to follow that advice.

It was on one of his inspection tours of downtown, as he liked to call them, that he had spotted Linda sitting on the bench staring wistfully at the coffee shop across the street. He surmised that Linda had frequented that establishment before she had fallen on hard times and, on the spur of the moment, he decided to talk to her. Even now he was not sure why he had done so but he had, much to his surprise. Again, it was quite by chance that he bumped into her after the end of her shift that same day. He had been strolling around the building to check for trash in the street and the employee parking lot when he had spotted her. Again on an impulse he had invited her to dinner, much to the surprise of both of them. Another inexplicable spur-of-the-moment decision!

Across town, despite being tired after a long work week, Linda lay in bed forlornly waiting for sleep to overtake her. The rich food, ultra-sweet desert and the later coffee had done a number on her, that and keeping half an ear open waiting for her children to come home. As she lay there, stray thoughts intruded on her mind, the way they always do when one is in bed and trying to fall asleep. She thought for a moment about Victor and then dismissed him from her mind. She would look into him the next day and speculation this late at night was pointless. Then she thought about her mother's comment about attending college to find a husband and even Victor's question about that. The reality, she knew, was far different and even now, after so many years and everything that had happened, she still smiled about meeting and hooking up with Michael.

It had been so sweet. One day a young man had come into the coffee shop and ordered a coffee to go. Over the course of several weeks, his visits became more frequent and he started to come in early and sit at the bar with a coffee and pastry, idly chatting with her between customers. Eventually he came in every day and a rapport was established between them, to the point that Linda started to look forward to him coming in every morning. He became the highlight of her day.

The shy customer, she learned, was Michael Woodman, a junior faculty member at Hathaway College, teaching economics or some such He was reasonably good looking and although he was on the quiet side, he did have an English accent and dressed well, so there was an immediate attraction. At first, Michael had given her the impression he was somewhat of a loner, being quiet and reserved, but he was always polite and always treated Linda as a person rather than just someone who served up coffee on demand. He was different and curiously, at least for her, he didn't seem to have the arrogance of most of the professors at Hathaway and certainly didn't give the impression that he thought he walked on water.

It took a while but eventually he asked Linda out. Even now, she was still amused by his clumsy efforts to approach her. When he first broached the subject of getting together outside of the coffee bar, Michael started to ask Linda if she would like to meet up for a coffee and then laughed at the thought. He was so flustered at suggesting that Linda would even consider having a coffee with him when that was all they ever did, he got quite red with embarrassment. After some to-and-fro banter, they had gone off and had a burger somewhere. After that the pair of them got together regularly, chatting away for hours about anything and everything. Sadly, things changed.

Linda was about to pursue that thought when she heard her children come in. It was late, later than she would have liked, but at least they were safely home. Suddenly she felt tired and then slipped into a welcome sleep.

CHAPTER 10

That week had been busy at the diner and this day, Friday, had been unusually hectic. For a small Arkansas town, it was unusual that there would be an eatery called *The Second Street Café* and that the place would actually be popular. Normally, most small diners tended to slow down towards the weekend but today had been an exception, with a constant stream of customers all day. By the time they had closed up, Bella, Michael and Andrew were tired and only too happy to go home and rest, and try to summon up the energy to start again the next morning. Fortunately, with the next day a Saturday, business should be slower than during the week and give them a welcome respite. Polite goodnights were exchanged and the three of them took off towards home in their separate vehicles.

Getting back to his motel, Michael unlocked his door and went inside. His room was somewhat depressing, but it was clean, a good size, cheap, quiet and satisfactorily distant from the expressway. He shucked off his shoes and soiled clothes, washed his hands and face and pulled on a T-shirt and a pair of sweatpants. He threw the dirty clothes into a hamper in the corner of the room and poured himself a rare glass of Scotch. As with most workers in the food industry, eating was the last thing he wanted to do after being around food all day long and Michael settled down with a cigarette and stared sightlessly at the television. Although virtually every TV station only broadcast the usual drivel, sitting there helped him relax and slowly drain his body of the adrenalin that had built up during the busy day. Occasionally he would glance around the room and smile to himself. It was not far short of a dump but at least the queen-size bed was comfortable, the easy chair was useable and the dinette table and chair where he sat to eat whatever he had prepared for himself, or brought in, was not too badly beaten-up or scarred. Even the tiny stove in one corner was relatively chip-free and serviceable enough for his needs. It was home and had been for several weeks now.

He stubbed out his cigarette, brushed his teeth and was about to strip off for bed when there was a knock on the door. Michael stared at the door, hesitated for a few moments and then padded over to open it. Standing there, slightly in the shadows, was Bella. She smiled slightly and held out a bottle of wine to Michael, saying "I hope you like red wine."

Michael just stood there and stared at her. He was surprised that she even knew where the motel was, let alone would visit him there, and at night too. Seeing her smile fade, Michael recovered himself and said, "Oh Bella….I'm…er…I'm sorry to be so rude….I just don't get too many visitors here."

Bella nodded but her smile looked increasingly strained. Seeing her expression, Michael added quickly, "I'm so sorry, won't you come in? I have completely lost my manners…it's….er…oh forget it, please come in and ….er…"

As Bella walked into the room, Michael saw her appraising the place and hastily said, "It's not much – actually it's more of a dump than anything but at least it's clean. Anyway, please grab a seat and I'll find a couple of glasses…hopefully there's a corkscrew somewhere." Bella smiled, it was fun to see the usually unflappable Michael caught totally off guard and dashing about like a teenager trying to take care of an unexpected visit by a new girlfriend. As she took in her surroundings, Bella was surprised, and rather pleased, to see no evidence of girlie magazines or X-rated movies in Michael's room.

After pouring two glasses and turning around, Michael saw that Bella was still standing just inside the door. "Oh dear, what am I thinking?" he said. "Please sit down…. oh, let me take your coat…. I assume that you can stay for a while." Then he laughed, adding, "That was a bit dumb, wasn't it? If you brought over a bottle of wine, it's a reasonable assumption that you might wish to …ah…stay for a while and drink it."

Bella laughed and slipped off the lightweight jacket, revealing a thin and well-fitting sweater that nicely outlined her body. Michael was startled. It was the first time he had seen Bella out of the slightly shapeless shirt she wore to the diner and he was even more surprised to see that she had a good figure. He took the jacket and laid it on the bed before sitting beside it and waiting while Bella settled herself in the armchair after turning it so that she faced Michael.

Silently they raised their glasses and toasted each other. "This is very good," said Michael. "Thank you for bringing it over."

"My pleasure," replied Bella. She took another sip, hesitated and then said, "We've been working together for some time but...er... we've never taken the time to ....um...socialize, have we?"

Michael shook his head and then added, "No, more's the pity". Then as their eyes met, both burst out laughing. "Well," said Bella. "That's got the social niceties out of the way." And she laughed again and slowly looked around the room.

"It's not much," said Michael. "But it's home – well, of a sort anyway." And he laughed too. "The good thing is that it's cheap, clean and quiet – what more can a man ask for?" He hesitated and then added, "Hell, some of the places I've stayed in were so small you had to leave the room to change your mind."

Bella smiled at the old joke, but she could well believe that Michael *had* stayed in places like that. As the wine slowly took effect, both relaxed and started to chat. First gossiping about the myriad and often slightly weird regulars that frequented *The Second Street Café* and then they moved on to more general topics.

Time passed and the barriers slowly dropped, letting them become increasingly comfortable with each other despite the awkward start to this most unusual evening. They laughed together at the antics of local, state and national politicians, dissected several new novels and bemoaned the dreadful television programing. Their tastes in music, mainly the 1960s and 1970s, were quite similar and both were surprised that the other was a closet fan of rock-and-roll.

As Michael poured the last drops of wine into their glasses, Bella glanced at her watch, exclaiming, "Oh dear, look at the time. Whatever must you think of me, dropping in like this unannounced and then hanging around all evening – you're probably anxious to get to bed?"

Michael simply shrugged. It had been the nicest evening he had spent in a long time and he had forgotten the pleasure he got from conversing with an intelligent and decidedly attractive woman. As Bella got to her feet and started to reach for her jacket, she stumbled slightly and fell into Michael's arms. He held on to her to stop her falling and then their eyes met. Without a word, Michael leaned over and kissed Bella, who hesitated for an instant and then returned his kiss.

Within seconds, Michael's arms tightened around her and as he gently pulled her against his body, Bella slipped her arms around him and they kissed more passionately. Slowly, tentatively, they started to gently run their hands over each other's bodies, still kissing deeply with lips parted and tongues exploring each other's mouths. Pulling back slightly from her, Michael started to caress Bella's breasts which, he was both surprised and pleased to find, were not constrained by a brassiere. Bella, in turn, slowly ran her fingers over Michael's chest and waist and then slid her hands down to growing bulge in his sweatpants, murmuring, "My, my, what do we have here?"

As Michael slowly raised and then peeled off Bella's sweater, she reached back and snapped off the light, leaving the room dimly lit only by the exterior porch light. They fell back onto the bed in each other's arms and explored each other's bodies with greater urgency as they kissed more passionately.

Suddenly Michael stopped, climbed off the bed and gently pulled Bella to her feet. Reaching down, he peeled back the bedcovers and then both of them almost crashed back onto the bed, hurrying to strip off each other's remaining clothes and make love.

Randy Cunningham stared hard at the papers and files spread out across his desk. He blinked a few times, got to his feet and walked slowly over to the coffee dispenser. After filling his mug, he took a few sips of the evil-smelling brew and went back to his desk. Once again he looked carefully through each file and then re-read his copious notes.

After receiving the go-ahead from Steve, Randy had contacted the FBI offices scattered across the nation from Pennsylvania to Utah in the west and from Illinois to Arkansas in the south. After that he contacted the state police headquarters in each of the states. As he expected, there were a number of unexplained and motive-less murders in several states. Eventually he got to his feet and made his way to Steve Wellington's office and after politely knocking on the open glass door, Randy entered the SAC's office.

Steve looked up and waved Randy to a chair. "Ah yes, Randy, good morning. Come and sit yourself down," he said in a vague, distracted manner.

Randy paused for a few seconds. He had been warned by his colleagues that Steve, for all his bonhomie, always had a lot on his mind and unless one waited for him to focus on who was in his office and why they were there, it was pointless saying anything. As one wag said, "If you start in on something at once, you can almost see the words going in one ear and pouring out of the other into a pile on the floor. No, wait a while and let him truly acknowledge your presence and connect the dots, and then you can talk."

"Really?" asked Randy.

"Yeah, he's been like that for years. Steve is brilliant when he hones in on something but if he isn't focused, then talking to him is as productive as talking to a brick wall."

After a few seconds, Steve's eyes locked onto Randy and he said, "Randy, I was just thinking about you. How are things going? Making any progress?"

Aware that he now had Steve's complete attention, Randy said carefully, "I've been looking into these serial killings."

"Serial killings?" said Steve. "Interesting statement. What's going on?"

"There have a number of killings, all with the same MO, that occurred in several different states over a period of months."

"And?"

"As I said, the killer used the same method, you know, a plastic bag and a garrote and in each case, there was no detectable reason for the killing. No murder was ever associated with a robbery or theft of any kind!"

"Any similarities in the victims?"

"None whatsoever and, as I said, each killing was apparently motiveless. It's almost as though the perp just happened upon the victim and offed him or her more or less on the spur of the moment."

"I'm not sure that I like the term "offed them" but I see what you mean. What I don't follow is the suggestion that it was a spur of the moment decision, especially if no theft occurred. Anyone who can murder half a dozen or more people, and I assume that there are probably more out there that we don't know about, without leaving any evidence or traces can hardly fall into the spur of the moment category. No, the murderer, be he male or female, planned things very carefully. But there has to be something that links these cases, so what have you got?"

"It's nothing definite but what I'm seeing is that each murder took place in the parking lot of a bar or the like that was in a small place a mile or two off an expressway."

"Go on."

"The impression I got is that the killer, and I assume it must be a man since it requires some strength to place a plastic bag over someone's head and then strangle him or her with a garrote. Anyway, I have the feeling that he picks an expressway, drives up or down it until he sees a likely exit and then locates a bar or roadside inn and waits for a suitable victim to turn up."

"Interesting theory. I assume that this vague pattern is the same in all cases?"

"Yes it seems to be. However, the latest case involved a shooting."

"The victim was shot? Surely that negates your basic hypothesis?"

"Perhaps. The perp used a potato as a crude but effective silencer and, again, there was zero motive for the killing."

"If, and that's a big "if", why did the killer change his MO? How do you know it's the same man?"

"The actual MO was different I grant you, but everything else was the same. However, this time the killer left behind a shell casing."

"He did? That's odd."

"What's even odder is that the fingerprint on the casing was that of the victim found in the parking lot of my father's place, one Clyde Wilkins."

"Oh?"

"I checked carefully and so did the local and State Police but there was no indication that Clyde Wilkins actually owned a gun. On the other hand, the man was a bit of a loner, so it's quite possible that he did own a gun. Most people around there did so and I doubt that Clyde Wilkins was any exception."

"I take it that you think that for once the killer took something from the victim, in this case a gun. Yes? Even if he did so, why change the MO? Surely that doesn't follow?"

"Maybe yes, maybe no. Did the perp get tired of strangling people and started to take the easier route of shooting his victims? After all, shooting someone is not as close up and personal as garroting or perhaps he just got tired of that approach to killing people."

"Ordinarily I would find it hard to accept this change in MO but that fingerprint on the shell casing does change things," mused Steve. He sat back in his chair and stared at the ceiling and thought hard. Randy was presenting a persuasive case and however unlikely it appeared to be, there was some merit to his conjectures.

Eventually he broke the silence, "So you are saying we have a serial killer who locates a slightly out of the way roadside inn, selects a victim at random and kills them, always using an expressway to get to and from the killing site, yes? What about geography – anything there?"

"Maybe. I did notice that there was a steady progression across the Midwest and now he appears to be heading south."

"Has there been anything recently?"

"Not for a month or two, at least not that I know of," said Randy.

"Hmm. So the killer has gone dormant. I wonder why? Has he holed up somewhere or did he just get bored with killing people? It's also possible that he can't find any likely locales or victims although, given the nature of human beings, I find that hard to believe. The other thing that is peculiar is that he left that shell casing behind. On the other hand, the killer, or one of the by-standers with a morbid interest in arcane artifacts, picked up the bullet. If my memory serves me right, that young man was killed by a through-and-through shot, yes?" Without waiting for a response from Randy, he continued,

"Leaving the casing but retrieving the bullet is definitely out of line with his behavior to date, unless of course he is just playing with us. That is always possible, isn't it?"

"I don't know sir. All I do know that there has been nothing of late – at least nothing has come in over the past few weeks."

"Huh. Okay, let's have a look at a map and see if we can see some sort of pattern in where he finds his victims."

As if on cue, Randy took the map out from the bundle papers on his lap and spread it out on Steve's desk. He slowly circled the location of each killing and waited for the SAC to draw his own conclusions.

Eventually Steve looked up. "I take it that there's no relationship between the killings and the phases of the moon?"

"None that I could find, no. Nothing simple like full moons or new moons – nothing like that. In fact, it seems that the skies were overcast when the killings occurred but it was never raining."

"I see. I assume that you checked that there are no psychopathic killers on the loose – you know, Charles Mason or Son of Sam types that escaped and are running around?"

"No, none at all. I also checked that no mass murderers or other psychopaths have been released from mental institutions. Nothing there either."

Steve was quiet again and then mused aloud, "So the evidence, such as it is, suggests a single perp who is very adept at covering his tracks but leaves a shell casing behind but collects the bullet itself. This same perp also used, until the latest murder, a bizarre method of killing people – one that I haven't heard of being used in decades, at least not since the heyday of the Mafia. He seems to pick the killing ground based on proximity to expressways and his victims are truly random. Nothing makes sense but then, most murders don't make much sense either."

Randy stayed silent. There was nothing he could say that would add to his chief's musings. Suddenly Steve focused his attention on Randy, "You think that the killer works on his own?"

"There's no reason to think otherwise. Besides, when two people are involved, the risk of gossiping or letting something slip is increased exponentially. If the perp did have an accomplice, how did they always agree on the victim, and the killing ground too for that matter?"

"Good point Randy. I cannot see two men or a man and a woman or any such pairing agreeing easily on who to kill and where. It's possible but unlikely."

He stared at the ceiling again and fell silent, thinking things over again. Eventually he said, "Okay, here's what I suggest we do."

"So, Bella, how did you end up here?" asked Michael.

"Is *here* referring to our fair town of Southampton, or are you referring to *here* in the sociological sense?"

"Either ….or… whichever you feel is more important. You are obviously intelligent and educated, so I am curious about both interpretations of *here*."

Bella smiled. Michael was obviously adept at avoiding talking about himself but since she had a captive and interested audience, she decided to open up a little…what harm could it do? Besides, it had been a long time, too long, that she had experienced the joy of relaxing in bed after passionate love-making.

"How I ended up here is a little convoluted. I did go to college…. the University of Missouri where I got a degree in sociology. In my sophomore year I met Charles and we dated on-and-off for a couple of years and got married in our senior year. He was a handsome man, an English major, and could quote poetry like there was no tomorrow. Coming from a small town like Southampton, I was swept off my feet and fell madly in love."

"And?"

"Ah well, it was all so predictable," Bella said sadly. "Charles persuaded me to give up my career….I was going to do a master's degree in social work…so that he could stay home and write the great American novel."

"Oh!"

"*Oh* is right," sighed Bella. "I got a job as a glorified typist in a law firm but because I typed fast and accurately, and could actually understand what I was dealing with, they paid me very well. It was boring stuff and I was miserable but, as I say, they paid well."

Michael slipped an arm around Bella and pulled her closer to his body. At first Bella tensed and then relaxed as she started to enjoy the warmth and comfort of his body. Yet again she wondered about the man and about what had prompted her to descend on him like this, not that she was complaining. For a moment, she interrupted her thoughts with a question, "I…er…do we have to worry about birth control? Um, you know how it is?"

"No, I had a vasectomy years ago…nothing to worry about there," said Michael flatly, remembering how Linda had pressured him to have one. He could still hear her acrid comment, "You are not putting that thing near me again unless you get it sealed off, Michael. I'm not going to get pregnant again…we've got two children already. So, take care of it or go without – it's your choice!"

Bella nodded. She was right, Michael obviously was one of those rare specimens who actually cared about whether he fathered children or not. She hesitated for a moment and then resumed talking.

"Anyway, bored as I was at work, I started to write short stories. Nothing too impressive but I enjoyed writing them and was able to explore various thoughts…you know how it is?"

"Yes," affirmed Michael.

"Well, when I came home after work, I always asked Charles about how the book was going. He was a bit non-committal but assured me that he was making progress and would tap on the pile of paper beside the printer."

"What was it like, the book I mean?"

"He wouldn't let me see it…his comment was that a work in progress was just that, in progress, and he didn't want to spoil the surprise for me with an unfinished and unedited manuscript."

"I have a feeling that this story does not have a happy ending," commented Michael.

"You've got that right," said Bella. "The situation was *status quo* for months and, to be honest, I just let things ride although I began to wonder when I noticed the paper pile hadn't grown in weeks. Then one day, I left the office really early. It was the birthday of one of the partners and we all got the afternoon off…"

"Uh oh!"

"*Uh oh* is right. I got home just after lunch and there was Charles in bed with the wife of our closest friends. Lots of screaming and recriminations….the usual…and then I threw them both out. It was at this point, still furious, I started to leaf through the so-called manuscript. It was drivel, complete drivel but what infuriated me more than anything was the fact that Charles had taken my short stories and incorporated them in his book…can you imagine?" Bella's voice rose. "Not only was he screwing my best friend, and in our bed at that, but he was stealing my writing and obviously was quite prepared to claim it was his own. I didn't mind that as much as that the fact that what *he* had written was such drivel. I felt like such a fool. The marriage didn't last much longer after that and the only good thing was that we didn't have any kids to deal with. Since we existed on my salary alone, we didn't have a whole lot of property to divide, and we went our separate ways. Fortunately I escaped having to pay him any alimony."

"Thanks Heaven for small mercies," commented Michael.

"You've got that right, have you ever!"

"And so how is it that you ended up here?"

"Within a few weeks of the break-up and divorce, my parents were killed in an auto accident. They didn't have much but they left Andrew and I this diner. Anyway, the two of us sat down and tried to decide what to do with it. The place was doing quite well but if we tried to sell it, we'd get nothing and we had to face the fact that our parents had sunk everything into the business. The long and short of it was that Andrew, who hated his job, and I decided to take the place over…and here we are."

"Interesting story. What did Andrew do before this?"

"He was an architect. He himself admits that he was a bit run-of-the-mill…you know, competent but certainly not gifted. Besides, there isn't too much demand for architects in Missouri, at least there wasn't back then with the way the economy was depressed, so we became restauranteurs or whatever people who run diners are called. Anyway, he does do a good job with our taxes and the business side of things, so at least he found something that he enjoys."

Bella chuckled and snuggled closer to Michael, "So there you have it, my life in a nutshell. No great cataclysmic events, at least not in hindsight, no exciting changes in fortune or anything like that and certainly no romance either." Bella paused, "Oh dear, that makes it sound as though I am just using you for sexual gratification. I....er...."

Michael laughed. "I know what you mean, so don't worry. Does Andrew have a girlfriend? Was he ever married?"

"Yes he was. Like me, no children which, given what happened, is a good thing."

"What do you mean?"

"Oh when we found that we had inherited this place, Andrerw, his wife and I met with the estate lawyer. Andrew's wife took one look at the town and shot off back to the big city just as fast as her car would go. Within a month or two, they were divorced and she's now married to an accountant or some such, and raising a brood of kids. Good luck to her, I say but also good riddance. Anyway, Andrew has a steady girlfriend and they are very happy. They'll probably get married one day and I am happy for them both – they suit each other."

"What about you?"

"What, do I have a girlfriend?"

Michael laughed again, "You know what I mean."

"No, I don't have a boyfriend, steady or otherwise. Let's face it; the pickings here are slim at best....oh damn, there I go again, you know, open mouth, insert foot!"

"Don't get your underwear in a wad – I know what you mean and no, I don't feel used or that you are here, here in bed, because you are desperate for male company."

"I'm not?"

"How should I know? Look, just enjoy being here and don't start fretting about what I think or don't think. In the long run it doesn't matter one iota, not at all."

In response, Bella just hugged him hard and then leaned over to kiss him. Within minutes they were fiercely making love again and any other thoughts vanished in the heat of their passion.

As the evening wore on, Victor felt tired and decided it was time to go to bed. Again his thoughts turned to Linda Woodman. That dinner with her had been a success and he had enjoyed her company. Should he ask her out again? He was undecided where things were going with her, if anywhere, but an enjoyable evening was simply that, an enjoyable evening, so why not?. As he made the decision, it suddenly occurred to him that perhaps he could help Linda by telling his head of security to start a search for the errant husband. Whether or not Michael Woodman could be found was one issue. A second issue might be whether he actually wanted to go back home and a third issue was if Linda would want him back. Whatever the outcome might be, at least Linda would have a handle on what her situation really was.

Victor thought about the matter for several minutes and then decided he would set his people on it. Linda most certainly had not asked him to do it and she might be resentful of his interference but for his own satisfaction, Victor made the decision to go ahead. He hated loose ends and if he was at all serious about the lady, then he or she and perhaps both had to know what the situation with her husband might be. He smiled. Was he serious about her? Time would tell and with that thought lingering in his mind, he prepared himself for bed but still wondered what it was about Linda that intrigued him.

Victor sat ensconced behind his desk and took that first welcome sip of Jamaican Blue Mountain coffee. It was one of his few indulgences and it amused Victor that despite being a billionaire, he was a relatively simple man at heart. Yes he lived in a nice house, had a driver and comfortable car, a housekeeper and a few other amenities that simplified his life but he was far from extravagant. His children and grandchildren were well provided for and his charitable donations and church tithes were extraordinary but, busy as he was, his life lacked something. He enjoyed working but the excitement and, yes, the challenge, was long gone. Did he need someone with whom he could share the excitement of living? Finding a bed-mate was easy and there was no shortage of willing women anxious to fill that role here in Pittsburgh and probably across the country. But meaningless sex was just that, meaningless – an exercise that kept the pipes clear but did nothing for him or his peace of mind. He sighed.

He thought again about Linda. He was about to set in motion a quasi-manhunt to find her husband but without the assent, permission or even the awareness of Linda. Again he wondered what her reaction might be to finding him. Did she want him back? He was, after all, the father of her children and that was a very strong bond but what was their relationship otherwise? Even if Michael Woodman was found and both he and Linda decided that things were well and truly over between them, was she interested in him, Victor? He had been assuming that Linda was attracted to him but was she? Was it just the arrogance of a rich man dictating the actions of others or was there something else there? He sighed again and muttered aloud, "No matter how old we are, how successful we might be, however much money we have, there are always imponderables in life. Balzac had it right when he wrote about The Human Comedy. Life *does* get in the way of all our plans." Silently he offered up a prayer thanking God for the many blessings in his life and for everything that He had enabled him to do in his life, finishing with a plea for wisdom regarding what he should do.

Finally he told his personal assistant to summon the Head of Security to his office. Within minutes, Vince Dodson appeared in his office. After signaling the man to take a seat, Victor said, "Vince, I have a job for you."

Dodson nodded and waited for the CEO to elaborate. Vince, a retired New York City police captain, was a very experienced investigator and loved his job but overseeing Bennet's small but efficient security force lacked the excitement and challenge of the NYC police force. He was well-paid but, if he was honest, Vince was slightly bored and this unexpected summons to the office of the boss possibly heralded a change from the norm.

"Vince," said Victor. "I want you to find someone for me."

Vince raised an eyebrow. This was something different. He could not remember the last time Mr. Bascombe had asked him to do anything other than the routine running of the security system and personnel. He nodded again and waited. As a retired cop, he was used to waiting for orders from on high.

Victor rapidly summarized what he knew about Michael Woodman and his disappearance and then looked at Vince, who stared off into space, digesting what he had just heard. Eventually he spoke up, "Did this Michael Woodman commit any crimes or is he wanted by anyone, you know, the mob or the like for gambling debts, anything like that?"

"Not to my knowledge, no."

"I assume that his wife contacted the police when he disappeared."

"I believe so, yes."

"Can I take it that there was no kidnapping or ransom, that sort of thing?"

"That is also true."

"I see." Vince paused and thought about things for a few seconds. "So, he just upped and left, did he?"

"Yes."

"What does his wife say?"

"I've told you everything that I know and talking to Mrs. Woodman is off limits."

"It is? Oh!"

"Oh?" asked Victor.

"That makes things a lot more difficult if I cannot talk to the lady." He was silent again before adding, "Well, I suppose I can talk to my contacts in the local police but I have to say, sir, this might not be easy – finding him, that is."

"But not impossible?"

"I cannot say but we can only try."

"Good, good," responded Victor affably. "Oh by the way, this is off the books."

"It is?" asked Vince in surprise and then he caught himself. This was the boss talking and if he wanted it off the books, then off the books it was! "I'll get right on it, sir."

"Good, Vince. Just keep me informed of progress, okay?"

As Vince left Victor's office, he thought about the assignment. He had very little to go on and idly he wondered what Mr. Bascombe's interest might be. It wasn't like him to dig into the private lives of his employees unless there was a very good reason but Vince could not see a connection between the boss and a lowly sales associate. It was all very curious but if that's what the boss wanted, then so be it.

Linda was enjoying a rare Saturday off from the relentless demands of retail. To her pleasure and relief, Damion and Rebecca were off with friends from school. She was glad that they had made some friends and things seemed to be going well in that regard. She had the house to herself for a change, at least for a little while at any rate. She switched on her computer and started to clear the packed Email in-box. It had been quite some time since she had had the luxury of just scanning and then deleting all the spam and other inessential items that came in every day.

After clearing away most of the in-box items and making a mental note to address some of the issues that demanded her attention, she sat back and Victor Bascombe suddenly popped into her thoughts. She hesitated for a moment and then clicked on Google and entered "Victor Bascombe, Pittsburgh Pennsylvania". After a while, the screen filled with dozens of "hits". Slowly scanning through them, she found one entry that looked the most promising and she clicked on it. Again the screen filled with information and Linda started to read through it carefully.

"Oh my," she said in dismay. "This is NOT what I expected, not at all," and she read the biography and pertinent information again. "Good Lord, what is he doing with me? He's a billionaire and I'm a near-broke abandoned housewife. This is ridiculous!"

The internet with its wealth of data informed her that Victor Bascombe not only was one of the richest men in Pennsylvania but, incredibly, was the owner of Bennet's Department Store, her employer. Not only that, he owned various radio and TV stations, was a major stockholder in numerous oil and gas corporations and was well-known as a philanthropist on a State and National scale. To her astonishment, and alarm, Victor was a college mate of the Governor of the State and was a frequent visitor not only to the State House but also to the White House.

"What the heck is he doing with me?" she asked aloud but the silent house did not respond. She went back to perusing the details of Victor's life and saw what she had already surmised. He had been married but his wife had died several years previously. He did indeed have children, two sons and a daughter, as well as several grandchildren. Apparently he lived in Pittsburgh because that was where he and his wife had been born, grown up, married and had their family.

As she digested the startling information, Linda wondered yet again how it was that Victor had happened upon her sitting on that bench downtown and then caught up with her as she had left work to go home. Since Victor was obviously a hands-on chief executive, she could well appreciate that he might have walked around Bennet's but why had he picked her? Was she that different from the other salespeople? Surely not. Given the hundreds of people who worked at Bennet's, why her? Besides, what on earth was a busy chief executive doing walking around downtown and could spare the time to talk to a lowly employee who was sitting on a street bench staring at a coffee shop?

Sitting back, she again addressed her empty house, "Why me? What have I got to offer this man who can buy anything he wants whenever he wants? It doesn't make any sense unless, of course, he sees me as some sort of charity case. If it's the latter, then all bets are off! Things might be hard but I sure as hell will not be some rich man's plaything. No, Mr. Victor Bascombe, if you only want to spend time with me because we're hard up, then think again!. You can employ me but you cannot buy me! That is just not going to happen." Suddenly Linda burst out laughing. What had Victor said to her? Something about just enjoying a pleasant meal with an intelligent man – well, he was right. She might never hear from him again. It was probably best that she didn't after what she had read about the man. There was no way she could even dream of dating the owner of Bennet's and she doubted that her looks or personality were so exceptional that Victor would fall for her. No, that was hardly likely. As he had advised, she could just enjoy a nice meal with an even nicer man and leave it at that.

Switching off her computer, Linda got to her feet and went into the kitchen to make some tea. All too soon she'd have to start preparing dinner and she might as well enjoy the peace and quiet of the empty house which would rapidly vanish when Damion and Rebecca got back. Besides, one never knew, perhaps they might bring some friends back with them. It would be a nice change to hear some young voices and laughter in the house. On the spur of the moment, she went round opening the blinds and shutters, flooding the house with sunlight. Whether or not her children brought anyone home, it was time that the place looked inviting. Curiously light-hearted, she busied herself making tea and then started sorting through the pantry and refrigerator looking to see what she could make for dinner. Again she laughed at herself. Fancy entertaining any thoughts of a relationship with someone like Victor Bascombe…the very idea!, and she laughed again.

As she chopped vegetables and started to brown ground beef in a skillet, Victor Bascombe popped up again into her mind. As she worked, Linda wondered how it was possible for a busy and important man like Victor to take time off and wander around downtown. Surely he had better things to do than waste time like that. She speculated for a few seconds on what he could possibly have been doing there in the late morning when it suddenly struck her. Men like Victor Bascombe could do whatever they wanted whenever they wanted and not only was it of no importance to her, it was none of her business. Shaking her head in exasperation, Linda devoted her attention to food preparation. "Grow up girl," she said aloud. "Do what the man says and just enjoy a good meal with an intelligent man."

CHAPTER 11

Bella awoke with a start and reached over to nudge Michael into wakefulness, "Hey, what's the time?"

Michael stared blearily at the clock radio beside the bed and said with a groan, "It's about 2.30 am."

"Oh my lord," exclaimed Bella. "I've got to get out of here."

"Why?"

"I should go home, that's why."

"By why do you have to go home…and at such a ridiculous hour?" asked Michael.

"Because…" and Bella hesitated, thinking 'Actually, why do I need to go home? It's not as though there's some sort of curfew imposed by strict parents and Andrew…well Andrew is off with his girlfriend and he certainly doesn't care whether I'm home or not. He's hardly going to check on what his sister is doing and if he did, he'd probably approve. Besides as co-owner of the diner, who's going to reprimand me or dock my pay if I'm not there sharp at 7 a.m.?'

Having decided that she really did not need to scamper out of Michael's room in the wee small hours, she swung her body on top of his and promptly started to explore his body. As his body started to respond to her kisses and caresses and Michael himself snapped into consciousness, the pair of them started to make love in the slow languid manner of long-term lovers until passion stepped in and the love making became fiercer.

Two or three hours later, Bella and Michael were fully awake and after a hot shower together, she gathered up her clothes, kissed him lightly and said, "Okay lover-boy, I'd best be off. As soon as I get home and change, I'll get to the diner and open up. So, dear man, I'll see you there is about 30 minutes, okay?"

"Of course," agreed Michael. "Besides I need to get back to work, if only to get some rest." He quickly grabbed Bella and hugged her tight before kissing her. "Wow, lady, you really are something else and thank you – what a marvelous evening…and night…and early morning!" and then he laughed. "All I can say is wow!"

Delighted, Bella hugged and kissed him before heading out the door, suffused with the warm afterglow of highly pleasurable coitus.

As she drove away, Bella thought about the previous evening. 'Did I really plan what happened? Subconsciously, I suppose I did. It would have been highly embarrassing if Michael had turned out to be gay or was one of those men who could take or leave sex, and usually left it. In either case, that would have ruined everything, so thank heavens that Michael doesn't fall into either category. In fact, he's quite the lover. Calm, considerate and remarkably good in bed - what a surprise. Man, that was good and I feel like a twenty-year old again. Oh I hope that the glow doesn't fade too soon.'

Arriving home, she quickly changed clothes and tended to her hair and make-up. As she walked downstairs, Andrew looked up from his newspaper and coffee and murmured, "So you've come home have you? Well, if you were out catting around, which I hope you were, I trust that you enjoyed yourself." He stopped talking and looked at his sister carefully, "Yup, I'm sure you did. That glow really suits you. Is that Michael's doing – in both senses of the term?"

Bella laughed, saying, "Hey, it's none of your business, dear brother."

"Oh I know it isn't but I can ask. Was it Michael?"

Bella laughed again and simply nodded. She did feel good and discussing things, even with someone as dear and close as her brother, could ruin what she was feeling. "Okay Andrew, I'm off to see the wizard," and then reddened. Andrew would inevitably take that the wrong way but then she really didn't care. Grabbing her purse, she walked out the door and climbed into her car for the short drive to the diner.

Navigating through the streets of Southampton, Bella thought about Michael. 'You really are an enigma, aren't you Michael? We've just indulged in the most intimate interactions between a man and woman and yet I know nothing about you. You are obviously intelligent and educated, and almost spiritual in your attitude towards work, other people and even our most irritating customers, but I know nothing about you. I wonder how you ended up here of all places. It's strange enough that Andrew and I are here but you? What are you doing here? Although you try to hide it, I get the sense that you are, or were, English and the soft British undertone of your way of talking tells me that. Not sure why but perhaps it's the words you use or the way you arrange your sentences. In that regard, you can never really talk like an American and certainly not like someone from Missouri. As for your love-making, well that *was* a delightful surprise. I really hope that it won't change things between us, like interfere with work. That would be dreadful because Andrew and I have grown to rely upon you. Hey ho, what seemed like a great idea last evening could have consequences, as most things do. Was I too aggressive? Should I have waited to check things out thoroughly before taking the plunge? Well, it's too late now and we'll have to just wait and see what happens next. At least Andrew isn't bent out of shape – in fact, he probably approves.'

She parked her car behind the diner as usual. She was just unlocking the back door when Michael arrived, exactly 30 minutes after she had left his motel room. Bella smiled to herself, thinking 'I doubt that he was in the military but he's as punctual as any officer I have ever known. That just adds to the mystery and, perhaps he was in the military although I doubt in one of our services. Maybe something in England, at least that's where I think you're from. Ah Michael, you are such a mystery. You really are a loner but on the other hand, you are so personable. I wonder if I will ever get to know you. Even if I don't, it will be fun trying to get know you better. Still, you are good in bed and at the moment, perhaps that's all I want from you?'

Steve Wellington sat down again and looked at Randy. "We really do have a mystery here, don't we? Your comments about the killer are pretty perceptive and I doubt that we would get anything useful from the profilers at Quantico. You could send copies of all your stuff to them but I should be most surprised if they come up with anything other than their usual generalized bullshit. No, what interests me more are your thoughts on the killer's movements around the country."

Randy nodded. He had been thinking of suggesting that they call in the Quantico profilers but then realized, like Steve, that he probably could not furnish enough information for a profiler to add anything useful to the precious little data they had assembled already. Not for the first time, he was fascinated and unsettled by the killer's uncanny ability to murder a number of people and completely avoid leaving any evidence. The only exception was the bullet casing that appeared to have come from Clyde Wilkins' gun. As the SAC suggested, that could have been an oversight or a clever piece of deliberate misdirection. Only time would tell on that. Carefully keeping a poker face, he waited for the SAC to make his suggestions.

"Okay Randy, let's assume that the perp was making his way East to West across the country and is now headed south. Given that scenario, perhaps it might be useful to take a look at motels and small hotels within, say, a 10-20 mile radius of each killing site. It might be a monumental waste of time and a lot of work but the perp must have stayed somewhere. Somehow I cannot believe he is staying in a tent or an RV. So, let's start to look for patterns of who stayed where."

"I thought about that, Steve but that's a lot of work and not all motels, especially not the smaller ones, keep good records."

"I know, I know, but at least it's somewhere to start. Tell you what, I'll have Ryan Whitcombe give you a hand. He's pretty reliable and I don't think he's got too much on at the moment, so he can get digging with you. Okay?"

Randy nodded. An additional pair of hands could lighten the load considerably with what might take weeks of patient searching. At least he would not have to go out in the field, what with internet searches and almost unlimited access to all sorts of information with the click of a mouse.

Steve, with a final glance at his youthful colleague, turned back to the papers on his desk but then said, "Hey, keep me informed of progress, will you?"

The doorbell rang and Linda, busy trying to get dinner together, called out to her daughter, "Rebecca, see who's at the door, would you?"

"I'm watching television," snapped Rebecca petulantly from the living room.

"Not now you're not," Linda muttered to herself and on the way from the kitchen to the front door, she snagged the TV remote and switched off the television, muttering aloud, "Next time, get up and do something to help."

Opening the door, Linda was astonished that a flower delivery person stood there holding out a huge bouquet of flowers. Surprised, Linda took the neatly wrapped bundle and politely thanked the man. Walking through the living room, she was amused to see that her daughter was staring open-mouthed at her and the bouquet she held.

"What's that, mom?" and in the next breath she added, "Why'd you turn off the TV? I was watching it."

"These are flowers and if you are too lazy to get up and answer the door while I'm preparing dinner, then you don't get to watch TV – that's why I turned it off."

"Who'd they come from?"

"I don't know yet," snapped Linda and went into the kitchen, trying to remember where she had put a flower vase. It had been so long since they had had flowers in the house that she had long since put the few vases they owned away somewhere safe, but where? Rebecca, now curious about this unexpected event, followed her into the kitchen and pulled off the card attached to the wrapping of the bouquet.

"Hey mom, they're from someone called Victor!"

"That's nice," said Linda distractedly as she opened various cupboards trying to locate a vase large enough to hold the flowers. Finding one, she focused on her daughter. "What does the card say?"

"Thank you for a very pleasant evening and I look forward to the next time. Warmest regards, Victor."

"Oh!"

"So who's this Victor person and why did he send you flowers, mom?"

"Because he's a nice man, that's why," said Linda and then, as she poured cold water into the vase, she thought to herself, 'That was nice of Victor but, as Rebecca said, I wonder why he sent them? I haven't even have time to call him or drop him a note to thank him for dinner. Actually, thinking about it, I couldn't do that anyway – I don't have any way of contacting him except through Bennet's and that would not be right. How very odd. He knows all about me, warts and all, but I know nothing about him, nothing at all except what I learned when I Googled him. That was so strange looking him up. Fancy having to check up on someone – that's one for the record books, isn't it? *Middle-aged lady seeks information on attractive stranger who took the same lady out to dinner and then disappeared in a puff of smoke.* What a hoot. Under other circumstances, Michael and I would have laughed about that.' She paused in her thoughts and then asked herself, 'Michael? I haven't thought about him in forever, so why now? Back in the old days, we would often laugh together about such things but that hasn't happened in a long, long time. Oh Michael, what happened between us?'

Sighing, Linda arranged the flowers and then took the laden vase into the living room, looking for a suitable spot to place them and then realized that Rebecca was staring at her curiously. "What?" she asked.

"You didn't say who Victor is or why he sent you flowers." Rebecca paused and then added, "Is he the reason that you got all dressed up the other night? What's going on, mom?"

Linda stopped pottering about and looked at her daughter. Rebecca had asked a valid question but it was one she could not answer. 'What *is* going on with Victor?' she asked herself. Idly she wondered what her children might be thinking about her getting flowers from a strange man. If nothing else, it would distract them from the perpetual time-wasting on Facebook or You Tube, or whatever it was they spent so much time on. She paused and thought about that. Now her teenagers were in a public school, their use of texting to communicate with former friends had diminished dramatically, presumably because their old friends had abandoned them, but they were establishing new relationships.

Again she sighed. Michael's departure had caused so many changes in all their lives but, she had to admit, things were slowly getting better. The children were still bratty but less so now, and even though she hated to have to go to work every day, it was oddly satisfying to actually earn a living and know that everything they now had came from her own efforts. This was something she never would have expected and she smiled smugly. Those self-indulgent selfish bitches that she used to run around with in the past were still selfish and self-centered and, she had to admit, they really were drones. Attractive drones but still pretty useless individuals with superior attitudes because they had affluent husbands. 'Well my dears,' she thought. 'Perhaps you also need to have a dose of reality. It's not pleasant, not at all, but perhaps then you might start to appreciate your husbands instead of making snide remarks about them all the time. Try going without for a while and then see how you like it.' She laughed quietly and then stopped, aware that Rebecca was still staring at her.

"What?"

"You still haven't answered me. Is this Victor person your boyfriend? Is he going to replace daddy?"

"To be honest, I just don't know. No-one can actually replace daddy but…."

"But what?" demanded Rebecca.

"Well your father disappeared months ago and we've not heard a word from him in all that time. He's gone but he's still your father. On the other hand, life has to go on."

Rebecca ignored her mother's closing comment and said, "Is he coming back?"

"Again, I just don't know but I doubt it. Do you want him back, Rebecca?"

Rebecca went silent as she thought about what her mother had asked. Did she want her father back? Did she even miss him? She knew that Damion could not care less whether their father was home or not, not now that he had made new friends and was getting involved in sports with his buddies at school. Eventually she said, "How did you meet him?"

"It just happened."

"How? Did you ask him out or something?"

"Of course not, Rebecca. I couldn't do that."

"Why not? I do it all the time."

"You do? Since when have you been asking boys out?" And Linda stared at her daughter. Suddenly she realized that her teenage daughter was developing breasts and was rapidly transforming into a very attractive young lady. 'Uh oh,' she thought. 'I'm going to have to talk about birth control and that sort of thing with her. I suppose I should do the same with Damion. If Rebecca has an interest in boys then it's likely the same applies for Damion. Oh Michael, where are you now that parenting has suddenly become more complex? Oh yes, you've fled the coup, haven't you? Typical!'

As Linda went back to getting dinner ready, she subconsciously started to muse about Victor. It was all so strange and, not for the first time, she wondered about his interest in her. What was in it for him? Anyone ostensibly that rich had his pick of female companions, anything form busty young air-heads to elegant and sophisticated ladies who didn't have to deal with bratty and ungrateful kids or scramble to get meals on the table every night. So why her? As she tipped the sliced and diced vegetables into the boiling water, Linda half-laughed to herself, thinking, 'Well, we'll put answering that question off for yet another day. If Victor does ask me out again, I'll just ask him why. But, on the other hand, do I really want to know? Probably not.'

Randy spread the map out on the conference room table and looked at his new partner, "Okay Ryan, did you have a look at the files and notes I gave you?"

"Actually I did…a couple of times."

"And?"

"To be honest, at first I thought you were crazy but there does seem to be some sort of pattern here. It's subtle but, like you, I sense some sort of pattern although it is hard to discern, isn't it?"

"Yeah, you're right but SAC Wellington thinks we might be on to something and, let's face it, if he thinks we're right, then…"

"If Steve agrees," said Special Agent Ryan Whitcombe. "Then you can bet there's something there. He is one sharp dude and he'll start to expect results in short order now that he's taken an interest. Okay chief, what do we do now?"

Randy was surprised and pleased that the more experienced agent was prepared to take directions from him, the new kid on the block. When his father had mentioned this whole business to him, Randy suspected that Big Jim was somehow setting him up for failure but now he wasn't so sure. His father had been a cop for a long time and had seen everything at least twice before. If he thought that there was something odd about the one murder he knew about, then his unexpressed opinion that similar cases were out there might prove to be correct. Somewhere, somehow there would be a key to the puzzle and, as his dad had said many times, nothing beat old-fashioned police work when you had mysteries to solve.

Snapping out of his reverie, Randy said, "Okay, Let's draw a line from say Columbus, Dayton or even Pittsburgh in the east to Denver or Provo in the west and then look to see where our murders lie in relation to that line."

"Why pick those places?" asked Ryan.

"I'm not sure why I picked them but I have a gut feeling everything has been happening in Middle America. Perhaps our killer dislikes Mid-Westerners? Anyway, it's somewhere to start...we can always change our focus if nothing pans out."

With that, the two men carefully placed a mark on each murder location. Sure enough, a certain pattern started to evolve. Looking at the drawn line and the scattered crosses marking the murders, Randy laughed. "That looks like one of those fancy regression lines I used to plot out in college algebra. Funny how all those hours spent slogging away at maths might actually prove to be useful. I wonder whether there are any more killings out there. I'll follow up with reminders to the various State Police but at least we have somewhere to start. Man, this is going to be a long slog."

Unaccountably, the diner was busy that morning and Bella did not have time to think about the previous evening although her brother would make the odd passing remark about it whenever their paths crossed between the dining room and the kitchen. Bella alternated between irritation at her brother's sophomoric humor and a secret pleasure that he knew she now had a lover, and one who appeared to have satisfied her. At least Andrew appeared to be pleased and even seemed to approve.

'Satisfied me?' She asked herself when she could stop running between dining room and kitchen. 'Now that's something I haven't thought about in years. Well, I suppose things were never that great with Charles but I didn't really think about *me* back then but that was a consequence, for want of a better word, of being young and in love…plus a whole lot of inexperience. My, my, how things have changed. It was fun when I was first divorced. Young, attractive, on the pill – the world was my oyster back then and it was like being a kid in a candy store but that soon paled when I realized that most of the men I met were simply using me. I should have known better but I shudder to think how many married men I took home with me at first without any idea that they had a wife and kids at home. Huh, I should have known. After the first couple of wham, bam, thank you ma'ams, it dawned on me that I was just a receptacle. It was fun while it lasted but it was over almost as soon as it started. Now, just when I thought I might be settling into celibate middle-age, up turns Michael. Fate, you really do a number on a girl, don't you?' and Bella went back to serving yet another plate of meatloaf, gravy, fries and green beans, the staple lunch-time diet of so many of their customers.

Out of the corner of her eye as she collected yet another brimming plate of food from the service hatch, she could see Michael concentrating on ladling out food. Again she marveled at his absolute concentration on the task at hand. Cooking and preparing food plates was hardly a major mental exercise but it was obvious that Michael took his work seriously. Not for the first time she wondered what he had done before ending up here. He didn't have the calloused hands and broken fingernails of a manual worker and he did not have the affect of a health care worker such as a doctor or dentist, and she could not envision him as a bank manager, an accountant or even an office worker or salesman. Nor did he have the dry, slightly caustic demeanor of a schoolteacher but nevertheless he did project the image of an educator. Then she stopped dead in her tracks, almost spilling the laden plate of food. 'That's it,' she decided. 'I'll bet he was some sort of college professor! Now I think about it, he really does remind me of some of my professors at college, albeit not as stuffy or self-important as many of them were. If that is the case, what on earth is he doing here, working as a cook in a small diner in Southampton, Missouri? One day I'll have to ask him about it but not yet, most certainly not yet. Unless I tread very lightly, I'll frighten him off and that would be a ridiculous price to pay for my curiosity! No, I'll let things lie….you never know, he might even tell me himself although I doubt it."

Then Bella shook her head in exasperation, thinking, 'What's wrong with you girl? If I asked Andrew's advice, which is unlikely, I know what he'd say, "Leave it be girl…don't fuck with it! Besides, who gives a shit? Just let it be!" and he'd be right. I'm acting like a giddy teenager. One night of fun and frolicking in bed and I'm already hearing wedding bells. What's wrong with me? Giddy teenager is right. Enough already!'

The morning dragged on and Randy and Ryan were hard at work compiling lists of every hotel and motel along their projected route. Eventually Randy straightened up and moved away from his computer. "Hey, let's get some lunch Ryan."

"Great idea. I'm famished – all this computer work is giving me a roaring headache."

As they sat munching on burgers, Randy said, "I'm shocked at just how many motels and hotels there are across Mid-America."

"It's not that surprising really," commented Ryan. "Let's face it, Americans are the most peripatetic people in the world and they have to have somewhere to stay when they are travelling, don't they?"

Randy looked at his colleague with surprise. Ryan was a big man and looked like the college jock that he probably was. Blond, broad-shouldered with a disingenuous face but obviously he was no dummy, otherwise he would not have become a Special Agent with the FBI. He waited for Ryan to continue, which he did after taking a sip of coffee.

"I used to know a senior maintenance engineer, you know the Mr. Fix-it, for a machine tool manufacturer. Anyway, he had the attitude that if any of his calls were less than 300 miles from home, he always drove there because he hated the hassle and endless delays of flying. I'm sure there are lots of men like that together with travelling salesmen and the like and they must stay somewhere on the road."

Randy nodded, "You're probably right but does there have to be so many of those places?"

"I'm afraid so. The real problem is that lots of those places are "no-tell" motels and their record keeping leaves a lot to be desired."

"That makes our job difficult, doesn't it, Ryan?"

"Yup but then if it were easy, anyone could do it and that's why the FBI pays us our big bucks."

"Big bucks?" laughed Randy. "In your dreams."

The afternoon wore on and both Randy and Ryan were very tired. They had located hundreds of lodgings on either side of the arbitrary line they had drawn across the middle of the country. Both of them stared balefully at the pages and pages of addresses and telephone numbers, and the odd Email address, of every hotel and motel. They had taken the precaution of compiling separate lists in case one or the other missed anything. Finally, they looked up and stared at each other. Randy nodded and said, "Let's hope we've got everything…what a chore."

"Yeah but a necessary one," opined Ryan. "Now what do we do with all this information?"

"Tomorrow we combine the lists and then start sorting."

"Sorting?"

"Well I think we can probably eliminate all of the large hotel chains and possibly most of the larger motels. Obviously we don't know how much money this guy's got but if he is travelling around and staying in motels, then he is likely to look for the smaller and cheaper ones. If nothing else, security is likely to be less vigilant in a smaller place, if it exists at all."

"That makes sense," agreed Ryan. "If he did stay in any one place for longer than a day or two, I agree that he'd have likely looked for somewhere cheap, at least I would think so."

"You're probably right, Ryan. Tomorrow we start winnowing down our list although I suspect it is still going to be difficult and time-consuming just to narrow down our search."

"I hate to agree with you Randy but that's what it looks like. I tell you man, give me an old-fashioned bank robber any time. Boring maybe, but much easier."

"Okay then we'll get started again in the morning," said Randy and the pair of them left the office, tired but satisfied with a good day's work. They had made a good start although both were aware that a daunting task lay ahead of them.

Vince Dodson sat behind his desk and thumbed through his notes. For the first time that he could remember, he had a case that yielded no clues, none at all, which he could follow. "How can someone disappear without a trace?' he muttered. For a moment he stopped and considered whether perhaps Michael Woodman had gone into a Witness Protection program. 'Nah,' he thought. 'That's unlikely. Surely they would have taken the wife and children into the program too.' Just in case, he decided he would check local and state archives to see if there had been any murders or other major crimes that Michael Woodman might have witnessed although even before he went that extra mile, he was viscerally aware that such a remote possibility was highly unlikely. He looked at his notes yet again.

The missing man seemed to be as pure as the driven snow. Not a single speeding ticket or a parking citation, nothing. His finances, while not spectacular, were sound enough and there was no evidence that he gambled, was a drug user or had extra-marital affairs. Even discreet inquiries of the security personnel at Hathaway College revealed nothing. As one man said, "Professor Woodman? He was one of the few faculty who didn't even flirt with the co-eds let alone get involved with any of them. Given what some of them look like and the way they dress, it's a miracle but that was the way he was. Good guy actually. Always said "hello" and he was just a nice man." No-one else at the college had anything negative to say. Basically, Michael Woodman was a good professor, worked hard, was always on time for lectures and seminars; even the students had nothing negative to say about him. No-one could understand why he had taken off the way he did – "Not like him at all" was the consensus.

Vince sighed. The missing man seemed to be a cross between Gandhi and Nelson Mandela. In his considerable experience,

Vince had always found that even the most innocent of people had something to hide but not this guy. That in itself was strange. He thought about his conversation with Detective Dick Schmidt, the officer to whom Linda had reported Michael's disappearance.

"She came across as a bitch on wheels, that one," said Dick and he drained his glass. As he deftly slid it towards Vince for a refill, he added, "So why are you interested in this guy, Vince? Hardly something that the head of security for Bennet's usually gets into."

"You're right there, Dick but when the boss, Victor Bascombe, says look into something, then that's exactly what you do. I grant you that it makes no sense but then very little that billionaires actually do make sense, at least to us ordinary mortals."

"Yeah. Hey, I wonder what it's like to be that rich…you know, you can do virtually anything and no-one can say or do anything about it."

"I dunno, Dick, but I doubt that we'll ever be in that position ourselves. On the other hand, I have to admit that Mr. Bascombe seems to be a decent sort and he's always been good to me, so I can't complain. Anyway, did you get anything useful out of Linda Woodman?"

"Nada. She was as astonished as everyone else that he had taken off without a word. I did get the impression that his home life wasn't the greatest but then whose is? What do they say? Three out of four marriages end in divorce – doesn't say much for most people, does it?"

"No," admitted Vince, thinking about his own home life. Things had been going bad for some time but retirement and the move out here had helped so that he and Madge were getting along better than they had in years. The increased income, a nice home and less pressure at work all helped. Snapping out of his reveries, he said, "So you didn't find anything noteworthy about the guy?"

"Nothing. It seems he took money out of an ATM the day he disappeared and some more about two-three weeks later, this time in a small town in Ohio but otherwise there's been nothing. He didn't even drain down the bank accounts and other than a single use of a credit card to buy gas, somewhere in Ohio, there's been nothing."

"Hmm. How odd," commented Vince. "What about his car? Anything there?"

"He drives a piece of shit Toyota, about as common as dirt and no, no-one has seen it either. The guy's just gone."

"I don't suppose anyone offed him and buried him in a landfill or under an expressway."

"Nah. I can hardly see the mob or a drug cartel going after an obscure professor from a small college. I did check all the hospitals and mortuaries in a 100 mile radius but no-one has reported an unclaimed body or someone even remotely answering his description lying in a coma anywhere. Sorry but you now know as much as I do."

Vince nodded and bought another round of drinks. At least the local detective had crossed all the "t"s and dotted all the "i"s – no complaints there but he was no further forward than before.

After a final read through his notes, Vince decided he had best bring Mr. Bascombe up-to-date on progress. He would not like what he, Vince, had to tell him but there was little he could do about it. Idly he wondered what the boss would tell him to do next. It occurred to him that if he was directed to try to follow in the footsteps of Michael Woodman, it could be a long, hard haul but then he was well-paid and he'd have access to a hefty expense account, so what did he care? Besides, Madge might even enjoy having him out of the house for a while.

CHAPTER 12

Randy and Ryan were poring over the large scale map of the United States trying to relate the sites of murders to Interstates and major highways. Concentrating, neither agent heard the conference room door open to admit Steve Wellington who asked, "So, how are things going? Making any progress?"

Both men straightened up and were surprised to see the SAC standing there. Randy broke the silence, "We think we are, yes."

"Okay," said Steve. "Fill me in."

"The crosses indicate the sites of the killings," said Randy gesturing at the map laid out on the table. "We've been able to add to their number by liaising with State Police and this is what we've found to date. It's possible that there are more out there but it's the best data we have so far."

Steve studied the map and the scattered crosses. Eventually he said, "Well it looks as though you might be right, Randy. Each murder seems to have occurred in reasonably close proximity to an Interstate. Right then, what are the large circles around each site?"

"We have assumed that killer probably did not drive for more than 1½ to 2 hours to find a victim so the circles are scaled to show an area that encompasses a distance of about 100 miles around each killing."

"I see that," said Steve. "Now some of the circles intersect, don't they?"

"Yes sir, they do. We think that the killer was holed up somewhere within that intersecting region or close thereto."

"Interesting theory. So what are you going to do next?"

"We've compiled a list of motels and smaller hotels in the vicinity of the intersections," said Ryan.

"Why only smaller establishments?" asked Steve.

"It seems logical to us that the killer would stay in a smaller place for several reasons, the most likely being somewhat lax security at smaller hotels and motels."

"How so?"

"If he stayed at a hotel, particularly one of a large chain, he would need to pay with a credit card and probably also provide his vehicle tag number. Also, most of those places have a manned front desk 24/7 and any comings and goings would be observed… not necessarily recorded, but an alert desk clerk might make note of someone making one or more trips out at night."

"Several trips?" inquired Steve.

"It is hard to believe that the killer found a suitable victim on every sortie he made. No, it's likely that he might have had to make several trips before he found what he was looking for, assuming of course that he had a particular type of victim in mind."

"Is there any evidence of that, a particular type of victim?"

"Apparently not but it seems most victims were people on their own either going into or leaving a bar at night," said Randy.

"Okay, that makes sense on all counts," said Steve. "So, what are you going to do next?"

Ryan sighed before saying, "Now the hard work starts, Steve. We'll have to identify and then contact every motel etc. within or close to the intersections."

Randy nodded and added, "The motel listings don't give us too much information about each place but at least we have somewhere to start. Since the killings seem to come in clusters, it seems reasonable to us that the killer likely stayed in one place for several days, possibly longer."

Steve grunted and Ryan added, "The trouble is, smaller motels might not always keep good records, particularly if the person paid in cash. As far as they are concerned, cash payments could be hidden from the IRS and simply pocketed."

"So No-Tell Motels complicates things?" suggested Steve mildly. "I can see why you both have some reservations. Of course, you could get lucky and find that the perp actually used his real name – stranger things have happened. On the other hand, given the fact that he has been careful not to leave any trace evidence at the crime scenes, I wouldn't hold my breath that he's done something that stupid."

"As you say Steve, possible but unlikely. So, we'll have to contact every single lodging place within our target zones and get information on who might have stayed there say two or three weeks before and after each killing. It is going to take time but we think that it's the best approach."

"Sounds good to me," commented Steve. "As you say, it's going to take time but I don't see that you have any other options. Well, good luck with that and keep me informed of progress, okay?" After that Steve headed back to his office satisfied that the two men were making progress, albeit slowly.

"Take time?" muttered Ryan. "It could be weeks or even months before we get everything together although it does seem to be a logical approach."

"Yes it does," agreed Randy. Looking at his watch, he added, "Let's get lunch and then we can divide up the work as best we can."

"Okay," said Ryan. "Let's hope the motels co-operate in giving us information. I hate the thought of having to make lots of field trips."

"Let's hope for the best. Burgers and fries?"

"Sure, why eat healthy when we can build our cholesterol levels," laughed Ryan.

The diner had been busy all week and Bella, Andrew and Michael were all happy with the thought that they would have Sunday off. The diner profits would have been increased by being open 7 days a week but, as Bella once remarked, "A girl's got to be able to sleep in at least one morning a week. How can I look cute and adorable if I'm dragging around every day?"

Andrew laughed. "You've never been cute and adorable in your life, at least not since you were about 4 or 5 but you do make a good point. Besides, my Angela hates me jumping out of bed so early every day when she looks forward to snuggling together in the mornings."

"Snuggling? You? Since when did you snuggle with anyone?" laughed Bella. Turning to Michael, she asked, "What do you think, Michael?"

Michael simply shrugged. It did not matter to him whether he worked 6 or 7 days a week since he really had no other pressing things to attend to, other than laundry on a regular basis. He had been so tired every day after cooking dozens or more breakfasts, lunches and dinners that he had had no time to even think about killing anyone. Besides, he reasoned, if Bella turned up at his motel room unannounced again, it might be difficult to explain where he had gone off to for several hours at night. He was getting into the swing of working long hours and one day he might be able to get back to his arcane hobby, as he called it.

It was bright and sunny Saturday afternoon and Michael slipped out back to smoke a cigarette and drink a coffee in the welcome interlude between lunch and dinner. As he sat soaking up sunshine and letting his thoughts drift, he heard the door open and then click shut, followed by tentative footsteps in his direction.

"Hey big guy, what's happening?" said Bella as she sat down on the bench beside him.

"Nothing much – just taking a break. No customers have suddenly shown up, have they?"

"No, it's quiet for a change – thank goodness. Got a spare cigarette?"

"Of course," and Michael pulled a pack out of his pocket, offered one to Bella and then lit it. For a several minutes, they sat quietly and companionably together, enjoying the peace and quiet. Eventually Bella broke the silence, "Hey Mike, are you busy later tonight…and tomorrow for that matter?"

"Not that I know of…why?"

"Well I thought that, if it's alright with you, I'd swing by later. If it's a nice day tomorrow, we might even go and do something, you know, drive around, have a picnic, something like that?"

"That sounds like a plan to me," replied Michael. "In fact, it sounds great. I have no idea of what is around here and I haven't had the time to go exploring."

"Okay then," said a delighted Bella. "It's a date." And then she immediately regretted what she had said, thinking, 'Damn, am I being too pushy? Why make a big deal out of spending the night and the next day with Michael, even going so far as to refer to it as a date? Talk about doing my best to frighten him off.' Stealing a quick look at Michael, she thought, 'He doesn't seem to be too put out at the thought of going on a "date" but I've got to be more careful. In some respects he reminds me of a nervous horse and I don't want to make him shy away. Oh shit, this boy-girl thing is such a pain at times!'

Michael smiled to himself. 'Bella is a truly nice person' he thought. 'and she wears her heart on her sleeve….rather endearing really. I wonder what her husband was like. He sounds like a self-centered idiot to me but then I didn't win any points in that area with my treatment of Linda. I like to think it was no-one's fault but that really isn't true. Obsessively working for tenure and promotion did a number on me and on our relationship. I acknowledge that it was a necessary exercise for me if I wanted to stay in academia but why did I let its effects drag on for so long after I became an Associate Professor with tenure? Not surprising that Linda switched off but the trouble is that it spilled over into my relationship with Damion and Rebecca. By the time I became aware of things, it was too late and the damage was done.'

He stopped thinking for a moment and then smiled at Bella, "You know, having a picnic somewhere that we can look at the developing fall colors might be great." He paused and then added, "You know what, spending the evening…and night…with you might be even better than the picnic."

Bella laughed, "I'm glad to hear it. Okay, I'll come on over say about 10….or do you want to come to my house? Andrew won't be home and…"

"Whatever you say, Bella. Just tell me what you've decided nearer to when we close up and can get out of here. As you have often said, let's take advantage of our day off. I only hope we're not too busy with the dinner crowd and end up exhausted."

"Don't worry about that, Michael. I'm sure we'll drag up some energy from somewhere," and she laughed again.

"Hey Randy," called Ryan. "I think I've got something."

"Really? What's that?"

"It looks as though one guy has stayed at several of the motels we have on our list and…" He paused dramatically before resuming, "He seems to have stayed in those places at various times some of which approximate to the dates of the murders."

"You are kidding! That's fantastic."

"Not only that, the guy registered as either Arthur C. Doyle or sometimes as A.C. Doyle."

"You have got to be kidding. Arthur C. Doyle…get outta here."

"Yeah, the guy obviously has a sense of humor. Fancy thinking we wouldn't spot that he was using the name of the originator of the Sherlock Holmes mysteries."

"Yeah but it's taken long enough for us to spot him, so why not have some fun at our expense?" Randy paused and then added, "On the other hand, he wasn't to know that we might be looking for him and if he's been getting away with using that name for months, why not continue to do so? Okay, where is he now?"

"I'll have to confirm it but I think he's somewhere close to Wichita, Kansas."

"He is? We actually know the place he's staying?"

"As I say, I'll have to check but it seems he's in a small motel, The Happy Highway Motel or the like."

A few minutes later, Ryan was able to say that this mysterious Mr. Arthur C. Doyle was indeed staying at The Happy Highway Motel and had been there at least three days.

"Right," snapped Randy. "Let's get some of the local agents there together with a SWAT team. With a bit of luck we've got him. Fantastic!"

"Should we tell Steve?"

"No. Let's wait until we've actually arrested him and then we can crow about it. I hate to say anything just yet given how elusive the guy is."

"You're probably right, Randy. Okay, I'll get onto the regional office and set things in motion. Let's hope we get him before he can take off again."

Arthur Cornelius Doyle stared balefully at the half-eaten Chinese take-out. The hot and sour soup hadn't been too bad but the chicken-fried rice had been dreadful and even the Fortune Cookie had been stale. This trip had been a bust from the get-go and the commission on the paltry sales he had recorded would not even cover gasoline and meals let alone the motel costs. While it had been pleasant enough to talk to his wife, the litany of woes from the home front simply depressed him. His oldest child, Johnny, had been growing like a weed for the past couple of years and now he had broken a leg at football practice. By the time he could play again, he'd need a whole now uniform. The youngest, Donna, had come down with a severe sinus infection and the antibiotic costs alone did not bear thinking about. As for Cathy, the middle child, Art Doyle was even less amused to hear that she needed orthodontics and that the down-payment to even start treatment would be about $2500. To cap it all, Sandy's Suburban not only needed new tires but was making ominous clunking noises when she drove.

Reviewing the telephone call and thinking about the past week severely depressed Art and he wondered what else could go wrong. As if on cue, there was a heavy pounding on the room door and a stentorian voice announced that they were the FBI and demanded that the door be opened. Confused and a little frightened, Art opened the door to face two large men in dark suits wearing sunshades with at least five heavily armed SWAT team members arrayed behind them in full battle gear.

"What do you want?" stammered Art.

"Are you Arthur C. Doyle?" demanded one of the suits in a threatening manner.

"Yes I am." There was a pause and he reached towards his back pocket for his wallet. Almost instantaneously, Berettas appeared the hands of the two men standing in the doorway and Art could hear the ominous snick of rounds being chambered by the SWAT team men behind them.

"Whoa," shouted Art. "I'm just getting my wallet."

"Just keep your hands where we can see them…no, put them behind your neck and we'll get your wallet for you," snapped what appeared to be the lead agent. "Now, just step back into the room and we'll check your I.D."

As the agents cautiously followed Art into the small motel room, they could see the remains of a Chinese meal, an open lap-top computer and the man's cell phone on the table. But, they were relieved to see, there was no evidence of a weapon of any kind. After handcuffing him, they quickly dug through Art's wallet and came up with a driver's license.

"So you are Arthur Cornelius Doyle, are you?" snarled the second agent.

"Yes. Why do you want to know and what's all this about?"

"Just tell us where you've been for the past few months and why you were there," ordered the lead agent.

"What?" exclaimed Art. "Are you kidding me? What on earth do you want to know that for?"

"We think that you are the perpetrator of a number of murders and your travels over the past few months coincide with those of the unknown killer."

"Oh get real," snapped Art. "I'm a salesman for Ascension Machine Tools and have been for years. Why on earth would you even think I could be a murderer?"

"Just tell us where you've been and why, and we'll decide whether you are the killer we're looking for. So, stand over there in the corner and stay there."

As Art followed orders, he realized that his life had just got a whole lot worse. 'What the hell is going on here?' he asked himself. 'One minute I'm trying to make a living selling machine tools and the next the FBI suspects me of murder. Sandy is not going to be pleased when she hears this although just how I explain it to her defeats me for the moment.'

Art listened carefully as he heard the lead agent speak quietly into his cell phone, "Yeah, we've got him. He says his name is Doyle, Arthur Cornelius."

The voice at the other end said loudly, "Cornelius, did you say? Not Conan?"

"Yup, it's Cornelius, Arthur Cornelius Doyle, according to his driver's license. Apparently he lives in Ohio."

"Okay, give me the license number and his address." said the other voice. "We'll check on it. I'll get back to you shortly – well done on catching him. Take him in for questioning, will you? I'll get you more information as soon as I can."

After hanging up, Randy turned to Ryan and said, "Okay, we've got an address for him and a driver's license number. Let's check both out and then send in some local agents together with the police as soon as we can get a search warrant. I think we've got him this time. I'll bet Steve will be pleased." He paused for a moment and picked up his cell phone to call the senior agent at Art Doyle's motel. "Hey Brad, it's Randy. Did you say the guy has a lap-top? He does? Good. Can you check on his movements over the past say 6 months? If he's a salesman, as he claims, surely he would have kept notes on where he was, who he saw, that sort of thing? Call me back when you've got something. In the meantime go easy on questioning him after you've taken him in. We don't want him lawyering up too quickly."

A few hours later, Randy and Brad spoke again. "I've been going over Doyle's customer contact notes on his lap-top."

"Really?" said Randy. "Find anything?"

"Well he was in the vicinity of the various places that you mentioned to me but…."

"But what?" asked Randy.

"He's made careful mention of the customers he saw, sales he made, where he stayed and everything else. You know, it looks like a typical sales rep's diary or daybook, or whatever they call those things"

"That's it?"

"I'm not sure what else I should be looking for but it all looks pretty innocent to me."

"What does he say about the killings?"

"He says he doesn't know what we're talking about. Claims not to have even heard of any of the places where the murders took place."

"Huh!"

"I've got Lance, my co-team member, going through his cell phone and checking through the calls he's made."

"Anything there?"

"Most of the calls seem to be either to his home or to potential customers. I can't see anything out of the ordinary."

"Look, this is one smart dude. You made sure that he doesn't have a burner phone or anything?"

"Of course. We found nothing. Are you sure that he's the one?"

"You tell me."

"When we were questioning him, his wife called. She was pissed that her home has been invaded by the FBI and the local police. Apparently they've been turning everything upside down, even rousting the youngest child out of her sick bed. That really got to Doyle and he's pretty angry now… and asking whether he needs a lawyer. In that regard he seems to be a bit clueless if he is a killer."

"Did he say anything to his wife?" asked Randy.

"Only to try to explain what he thought was going on, and she didn't take it too well. I gather the poor schmuck works pretty hard but doesn't make a whole lot of money and, from what I gather, they are having some financial problems at the moment. Nothing too serious but it seems he's worried about paying all the bills." Brad paused for a moment or two. "Look Randy, I've got to tell you, I just don't see this guy being a serial or any other type of killer. Hey hold on a minute, Lance wants to talk to me. I'll call you back."

After about 15 minutes, Brad called Randy back and said quietly, "Ah Randy, we have a problem."

"He lawyered up, did he?"

"Actually no although I think he's thinking about it. In fact he virtually asked our advice on what he should do. He made the point and I quote, *"Look, I know I'm no rocket scientist but even I know I cannot prove a negative. There is no way I can prove that I didn't murder anyone and you people should know that!"* He had a point."

"So what's the problem?"

"Well Lance has been carefully checking the guy's cell phone records and matching them with the home phone records that your guys sent to us. He's also been looking at his log book for all his travels."

"Go on," said Randy flatly as a sick feeling started up in his gut.

"It seems that virtually every time that a murder was being committed, our Arthur Doyle was either talking to his wife on the phone or meeting with clients. Bit surprising that he met with people in the evenings but I suppose he had to wine and dine them to make a sale. Anyway, it looks as though he's got some pretty solid alibis and he has hotel and restaurant receipts to support what he says. Lance will follow up with the clients but it doesn't look too good as this point."

"Are you sure about this?"

"Pretty sure. There is one murder that happened when Doyle was not talking to his wife or meeting with a customer but he was about 200 miles away from where the murder occurred. Let's face it, a 400 mile round trip tends to rule out that possibility."

"Oh shit!" exclaimed Randy.

"As I told you, I think we have a problem," said Brad.

"Damn right we do. Now what do we do?"

"You are asking me what to do next?" asked Brad. "It's your call what we do now."

"This is not good news. Tell you what, I'll have a word with my SAC and get back to you ASAP. Thanks for the heads-up Brad."

As Randy feared, the meeting between he, Ryan and Steve did not go well. After listening to them, Steve sat back and stared at the ceiling, his habitual pose when he needed to think. Eventually he said, "Okay, I can see that a number of things pointed towards this Doyle fellow and calling himself Arthur Doyle or Arthur C. Doyle, if that's his name, would be an obvious clue. Actually that would have been quite clever really. Not only that, like you guys, I hate and completely mistrust coincidences but it looks as though the near-impossible actually happened. Well, I can only advise you to turn the guy loose with apologies and hope that he doesn't go to the newspapers with this."

"Let's hope not," said Ryan. "I gather from talking to Lance in Wichita that Mr. Doyle is pretty steamed up, wanting to know how all this happened. He claims that we've caused problems between him and his wife, unnecessarily blackened his reputation with his customers and he's worried sick that he could lose his job because the FBI was investigating him. Apparently his firm did not take kindly to our guys inquiring about one of their salespeople. I hate to say it Steve, this is a real mess."

At which point, Randy chimed in. "Look Steve, I'm sorry but this is probably all my fault. It all seemed so likely when we found this Doyle guy."

"Don't I know it," sighed Steve. He paused for thought again before saying, "Okay, turn him loose with profuse apologies. I'll get onto *my* boss and see if we can give him some sort of financial compensation and let's hope that will settle the problem." He stopped and looked hard at his two agents.

"You know, I really do hate coincidences and it seems as though you two turned over a doozy this time. Even I was convinced you'd got the killer but apparently not. Well, when all else fails, go back to the drawing board and try again. There has to be something out there." He paused and then offered a thin smile. "This time guys, if you find someone with the name Agatha Christie or even an A. Christie, be a little more cautious, okay?"

On their way back to the conference room, a chastened Randy said to Ryan, "What a total bummer. I really thought we'd got him, didn't you?"

"I'm afraid so. I suppose we should have known when it seemed almost too perfect and that Arthur C. Doyle name really got me. So Randy, what do we do now?"

"We do as Steve said. We get back to work but before we do so, let's have another think through to check that we really are on the right track but, for the life of me, I can't see any other way to find this killer. You got any ideas?"

"Not me although getting some lunch sounds like a good idea."

"Yeah, why not? When all else fails, let's feed our faces." Randy paused and then added, "You know, if that damn killer knew what we'd been doing, he'd probably be laughing his head off at us. I tell you Ryan, he must have made a mistake somehow, somewhere. No-one is that good but what else can we do at this point?"

"Hell, why ask me? My last good idea didn't pan out too well, did it? Nah, let's get some food. Maybe inspiration will hit us....

along with gastritis from those lousy burgers you like to eat. Hell, even my wife's cooking tastes better, which is saying something."

Randy grunted. Ryan was right on all accounts, including the indigestion.

CHAPTER 13

After listening carefully to Vince Dodson's report, Victor Bascombe sighed and shook his head, "So Michael Woodman has literally disappeared without a trace?"

"So it appears, sir," said Vince. "The local police have nothing and my own discreet and very unofficial inquiries with the IRS and Social Security indicate no activity in months. Of course, they do not always keep those records right up to date, so it's possible that he is out there somewhere. I even wondered whether he might have gone into the Witness Protection program but that seems to be a bust too."

"Hmm. This is very strange," said Victor.

"That it is, sir, that it is," agreed Vince. He paused and then asked, "Do I take it that you do not want me to talk to Mrs. Woodman?"

"No I do not." Victor paused in turn before saying, "I assume that the police have heard nothing from her regarding her husband either?"

"No. From what I can gather, she has made the best of it and simply got on with her life. Oh yes, I did talk to the people at Hathaway College and no-one has heard a thing either. The disappearance of Professor Woodman is as much a mystery to them as it is to the rest of us."

"I assume that there's been no credit card activity or withdrawal of cash from an ATM?"

"He did make a couple of ATM withdrawals and paid for gasoline with a credit card on one occasion since he left. That occurred in some small town in Ohio but there's been nothing since then for months."

"What's he been living on? I gather that neither he nor his wife were particularly affluent."

"No they weren't. They did not exactly live from paycheck to paycheck but there's no evidence of lots of cash being secreted away anywhere. College professors are scarcely rich and any money they both might have had when they were first married went into buying that house. No, I could not find anything there. Besides, someone at the bank would have noticed if he'd emptied a safe deposit box before taking off. As I say, they met their bills and not much more. In fact, from what I can tell, Mrs. Woodman has been struggling financially since he took off. I believe she's working here at Bennet's."

Victor greeted that last comment with silence while Vince looked narrowly at his boss and thought, 'So that's what this is all about. If the woman is as attractive as that Pittsburgh detective Dick Schmidt had said, then perhaps that's where Mr. Bascombe's interest is coming from but given his wealth, power and influence, why would he be interested in someone as cold and downright bitchy as Dick implied? Oh well, ours is not to reason why.' Vince waited a few beats and asked, "What would you like me to do next, sir?"

"Good question, Vince, good question. What are your thoughts on the matter?"

"Mr. Bascombe, the situation is rather like Earl in that Dixie Chicks song, you know the one where they sing about Earl going missing but no-one misses him. What we have here is something similar. Michael Woodman has gone missing and no-one really seems to care except for his wife and children and I don't they are too cut up about him being gone." Vince paused and looked at his boss. "As far as the police are concerned, the guy has committed no crimes, so their interest is now minimal. It seems to be highly unlikely that some Mexican drug cartel or the mob or anyone like that is after him because he seems to be as white and pure as the driven snow. He's just gone."

"Hmm. Okay, so tell me, where did he drop off the radar?"

"His last sighting, actually the last electronic trace of him from a credit card or an ATM machine was in Cambridge, Ohio, somewhere off I70. As I said, that was months ago and there's been nothing since then."

Victor was silent as he digested what Vince had told him and then he grunted, "I wonder why he went there? Hmm, how odd." He thought for a moment or two before saying, "Isn't there some way of tracking someone from their cell phone? I recall seeing that being done on one of those detective shows on television."

"Ordinarily yes, that is true. Unfortunately, when Michael Woodman left home, he also left behind his cell phone and even his checkbook. I'm afraid we cannot find him that way, no."

"I should have known it wouldn't be that simple," said Victor. "If it were, the police would have dug into that, wouldn't they?"

"Yes sir," agreed Vince and he sat back to await further instructions. He did not have to wait long.

"Alright then, Vince, I think the way ahead is straightforward, isn't it?"

"It is?" asked Vince in astonishment and then hurriedly changed his response to, "I'm not sure what you mean, sir."

"All I can see is that you should pack a bag, say goodbye to Madge for a few days and chase after the man…follow in his footsteps, so to speak."

Vince was silent but he was thinking, 'Whatever is going on here? Mr. Bascombe is very serious in finding out where this man has gone but I really don't understand why. Of course, that's no matter to me since he's paying to do a job and that's what I'll do.'

Seeing Vince deep in thought, judging by the distracted look on his face, Victor added, "You will have a generous *per diem* as usual and use the corporate credit card as and when you need it Take as long as you need but I should like a weekly update by telephone, not by Email.…you understand, of course."

Vince nodded. It was not the first time that his boss had asked him to do something "off the books" and he doubted that it would be the last. As long as he did not have to do anything illegal or immoral, he would obey orders to the best of his ability. After hesitating for a few seconds, he said, "Certainly Mr. Bascombe. I'll get started today." He laughed and added, "I imagine Madge will be only too happy to have me out from under her feet for however long this takes."

Victor smiled, saying, "It's funny how that works, isn't it? But I'm willing to bet that she'll start missing you after only a day or two.

Anyway, good luck with the search and drive carefully. I shall look forward to hearing from you in a few days…and thank you."

Vince nodded again and left the CEO's office. He still wondered what the old man's interest might be but since he would be substantially adding to his income while he was away, he really didn't care about the reasons for his search.

On his drive home, Vince called his wife and filled her in, to a limited degree, on what was going on and asked her politely to pack a bag for him. He would take Madge out for a nice lunch, kiss her goodbye, fill the car with gasoline, buy a bottle of scotch for the room and be on his way by early afternoon. Aloud, he told his car, "The game's afoot, Watson, the game's afoot", unconsciously following the lead of the FBI agents Randy and Ryan in trying to chase down the elusive and purported Arthur Conan Doyle in Kansas. As he headed home, he decided that he would book a hotel room in wherever that place was in Ohio that Woodman had stopped first and perhaps also book rooms in what he deduced from the map as logical stopping points thereafter. He was secretly delighted with his assignment. At last he had a real task of detective work ahead of him.

Senior profiler Irving Latimer sighed and smacked the file on his desk in frustration. He had been doing his job for a good many years but for the first time in his career, he was at a loss on how to proceed. In the end, he decided to call Special Agent Randolph Cunningham to check whether the agent had any further information for him.

"Special Agent Cunningham?"

"Yes?"

"I'm Senior Profiler Irving Latimer at Quantico. I've been going through that file you sent me."

"Yes sir," said Randy, surprised at being called by such a senior person.

"There isn't much to go on, is there?"

"I'm afraid it's all we've got, sir."

"Oh I believe you. But…" and Irving paused to gather his thoughts. "There are a lot of odd things about this killer, aren't there?"

"I think so, yes," agreed Randy. "What strikes you in particular, Agent Latimer?"

"Well for a start, the guy never leaves any trace evidence and, let's face it, he seems to be using an arcane method of killing his victims, apart from that one shooting."

"Yes, that's right."

"I also gather that he doesn't steal from his victims, that right?"

"As far as we can tell, robbery does not seem to be a motive, no." Randy hesitated and then added, "But it is possible that he took a gun from one victim but we cannot confirm that."

"Ah yes, that was the instance of a later killing where a spent cartridge was found with the fingerprint of a previous victim, yes?"

Yes, that's right."

"Well Randy, this is all very puzzling."

"Yes?"

"We have a perp who apparently kills for no obvious reason and does so randomly and in different locations using a very odd approach to killing his victims. He does not rob his victims other than the possibility that he took a gun from one victim. No-one seems to have seen him come or go and he, assuming that it is a "he", has never left a trace. Now it seems, based on what you've sent me, that he has gone quiet for quite some time." Irving sighed before continuing, "In my experience, killers like this usually keep on going, and often escalate their activities, until they either are caught or they give themselves up….but not in this case. Not only that, there appears to be no rhyme nor reason underlying his selection of victims, other than random opportunity and, based on your data, the killings have nothing to do with a full or any other phase of the moon, or the time of the month. The spacing of the killings is also very arbitrary. I have to say, I am really at a loss."

"I'm sorry to hear that, sir," said a disappointed Randy although he had had no real expectations of help from Quantico.

"You are sure that there has been nothing else for several weeks if not months?"

"Well nothing has been reported to us. I did check again recently with the State Police in a number of states and, as I said, there appears to be nothing untoward out there in terms of random killings."

"I was afraid of that," said Irving. "The only positive thing I can tell you is that your surmise that the killer picks targets off Interstates would appear to be correct although other than convenience of access, I can't see any other relationship in any of the killings." He paused before adding, "I've got to tell you, there is one thing that is strange to me, and that is the random and almost arbitrary spacing in the various killings. What is equally odd is that the killer has been inactive for so long."

"Oh?" said Randy.

"In my experience, as I have just said, most serial killers, if that *is* what we have here, normally accelerate their behavior, not space them out over different intervals. That is far from common and it makes me wonder what makes this particular killer tick."

"So what do you make of it all?" asked Randy, feeling a bit foolish in posing such a question.

"Believe it or not, this killer does not match the usual profile of a psychopath, if indeed such a beast actually exists." Latimer paused again. "Let me express that differently. This particular killer is not behaving like any other psychopathic killer that I have come across, and I have come across many of them in my time. Look, let me think about this a bit more. There is something here but I'm not sure what. There has to be something about the victims that sets our killer off. I know people go off the rails and will start to randomly kill people – there have been lots of incidences like that over the years in New York, Austin and so forth, as well as the various high school shootings. However, in most cases of mass or multiple killings, they all occurred in the same place, not spread out as with your guy, and certainly not over the time span we've got here. Look, as I said, let me mull this over some more. I cannot see anything obvious but there has to be something. I'll get back to you as soon as I can. My advice is to keep plugging away and we'll all hope that something breaks loose."

"I understand," said Randy.

"I'm sorry not to be able to offer you more help. If anything else comes in, don't hesitate to contact me. Frankly, I am as puzzled as you are and I share your frustration. So Randy, we'll file the matter for the moment but, as I say, keep me informed of any and all developments."

"Yes sir," said Randy, thinking 'Steve was right. Quantico cannot help us… Ryan is going to be disappointed too. Ah well, back to the drawing board.'

Shortly after Irving Latimer had rung off, Randy and Ryan were sitting side-by-side in a local bar, morosely sipping on drinks and silently staring into space. Eventually Ryan broke the silence, "Okay chief, what do we do next?"

"I hate to say it, Ryan, but if Quantico can't help us, then it's up to us."

"Yeah, I figured as much. Trouble is, Randy, we've done a whole lot of work and the one lead that looked promising proved to be an embarrassing bust."

"Don't I know it," sighed Randy. He drained his glass and turned to Ryan, "Another?"

"Sure…why not? There's not much else going on. Reminds me of many an evening I spent back in rural Iowa. *Boring*!"

As they worked on their replenished drinks, Randy suddenly smacked his glass down. "Hey, you were a country boy, weren't you Ryan?"

"Sure was. What of it?"

"Actually, so was I. Anyway, something suddenly struck me." He turned and looked directly at Ryan, and asked, "What was a common feature, for want of another word, of country life?"

Puzzled, Ryan thought for a moment or two and then said, "That there's nothing much going on other than cattle mooing, wheat and cornfields, farms - that sort of thing?"

"Yes, of course, but what else?"

"I'm not sure where you're going with this, Randy."

"What I'm saying is that rural areas are usually pretty quiet at night – you know, not much stirring, right?"

"Right. So what?"

"The thing I remember growing up was that while the roads might be empty, that didn't stop people from sitting on their porches and staring out for hours just to see who or what came down the road. They tended to do that all day and all night where I grew up.

Even little old ladies would peer out of their windows at odd intervals just to check what was passing."

Ryan stared at Randy and thought hard. "You know, you're right. Those old people knew everything that happened within eyesight of their homes." He stopped and wrinkled his brow. "You know Randy, I think I know where you're going with this. Wow!"

"Wow is right. The perp had to drive down one or more roads to get to his killing site and not all of those roads were completely deserted. My betting is that houses or farmsteads lined many of them."

"You may be right," interrupted Ryan. "It's possible, just possible, that one or more people might have seen his car. I know that lots of old biddies and grandpas might be the ones looking out but that don't mean they didn't see anything. Nor does it necessarily mean that they don't remember seeing something."

"Right!" said Randy. "I know lots of old people have fading memories but the fact that a killing happened some place down the road from them might just prompt a memory. Hell, what have we got to lose by pursuing that line of inquiry?"

"Nothing, Randy, nothing. Besides, it sure beats talking to endless hotels and motels across the mid-West."

"Okay...tomorrow we get back to work. You know what?, I'll even discuss this with Steve. He might have some suggestions for us."

After listening to Randy, Steve thought hard and then said, "Okay, you and Ryan drive out that way...Ohio wasn't it?"

"Yes, Steve. The nearest reasonably large town seems to be a place called Cambridge."

"Okay, the pair of you get up there – it's about 650 to 700 miles so you might get there in a day if you start early enough. After that, start interviewing motels, something might shake loose." He paused and then said, "Remember that your *per diems* are limited so don't even think about finding four star hotels or expensive restaurants to eat in. This is an off-chance operation so you have a limited budget. Remember, if something does break loose, let me know and I'll contact the regional FBI office up there. In fact, as a courtesy, I'll let them and the state police know that you are on the way. We don't want to ruffle any feathers, do we?"

After kissing Madge goodbye, Vince climbed into his car and drove towards I70 and headed west towards Ohio. He reasoned that the town in Ohio where Michael had gassed up his car and got some money from an ATM was a likely starting point for his search. He knew that finding the man would not be an easy task because, unlike New York, the United States covered a huge area and contained some 300 million people. In New York, back when he was on the force, finding someone was relatively easy despite the 8 or 10 million anonymous people who lived in the five boroughs. As he well knew, once there, few people actually left the place and there was always somebody who knew someone who in turn knew someone else who knew the quarry. Finding people was just a matter of time and patience despite the claimed anonymity and isolation of New Yorkers.

As he drove, Vincent mused that finding the elusive Michael Woodman might not be be that simple or straightforward. Although sparing with the details, over lunch he had mentioned to Madge that whereas Michael Woodman had hopped off I70 to gas up his car and get some cash, after that he could have gone anywhere. He could have gone to Columbus and then hopped on I71 and headed southwest to Cincinnati or north to Akron or Cleveland although why he would go to either of those two cities was beyond him. On the other hand, if he had continued on I70 and reached Indianapolis, he could have taken I65 north to Chicago, I65 south to Louisville and then onto Mobile and New Orleans, taken I74 west to Cedar Rapids and Des Moines or simply stayed on I70 and headed west to St. Louis and Kansas City.

"So how will you find him, dear?" asked Madge.

"I have no frigging idea," moaned Vince. "But if the boss wants me to find the man, then that's exactly what I have to do."

"It all sounds rather difficult," sympathized Madge.

"It is," said Vince and promptly decided not to discuss the matter further. Not only was it a bad idea to discuss his work in a public place with his wife, he realized that he was probably breaking his employer's confidence….a very bad idea. He swore his wife to secrecy but Madge, having been married to a senior NYC police officer for decades, was well aware that she could never discuss her husband's work. Vince's final words on the subject were to the effect that trying to find the missing man in the contiguous United States was like looking for the proverbial needle in a haystack. The thought depressed him, so why spoil a good lunch?

As he drove west, Vince mulled over the question where Michael Woodman might have gone after reaching Indianapolis, assuming of course that he had traveled that far although that was quite likely. Starting to be lulled into sleep by the steady thrum of tires on the roadway and in an attempt to fight the soporific effects of driving on a full stomach after a good meal, Vince began talking out loud. "Okay, Professor Woodman, where *did* you go? I suppose you might have gone all the way out west to California but when you think about how far away that is and the outrageous cost of living out there, that surely would not be your first choice of destinations. Likewise, why on earth would you even consider heading north? Surely a big city like Chicago would hold no appeal for you and the weather ain't too good even further north. I don't see Akron or Cleveland holding much appeal either. So, Michael Woodman, did you go south towards Louisville, Tennessee and into the Southern States, continue going west into Kansas and Colorado, or even south into Missouri and Arkansas?

"Ah man, you didn't give me much to go on, did you? On the other hand, you weren't to know that I would be coming to look for you either. Although you only gave me a little bit, you did give me a possible starting point for finding you. The trouble is, I doubt that anyone would take much notice of an ordinary-looking man like you or a man driving a non-descript car. Not having a good photograph of you doesn't help either. I've got to say, Michael, that "mug shot" of you on the Faculty Directory of Hathaway College would probably fool your mother…I hope that's not the way you look in real life." Vince sighed. He was pleased that he had thought to download a picture of the man from the Hathaway College website but it was far from sharp and looked to be several years old. He sighed again and thought about what he would do when he reached Cambridge, Ohio which apparently was one of Michael's stops after leaving home. Judging by the internet information, it was a pretty small place and he knew that there were no four star hotels anywhere close. Aloud, he commented, "You know, Michael, you really are a pain in the ass. Why didn't you stop in a large city so that I could find a luxury hotel and maybe eat in a really good restaurant? I know things must have been bad at home for you to up and leave like that, but must I suffer too?"

Eventually Vince pulled into the convenient store where Michael had filled his car and, after gassing up his own vehicle, he went inside. The clerk, a man in late forties, looked up and asked, "Can I help you?"

"Perhaps," said Vince and pulled out the photograph of Michael. "Do you remember this guy?"

The clerk stared at the photo and then slowly shook his head, "No, I can't say I do? What's he done?"

"Nothing that I know of," replied Vince.

"Then why are you looking for him?" asked the clerk reasonably.

Vince shrugged and spread his hands, saying, "Would you believe a missing heir to a large sum of money?"

"Not really, no."

"I thought as much" sighed Vince who then pulled a $10 bill out of his wallet and offered it to the clerk. "The guy was in here some months back and I wonder whether you might remember him.

After pocketing the bill, the clerk laughed, "Man, I can't remember who was in here last week let alone a few months ago."

Vince shrugged again, saying, "Well, it was worth a try." He thought for a moment and added, "Are there any cheap motels around here? You know, mom and pop operations, that sort of place?"

The clerk looked at the expensive suit Vince was wearing and at his even more expensive car parked outside, and said, "Yes there are but I doubt that they would suit someone like you. Anyway, you'll find that sort of place off I70, back towards where I70 and I77 intersect but as I say, you'll probably want to head on to Columbus or go back to Wheeling if you want one of the better hotels."

"Thanks," nodded Vince and headed out the door, thinking a small, modest and cheap mom and pop operation might be just be Michael was looking for when he got here. He decided that he would look at a map and do some research when he booked in his hotel. Hopefully all of them would be listed on the internet but he suspected that he would not be that lucky.

After checking in, Vince sat down with his Rand McNally road atlas and stared at the map of Southern Ohio. He then got out his laptop and looked carefully at what surrounded the town and was close to the two intersecting interstates. There were several motels and some appeared to be the sort of place that he surmised Michael might have stayed at. Deciding, he got back into his car and headed towards I70 and started to look at what motels were close to the interstate.

The first places he stopped at proved to be a bust and some had closed down but then he saw *Sans Souci Motel* tucked into a clearing off the interstate. Vince walked inside and was greeted by an older man sitting behind the desk.

With nothing to lose, Vince pulled out Michael's photograph which, together with a $20 bill, he handed to the clerk, "Does this man look familiar to you?"

The man examined the photo carefully, thought for a few moments and said, "Maybe. Have you any idea when he might have stayed here?"

"Several months back, I think," said Vince.

"Hmm," muttered the man and then switched on a somewhat dated computer, After it had warmed up, he scrolled through several months' worth of entries. Looking at Vince, he said, "We're not too busy most weeks and back then, we were far from busy." He glanced at the computer screen and said, "Ah yes, I remember him now. It seems he paid cash and stayed 4 nights…we even gave him a special rate because he was here for more than a single night. Not like most of our guests. He said his name was Michael Woodman…is that the guy?"

"It is indeed," said Vince. He paused and the asked, "Was there anything special about him that you remember?"

"What sort of thing?" asked the clerk.

"Anything that you can recall."

"It was several months ago so, no, nothing comes to mind." He stopped and thought before adding, "I did notice a slight British accent."

"You did?" asked Vince.

"Yes, I was stationed in England when I was in the Air Force back in the 1960s and I picked up that he might have been from there."

"Did you ask him about it?"

"No. He kept himself to himself and I really didn't get to talk to him. I'll tell you one thing though, he was very neat and tidy. The motel room was very easy to clean. I know he smoked the odd cigarette or cigar but always outside so there was never any odor in the room."

"Did anyone ever come to see him, ask about him at the desk or go into his room?"

"Not that I can recall," said the clerk. "As I say, he was quiet and kept to himself. I'd say that he was almost a model guest." He paused and then added, "Funnily enough, now I come to think of it, I remember hearing something about an off-duty police officer that was killed up I71 a ways. Created quite a stir at the time, it did. From what I gather, it's still unsolved."

"That's interesting," commented Vince dryly and then promptly dismissed what the clerk had said. He was not interested in stray murders in rural Ohio several miles away. His primary focus was where Michael had gone next rather than where he had been or what had happened around him.

After exchanging a few more words, Vince took his leave after ensuring that Michael had not left a forwarding address or mentioned where he might be going.

Later, back in his room, Vince took another look at the map. "Well Michael, at least we know where you stayed and for how long," he said aloud. "I wonder why you stayed here for several days….this place is hardly a bustling metropolis so you must have had a reason but why is beyond me. Okay then, where might you have gone next?"

After drawing a circle around Cambridge on the map, Vince decided to take a nap before going out to get a drink and dinner somewhere. "Slim pickings around here when it comes to places to eat but I'll bet there are bars aplenty." he muttered and then stretched out on the bed.

Randy and Ryan pulled up in front of the Holiday Inn and climbed out of the car. It had been a long drive and they were stiff from sitting so long. They took their bags out of the trunk and headed inside. At least they would be able to get a good night's sleep and a decent meal.

Later, after eating dinner and having a night-cap, they agreed that they would start to check out all the motels in the area after they had had breakfast. As Randy said, "I'm still not clear as to how many there are around here but if we make an early start, we might get lucky."

CHAPTER 14

Victor smiled at Linda and said pleasantly, "I'm glad that I could persuade you to have dinner with me again, Linda."

"I'm still uncomfortable being here," she replied. There was a pause and then she continued, "Let's face it, Victor, or should I address you as Mr. Bascombe?" The question hung between them, raising an inviable but tangible barrier.

Victor just looked at her without responding. He was well aware that his guest was slightly uncomfortable and whereas he regretted that he had not told her who he was, he also knew that if he had told Linda that he was the owner and CEO of Bennet's, she would never have agreed to have dinner with him. Shades of the old tale of the prince and the pauper. Another factor, albeit less important, was the age difference between them although the difference was probably less than 20 years, virtually nothing in this day and age.

Eventually, Linda broke the silence, "Well?"

"Well what?" asked Victor gently.

"Well how do I address you?" asked Linda. She paused again and then said, "I am frankly puzzled what I am doing here with you."

Victor simply raised an eyebrow and smiled gently.

"Look….um….Victor…er…why did you invite me to dinner?"

"I enjoy your company, that's why."

Linda blinked and then said, "Look, you are a billionaire and you are my employer. You have can pick and choose between hundreds if not thousands of women…not only here but all over the country. So, why me?"

"Good question, Linda, a very good question." Victor took a sip of wine and then looked at Linda over the rim of his glass, before setting it down again. He flicked the glass with his finger, listening to the ring it made. He sighed, smiled and touched the glass to stop the ringing. Finally he said, "I work hard and, as you say, I am rich and possibly I could have anything I want whenever I want it." He paused and took another sip of wine. "However, wealth, as you probably know, does not buy happiness…in fact there are many, many things that money cannot buy. In many respects, extra-ordinary wealth often comes with extra-ordinary problems and responsibilities."

Linda snorted quietly but listened carefully to what Victor had to say. He was revealing a gentleness that belied the power and influence that he could exercise at the drop of a hat. Avoiding a response, Linda just nodded.

"Not too long ago, a man won several million dollars in the lottery and, after all the dust had settled, he commented that the first thing one should do after winning a lot of money is get rid of your family and friends."

Linda looked at Victor incredulously, asking, "He said what?"

"One has to get rid of friends and family."

"Why on earth would he say that?"

"Apparently he had given everyone quite large sums of money and within a matter of months, his gifts had been squandered and some relatives even had to declare bankruptcy. His generosity turned out to be more of a curse than a blessing."

"Oh!"

"So, in a very roundabout way, that is why I never talk about what I do or don't have. In fact, other than a few indulgences like my car and driver, a housekeeper and eating here regularly, I live relatively simply." He shrugged and continued, "Since my wife died, things….well…..things changed."

He stopped talking and sipped his wine again. Eventually he looked at Linda, "It is difficult to answer your question because, to be honest, I really don't know "why you", as you put it." He gestured at her dinner plate, "Please eat your steak – it is getting cold and so is everything else. As I said before, there is no crime in enjoying a nice meal with an intelligent man."

Linda smiled and sliced off some beef which, after chewing, she washed down with wine, and said. "No, as far as I know, there is no crime in dining with an intelligent man and eating a steak this good is a delight. For that I thank you." She took a sip of wine before saying, "Look Victor, I have to ask you what am I doing here with you? I know I am reasonably attractive..."

"Very attractive" interjected Victor.

Linda dipped her head in acknowledgement of the compliment but resumed, "Be that as it may, I am a lowly sales clerk in your department store selling bed linens, my finances are a shambles, I have two teenage children and a wayward, no a missing husband. What can *I* offer you?"

"There is you," said Victor and smiled. "Frankly, I don't know what it is, Linda, but I feel a connection with you. I am very well aware of your circumstances but so what?"

"Oh Victor," cried Linda in exasperation.

"Oh Victor nothing," he responded. "I enjoy your company and, as I implied, I really don't care about your circumstances, as you put it."

"But *I* do! No matter how enjoyable I find your company and regardless of the excellent meals you place before me, I will not be a charity case. Things might have gone wrong in my life and I am sure that I caused most of my problems but I don't need your pity. So..." and Linda started to get to her feet.

"Linda, please sit down," ordered Victor but in a gentle tone. "Let me assure you that I do not look upon you as a charity case nor do I feel pity for you. Sympathy yes but not pity. I have too much regard for you to treat you otherwise." He paused and drank some more wine. "I enjoy your company and you are very easy to talk to. As I have said, why don't you take a moment and just enjoy a good meal with, I hope, pleasant company. There are no strings attached and there never will be. As for being a sales associate at Bennet's, that is hopefully not something to be ashamed of and if it doesn't bother me, why should you care?"

Mollified, Linda resumed her seat and drank some wine to calm herself. Victor's words were oddly satisfying although she still wondered about his interest in her. Perhaps he was right. Why not simply enjoy a good meal with very pleasant company? Suddenly she laughed. "I am sorry Victor. I am being churlish and I apologize. You are being very kind to me and I am being a pain….I'm sorry."

"Think nothing of it," said Victor. "Changing the subject, do you miss your husband? Michael isn't it?"

"Do I miss Michael? Yes and no."

Victor raised an eyebrow.

"Obviously I miss the security of his income – his leaving us caused a lot of problems, financial and otherwise, but we are coping. I miss him when the children have problems with their homework and I have to deal with their raging hormones – that is difficult for a single parent, especially for a mother with a teenage son. I never had to think about such things before."

"Oh I'm sure that you are coping very well."

"I'm not sure that I am but I do my best. Actually, when you think about it, I really have no alternative."

Victor laughed, "Welcome to parenthood in the 21st Century."

After that, they chatted away about children, schools and homework as well as the problems that teenagers experienced the world over. Both tactfully avoided the question of the cost of clothing and electronic gadgets but Victor shared with Linda some of his enjoyment, and disappointment, with his grandchildren.

"I thought raising two boys and a girl was difficult but it is really difficult to resist the urge to interfere or to give advice when you see the scrapes that they and their own children get into. You suddenly realize that your children and grandchildren have the right, if not the need, to make their own mistakes and, hopefully, learn from them."

"Did your children want to come into the business…work at Bennet's?"

"Not really, no and I certainly did not push the issue."

"What do they do?"

"My oldest, Jonathan, is a physician – a heart surgeon actually whereas William is an engineer. My daughter trained as a teacher but got dragged off to be a wife and mother by her husband Arthur. I am glad to say all three are happily married and they have blessed me with a parcel of grandchildren."

"I am so happy for you," said Linda and gently probed him about his family, curious to know more about the man, and enjoying just chatting about mundane things. As for her concern over what Victor saw in her, that evaporated in the fumes from the delicious wine he had ordered. Suddenly she felt relaxed and happy. As he had advised her, she settled back and started to enjoy a good meal with pleasant company…and relished not having to take care of the ever-demanding Damion and Rebecca.

Michael flopped down on the rather uncomfortable armchair in his motel room. Despite being a Tuesday, the diner had been busy all day and he was tired. The smell of fried food and cooking oil permeated everything, even his hair, but he was too tired to get up and shower. He poured himself a stiff drink and lit a cigar but not before opening the window to air the room. As the Scotch slowly took effect, he relaxed and started to think about the past weekend. Bella had certainly been right when she predicted that they would spend an enjoyable, and very energetic, night together…and the following morning for that matter. What was really enjoyable, however, was to take off and go into the country to look at the beginnings of the Fall foliage and have a picnic. He could not remember the last time he had done that. Teaching, tutoring, coping with the children and too many other things had taken up his life and suddenly he felt a pang of regret at what he had missed. It was easy to blame Linda for what had happened in their marriage and in his life but he had to share the blame equally. He and Linda had drifted apart and he had done nothing to prevent or to slow its progress. As he sipped on his drink, he asked himself whether he actually missed Linda and the children.

As he thought about it, he slowly came to the conclusion that whereas he and Linda were nice people, they should never have married. It was all so exciting and fun at first but when reality had eventually hit home, neither of them were prepared for the responsibility of marriage and raising a family. For a moment he wondered how Linda was coping without him but had to accept the fact that she was probably managing very well and might even be thriving. Money was obviously tight but if the lack of spendable cash got her out of the clutches of her so-called friends, it could only be to the better. In his opinion, those friends were idle drones and he surmised, accurately as it turned out, that if she could not keep up with their thoughtless spending, they would want nothing to do with her. It was probably hard on Damion and Rebecca not to have the latest electronic gadgets, hot fashion clothing and the like but they would learn, and hopefully appreciate, that such indulgences came at a price. Regardless of the circumstances, learning that they could not have anything and everything they wanted was a valuable lesson which would stay with them for the rest of their lives. Their friends at school, spoiled rotten and most of them rude and unpleasant, would probably have ditched them when they could no longer keep up but at least Damion and Rebecca would understand what true friendship actually meant.

As he drained his glass, Michael realized that he really didn't miss his wife or children. It was sad but he suspected that they did not miss him either. They were all building new lives, even him here in Southampton, and all four were likely better off than ever before. As he got ready to go to bed, he concluded that whatever the cosmic plan might be and however painful the process, they all had better futures. He laughed aloud – it was funny how things worked out.

Randy and Ryan had had a frustrating morning and were heartily sick of talking to desk clerks at what seemed like a couple of hundred motels. Driving from one place to another and getting in and out of their vehicle at each motel was wearing on them. They had always tried to be polite with the desk clerks they interviewed but after so many, politeness was starting to fail on them and they were drained.

Eventually they pulled up in front of the *Sans Souci Motel* and Randy walked in, closely followed by Ryan. The door slammed behind them as they marched almost in step to the desk.

"Are you the proprietor of this establishment?" demanded Randy.

Jerry Weatherly, Major, USAF (retd.), looked up from the newspaper he was reading and said quietly, "Yes."

"We are Special Agents Cunningham and Nelson of the FBI."

"How nice for you," said Jerry pleasantly. Back in the day, he had captained a B47 bomber during the cold war, flying out from England and patrolling the English Channel, the North Sea and the Arctic Ocean, and he was unimpressed by two self-important and likely junior FBI agents. "Do you have identification?"

Randy paused and then irritably flipped open his folder to show his badge, Ryan doing likewise.

Jerry nodded and said, "Gentlemen, what can I do for you? What brings you to my humble establishment?"

"We want to know who has been staying here."

"Oh?" said Jerry. "Well I must tell you, there are some problems with that request ... no, your demand."

"There are?" snapped Randy. "And what might those problems be?"

"Well firstly, I believe you might need a warrant before you can demand to have access to my records. And then there is the lack of specificity."

"What do you mean by lack of specificity?" asked Ryan.

"By that I mean are you asking about who is staying here now, who was here this past week, past month or what?" said Jerry amicably. "We are far from a large or ultra-busy establishment but we do have a fair number of guests staying here at one time or another."

Randy and Ryan looked at each other. This man was no pushover and they realized that unless they modified their behavior, cooperation was not likely to be forthcoming. Randy nodded and, admitting defeat, said, "I'm sorry, let's start again. We've had a frustrating morning and we're getting tired, hungry and very irritable but to take it out on you is both unfair and pointless."

Jerry nodded and waited for the G-man to continue.

After collecting his thoughts, Randy asked, "We are interested in knowing whether a man stayed here over a period of days..." and as Jerry started to shake his head, he hurried on, "Not recently but a few months back. Did anyone stay here for several days?"

Jerry looked at Randy and Ryan curiously while checking that his computer was up and running.

Randy, catching Jerry's expression, asked, "You look surprised at my question. Surely it's not that out of the ordinary for someone to ask about people who have stayed here?"

"Not really, no. What I do find surprising is that I have been asked more or less the same question two days in a row."

"What?" asked Randy and Ryan almost in unison. "Did you say someone else has been here asking about a guest staying here months back?"

"Yes. A man came by yesterday asking the same thing."

"What did he look like, this man? Did he give you his name?"

"No. There was no reason for him to do so." said Jerry, neglecting to mention the $20 bill. "Anyway, he showed me a photograph of a man and asked whether I had seen him."

"And had you?"

"Yes," and he told them the dates when Michael had stayed at the motel. "He was here for four nights. He paid cash so he got a special rate."

"Did he leave a name and address?"

"Name yes – he said his name was Michael Woodman – but as for an address, no. However, I did pick up on a faint British accent but nothing else comes to mind except that he was quiet and kept to himself." After he had collected his thoughts, he added, "No, before you ask, I did not register what car he was driving or its license plate but I think it was a reddish color and looked to be a foreign vehicle. Probably a Nissan or a Toyota….something like that.

As Ryan noted down the information, Randy asked, "This man who was here yesterday, what did he look like?"

"He was middle-aged, late forties or early fifties, well-dressed and driving an expensive late model vehicle….looked like a Mercedes. Black it was."

"Did he say why he was looking for this Michael Woodman?"

"No."

"Anything else that you noticed about him?"

"Not really but judging by his accent, he was from New York or Boston, or even Philadelphia….certainly somewhere on the Eastern seaboard."

After a few more minutes, Randy and Ryan took their leave, thanking Jerry for his help. As they drove back to their hotel, they discussed what they had heard.

"Could this by our guy?" asked Ryan.

"I assume that you are talking about the motel guest, not the guy asking about him. Whether it is him, the motel guest, I don't know but the dates certainly match and so do the circumstances. You know, a small, slightly out-of-the-way motel, proximity to a couple of Interstates. He could be," said Randy. "I hate to jump to a quick conclusion but this does look promising. If nothing else, we do appear to have a name." He paused and then said, "Who the hell was this guy that was looking for our man?"

"Assuming that Michael Woodman is our man the serial killer, it is strange that someone was here yesterday asking about him. I wonder what that's all about."

"Hopefully we'll soon find out but now we do have a possible name for our perp."

As they pulled into the car lot, Randy spotted Vincent's car and, pointing at it, he said "Maybe we'll find out who he is and why he's asking about this Michael Woodman sooner than we thought."

"Let's hope he's in the bar but before we go looking for him, I need to take a shower. This has been a long day and I'm willing to bet that it's likely to become even longer once we start talking to this fella, whoever he is."

"I think you might be right," said Randy. "Okay, let's meet up in the bar in say 30 minutes. Hopefully the guy will be still enjoying Happy Hour if they have one here."

After they ordered their drinks, the two agents surveyed the room and spotted Vincent sitting at a small table, his back to the wall and carefully but unobtrusively checking out who was coming and going in the bar. Nodding to each other, Randy and Ryan walked over to Vincent's table and stood over him, flashing their badges.

"Do you mind telling us who you are?"

New York City police captains, whether active or retired, are not easily intimidated and Vincent Dodson most certainly was not intimidated by two young and presumably relatively junior

FBI agents. To him they looked as though they were fresh out of Quantico. Mildly he said, "I do mind."

Randy blinked. This was the second time on the same day that his badge had had no effect on people. As Ryan started to straighten up and try to impress the man at the table with his admittedly large build, Randy hurriedly said, "We really would like to see some I.D. We can't force you of course, but we are here conducting a Federal Investigation and it seems that you might be here for the same reason."

"I doubt that," said Vincent but he fished out his wallet and showed the two agents his Private Investigator's License and handed them each his Bennet's Head of Security business card.

After scanning his card, the two agents handed over their own cards and then asked politely whether they could join him. After they got seated, Randy said, "I get the impression that you were a cop at one time."

Vincent nodded and said mildly, "I'm a retired police caption from the New York City Police."

Randy and Ryan exchanged glances. This was a wholly unexpected development. What was a retired NYC cop, a captain no less, who was now the head of security of a very large and prestigious department store doing inquiring into someone who might be a serial killer?

When they were all settled and the formal introductions were complete, Vincent said, "As you can see from my business card, I'm Vincent Dodson but people who know me call me Vince." He looked hard at Randy and Ryan before saying, "Okay, what's all this about a Federal Investigation?"

"Before we get started on that," said Randy placatingly. "Do you mind telling us why you are looking for someone called Michael Woodman?"

Vincent thought for a few minutes and then said, "Actually I am looking for a missing man whose name happens to be Michael Woodman." He paused and took a healthy swig of his drink. "It seems he just up and left home without telling anyone why or letting anyone know where he was going."

Randy and Ryan looked at each other again before Ryan said, "So, what's your interest in him?"

"Me personally?" said Vince. "I have no interest in him but my boss, Victor Bascombe, Chairman and CEO of Bennet's, asked me to find him."

"Why did he do that?" asked Randy.

"I have no idea but when a billionaire, who also happens to be your boss, asks you to do something, then that is exactly what you do."

"That has a familiar ring to it, doesn't it Randy?" said Ryan. Turning to Vincent, he added, "The circumstances may be different in the FBI but the outcome is the same."

"I don't suppose he told you why he was interested," said Randy.

"No and I think his reasons are beyond my pay grade."

"Hmm," muttered Randy and thought for a few moments. 'Vince seems to be on the up-and-up although it is odd that his boss wanted him to find a missing man. The only logical explanation is that there's a woman involved and I wonder who she might be? It's not my problem but this is one very weird coincidence.' Turning to Vincent, he said, "We are actually looking into a series of random murders that have been committed across the Mid-West."

"Oh?"

"What appears to have been the first one was committed about 50 or 60 miles north of here, up I77." He paused to take a breath and Ryan took over the narrative.

"Careful investigation and checking of unsolved cases sent to us by the State Police in different states across the country showed a pattern. Actually it would be more accurate to say that there was a trend rather than a clear pattern."

Resuming the narrative, Randy said, "As we looked into the killings, it looked to us that they were all committed a few miles off an interstate, presumably to ensure easy access to and from the murder site. But there were some odd aspects to these killings."

"Just how odd were these aspects?" asked Vincent. He stopped and then said, "Okay guys, you've got my interest but I think it's time for another round." As Randy and Ryan started to fish for their wallets, he added, "Nah, it's on me...actually it's on my expense account so put your money away." And he signaled to the bar tender.

After sampling their drinks, Vincent asked Randy, "Now that we've taken care of the urgent matter of booze, tell me what these odd aspects were."

"For a start, with most of them the killer used a garrote."

"A garrote? Man, I thought that only the Sicilian Mafia did that. As far as I know, garroting went out after the repeal of Prohibition."

"There was one instance of someone being shot," said Ryan. "But we'll get to that in a minute."

"Anyway," resumed Randy. "The killings were spaced out at irregular intervals and they were always in different places." He held his hand, adding, "And before you ask, we could find no relation between the killings and the phases of the moon or days of the month. There was nothing like that."

Vincent nodded.

"Not only that, there seems to be nothing in common with any of the victims. There were men and women and even a college student but race does not seem to be a factor in the killings."

"Another odd thing is that no robberies were committed by the killer," interjected Ryan. "However, we think that our killer did take a gun from one victim which he used in a later killing."

"He did? How do you know that?"

"The killer never leaves a trace after the killing except in the last instance. It seems he left a spent cartridge behind but the finger print on the cartridge belonged to an earlier victim, so we think the killer took the gun from that victim – and that's the only instance when he apparently took something from a victim."

Vincent went silent as he digested what he had just heard. "So, the only thing in common with all the killings is that they occurred somewhat close to interstates, is that right? Of course no-one saw a thing, did they?"

Randy and Ryan nodded in agreement.

"Then it appears," continued Vincent. "That the killer used an arcane method of killing which he then substituted with a gun that he possibly took from an earlier victim. What about a silencer?"

"He used a potato," said Ryan.

Vincent laughed, "Well at least he didn't use a pillow." He stared into space for a few seconds and then said, "I can see your interest in all this but I have got to tell you, *my* Michael Woodman is a college professor and seems to be as white and pure as the driven snow. I just can't see him suddenly turning into a serial killer. As far as anyone knows, he just got fed up with his wife and the kids and simply took off to parts unknown. Frankly guys, I just don't see it."

The three men continued to talk about the killings and the wayward Michael Woodman but could reach no conclusions. Eventually Vincent said, "Okay, we're not getting anywhere fast here. Let's get some dinner – it's on me, okay?"

After a final night-cap in the bar, Randy said, "Look, I don't know what your plans are in your search for this Woodman fellow...."

"Frankly, neither do I," said Vincent.

"Well, we might have a lead, if that's what it is," said Randy. "What we were thinking is that we would drive on to the approximate location, as far as well can tell, of the next killing and start asking questions at small hotels and motels within say 50-100 miles of the killing. Want to come along?"

"Sure, why not?" said Vincent. "That sounds like as good a plan as any, besides a third hand could lighten the load for you." He laughed. "You never know, you might find your killer and I might find my missing husband. What a hoot it would be that they are one and the same but I doubt it."

"Okay," said Ryan. "After breakfast, let's saddle up and head west." He looked at Vincent and added, "Hey thanks for the drinks and dinner - much appreciated."

Vincent just nodded. He knew what travel was like on a Government *per diem* and he was grateful that a tight travel budget was not a problem for him.

Later, as he lay in bed, Vincent thought through everything that he had heard. Was it possible that Michael Woodman was actually a serial killer? Stranger things had happened, as he well knew, but this seemed to stretch credulity to a breaking point. On the other hand, he reasoned, he had nothing better to go on, so why not go with the two FBI agents. Before this evening, he had had no idea where he should go next and the suggestion of Randy and Ryan was as good an approach as any. Just as he was about to drop off to sleep, he jerked awake and decided to call Madge. She would be interested to learn where he was off to next although there was no way he could tell her that the FBI suspected that Michael Woodman was a serial killer. 'What a ridiculous notion' he thought as he hit the auto-dial for home on his cell phone.

CHAPTER 15

After the two FBI agents and Vincent had booked into their hotel just outside of Indianapolis, they met up in the bar. It was not the greatest hotel but, in deference to the limited *per diem* expenses for the Government agents, Vincent agreed to stay at a modestly-priced hotel rather than what his expense account would have permitted. "All in a good cause" he muttered. "The sacrifice will be worth it if I can locate Michael Woodman and the company ain't too bad either."

"Okay guys," said Vincent after they were seated at a table with stiff drinks placed before them. "What do we have?"

Randy, after a healthy sip of his bourbon and water, said, "It seems we have two murders committed relatively close to here. One that was up north on I65 and another to the south, also on I65, but it occurred about 3 weeks later."

"Huh!" muttered Vincent. "So, according to you, the first of these murders was about 6 weeks after that one in Eastern Ohio and the other nearly 10 weeks later."

"That's about right," agreed Ryan.

"That raises an interesting question, actually two questions," said Vincent.

"And what might those be?" asked Randy.

"The first question is where your killer and my Michael Woodman were between the time in Eastern Ohio and here. If we assume that they are one and the same person, where did he or they for that matter hole up for so long?"

"And the second question?" asked Ryan.

"The second question is what did he live on during all this time?" asked Vincent. "I am referring of course to Michael Woodman."

The two agents looked at him and then at each other. Vincent had a point. Where had the killer gone to and if he indeed was Michael Woodman, what had he been living on since he had not used an ATM? Eventually Randy broke the silence by commenting, "Do you think he might have shacked up with some woman?"

"It's possible," agreed Vincent. "However, I gather from the local cops who looked into his disappearance that Michael Woodman was no womanizer, something that I concluded from my own inquiries. While it is possible that he hooked up with someone, it doesn't seem that likely. Either he must have been extra-ordinarily fast on his feet to hook up that quickly with a woman or he lucked into finding a druggie or some desperate woman needing company. To be honest, he's not bad looking but I cannot see him sweeping some woman off her feet to the degree that she would take him in and let him live with her that quickly."

"And your point is?" asked Randy.

"My betting is that he got some sort of temporary employment, you know, got paid under the counter so-to-speak and moved out of the motel into a boarding house for a period of a few weeks."

"You may be right," agreed Ryan. "Trouble is, how do we check out either possibility?"

"We probably can't" sighed Vincent. "Of course, it is always possible that Michael, or your killer, made his way here almost immediately after his four days near Cambridge. After that, it would be the same scenario, you know two or three days in a cheap motel and then a move into a boarding house and probably finding a temporary job to get some income." He looked at the FBI agents and asked, "Any chance that you can check with Social Security to see whether any contributions were made recently in the name of Michael Woodman?"

"Officially, no," said Ryan. "It's possible we could ask unofficially but our boss might not be too pleased if we did that, especially if it turned out that your Michael Woodman was not the killer."

Vincent nodded. If he were back in Pittsburgh, he would have asked one of his hacker contacts to check out Michael Woodman but out here? No way! The three men drank some more and then Randy broke the silence.

"Well I suppose the next step is to go back to checking out hotels and motels around here, you know, within driving distance of the murders."

"Yeah," agreed Ryan. "What a pain." Then he brightened, "At least we now have three of us to make inquiries." He looked at Vincent and asked, "Can you get us copies of that photograph? If Michael Woodman is the killer, it might help identifying him."

"Sure thing buddy," agreed Vincent. "I'll download it from the Hathaway College website later. One other thing strikes me. Even if, and that is a big *if,* Michael Woodman is your serial killer, you really don't have anything with which to pin the murders on him. As far as I can see, it is all circumstantial evidence and any good defense attorney would rip your case to shreds."

"You are probably right, Vince, but if we can find the man, then we may be able to get him to admit something when we interview him."

"That's possible," agreed Vincent. "But I have to say that anyone who's as canny as you say the killer appears to be is unlikely to say anything without a lawyer being present or even agree to be interviewed."

"You may be right," said Ryan. "However, we can but try."

After discussing things a bit more and then having dinner, the three men agreed to meet up early the next morning and get on the road to check out motels. None of them felt particularly hopeful of what they would find but all three felt they had at least made some progress.

Back in his room, Vincent telephoned Victor to fill him ion on his progress. After outlining what he discovered regarding Michael's travels and stopping points, he hesitated and then said, "We might have a problem, sir."

"And what might that be?" asked Victor.

"Well it seems two FBI agents might also be looking for Michael Woodman."

"They are? What on earth for?"

"It seems that there is a serial killer out there who seems to be following the same travels of Professor Woodman."

"Are you telling me that the FBI suspect Michael Woodman of being a serial killer? What gave them that idea?"

Vincent then explained the location of the killings that they had tracked so far and how Michael seemed to always stay within driving distance of each killing.

"Good grief," exclaimed Victor. "How can that be?"

"I admit that it's all circumstantial and may just be a coincidence but, I have to say, I really don't like coincidences, especially not ones like this."

"Do *you* think he's a serial killer, Vince?"

"I find it hard to believe based on what I have learned about the man but anything is possible."

"This is incredible."

"I agree but we'll know more once we track his movements further."

"What are you doing in that regard?"

"I'm going along with the FBI guys."

"And what does that entail?" asked Victor.

"What we are doing is finding a motel that is within say 100 miles of a killing and then checking to see whether Michael, or the killer, might have stayed there for a few days. I know it's only circumstantial evidence, as I said, but this approach does give me something to go on. Of course, if Michael is the killer and has stopped offing people, then finding him will become a whole lot harder."

"Hmm," muttered Victor, who paused for thought before saying, "So it is possible, however unlikely, that Michael Woodman suddenly turned into a serial killer after leaving home. If he is that killer, what on earth would make him do such a thing?"

"That's one for the psychologists, isn't it? As I say, it might all be coincidental but one does wonder why Michael would have picked those locations to hole up for a while. There may be a simple explanation but I just don't see it. On the other hand, it really isn't too clear why the man just upped and took off either."

"Well, just keep me informed, will you?"

"Yes sir."

"I really hope that what those FBI agents are saying is not true. If it is, Linda and the children will be really distraught. Frankly I don't know how anyone can deal with something like that. As someone once said, the road to hell is paved with good intentions and what started out as a simple effort to locate a wayward husband seems to be turning into something that no-one could have anticipated." Victor fell silent and then added, "Well, just keep me informed on progress."

Michael and Bella lay snuggled together in post-coital bliss. It had been a busy week but today, Saturday, had not been as frantic as it sometimes could be at the diner. They had the next day to relax and have fun away from the ever present demands of feeding people during the other six days of the week.

"Michael," said Bella tentatively. "Do you like it here?"

"Here in Southampton?"

"No, I mean here in this motel."

"Not particularly but it is convenient."

"Look….um…" started Bella hesitantly. "I'm wondering….er… well I'm wondering…" and her voice tailed off.

"What are you wondering Bella?" asked Michael.

"It's like this," she said. "Andrew is hardly home any more. He spends almost every waking hour with his girlfriend and he's told me that he is thinking of moving in with her. You know, getting married and all that. She has a son and Andrew adores him, so…."

"So?" asked Michael in a neutral tone.

"Well, I'm wondering whether you would consider giving up this place," said Bella, waving a hand at the room. "You know, moving in with me."

Silence.

"It would save you money and….er….I have a fairly large house which, frankly, is too big for just one person. You can have the spare bedroom and there's no pressure from me." She was silent, waiting for a reaction and when it didn't come, she hurried on, "Look, it makes no sense to me that you are stuck here in this motel, spending out on room charges every week when you could live rent-free with me. After all, we get on well, don't we?"

Michael stared up at the ceiling. He had been half-expecting this suggestion from Bella and it did make sense. The motel room sucked, even he had to admit that, and moving in with Bella would be definitely better than staying here and would probably be more comfortable for both of them. It would be more difficult, if not impossible, to resume his "hobby" but it had been so long that he had killed anyone that he now wondered whether he could even do it again. The urge seemed to have dissipated which was doubtless a good thing because sooner or later he might make a mistake and end up getting caught. Then he thought about Linda. He had not thought about her in months but he was still married and he did not know how Bella might react to hearing that. Would she just up and leave, and fire him from the diner? He didn't want to have to move on but continuing to live in limbo didn't appeal either. Eventually he spoke.

"Bella, that's a great idea but…"

"But what, Michael? Is there something wrong…something you haven't told me?"

"Yes…and yes." and he fell silent, steeling himself for what might be a massive blow-up after he told Bella the truth, or at least part of the truth.

"So, what dark secrets have you been keeping from e?" asked Bella jokingly.

"I'm married," said Michael flatly.

"I figured as much," said Bella. "So, tell me about that."

"I used to be a college professor, at Hathaway College in Pittsburg."

"I knew it!" said Bella triumphantly. "I thought that you were a teacher or a professor the first moment I set eyes on you. Anyway, go on."

"One day, months ago, I just got fed up with everything….the college, my wife, the ungrateful and self-centered kids, everything! So I just upped and left."

"You left? Just like that?"

"Yup!"

"Really?"

188

"Yes. I simply packed my bags and left everything behind. I withdrew some money from an ATM, filled up the car and took off, never to look back."

Bella was silent for a few minutes. Somehow she was not too surprised to hear that Michael was married with children. He had that settled look of a married man, whatever that settled look might be. It really did not come as a shock to her that he had simply taken off and left everything behind. He had always given her the impression that he was somewhat of a loner. Quite personable, friendly and even easy to talk to but there was an inherent remoteness about him which she picked up on, ascribing this characteristic to his being a professor, someone who operated on a different plain to the rest of humanity. Eventually she broke the silence by asking, "What are their names?"

"Linda and the children are Damion and Rebecca. They are teenagers and, like all teenagers, are only concerned with themselves, their friends, computer games, texting…you know how it is these days."

"Actually I don't know but I'll take your word for it," said Bella. "Anyway, have you been in touch with them…or even thought about them? You know, checking on how they are, that sort of thing?"

"No. Sad to say, I haven't. It sounds petty but they really didn't give a damn about me when I was living at home and I'm willing to bet that they still don't. Besides, what can I say to them after all this time?" He fell silent again, thinking about the futility of even trying to get in touch with Linda let alone the children.

Misinterpreting his silence, Bella asked, "Do you miss them?"

"No, not at all. It is a shame and I am saddened to have to admit it but I really don't care, Maybe in time when the scars have healed over I will think differently but for now? No."

"As you say, it is a pity but what you are telling me has happened to thousands of families all over the country, and probably the world. The good thing is that you didn't leave them destitute."

"I suppose," said Michael flatly. "No, I didn't drain the bank account or run up huge credit card debts but after I left, the household income went with me. That alone must have caused a whole host of problems, Linda not having had to work for years."

"What did she do if she didn't work?"

"Spent time at the gym or the country club, and gossiping with her friends, that sort of thing. Just filling in time but for what, I have no idea."

"Oh! How sad."

"Yes but it was typical of her and her so-called friends. I imagine that once Linda had to go out and actually earn a living, those friends of hers would have dropped her like a hot potato. I doubt that Damion and Rebecca would have been able to continue to go to that fancy private school either." He laughed wryly. "Fancy them having to mix with the hoi-polloi at school."

"Hoi-polloi? What a strange expression."

"You know what I mean. They would no longer be able to look down on other kids at public school. It might have even been a good thing for them because humility is good for the soul, or so they tell me."

Bella thought for several seconds and then said, "Nothing you've told me changes anything. So are you going to move in or what?"

Michael laughed, hugged Bella and said, "Okay, okay, I surrender. When do I exit this palatial motel and move in with you?"

"How about tomorrow?" and she slid on top of him before adding, "But first we might as well not waste this wonderfully comfortable bed." As she ran her fingers over Michael's body, she laughed and said, "Funnily enough, I shall miss our trysts here in my favorite No-tell Motel. Whatever will we do on a Saturday night now?"

"Oh I can think something," said Michael as he grabbed her. "That is not going to be a problem, not at all."

After he had heard what Vincent had to say, Victor realized that his good intentions were likely to misfire, and do so very badly. Of course he could do nothing until the situation became clearer but now even telling Linda that he had initiated a search for her missing husband might have dire consequences. He decided that the least said the better and that he should proceed with Linda as though nothing had happened and that he knew nothing about Michael's disappearance. After mulling things over, he picked up the telephone and called Linda.

"Linda," said Victor when she picked up the phone. "You sound a little distraught."

"I am, Victor, I am."

"What's going on?"

"I finished my shift late today….I was dealing with a difficult customer and I wasn't about to walk out and turn her over to someone else."

"Good for you but I still don't see why you are that distraught. You've worked late on more than one occasion. So what happened this time?"

"As you say, I have worked late on many occasions but this time I had to rush to the supermarket and get things for dinner since there really was nothing in the house. Then, after I had prepared everything and put the shepherd's pie into the oven and even baked an apple pie, my dear children told me that both of them were going over to friends' homes and didn't want dinner. It makes me so mad."

"Did you say shepherd's pie?"

"Yes. Why do you ask?"

"Well, I hate to think of all that effort going to waste, so can I invite myself over to eat with you? That apple pie also sounds delicious."

"Victor, I hate to say it but I'm really not that good a cook and you might be disappointed."

"I'll chance it. Look, let me bring over a bottle of wine and that will give me an opportunity to discuss something with you."

"Er…oh damn, I don't have any ice cream to go with the apple pie."

"Don't worry, I'll bring over both vanilla ice cream and some wine. When should I come to your house?"

"Victor, I hate to disappoint you with my poor cooking…"

"Nonsense, I'm sure it will be delicious. So, what about in 45 minutes or so? I assume that casual dress is fine?"

Admitting defeat but secretly pleased to see Victor again, Linda agreed and then rushed off to shower and change into jeans and a baggy sweater. As she dried her hair, Linda suddenly wondered what Victor wanted to discuss with her. That was so unlike him that she was intrigued. They had had dinner together several times and,

Linda had to admit, she really enjoyed Victor's company. Charming, urbane and with a wicked sense of humor, he was an ideal companion and someone she enjoyed being around. Her initial reservations over dining with her employer had evaporated as she realized that it did not bother Victor in the least and he certainly did not care what their respective roles might be at Bennet's. As she carefully applied make-up, Linda smiled. This would be the first time that she had entertained anyone in her home since Michael had left and, truth be told, she was looking forward to it.

Victor sat back and looked at Linda, "I don't know why you are so self-deprecating about your cooking. That was delicious. I have to say, I don't recall ever having shepherd's pie that tasted like this. What's your secret?"

"Actually Michael taught me how to prepare that way."

"Really?"

"Yes. Apparently what he showed me, and he is no cook, is the English way and I like to cook it because it will last for more than a single meal which is an important consideration for a working mother."

"I can understand that," Victor said. Then he added, "I mentioned to you that I wanted to discuss something with you, didn't I?"

"You did…I'm all ears."

Victor hesitated for a beat or two and then said, "I really enjoy your company and you must surely know that I am very fond of you. I think you have similar feelings about me…," and he looked directly at Linda, who ducked her head in acknowledgement, not trusting herself to speak.

"As I say, I am very fond of you and I really enjoy spending time with you. I think that perhaps it's time for us to move to….er…move to another stage in our relationship."

Linda said nothing but thinking, 'It's funny but I was so worried when this subject would come up but now it doesn't scare me at all. Victor is really a dear man and I wish I didn't have the specter of Michael hanging over me. How can I get involved with Victor when the situation with Michael is unresolved? I no longer give a damn about him but moving on is impossible until I know where he is and whether he would give me a divorce. A divorce? Wow, is that what I'm thinking about with Victor? I was very anti-men for so long it is scarcely credible that I should even think about dating again let alone having a relationship with a man. Funny how things change with time'

Seeing the interplay of emotions on Linda's face, Victor thought, 'So I've touched a nerve here. I think she cares more deeply for me than I, or she, ever suspected'. He waited until Linda's brow cleared and then said, "In a few weeks there is a gala event that I really have to attend. In short, I would be pleased, very pleased in fact, if you would accompany me." As Linda started to speak, he held a hand up, "I know, I know, you have nothing to wear, you would be embarrassed to be seen in public with me, you won't know anyone…. blah, blah, blah!"

"Victor, you know I would love to go with you but it really isn't possible, is it?"

"Why not? I would be delighted to help pay for a new dress – that is only fair if you have to get one to attend some big social event at my invitation. So that is not a consideration…and I don't want to hear any protestations about it. It's only fair."

Linda blinked and looked carefully at Victor, thinking, 'He wants to buy me a dress? That's incredible. Ordinarily I would refuse but as he said, this is different.' Eventually she said, "I really appreciate that offer and, under other circumstances, I would be delighted to accept but a new dress is not the only consideration, is it?"

"What else is there that bothers you?"

"Victor, let's face it, I'm a lowly sales clerk at Bennet's, a store that you own. Regardless of the facts of the matter, everyone who sees us together will think that I am some slightly dated popsy that you took under your wing to show off in public and screw in private. What people think about me is irrelevant since I went through a whole lot worse when Michael first left but I really do worry about your reputation. Many of the people at that event may have seen me at Bennet's, and I know my former friends are well aware of where I work and who you are. No, the gossip will start the minute we are seen together. So, dear Victor, I cannot agree to accompany you much as I would like to."

Victor laughed. "I thought you might say something like that and I appreciate more than you could ever know your concern for me and my reputation. Frankly, what other people think doesn't bother me one iota but anything that makes you in the least bit uncomfortable is something we need to deal with."

Linda nodded and then asked, "Just how can that be done?"

"Ah yes," said Victor. "That is what I wanted to discuss with you."

Linda raised an eyebrow, looking even more appealing to Victor than she realized and making him smile.

He hesitated and then said, "You know that coffee shop on Main Street, the one you were staring at wistfully when we met?"

"Of course I do. I spent many, many mornings and afternoons there at one time. What about it?"

"Well I bought the place."

"You did? What on earth for?"

"I want to expand the place and I want you run it. We will be partners in it, me being a silent partner of course, but you will run it."

"What? You're crazy, Victor," exclaimed Linda.

"No I am not. With proper management, an expanded menu and upscale decor would turn that place into a gold mine. You know a lot about running a coffee barista and that, combined with your inherent good taste and style, almost guarantees success. Obviously I would leave all the details to you and provide you with a substantial amount of working capital but, in essence, the place will be yours. I have no doubt that it will become a really good investment."

Linda simply stared at Victor for several minutes, her head in a total whirl. Suddenly she jumped to her feet, dashed around the table and kissed him on the lips, hard and with genuine passion.

"Oh Victor, are you serious, really serious, about this?"

"Yes, of course I am. I think it will be an ideal arrangement not only from a business perspective but it would solve no end of problems and issues with us. So, what do you think?"

"Victor, I don't know what to think or even what to say. This is a dream come true." She looked at him again before saying, "You really mean this? You are not just making fun of me….you know, raising my hopes only to dash them down?"

"Nothing could be further from the truth, my dear Linda," said Victor reassuringly.

Linda sat down and stared the length of the table at Victor before saying, "Oh Victor. My dear Victor. Thank you, thank you." And then she burst into tears, her heart almost bursting with happiness, alarming Victor who was at somewhat of a loss over what to do next or even why Linda was suddenly crying.

Randy and Ryan entered the office of yet another small motel. It was the fifth or sixth that they inspected that morning and they were heartily sick of dealing with uncooperative desk clerks. Seeing the young man behind the counter covered in tattoos and sporting both ear-rings and nose rings as well as almost recoiling from the strong smell of marijuana wafting towards them from behind the desk, their hopes plummeted.

"Help you?" inquired the young man.

"Yes, have you seen this man?" and Randy held out the photograph of Michael together with his badge.

"No, can't say I have. What's he done?"

"Probably nothing…we're just asking."

The young man shrugged and looked as though he couldn't wait to take another toke on his joint or bong, or whatever he had been using before the two agents had walked in. Then obviously a thought worked its way through the tortuous pathways of his brain, "When was he here?"

"A few months back."

"Oh well," and the young man shrugged again.

"Oh well what?" asked an irritated Ryan.

"I've only been here a couple of months so I wouldn't have known if he was here or not." He paused, thought for a minute and then said, "The guy who was here before me, he might know but…" and there was another pause, "I don't know his name or where he's gone."

"Fine," snapped Randy, wondering whether he should arrest this guy for drug possession but decided it wasn't worth all the paperwork he'd have to fill out. "Okay then, can you look up who has been staying here…you know, do you have a guest book or something?"

The man stared at him for several seconds before answering, "I dunno about that but it might be in the computer. Want me to look for you?"

Ryan, ready to leap over the counter and beat the stoner to a pulp, gulped and then said pleasantly, "That would be nice. The man's name is Michael Woodman. Check back over the past several months, will you?"

Moving at the speed of molasses in winter, the young man eventually found the right information on the ancient computer and said, "Yeah, he was here…Michael Woodman…paid cash he did, stayed for two nights."

Gritting his teeth in frustration, Randy asked, "I don't suppose he left a forwarding address or a contact number, did he?"

The young man peered blearily at the computer screen, slowly shook his head and said, "Nah, nothing like that."

"Well sir," said Randy. "Thank you for your help."

"Yeah, fine," said the young man and then asked, "Hey, if he shows up here again, shall I tell him you were looking for him?"

"No, that's alright but thanks anyway," said Ryan.

As the two agents started to leave, Randy turned back and commented, "You do know we are Federal agents, don't you?" Getting no reaction from the young man, he added, "We could arrest you for drug possession."

"Yeah, yeah," said the young man dismissively but at the same time holding tightly to the counter to avoid falling over.

As they climbed back into the car, Randy looked at Ryan and nodded back towards the motel. "Somehow I don't think he's active in the local Mensa group, do you?"

"These days you can never tell," sighed Ryan. "You just never can tell but somehow I doubt it – the Mensa thing I mean."

"Ah well, let's get back and meet up with Vince. At least we now know Woodman stayed here for a couple of nights but, as Vince has said, it probably doesn't mean diddly squat because it's all circumstantial."

CHAPTER 16

Vincent, Randy and Ryan met up again at the bar in yet another hotel after a second fruitless day of inspection and interviewing of motels and their managers spread out over a wide area. All three had to admit that they had found nothing.

"I tell you, Vince," said Randy. "It is amazing just how many of those places have been forced to close down over the past few months."

"Not only that," chimed in Ryan. "The smaller places that haven't closed are either under new management or are being renovated."

"I take it then," said Vincent. "That the closed motels, those under new management or the rest that are being renovated have no records beyond the past couple of weeks."

"You've got it," affirmed Randy. "Even the motels that have been open for some time don't seem to have any viable records for more than a couple of months. All in all, we've just got one big bust."

"Well, so much for tracking Michael Woodman or your killer, regardless of whether they are one and the same person or not."

"Correct," yawned Ryan. He was tired and by now thoroughly disenchanted with this whole search process. It had been exciting at first, especially when they had a possible lead with this Michael Woodman individual, whoever he might be, but now? Now it was just routine and lots of tedium. He drained his drink and offered to get another round.

"Sure, why not?" said Vincent. "It's not as though it will do any damage to our mental processes. This search business is growing older by the day."

"Don't I know it," agreed Randy. He then paused and added, "The funny thing is, this whole business started quite near here…you know, within our 100 mile radius rule."

"It did?" asked Vincent curiously. "How did that come about?"

Randy succinctly summarized what had happened at his father's bar and then how, on a later visit home, his father had told him about the killing of Clyde Wilkins. Randy had followed up on his father's particular murder when he came across the report of the shooting of Matt Levine.

"How do you know they are related?" asked Vincent.

Randy explained about the spent cartridge case found at the site of the Levine killing having Clyde Wilkins' fingerprint on it although no-one could account for the missing round itself. "So Vince," he added. "We have the anomaly of the killer actually leaving something behind at the scene, something he's never done before, together with him taking something from a previous victim."

"How very strange," commented Vincent. "Carelessness at the scene of a killing, if that's what it is rather than a deliberate piece of misinformation, and a change in the MO and everything now nicely wrapped up in a vanished and traceless killer and/or Michael Woodman. So what do we do now?"

"The only thing I can think is to try to find him by checking on motels in our 100 mile radius around the Levine killing," said Randy.

"The good thing is that the area around the Levine killing is a bit more rural," said Ryan. "So it's possible that someone might have noticed a strange car coming and going on one of the roads from the interstate to the bar where he was killed."

"Hmm, it sounds feasible," said Vincent. "Trouble is, everything happened several months back and who is likely to remember one single car after all this time?"

"You may be right," agreed Randy. "However, at this stage, we've got nothing else to go on."

"I don't suppose anyone has reported any other unsolved or random killings since then?" asked Ryan hopefully.

"No," said Randy. "You suppose correctly. I checked with Steve about an hour ago and there's been nothing reported to us and it makes me wonder why our killer has gone silent for so long? It don't seem like him at all."

"Perhaps he just got bored," ventured Ryan.

"Either bored, arrested for something else or simply died."

"Arrested?" commented Vincent. "Now that's a possibility, isn't it?" He turned to Randy and asked, "Can your people check whether someone in possession of a gun has been arrested in the past few months? It might also be worth asking whether Michael Woodman got arrested and/or locked up too."

"I can try," said Randy. "But we're in the South and I shudder to think how many people, with or without guns, have been arrested over the past few months. There are probably hundreds if not thousands of arrests every Friday and Saturday all across the South. As for carrying a weapon, everyone has a gun…you can't call yourself a man unless you're carrying in these parts."

Vincent sighed. Randy was probably correct but they still had to try. Even he was now starting to feel that the search for Michael Woodman was becoming pointless. He could have gone anywhere and the likelihood of the owner or manager of an out-of-the-way motel admitting to a cash-paying person staying for one or more nights was remote at best. Avoiding reporting income was as prevalent as making moonshine and equally profitable.

Eventually and with great reluctance, Randy smacked his glass on the table, "Okay, we have to admit that we are just marking time."

Vincent and Ryan looked at him.

"So, let's call it a day." Randy turned to Vincent, "Look Vince, I think we should head back to Kansas City, our headquarters, and report in. We'll have to tell our boss Steve Wellington about our lack of success. However, if you can spare the time, why not come with us and meet him? He might have some ideas of where we go next but I somehow doubt it. On the other hand, its possible he'll have some insights regarding your Michael Woodman and may even be able to help you find him."

"Thanks," said Vincent. "It can't hurt and I suspect that you've got far more resources available to you than I could ever have. What about the Levine killing? Should we take a look at motels there?"

"I hate to admit defeat," said Randy. "But I feel that it would simply be another wasted two or three days asking around for information on our killer. Frankly, it's been too long. Besides, as you so correctly said Vince, it is all circumstantial anyway. Even if we did locate a possible lodging for the man, the fact that's he's gone quiet for an extended period tells me that he is well and truly off the radar now and we have no idea where to look next." He paused and then said, "No, let's man up and go to Kansas City and report in. I honestly don't see any real or viable alternative."

"Not only that," chimed in Ryan. "They've got some great restaurants in KC and quite a few really good hotels…you know, places more in keeping with your tastes," and he laughed. "You might as well run up that expense account after slumming for the past few days."

Later, back in his hotel room, Vincent telephoned Victor and to fill him in progress, such as it was.

"So Michael Woodman has simply disappeared, has he? Well, so much for him being a serial killer," said Victor.

"I was always a bit doubtful about that but I do dislike coincidences and it was just possible, however unlikely."

"Visiting the FBI field office could prove to be helpful, if not now but possibly in the future," said Victor. "Making a few friends and allies never hurts. We never know when we might need them in the future." He was silent for a few beats. "Okay, go to Kansas City and see if they can check with Social Security if any filings have been made for Michael Woodman. You never know what'll turn up. Anyway, thank you for all your efforts. When should I expect you to return to Bennet's?"

"I expect I'll spend a day or two in KC with the FBI and then head on back. So, I should be back at work in three or four days."

"Good. I'll look forward to it," and Victor hung up the phone.

After thinking about what Vincent has said, he smiled again. Fancy anyone thinking that Michael Woodman could be a serial killer…it was laughable. On the other hand, where *had* the man gone? At least with the FBI was involved, they could rule out Michael being killed, arrested or anything like that but that still left Linda, and himself for that matter, hanging with regard to her errant husband.

His thoughts then turned to the dinner with Linda at her home. Her sudden breakdown had alarmed him and he had jumped up to take her in his arms and tried to comfort her. Eventually the tears had subsided and, after wiping her eyes and blowing her nose on a handy tissue, she had murmured into his chest that she was sorry to have frightened him with her tears of happiness. "Victor, this is the first time I have cried in a long time but this time wasn't because I felt sorry for myself but…but because I am so happy. Thank you, thank you."

When they had resumed their seats and the embarrassment of the tears was safely behind them, Victor said mildly, "You realize of course that as a business owner, you need no longer worry about what people say about you, or about me for that matter."

Linda blinked and stared at him, the import of his words stunning her. "Are you saying that because of all this…you know, the coffee shop…we can now go out in public?"

Victor simply nodded. Linda thought for a few moments and then said, "Is this why you bought that place? Is it just a means of justifying us being together?"

"As I already said, Linda," said Victor calmly. "It was a sound business proposition and anything else is a welcome fall-out but certainly not the primary reason." As Linda started to protest, he held up a cautionary hand, "Linda, fond as I am of you, as I have already said, I base my decisions and actions on sound business principles, not emotions."

Linda was silent and then said simply, "Thank you." Then she jumped up, raced around the table and kissed him again, hugging him tight. She was sensible enough to appreciate that Victor's actions were not wholly based on sound business practice but she was also aware that he was making a firm declaration of the importance of their relationship to him, and was silently signaling that he wanted her to be a larger part of his life.

After they had settled back down again, Linda eventually said, "Victor, this whole thing comes as a complete surprise and I cannot quite take it all in. I understand, and appreciate, the subtext of what is going on and, honestly, I should love to have a larger role in your life. But….” and she hesitated before continuing, “I am still married to Michael and until that situation is resolved, I am a bit worried about getting involved with you. The trouble is, I have no way of getting in touch with him. If I could, I would love to either legally separate or even get divorced but to do so, I have to be in contact with him, something I have idea of how to do, find him I mean.”

Victor hesitated and thought carefully about what he should say next. If he told Linda that he had already initiated a search for her husband, she might take offense but it was always possible that she would be grateful, if not relieved. Eventually he decided, “Linda, my head of security, Vincent Dodson, is highly experienced former police captain. How would you feel if I asked him to look into Michael’s disappearance, you know try to find him?”

“I would be very grateful. This situation cannot continue but I can’t afford to pay him to find Michael…that is far beyond my budget.”

“Again, getting Vincent to look for Michael is another sound business decision. The last thing we want is for you, I mean us, to turn the coffee shop into a thriving business only to have him turn up and demand a share of the profits. The thought of him trying to divorce you and claim alimony doesn’t bear thinking about. That would not do at all.”

Linda paused for thought. What Victor said made sense and if she could resolve the Michael situation, then life would get to be a whole lot simpler. She looked at Victor and said, “If it’s alright with you, then I would be most grateful if Vincent, it was Vincent wasn’t it?, did start looking for Michael. Once he’s found, then I can take action.”

Victor clapped his hands, saying, “Great. I shall take care of it at once.”

After that they went on to talk about other things although both were aware that the Pandora’s Box of romantic involvement was now half-open, and both were secretly pleased.

It was early evening and Bella and Michael sat out on the porch, enjoying the cool autumnal air. It had been yet another busy day and both were tired but happy to be able to relax in each other’s company. Michael, sipping on a scotch and water and smoking a cigar, thought about recent events. Moving in with Bella had been a great success, what with Andrew now moved in with his lady friend Angela and ensuring that they had the house to themselves. He felt a sudden spurt of happiness. It was strange how things had worked out and he idly wondered what the future might bring. Bella did not seem to be in the least concerned that he was married but, like most women, she would probably eventually want to have a more permanent arrangement. This was fine with him but, sooner or later, he would have to get back in touch with Linda and suggest a divorce. He surmised that a legal separation would not cut it with Bella in the long term but that presented a problem of what he would say to his wife when they did get back in touch. It was quite possible that if she learned that he was involved with another woman, Linda might dig her heels in and refuse to divorce him. On the other hand, she herself might have hooked up with someone and be all too happy to be rid of him.

As he mused, Bella rested her head on his shoulder and left him to his thoughts. He was obviously processing something and experience, as well as instinct, told her to let him be. He would share his thoughts with her in due course. As she listened to his quiet breathing, Bella wondered whether Michael might ever want to go back to teaching. It amused her to think that she could end up with a professor as a lover and then, perhaps, a husband. Andrew would probably pull her leg unmercifully over that but at the same time, she was secretly pleased and proud that someone like Michael wanted to be with her. Bella knew she was above average in intelligence but it was beyond her wildest dreams that she would ever hook up with someone like Michael here in dear old Southampton. That sort of thing just didn't happen.

Michael, feeling Bella relax and snuggle closer, half-closed his eyes and let his thoughts drift. For the first time in ages he thought about his killing spree. 'Did I really do that?' he asked himself. 'I know I did but what prompted it? I cannot believe I was working out some deep, dark hatred for humanity that I'd harbored for years or that I was paying back stray persons for all the injustices landed on me by my parents, Linda, the children, that bloody college. Surely that's not the case. If things had been different, I suppose I could talk to a counselor but that would be an open invitation to disaster, and I certainly cannot tell Bella. Even she might balk at associating with, or even marrying, a serial killer. If I were a devout Catholic, I suppose I could make use of the seal of the confessional and talk to a priest although he would probably try to push me into going to the police. There is of course the dichotomy of being a devout Catholic and a serial killer.

'Oh well, I'll have to shelve this for the moment and come back to it later.' He stared off into the night and smiled, 'We've been together only a few weeks and here I am already thinking about marriage. I never thought that was something I'd ever want again and now here I am giving serious thought to it.' He stopped thinking, gathered Bella up into his arms and kissed her. "Hey lady, time for bed. We've got another busy day ahead of us tomorrow and I would not want Andrew telling us that we're slacking."

"He wouldn't dare!" snapped Bella but laughing. "Besides, you cannot imagine how many days he turned up tired and bleary eyed when he first hooked up with Angela. Turnabout is fair play. But I agree, it is starting to get cool and that bed upstairs is starting to be awfully appealing."

She peeled herself off Michael and, taking his hand, led him inside and upstairs. As she had said, bed sounded very inviting, especially when it would be shared with the man she loved.

After listening to Randy and Ryan, and taking careful measure of Vincent, Steve Wellington nodded. After the disaster over Arthur Cornelius Doyle, he was understandably wary of making any assumptions regarding this Michael Woodman fellow. As Vincent had said, it was all circumstantial. Even though he could not bring himself to accept such a wild collection of coincidences, he was experienced enough to know that pursuing the matter further would only be a waste of time and resources. Not only that, the last thing he needed was a failed criminal prosecution following so soon after the Arthur C. Doyle fiasco; that might do severe damage to his reputation and career.

Steve looked hard at Vincent and then asked, "Tell me about this Michael Woodman person you are looking for. What's that all about?"

Vincent hesitated. This was starting get into confidential matters that Mr. Bascombe might not want to have discussed, especially not with the FBI. There was nothing illegal or criminal about looking for a wayward husband, regardless of whether he was married to an employee or not. On the other hand, when a powerful man like Victor Bascombe starts to look into the life of an employee, especially an attractive female, then gossip about it might start to spread like wildfire, ruining lives and reputations. One incautious comment could lose him his job, and everything that went with it, not something that Vincent wanted to have happen.

"Mr. Bascombe, the CEO of Bennet's, a large department store in Pittsburgh, asked me to see if I could find the husband of one of the sales associates at the store. Apparently the man took off without giving anyone any warning and for no obvious reason and Mr. Bascombe asked whether I could help locating him."

"And why would he do that?" asked Steve.

"Mr. Bascombe is a billionaire and, as you well know, billionaires can do almost anything they want, and when they want to for that matter."

"Don't I know it," sighed Steve. "Okay, for reasons best known to himself, Mr. Bascombe asked you to look for this woman's husband."

"Correct."

"I assume that this man left home abruptly."

"He did. As I said, one day he just took off without telling anyone…he even left his laptop and cell phone behind."

"Hmm. That's somewhat unexpected. In this day and age, I cannot imagine anyone leaving home without either of those. I have to pry that smart phone out of my daughter's hand at night when she goes to bed, and she's only nine!" He paused and then asked, "What can you tell me about the guy?"

"He is, or rather was, a professor at a small college, Hathaway College, in Greater Pittsburgh."

"Any problems with a female student or possibly a female colleague?"

"No. Nothing there. That in itself is astonishing. I tell you, Steve, when you look at those co-eds with their plunging necklines, short shorts and sexy behavior, I cannot believe he wasn't tempted to nail one." Vincent stopped and reflected. "When I walked around that campus, my eyes were out on stalks most of the time. Talk about walking wet dreams. Anyway, apparently our Professor Michael was as pure as the driven snow in that regard. With regard to finances, Michael Woodman, or rather he and his wife didn't have any debts to speak of – the house was even paid for. They were comfortable, not affluent, but comfortable. As I say, he seems to be lily white in character and behavior."

"He was? How unusual. I suppose there's no history of drugs or gambling – that sort of thing? No other woman out there that he was carrying on with?"

"Again, nothing. I gather that his wife kept him on a fairly tight leash but I could find nothing on him. The same goes for the local police who looked into his disappearance."

"So, you say that there are no mob or drug carter issues. I don't suppose he could have gone into witness protection, or did he?"

"Not that I could tell. I did check the local and state records and there haven't been any major crimes or murders anywhere near the college or where he lives in a couple of years. So it's unlikely that he needed to be secreted away somewhere until a trial. That possibility just don't fly."

Steve Wellington went quiet as he digested what he had been told. Nothing made sense to him although he knew that people often just took off for myriad reasons but usually it came down to heavy debts, sex, drugs or gambling issues, none of which seemed to apply here. He turned to Randy and asked, "You checked arrest records and hospital admissions, that sort thing?"

"Yes sir, we did. We could find nothing. No unidentified men have turned up anywhere, at least none so far this year. We can keep digging but..." and Randy spread his hands helplessly.

Steve fell silent again and thought things through. Eventually he said, "I've got to tell you that this Michael Woodman just doesn't fit the usual profile of a serial killer. I can forward your information to the profilers at Quantico but I wouldn't hold my breath on that.

The last time we talked to them, they were as mystified as us about the killer and I'm afraid that they might just laugh if we suggested that a college professor was randomly killing people. That just doesn't compute, does it?"

Vincent, Randy and Ryan all mutely shook their heads. Whatever their intuitions, instincts and experience might tell them, the preponderance of evidence suggested that the missing Professor Michael Woodman was about as unlikely a serial killer as Big Foot, and apparently was as difficult to find. Where had the man gone? The why was unanswerable but, as someone once said, most men lead lives of quiet desperation so his taking off might simply be a consequence of an unhappy home or professional life, not uncommon in today's high pressure life.

Finally, SAC Steve Wellington said, "It seems we have hit a brick wall. As Vince said, even if we do find the killer and/or his possible alter ego Michael Woodman, there's absolutely nothing that we could pin on him or them. So, it looks as though we'll just have to consign this matter to our own dead file….not something I like to do but I see no alternative." He turned to Vincent, "As a favor, we will check with the IRS and Social Security to see whether anything has come in about your Michael Woodman…did you give Randy his Social Security Number?" Seeing nods of assent from Vincent and Randy, Steve continued, "As I said, as a favor we'll check on this and let you know what we find. If we can locate him, that'll at least help you."

He got to his feet and held out his hand, "Thank you for helping Randy and Ryan. We'll be in touch."

"Vincent nodded and shook the SAC's hand. He was going to invite them all to lunch but Steve Wellington's dismissal was evident. An invitation to lunch could possibly be misinterpreted.

After saying goodbye to Randy and Ryan with the customary promises to keep in touch, Vincent left the FBI building, climbed into his car and headed back to Pittsburgh. It would be a long drive and he was disappointed at his personal lack of success. As he drove, he thought about the unidentified serial killer, the vanished Michael Woodman and the odd series of coincidences surrounding Professor

Woodman and the various killings. Nothing made sense but, as SAC Steve Wellington had said, what could they do about it if the unlikely and the improbable were actually the case? There simply was no incriminating evidence.

He would report back to Mr. Bascombe and hope that the FBI might come up with something about Michael Woodman. As for him being a serial killer, it was best to bury that suggestion. If Mr. Bascombe was going to get involved romantically with Linda Woodman, the last thing he would want to hear was that the woman's husband randomly killed people for no apparent reason. Vincent did not relish the thought of being the messenger conveying that sort of message. All too often, the recipient of bad news would kill the messenger and self-sacrifice was definitely not on his personal agenda.

Steve Wellington sat behind his desk and stared balefully at Randy and Ryan. He was irritated at their lack of success in locating or identifying the serial killer but he had to acknowledge that they had done everything they could. To suggest that a wayward college professor was a serial killer was almost laughable but stranger things had happened in his long career and he was not about to dismiss it out of hand.

"Well gentlemen," he said. "You tried. If you find anything out about this Woodman character, let Dodson know, okay? It is possible that Professor Woodman and the killer are one and the same person, however unlikely that might be. So, once we locate the guy, get someone from a local office near to him to discretely look into the man and keep a watchful eye on him. Nobody, I repeat nobody, is that good and sooner or later he'll trip himself up. Then we'll be ready for him." He fell silent again and then mused aloud, "I wonder what the killer was thinking when he killed those people? What was it about them that prompted him to murder them? Maybe Quantico can offer some insights there? That at least would help in identifying the killer. I tell you, true randomness in events is the province of nuclear physics, not human behavior. There has to be something connecting these victims but what is it?"

Neither Randy nor Ryan spoke. They had nothing to say.

Steve sighed yet again. "Okay guys, wrap things up here, check with the IRS and Social Security, keep Vince Dodson in the loop on Woodman and let me know if something, anything, turns up."

CHAPTER 17

Michael and Bella were lying snuggled together in bed after a sedate session of lovemaking. It had been yet another long day and now they were nicely relaxed, allowing their thoughts to drift. Eventually Michael broke the companionable silence, "I think it's time to get rid of Wilma."

"Wilma?" asked Bella in mock horror. "Who is Wilma? Don't tell me you've got another wife out there?"

"No such luck," said Michael, earning a painful poke in the ribs from Bella. "Wilma is my old car and she's showing unmistakable signs of age and decrepitude…a bit like me, I suppose."

"Far from it, big boy" said Bella. "At least, not that I've noticed," as she gently patted his penis. "This boy's still pretty active."

Michael laughed and said, "No, it's time to trade her in and get something a bit more reliable."

"Do you need another car?" asked Bella.

"It's probably not essential but Wilma is beginning to act up and, like it or not, I need to get another car. After all, I can't rely on you to drive me around all the time."

Bella digested his comment before saying, "Well, you can afford it, so why not?" She paused and then said, "What are you thinking of getting?"

"I'm not sure but perhaps an SUV or something. I'll start to shop around and see what I can get."

Accordingly, Michael went on line and researched available new and used vehicles and made his decision. After making sure that the diner had a fill-in cook, he took off one Saturday to a neighboring larger town and went through the tortuous and time-consuming process of trading in Wilma and arranging financing for a newer vehicle. Now that he had a fixed address and a steady income together with a good credit score from his previous life, the dealer was only too happy, eventually, to let him take possession of a Ford SUV and drive off back to Southampton.

The next day, he and Bella went off for a drive into the countryside in the new vehicle and Bella barely suppressed her happiness that Michael now appeared to be settled into his new life. A new life centered around her, the diner and Southampton in general. She knew that it had taken a lot of thought for Michael to make this decision and she was happy for both him and herself that they were together and settled. Sooner or later Michael would make a decision regarding his estranged wife back in Pittsburgh but that, she knew, was something he would have to deal with on his own. Bella was also aware that Michael was far too intelligent and educated to remain satisfied as a short-order cook in a small diner. Sooner or later, she had little doubt, the academic life would starting to loom large in his thoughts but when, and how, were problems that she and Michael would have to face eventually. Michael's purchase of a new vehicle was the first straw in the wind.

Winter was looming on the horizon and Bella was starting to make plans for the coming Christmas season. She and Andrew had always catered a Christmas party for their regular customers and this year would be no exception although she was secretly pleased that she, and Andrew, had their own loved ones with whom they could celebrate the season. As she thought about Christmas gifts for Andrew and Angela, she wondered what she should get for Michael. She had, of course, dropped hints to him as to what she needed or might like as a present, Michael, however, had remained stubbornly silent regarding any needs or wants that he might have. Traditional favorites such as ties, after-shave, sweaters and the like were good standbys but they lacked inspiration or originality. Eventually she decided that she needed to consult Andrew and his girlfriend Angela.

After listening to Bella, Andrew said, "I can see your point. Michael seems to be so self-contained and self-sufficient...he always gives me the impression that he doesn't need or want anything, which is hard to believe in this day and age."

Then Angela chimed in, "Does he read much, you know, novels or mysteries?"

"Not really," answered Bella. "By the time evening comes, we're both so tired from the diner that all we do is watch a little television and then fall into bed."

"What about Sundays?" asked Andrew.

"Oh we tend to lie in and…er…you know…we lie in," said Bella and then blushed, causing both Andrew and Angela to laugh.

"Yes we do know," laughed Andrew. "But you surely don't do that all day, or do you?"

"No, of course not," said an embarrassed Bella. "We used to get out and have picnics and explore the surrounding country but with winter almost here, getting around is not that much fun what with the wind, rain and falling temperatures."

"No, I suppose not," said Angela. She thought for a moment and then said, "Didn't you say he used to be a professor?"

"Yes, I did."

"What did he teach?" asked Andrew.

"I believe it was economics but he really doesn't talk much about it," said Bella. "It's almost as though that was another lifetime for him…something in the past that he's put behind him. He doesn't seem to want to go there anymore."

"Have you talked to him about going back to teaching?" asked Angela. "I know we all appreciate what he does at the diner, but is that challenging enough for him?"

Both Bella and Andrew looked at Angela in surprise. This was the first time that she had identified herself as part of *The Second Street Café* family.

"Where are you going with this, Angela?" asked Andrew.

"Look, it seems to me like a bit of a waste of a fine mind for Michael to be a line cook when one glance will tell you that he is far too intelligent to be spending his time serving up hash-browns and meatloaf to our less than intellectual customers."

As Andrew and Bella started to protest, Angela continued, "Hey, don't get me wrong. I'm not knocking our customers or denigrating what Michael does but….well, it just seems a waste to me."

"I can see that that," said Bella reflectively. "But he seems to be happy enough and Andrew and I are delighted that he's here. I'm sure that you're aware of the problems we've had in the past over getting and keeping someone reliable for the kitchen. At times it was almost a nightmare for us."

"Look, if it's a cook you want…well, that's something I could do," responded Angela.

"You could?" asked Bella and Andrew almost simultaneously.

"Yes," said Angela simply.

"I knew that you could cook," said Andrew. "But as for working at the diner, is that something you'd want?"

"Actually, yes. I'm bored silly with that dead-end office job I've got and the pay isn't that good either," said Angela as she looked from one to the other. "Look guys, Andrew and I are engaged and soon to be married and then …well, I know that I'm already part of the family now but our marriage will make it official," and Angela reached over to touch Andrew's arm. "So, I want to make a real contribution rather than simply keeping a bed warm at night for Andrew. I don't mean to suggest that I want to push Michael out, not at all in fact because he's part of the family too now. No, I feel we should encourage him to realize his full potential, as those feel-good preachers, motivational speakers and pop psychologists like to say."

Silence greeted her words as Bella and Andrew thought over what she had said. Were they holding him back? Both of them knew that if someone really wanted to do something, then virtually nothing or no-one could hold them back but sometimes people just need a nudge, a little encouragement, to take that first step. All too often, a person's dreams and aspirations could be destroyed by a negative comment, a cruel remark or even outright ridicule but what if that person only needed a slight push or even a mild suggestion that this is what they should consider doing?

Eventually Bella leaned over and hugged Angela, saying "You're one smart chick, aren't you girl? I come over here asking about Christmas gifts and here you are, revamping the diner…and possibly for the better." She turned to Andrew and said laughingly, "What's Angela doing with you? I always knew she was intelligent but here she is, pointing the way forward for us all and with such style."

Angela ducked her head demurely, saying "Aw shucks, it ain't nothing."

After that interchange, the discussion returned to gifts and present giving but even as the three of them talked about Christmas, Bella's mind was churning fiercely. The diner was doing well, at least well enough to provide a comfortable living for them all, but for how much longer? The population of Southampton was aging and industry was slowly but surely contracting here in town and throughout the county. Sooner or later they would be forced to scale back operations, sell out or even shut down. *Status quo* didn't stay that way for long and, like it or not, Bella knew that she and Andrew would have to initiate discussions on what the mid- and long-term plans should be. Encouraging Michael to go back into teaching might be the first step in re-shaping all of their lives, and not just for her and Michael. The new car was a start and she knew, viscerally, that Michael would probably also start sorting out his tangled marriage. At least he was now reasonably secure financially.

Vincent was seated at his desk, checking the routine paperwork for a large and successful department store, when his phone rang.

"Yup?" he said, still distracted by the paperwork spread out across his desk.

"Do you remember asking me to check on someone?" asked Greg Reynolds, Bennet's finance and credit officer.

"Er…remind me who you are talking about, Greg," said Vincent.

"Someone called Michael Woodman."

Immediately Vincent's focus snapped to attention, "Yes, yes I do. What about him?"

"Apparently this guy just applied for a car loan."

"Really? Look, come up to my office and fill me on this, okay?"

Greg promptly collected his notes and quickly went to Vincent's office. When the boss wanted information, it was usually important and most of the time he wanted it immediately.

Hearing the polite knock on his door, Vincent called out for Greg to come in. After entered the office, he sat down across the desk from Vincent and handed over a folder.

"Okay," said Vincent. "Where was this car purchased…..and when for that matter?"

Relying on his exceptional memory, Greg said, "A few days ago. It took a while for it to go through all the credit reporting services but, if it's the same guy, which he appears to be based on his social security number, then he bought a new car in Arkansas."

"Arkansas? What's he doing there?"

"Not sure about that, chief, but it seems he's working at a small restaurant or, more likely a diner, there. A place called *The Second Street Café*. It's not clear how long he's been there but that's where he's employed and the credit bureau also gave us an address. Funny thing is, that house where he's living is owned by someone called Bella Summerfield, who also seems to be co-owner of that diner with a brother, Andrew Summerfield."

"Really? Did you find out anything about these Summerfields?"

"Both are divorced. Based on what I got through one of those people search sites, I gather that their parents had lived in Southampton for years and died there. Since both Bella and Andrew moved to Southampton after the death of their parents, I surmise that they inherited the diner from them….not that it matters really."

"No, it really doesn't. Okay, what about any financial data on this brother and sister?"

"Both seem to be sound financially and have good credit scores. There's no evidence of law-suits, arrests or convictions, bankruptcies or anything negative about them, and certainly no criminal records. I gather that both are college graduates." Greg hesitated before continuing, "Do you want me to dig deeper into their backgrounds? I could get…er…one of our contacts to do some in depth searches, if you get my menaing?"

"No," said Vincent. "I can't see a need for it." He paused for thought. "So, Michael Woodman seems to have moved in with the divorced Bella Summerfield and works at the diner. I wonder when that happened but I somehow feel it wasn't all that recent."

He leaned back in his chair and looked at Greg Reynolds. "You did very well, Greg…thank you. I'll take it from here. If anything else turns up, let me know but I think I've got everything I need."

Greg Reynolds nodded and left the office, mystified as to why his boss wanted all that information but he decided, sensibly, that it was not his concern and by the time he returned to his office, the matter had been filed away in his memory banks. The main thing was that the Head of Security was satisfied with the job he had done and, presumably, that would be reflected in his year-end bonus.

Vincent read carefully through the information that Greg had assembled and sat back for a few minutes thinking about it. Eventually he picked up the telephone and called Victor Bascombe's secretary and asked whether the CEO was available to meet with him. Receiving an affirmative, he picked up the file headed towards Victor's office. Once there, he filled Victor in on what he had learned.

"Now that is interesting," said Victor. "That rather puts paid to any suggestion that Professor Woodman is a serial killer, doesn't it?"

"I'm not sure about the time line but, by and large, I think that you might be right," said Vincent.

Victor sat back and looked thoughtfully at Vincent. "Okay, it seems as though we might have found the man…well done."

"Actually, I have to give credit to Greg Reynolds. It was he who found all this out."

"Well, kudos to him," and Victor fell silent, thinking, 'Somehow I have to raise this with Linda and find out what she wants to do next. The ball is in her court now.' Aloud, he said, "Thank you Vincent. Have you told the FBI what you've learned about Woodman?"

"Not yet, no. I thought I'd run everything by you first."

Victor nodded and then said, "Fill them in…if only to keep up a working relationship with them. As I have said, any favors we do them might come to be useful down the road. Right then, thank you…you've given me something to think about." He paused before adding, "Let me know if anything else turns up and, indeed, what the FBI think."

"Yes sir," said Vincent, and headed back to his office, his job done with regard to Michael Woodman. What happened next was up to Mr. Bascombe and the FBI, but first he had to call Randy at the Kansas City Field Office and fill him in regarding what they had learned about Michael Woodman. Idly he wondered what Randy and Ryan would do next. It was one thing to know where a missing husband had turned up but another matter to prove that the man was a serial killer, if indeed that was what he was.

After hanging up the telephone with Vincent, Randy quickly told Ryan what he had heard. "What if this Woodman guy isn't our killer?" asked Ryan.

"He may not be but my gut tells me that he and the killer are one and the same person."

"But why has he been quiet for so long? Surely that doesn't seem to fit the pattern." Ryan was quiet for a few seconds and then added, "Even if Woodman is our guy, so to speak, we've only got circumstantial evidence at best and, let's face it, that evidence is pretty thin. I'd hate to go off on another wild goose chase, especially not in Arkansas with winter coming on."

"I hate to agree with you but..." and Randy hesitated. He took a mouthful of coffee and nearly spat it out. Slamming his mug down, he said, "Why is it that the military always supplies great coffee but I have yet to drink any in a police station or an FBI office that doesn't taste like motor oil, and used stuff at that. Is there some arrangement with Maxwell House or Folgers that ensures we always get the dregs?"

"Nah, it's just that coffee gets made first thing in the morning and it hangs around stewing all day. The stuff I drink at home doesn't taste like that."

"Huh, and you're a bachelor. I tell you Ryan, I love my wife dearly but she's no cook and can even burn boiling water. Nevertheless, even her coffee don't taste this bad. No wonder that there's a coffee shop within striking distance of every police station in the country. Must be some sort of conspiracy." Randy snorted and then said, "Well, let's go talk to Steve and see what he thinks. I dread the thought of another road trip but if the boss says do it, well...."

After hearing what Randy and Ryan had learned from Vincent, Steve Wellington said, "Looks as though your work with Vince Dodson has paid dividends...which I'm glad to hear. But, and this is a big but, are we that much farther forward? We still can't be sure that he's our killer…the evidence just isn't there, is it?" Steve paused for thought before saying, "Pulling him in for an interview probably won't work. Not only is it unlikely that he'll talk, it will only alert him to the fact that we're onto him. Either he'll take off again or simply stop killing people for good. Getting him to stop wouldn't be a bad thing but, like you, I really do want to nail him. The question is, how do we do that?" He was silent again, gently tapping a pencil on his desk and staring off into space. Finally he looked at his two agents, "I hate the thought of sending you two out again and getting the local police involved down there might cause more problems than I want to think about, especially if this Michael Woodman isn't the killer. No, maybe we can get a field office down there to put someone onto him, you know, watch his movements and see if he makes a move. Surely he's going to break out again…I cannot believe that a serial killer can simply stop what he's been doing and go back to an ordinary life. That's hardly credible." Steve fell silent again.

Randy, slightly uncomfortable with the silence, said, "Can we do that? Get one of the local agents to stand watch on Woodman?"

"I don't see why not. I can't believe that the field office down there is all that busy and they may be only too pleased to lend a hand. If they balk at it, I can always go through Washington but I hate to get the big guns involved when all we're doing is following up on a hunch. No, I'll ask them personally and we'll go from there."

Special Agent Matt Downey was excited. He was not long out of the Academy and already he was on a stake-out. It was a bit boring, he had to admit, but it was a whole lot better than shuffling paper behind a desk, a task assigned to every newbie across the country. As he sat in his car, listening to the radio, Matt felt sorry that he had stopped smoking three years previously. Tobacco had many disadvantages but at least smoking did help the time to pass. He glanced at his watch. In another few minutes, the woman and man would leave the house and go the diner and, if they followed their regular pattern, they would stay there all day and often well into the evening. After two weeks of surveillance, Matt could recognize each and every customer that went into the diner. He was tempted, at first, to go in and get something to eat, if only see why the place seemed to stay reasonably busy all day. While the place was hardly packed, there was a steady stream of customers and that alone was surprising in a small town like Southampton.

Matt longed to get out of the car and stroll around, if only to stretch his legs and unkink his back but he knew that the one time he did such a thing would be the day that the guy took off and killed someone. No way could he explain that lapse. Likewise, much as he'd like to bring along a book and read, he knew that once he got involved in the plot, he devoted his entire attention to it and with his luck, that would be when the putative killer took off or when someone might go into the diner and shoot it up with an AK-47. No, best to suffer in silence and do his job. If he let anything happen, he dreaded what damage it might do to his career. Arkansas was bad enough but he knew that there numerous postings that could be a lot worse. Fortunately Matt was not on stake-out every day but it was often enough for his girlfriend to start making remarks about him possibly having another woman on the side. Trouble was, he couldn't discuss it with her and had to suck it up while trying to placate her annoyance at not seeing as much of him as she'd like.

Sheriff's Deputy Jack Ormsted was a 15 year veteran on the force. Tough and experienced, he was a non-nonsense cop and loved his job. It was not as exciting as his tours of duty as a combat MP with the U.S. Army, and his current duties were nothing compared to his service in Iraq and various other hot spots but he was happy enough. He was big man, hard, lean and very fit and easily handled the odd rowdy and sometimes belligerent drunk on a Friday or Saturday night but was compassionate enough to listen patiently to little old ladies who had had their sleep disturbed by odd sounds in the middle of the night and promptly called the police to investigate. Most of the time it was a raccoon tipping over trash cans but every so often it might be high school students working off their hormones by getting into mischief. Jack handled it all and was efficient, nothing bothering him and, as an ex-MP, he was a strict by-the-book man. His reports were a model of concise summaries of what the incident had been and what he done to take care of the problem regardless of what was involved.

When Mrs. Simmonds had reported that she had seen a black car parked on her side road several times, Jack took notice. Mrs. Simmonds was not one of his regulars, as he referred to the gentlemen and ladies who called in on a weekly basis to report incidents that ranged from stray dogs, cats stuck in trees and even the odd siting of an alien space ship. No, Mrs. Simmonds was sane and sensible and did not bother him unless she was genuinely concerned about something. Accordingly, Jack drove his cruiser slowly down the street and made a mental note of both the position of the car, the license tag and the fact that the car, a late model black Chevy, was occupied by a young man staring vacantly into space. Nothing struck him as too unusual or alarming so Jack continued to patrol the town. When, two or three days later, Jack took another drive down Mrs. Simmonds' street, he saw the same car and same driver although it was not in exactly the same spot. He drove around the block and after stopping a few yards behind the car, he called in the license tag and was surprised to learn that it was a Government issue vehicle.

Surprised, Jack climbed out of his cruiser, checked that his weapon was easily accessible and walked up to the car. He tapped on the window, signaling for the driver to wind it down. Startled, the driver looked quickly at Jack Ormsted and wound down the window with one hand while reaching into his jacket inside breast pocket. Immediately Jack's Beretta appeared in his hand and he snapped, "Now sir, I want you to place your hands on the dashboard where I can see them."

When the driver complied, he said, "Now sir, I want you to slowly turn off the engine." Jack watched carefully as the driver did as he was told and then said, "Now, I want to see some identification. So, slowly and carefully, get it out."

The driver fished into his inside breast pocket again and pulled out a black leather folder which he offered to Jack. Taking the proffered folder in his left hand, Jack backed up from the car door just in case the driver decided to swing it open and, keeping his weapon aimed at the driver, he glanced down at the folder. Then he looked again. He had seen FBI I.D.'s before and, as always, was astonished at how small they were, almost like a child's play police badge.

He looked at the driver again, carefully, and then said, "This says that you are an FBI agent?"

"That's right," said the driver. "I'm Special Agent Matt Downey."

"Well now," said Jack, cynical and cautious as always. "Let's have a look at your driver's license just to make sure, shall we?"

The driver slowly pulled out his wallet and carefully handed over his license and insurance papers. After examining them, Jack holstered his weapon, saying, "It's looks as though you are who you say you are. Okay then, do you mind telling me what you're doing here?"

"I'm on a stake-out," said Matt.

"A stake-out for what, or rather for whom?" asked Jack.

"A person of interest," said Matt simply.

"Look Special Agent Downey, we don't get an FBI agent here in our small town on a regular basis. In fact, I can't remember the last time we had a Feebie here and certainly not on a stake-out. So to avoid any misunderstanding, who are you staking out and why here?"

Matt hesitated. This was not something they had covered at the Academy but he was sensible enough to know not to piss off a local police officer, and certainly not someone who looked as tough and competent as this man. Deciding, he said, "Look, do you mind getting in the car? I don't want to draw too much attention to my being here, at least no more than I have already."

Jack nodded and walked around the rear of the car to climb into the front passenger seat. After he was settled, he looked at Matt inquiringly. Slowly and with some reluctance, Matt told Jack about his mission.

Victor stared hard at the folder Vincent had given him. So Linda's husband was in Arkansas, presumably living with someone or least staying at her house. The fact that he had just bought a new vehicle from a reputable dealer and could get financing from a large finance company indicated that he had lived in that place long enough to be considered a viable candidate for a car loan.

Reviewing the financial data, Victor could see that *The Second Street Café* was doing reasonably well, about right for a diner in a small Arkansas town and he assumed that the personal finances of this Bella woman were probably sound enough, since there were no indications of a looming financial crisis. The question he had to consider was why Michael was staying at that house. Was he there because it was convenient for his employment at the diner or could he be there as a companion and lover for the woman? If it was the former, the situation vis-à-vis Linda was wholly different than it might be if the latter arrangement applied.

Victor now had to address the issue of what to do next. He and Linda had been lovers for some time, to their mutual pleasure and satisfaction. However, both acknowledged the fact that things could not continue as they were for much longer. At first, sneaking away for pleasurable meetings in a convenient downtown hotel or going to one or other of their respective homes during lunchtime or the early afternoon had been quite exciting. They had even been able to spend the night together on the odd occasion that her children had had sleep-overs at the houses of their friends, but both knew that it was rapidly approaching the time when a more permanent arrangement would have to be made. As Victor ruefully acknowledged, if Michael was hooked up with this Bella Summerfield woman, then he might be very amenable to divorcing Linda. On the other hand, if he was just a glorified lodger, then he could still lay claim to being married and that would raise all sorts of complications now that the revamped coffee shop was proving to be a big success.

Deciding, he invited Linda to have lunch with him in his executive office and, as they sipped their coffees, he broached the subject of Michael and what Vincent had learned about him. He glossed over the details of how Michael had been found and certainly made no mention of the wild suggestion that the FBI were wondering whether Michael Woodman, her husband, might be a serial killer.

Linda listened in silence and then sat back, staring into space. That Michael might have hooked up with some woman came as a surprise but that was not as astonishing as the news that he was working in a diner in semi-rural Arkansas and had been able to purchase a new vehicle based on his income at that diner. She had been a little hurt that her errant husband appeared to have set up house with some woman, if that indeed was the case, but given her own liaison with Victor, she could hardly blame him. Now that the situation regarding her husband now seemed to be a little clearer, she had to consider whether she really did want a divorce or was it possible that she might want him back in her life?

Getting to her feet, she quickly kissed Victor, saying, "I've got lots to think about. Can we get together later tonight…no, better tomorrow after I've had a chance to digest everything." She smiled fondly and said, "Thank you for lunch and do thank Vincent for getting all this information together."

"Not a problem on either count," smiled Victor. "It was a pleasure and I shall look forward to getting together tomorrow…just give me a call, okay?"

CHAPTER 18

"Okay," said Sheriff's Deputy Jack Ormsted. "You've got my attention. Are you telling me that the FBI suspects that a man who was once a college professor and is now a short-order cook here in Southampton, Arkansas is a serial killer?"

"Yes" affirmed Matt succinctly.

Jack looked at him in astonishment, "You have to be kidding!"

"That's what they told me."

"So, we have a former college professor who, for reasons best known to himself, dropped out and travelled around for a bit before ending up here and finding work in a diner. A diner, I might add, that has been a popular eatery in this community for a long time. Andrew and Bella Summerfield, and their parents before them, are fixtures in the community and are very well regarded. I just can't see them hiring anyone with a shady past, especially not a serial killer." Jack sighed and then said, "Look, I've had a lot of experience and I can tell you that people drop out or simply take off for many reasons, reasons that don't make a whole lot of sense to anyone but themselves."

He fell silent, thinking of all the military men and women that he had known over the years that had done just that. The fancy name for this was PTSD but the bottom line was that people simply decide that everyday life was not for them. They had seen and been part of so much violence, pain and death during warfare that not only did they not want to be reminded of it, they just wanted to run from it. Consequently, just like a snake shedding its skin, they wanted a whole new life. In his opinion, it was more than likely that something comparable had happened with this Michael Woodman person and his dropping out of society was not all that extraordinary and certainly was no crime.

Jack Ormsted had not had that much experience with murders or the people that committed them but he had got to know the man in question from his periodic visits to *The Second Street Café*. Whatever else Michael Woodman might be, he was a most unlikely candidate to be a serial killer. Finally he broke the silence.

"Look, I know you've been assigned to this stake-out but I have to tell you, I just don't see it. That guy in there works from early morning until well into the evening six days a week. The diner is closed on Sundays and I know that he and Bella spend their Sundays relaxing and recovering from the week. Sometimes they do go off driving around the country – I've seen them, so I know – but most of the time, they are home-bodies. I just don't see how this Woodman guy would ever find the time or the energy to be a serial killer." He paused before adding, "Not only that, I haven't heard of any unsolved murders around here or even anywhere in the county this year. From what I gather, serial killers don't just stop and if your guy is a psychopath, then surely he would still be doing things, not working as hard as he does every day of the week and on Saturdays. I'm sorry but I just don't buy it."

"Apparently, the Kansas City Field Office think he committed these crimes months back, after he left home in Pittsburgh," said Matt defensively.

"Really? Well I suppose anything's possible but just go into the diner and see if you can meet him. Actually you might find it easier to go round the back and chat to the guy when he's taking a smoke break during a slack period at the diner. After you get a chance to talk to him, I think you'll change your mind." Jack looked at Matt and then added, "However, if it was me, I'd ditch the suit and tie – nobody would ever believe that a buttoned-up individual like you just happened upon a short-order cook and stopped to have a chat. You might as well wear a flashing neon badge announcing who you are."

Matt nodded. Talking to the suspect was a great idea. If the local cop was right and Michael Woodman was really that unlikely a suspect, he'd report that in and, hopefully, be assigned to something else.

"Bella," said Michael quietly.
"Yes darling, what is it?"

"You mentioned some time back something about me going back into teaching."

"Yes?"

"Where did that idea come from?"

"I saw an advertisement in something I was looking at when I was in the beauty salon." This was not actually the case since Bella had gone online to see if there any opportunities in education within driving distance of Southampton. She rationalized that a small white lie would do no harm, especially if it made her man happy. "It seems that a college is looking for faculty in a number of different fields, one which was economics. Wasn't that what you used to teach?"

"Yes but are you sure about all this? What's the name of the college?"

"Not one that I've heard of, but that doesn't mean a whole lot. I think it was called Hope State College…in Hope, Arkansas, down near Texarkana."

"Hmm, that's interesting. I wonder how I can find out more about this."

"Why not go online and see what their website says. What have you got to lose?" said Bella, pleased that Michael was showing some interest. Although she would never admit it to anyone, least of all to herself, Bella was worried that eventually Michael would get bored, if he wasn't already, with being a short-order cook. It was hardly in keeping with his education or his intellect. Sooner or later he might simply take off, the way he had with his wife and children. Although the circumstances between then and now seemed to be completely different, she was insecure enough to be troubled about what could happen. As she muttered to herself one day when applying make-up before going into work, "Better to be proactive than to sit back and wonder what happened if Michael gets too bored and fed-up and just takes off! By then it would be far too late to do anything."

The following Sunday, after breakfast, Michael sat down at Bella's computer and logged in to the Hope State University website. As Bella had said, they were indeed looking for faculty at both the Assistant and Associate Professorial rank. Looking over his shoulder, Bella asked, "What's the difference between an Assistant and an Associate Professor, other than academic rank. Is it important?"

"Oh yes," said Michael. "An Associate Professor usually has tenure and one only reaches that rank after about 6 years as an Assistant Professor."

"What's the significance of tenure?"

"A tenured professor basically has a job for life…you have to really do something terribly wrong to get fired. The other thing is that if you are turned down for tenure at one college, then no other institution will take you on. In other words, if you apply for promotion and tenure and it is not granted to you, then your academic career is effectively over."

"That seems a little harsh."

"Maybe, but that's the system."

"Did you…er…have tenure when you were teaching?" asked Bella.

"Yes I did," said Michael flatly.

Bella, thinking that at least being turned down for promotion and tenure was not the reason he left home, went on to ask, "Is tenure hard to get?"

"It depends on the field, but no, it is not easy. You have to show that you have achieved National recognition in your chosen field, you know, publish lots of papers and often write at least one book. In science it is somewhat easier because you can get various grants to support your research and the bigger the grant, the better your reputation which helps immeasurably in the tenure process. In soft subjects like the arts, getting grants is well-nigh impossible and that makes the tenure process really difficult."

"But you made it?"

"Yes. It was difficult and challenging but I did make tenure."

Bella nodded and sat back in her chair. Despite having lived in the United States for decades, Michael still retained the British tendency to downplay difficulties and she wondered just how "difficult and challenging" it had been for him. Could that have been a factor in the break-up of his marriage?

As Michael also sat back, staring at the computer monitor and lightly tapping a pencil against his front teeth, Bella could see that he was deep in thought. Although reluctant to interrupt his thoughts, she wanted to know what he was processing through.

"Michael, you look…er…you look both pensive and, I don't know, worried or at least concerned about something. What is it?"

"I hate to admit it but applying for a position at this place, well…," said Michael with a negligent wave of his hand at the monitor screen. "It is not that simple."

"Why not?"

"Well, for a start, I have to show proof of my education which in itself is not that difficult because I can contact my own *alma mater* to get my transcripts. But my application must include references and I'm not sure whether anyone at Hathaway will be that keen to help me after I just walked away from the place."

"I can see that but surely they would be honest in what they say about you?"

"Possibly….probably," admitted Michael. "But say Hope State College did offer me a job. I'd have to get back in touch with Hathaway College and arrange for them to collect together all my teaching notes, files, books and so forth. They might agree to ship them but I suspect they may insist that I get them in person. Not only that, I'd have to ask Linda to pack up all my clothes, my laptop and all that stuff and ship it down to me. I just don't know how the College or Linda might react if I suddenly made those requests after months of silence. Frankly, I just don't know how that would go down."

Bella nodded. Although going back into teaching had seemed like a good idea when she raised it, she could now see that it involved far more than she had anticipated. Hesitantly she asked, "How do feel about contacting your wife? Did you part on good terms?"

Michael laughed. "We didn't part on *any* terms…I just upped and left. Whether Linda has come to terms with that or if she harbors a deep and visceral hatred of me for leaving her and the children… well, I just can't answer that."

"Would she want a divorce or is it possible that she might try to persuade you to come back home?"

"I have no idea. Frankly, going back home, which is no longer my home anyway, really isn't an option. As for a divorce, unless she wants one, then what would be the point?"

Michael's comment stunned Bella. The implication was that he saw no reason to be officially and legally single again and that effectively ruled out him marrying her. Was she just a convenience, a bed-mate, only for as long as it took for him to build up his finances before taking off again? A pleasant way of passing time until boredom or something else sent him on his way again?

Her dreams of their future together were starting to go up in smoke and she was deeply perturbed, if not angry. Bella was about to snap at him when she realized that it was her prodding that had started all this. She was mature and sensible enough to know that most actions can have unintended consequences and what she had just heard was a prime example of what can happen. Before saying or doing anything, she knew she had to calm down and then gently, carefully broach the subject of their long-term future. Getting to her feet, she said, "Okay, I'll sort something out for lunch," and leaned over to lightly kiss Michael on the forehead but thinking, 'I'll get back to this another time. Pushing Michael would not be sane or sensible. Huh, that'll teach me to make assumptions!

Linda set the table and called Damion and Rebecca down for dinner. For a change they were both home and appeared to be in good moods, at least they were not as snappy and snarly as usual. Not for the first time, Linda wondered whether there were *any* non-dysfunctional families since, in her experience, everyone had problems with their children. Nevertheless, after thinking long and hard about her relationship with Victor and the unsatisfactory situation with Michael, Linda decided it was time to broach the subject with her children. Although she really did want her children to approve of and even like Victor, Linda was realistic enough to know that both of them would be off to college, gone from home and embarked on their own lives and careers within a few years. In contrast, what she was thinking about with Victor would likely determine what the rest of her life would and could be like. Her children were obviously a strong determinant on what she could do now but her future was in her own hands, not theirs. She remembered the words of the husband of one of her former friends when his wife paid more attention to her daughter than to him, "Look, just who are you married to? Is it to your daughter who seems to want to run your life and screw up any happiness that you might have while doing nothing about her own miserable life, or is to me? Make your mind up about this before it is too late." Linda was not about to make that mistake because, from personal experience as well as that of others, she was very aware of what happens when a mother devotedly caters to her children rather than to her husband. Marriage and parenthood was a delicate balancing act but most men, when marrying a single parent, want to be the foremost person in that woman's life, not her children since they leave home all too soon, leaving the mother stranded and alone.

As she watched her children scarfing down their meals, Linda said, "Hey guys, what do you think of Mr. Bascombe…you know, Victor?"

Both children stopped eating and looked their mother blankly, "Victor?"

"Yes Victor, you the man that you've had dinner with several times, both in a restaurant and here at home."

"Oh that Victor," said Damion dismissively, almost as though there was a legion of men that he and Rebecca had dined with on numerous occasions.

Linda blinked in surprise. She knew that teenagers customarily were self-absorbed and showed little consideration for others but were her children really so self-centered that they paid no attention to what might be happening in their mother's life? Obviously so, and that set her back a bit. After a short pregnant silence, she changed tactics.

"Do either of you ever think about your father…you know, want him back or anything?"

Damion and Rebecca looked at each other and shrugged. To them, their father was long gone and out of their lives. What did they care about the man who had abruptly left home and wreaked havoc in their relatively young lives? Depriving them of new clothes and essential things like the latest and greatest cell phones, lap-tops and computer games was bad enough, but forcing them to go to a public school and leaving all their old friends behind? That was unforgivable, so what did they care about their father? Eventually Damion spoke up, "Mom, dad's been gone for a long time. Even when he was here, we didn't have much to do with him, did we? Did he really care about us?"

Linda stared at her children in silence. Her son's comments made her sad because, she had to admit, she herself had caused many of the problems. It had been far too easy to spend her time with her dis-satisfied and unhappy friends who groused unceasingly about *their* husbands and children. Their attitudes had rubbed off on Linda and slowly but surely she had slipped into treating her husband as someone who was just *there*, a person to acknowledge but to disregard most of the time. That had a similar effect on her children and, as a result, even over dinner when Michael had something important to say or wanted to talk about things at Hathaway College, all three simply looked away and paid him no attention. Thinking back, it appalled her that she had not allowed him to bring home anything related to his work. As for him having a study or somewhere that he could retreat to when he need peace and quiet, or even space where he could relax and ruminate over things - that was something she simply refused to permit. Where had the joy in their marriage and in each other gone? It was too late now; all she could do was to avoid doing anything like that again, not now and certainly not in the future.

"Well, okay," said Linda at last. "Is that what you think too, Rebecca?" Receiving an affirmative nod from her daughter, Linda continued, "In which case I have some news for you."

Again both children stopped eating and looked at their mother. Now she had their attention, Linda swallowed hard and said, "Well my dears, I'm thinking of getting remarried."

"Married? Who to?" asked Damion. "What about dad?"

"Your father has gone and we've not heard a word from him in a long time."

"Do you know where he is?" asked Rebecca.

"He's in a small town called Southampton…it's in Arkansas."

"Where's that?" asked Damion.

"Southampton or Arkansas?" asked Linda.

"Either – both," said Damion.

"Arkansas is a Southern State, It's between Missouri and Louisiana and sandwiched between Mississippi and Oklahoma."

"Oh" said Damion and Rebecca almost in unison, clearly demonstrating their complete ignorance of the geography of the contiguous United States.

Linda shook her head sadly, thinking, 'What has happened to the educational process in this country. These two behave as though they have never heard of any of those states.' Patiently she said, "One of our recent presidents, William "Bill" Clinton comes from Arkansas." Seeing the mystified looks on their faces, she added, "Surely you've heard of the Clintons, or have you?" Again negative shakes of their heads and Linda gave up.

"Well anyway, I want to marry Victor Bascombe."

"Really?" said both children, again almost in unison. "Why do you want to do that?"

"Why not is the simple answer to that," said Linda and immediately regretted snapping at her children. This conversation was not going well and getting irritated with Damion and Rebecca certainly was not helping. She paused for a beat or two, trying to calm herself. "Victor and I care a great deal for each other and we both feel that being together is the right thing to do."

"Oh!" said Damion. "When did this happen?"

"Over time," said Linda and, seeing the confused looks on their faces, she added, "Guys, I know a lot has happened recently, you know, new schools for you, financial problems, the Coffee Shop and things, but I do have a life other than running around after you two."

"What about dad?" asked Rebecca. "What does he say about … about you remarrying?"

"He doesn't know yet…I'd thought I'd tell you two first."

"So how you know where dad is?" said Damion with sudden and unexpected maturity. "Did you get a private detective to look for him?"

"In simple terms, yes," agreed Linda. Again she paused. "When I realized that it was all over between your father and me, well I decided that I needed to find him so that….well, so that we could get divorced."

"Divorced?" said Rebecca, almost in horror. Divorce was something that happened in other families, not in theirs.

"Yes, I'm afraid so," said Linda. "Look, a lot has happened, since he left us and life was very hard for several months, as you well know. But we have survived. You two seem to like your new schools and have lots of friends now….you both seem to get on just fine without all those fancy and very expensive gadgets that you wanted every few months. Not only that, the Coffee Shop is starting to do quite well. I know it has been taking up a lot of my time but that doesn't seem to have adversely affected either of you and it certainly has not stopped me loving you.'

She paused and looked at her children. "Anyway, things seem to have settled down and we've all made the best of our situation. I just want to add to that happiness by marrying Victor and that can only happen if your father and I get divorced."

Silence greeted her words. Neither child appeared to be terribly upset by the news but, Linda knew, the fall-out had yet to come. For their father to drop out of their lives with his sudden disappearance had been a blow, even if neither seemed to be bothered by it. However, to hear that their mother was thinking of replacing him by someone they barely knew….well, that was another thing altogether.

After quickly finishing their meal, Damion and Rebecca looked at each other and, with the invisible signal that passes between siblings, they collected their plates and deposited them in the sink before taking off upstairs, obviously to discuss this news. Linda, watching them go, felt torn. Perhaps she had not handled things as diplomatically as she might have done but at least they now knew. Would they be accepting of Victor even if their father appeared to be gone from their lives? For a moment, Linda wondered whether she should have sought the advice, and possible assistance, of a counselor. 'Well,' she decided. 'It's too late now. I'll just have to wait and see what happens next. I wonder whether Victor and I should take them out for a meal so that they can be with us altogether now that they know about what we feel for each other and are thinking of doing. Hmm, I'll have to discuss this with Victor. Now that I come to think about it, I wonder what his children, and his grandchildren for that matter, will think about us getting married. They've only met me a couple of times and I have no idea whether they will approve or not. Oh Michael, even in your absence you seem to be able to cause problems, dammit! Actually now that I've raised the question of divorce, I wonder how you're going to feel about it, Michael. Will you simply agree or are you going to fight it? Oh well, that's just another brick in the wall.' Shutting down her thoughts, Linda finished her meal although she really was no longer hungry; she went into the kitchen to put the dishes in the dishwasher and decided what to do next. She'd call Victor later and fill him in on what had transpired with Damion and Rebecca. Hopefully he'd come up with some good advice.

Michael, sitting out back of the diner and smoking a cigarette, thought about the whole business of going online, the possibility of getting back into teaching and his relationships with Linda and Bella. He had noted Bella's reaction when he had idly commented that divorce was not that important to him. That really wasn't what he truly believed; at least he hoped that it wasn't. What he had meant to say was that as far as he was concerned, he and Bella were a couple and a piece of paper would not change that. Nevertheless, he had been thoughtless and the damage was done. Now that the issue was dead center and to the forefront of their relationship, Michael knew he had to do some careful damage control. It was possible that Linda might welcome a divorce, but what if she refused? He realized that sooner or later, probably sooner, he'd have to get in touch with her and open a dialogue. Depending on how that went, well, then he'd know what to do next. For a moment, he wished he had a close friend that he could discuss things with but the only person he was close to was Bella, and was she the right person with whom to mull things over? He sighed loudly and then felt Bella's light touch on his shoulder. Startled, he looked up at her.

"Hey, what's up?" asked Bella. "Is there something bothering you?" She paused and then said softly, "Look Mike, you know I love you and you can tell me anything. If something *is* troubling you, I am only too happy to listen."

Michael smiled warmly and gently laid his hand on top of Bella's. "Yes, my love, a whole lot is troubling me." He sighed again. "This is not the time to discuss anything but I should like to talk things over after we finish here tonight." Seeing Bella's slightly stricken look, he added, "No, there's nothing wrong but everything's suddenly become complex and confusing, and I, no we, need to see how it can get sorted out" Seeing that the worried look had yet to leave Bella's face, he added, "I don't know how you feel about getting married but that's something I want. However, we can't even think about it until I resolve the situation with Linda and, hopefully, I can get a job that will give us both the life we deserve….and that's what I want to discuss with you."

Flooded with joy and relief, Bella leaned over and kissed Michael. "Okay, Mike, we'll talk about it later, if that's what you want? Hopefully we can close up early tonight and we can curl up at home with some good wine and talk about things. Okay?"

Michael nodded. Perhaps his lamentable efforts at damage control were more effective than he had hoped. But now he had to get back to work; there were hungry customers inside and sitting out here was not getting them fed.

After shutting down the speaker phone, Randy looked pensively at Ryan, "Well, what do you think about what this agent…er… Special Agent Matt Downey just said?"

"He does seem to have a point. If even that local cop has laughed it off that Michael Woodman might be a serial killer, then he might be wasting his time continuing his surveillance." Ryan sipped at his coffee before continuing, "From what he told us, this Woodman guy seems to be lily white and pure…and far too busy being a cook to even think about going off and killing people. Of course we don't know how long he's been there but obviously long enough for everyone to think the world of him and give him sterling character references. Like you, I tend to question what a newbie agent might think but I do give credence to the opinion of a cop who's been on the job for several years and was a military policeman before that. That guy will have had a whole lot of experience and, frankly, we shouldn't take that too lightly."

Randy sighed, "I agree with you Ryan." He smacked the table in frustration and muttered, "So, what do we know? This is the second hot lead that suddenly got cold and I'm fresh out of ideas. We have no idea who the killer might be and scouting around endless motels across the country hoping to identify him does not look appealing, not at all. Shit!" He looked at Ryan, "Okay, let's go and talk to Steve. I hate to admit defeat but is there any alternative? No, don't answer, that was a rhetorical question. Ah well, let's get it over with."

After listening to them, Steve sat in silence for a couple of minutes before saying, "This is all very underwhelming. That fiasco over Arthur C. Doyle was embarrassing, but at least you didn't try to get Woodman arrested. Gut feelings and instincts are all very well but they don't get us convictions. Much as I hate to say it guys, I have to agree with you. Running around the Mid-West trying to find where our killer might have stayed would get old very quickly and, as you say, may not give us any useful insights. Pity about Michael Woodman but it does look as though he isn't our man. Of course, if the killer does start up again and assuming that Woodman *is* our killer, then at least we know where to start.

"However, like you, I'm not holding my breath and I can't see the field office down there being too keen on assigning one of their agents to sit around waiting for something to happen. Like us, they're probably short-staffed and losing one of them on a thankless task for us won't cut it." He paused for thought as he ran through all the political and strategic ramifications of what he was about to say next. "Okay, let's call it a day on this. In the unlikely event that Michael Woodman is our killer then as I said, we have somewhere to start. However, I do find it hard to believe that a serial killer can just shut up shop and stopping killing for an extended period. The psychologists and behavioral scientists always say that for a serial killer, killing people is an addiction just like heroin and that need, if you will, doesn't just disappear or go dormant for very long. So, keep a watchful eye on things but go back to whatever it was you were both doing before all this. If anything turns up, let me know." He sighed and muttered, "Yet another hot lead gone cold although even I find it hard to believe that a college professor could be that skilled over leaving no clues behind. Hopefully something will turn up, and soon."

Victor listened carefully to Linda's account of her dinner with Damion and Rebecca. "So, they weren't too unhappy at the thought of us getting married?"

"Frankly, I'm not sure what they think," sighed Linda.

"It's the nature of the beast for teenagers to think differently from adults…to be rebellious. Do you remember how horrified *our* parents were when we listened to Chuck Berry, Little Richard, The Beatles, The Stones and even Buddy Holly? Now that music and those musicians are revered icons of music."

"I'm not sure what that has to do with modern teenagers," said Linda.

"Probably nothing," agreed Victor. "What I am saying is that I'm not sure that modern teenagers are that much more selfish and self-absorbed than we were at that age. The pressures on them are possibly greater than those we experienced and their world of computers, cyberspace and texting is wholly different from what we knew. And this new world of discussing things on Facebook and Twitter is unfathomable to us. Anyway, as far as I can see, the best thing to do is nothing…you know, say nothing and let them work things out for themselves."

Even as he spoke, Victor was aware that he had not addressed the unspoken question hanging between them. What did his own adult children think about Linda? Although virtually nothing that he did would have more than a minimal impact on their lives, he wanted his offspring to like Linda and welcome her into the family. If they didn't, then so be it. However he could appreciate that things were more difficult with Damion and Rebecca because they lived at home and it would be several years before they were off to college and she still had to deal with all the tantrums and torments of adolescence.

He cleared his throat and then asked, "To slightly change the subject, what do you think Michael's reaction might be to our news?"

"I have no idea. Hopefully he won't make a fuss or anything… he could hardly do that since he just upped and left us all. But if he could disappear like that without warning, then he might be capable of anything."

"Well I suppose we'll just have to test the water, won't we?"

"And how do we do that?" wailed Linda. "I don't even have a lawyer."

"That, my dear, is the least of our problems. I have more lawyers on retainer than you can shake a stick at. I'm sure that at least a couple of them handle divorces or they have partners that specialize in family and marital affairs. Just leave it with me and I'll get someone suitable to work with you." As Linda started to protest, Victor held up his hand, "No, don't start worrying about the cost. This is something we are doing together and the cost will be minimal." As Victor said it, he smiled to himself. 'I suppose legal fees of $300-500 an hour are insignificant to a billionaire like me but Linda would be horrified if she knew the real cost. Fortunately she'll never know otherwise I know that she'd just stay married, which would be unacceptable.'

CHAPTER 19

It was Saturday night after a long and busy week at the diner. Michael and Bella had made love and now Bella was curled up next to Michael, lightly snoring and thoroughly relaxed. Michael, although tired, lay awake thinking. The immediate crisis with Bella had been resolved but he could feel the need to kill growing within, an urge that grew stronger every week. Soon, he knew, he would have to take action but how could he do it without alerting Bella and driving her to ask where he had gone at night? As he thought about the whole marriage question, a plan began to take shape.

If he and Bella were married, then he would always have a safe haven to come back to without too many questions being asked, as long as he was active in the early evening, after nightfall but not so late as to arouse comment or suspicion. The next question was how could he arrange to be out during the evening, again without eliciting comment? If he got appointed as Faculty at Hood State College, then ostensibly staying late at the college to finish off a project or grading papers would provide cover for coming home late, provided that it was not too frequent. That would give him some freedom to kill without it being obvious that he was doing so. Finding victims and covering his tracks would be difficult but he could work on that as he became active again.

Getting a faculty appointment at Hope State College might be a challenge but he did have a good reputation and provided the dean and faculty at Hathaway College were amenable to giving him a strong reference, then he stood a good chance. Approaching Hathaway College would require some diplomacy but he thought that he could manage to persuade them to help and to let him have all his teaching materials. As he thought about Hathaway, he realized that he would also have to discuss things with Linda. If he spoke to her in person after they had been in contact by telephone, a conversation that he was not looking forward to, then it was possible that she might be more amenable to giving him a divorce as well as letting him collect his stuff from the house. Seeing the children would be awkward but that likewise was manageable. If he arranged things properly, he might be able to go to the house and avoid even seeing them. It was sad that he had so little affection for his children but that was reality for him.

As he thought about things, Michael realized that he could actually kill someone on the drive to Pittsburgh and then again on the way back since, by any estimate, it would be at least a two-day drive. If he was careful, paid for everything in cash and used a false name, he should be virtually invisible. As he processed things through, Michael could feel himself getting aroused at the thought of again killing someone and involuntarily his arm muscles also tightened, pulling Bella tightly against his body. As she stirred, he quickly forced himself to relax. No need to alert Bella that he was lying awake thinking about things in the middle of the night – that might elicit far too many questions.

Relaxed again, Michael started to think about what victims he should select and gradually dozed off into a sound sleep.

"Vincent," began Madge. "Whatever happened over that man Mr. Bascombe sent you to find? What was his name again?"

Ignoring the question of Michael's name, Vincent replied, "One of my people actually found him through an online search. It was a bit of a fluke but at least we now know where he is."

"So, where is he?"

"Down South," said Vincent vaguely. Despite Madge's discretion, he still was reluctant to share too much information.

"Hmm," muttered Madge, well aware of what Vincent was doing. "So is it all over for you with him?"

"That I'm not sure about." He looked hard at his wife before continuing, "Mr. Bascombe mentioned something about his lady-friend wanting to divorce him and if the guy actually comes back here, I'm sure that he'll want me to keep a weather eye on things and possibly be there if the two of them meet up."

"Is he likely to cause any trouble?"

"I have no idea but I am the Head of Security for Bennet's and if I'm told to ensure that there is no trouble, then that's what I'll have to do. It's hardly likely that a college professor will do anything rash and, based on what I've learned, I just don't see him as a likely battery or homicide threat."

"I can understand Mr. Bascombe being cautious. Killers come in all shapes and sizes and one never knows about people."

"You're right there, Madge. One never knows but still and all...." and Vincent got to his feet, starting to help clear the dinner table. As he took the plates and silverware into the kitchen, he suddenly had a funny feeling about Michael Woodman. Could there be any connection between Michael Woodman and the serial killer that was the focus of the FBI's search? Surely not but he still felt slightly uneasy. Was it his cop's instinct clicking in? He'd know more when he actually met Woodman, if that ever happened but for the moment he decided to keep his thoughts to himself. No point in upsetting Mr. Bascombe or worse, alienating his wife-to-be.

As he stacked the dishes in the dishwasher, he asked idly, "Have you tried that new coffee shop on Main Street? What's it called?"

"*The Café on Main*, and yes, I have been there - it's great. I love it and those pastries they serve – well, they're just to die for. We've got to go there together. Take some time off work and we'll go there for coffee or tea one day, in fact the sooner the better."

Vincent smiled at Madge's gushing. It was seldom that she enthused about anything and he resolved to make time in the next day or two to indulge her wish. Then his mind involuntarily turned back to Michael Woodman. Like police officers the world over, he disliked and distrusted coincidences and, despite his reservations over whether the man might actually be a serial killer, he was experienced enough to know that nothing could be ruled out. He made a mental note to keep in touch with Randy and Ryan just in case something turned up.

The diner was officially closed for the evening and Michael, Bella and Andrew were seated at a table eating the dinner that

Michael had prepared. As they sat eating and casually chatting about the day's events, Andrew suddenly said, "You know Michael, you really are a pretty good cook. This meal is delicious." He paused and then added, "I'm really surprised, and pleased of course, that after cooking all day, you can still summon up the enthusiasm to try something new for us. Thank you."

Bella looked up in surprise. Andrew was normally very reserved and for him to be complimentary was the exception, not the rule. "Hey Andrew, what gives?" she asked. "Since when are you being nice to Michael?"

"I'm never not nice to him," said Andrew defensively.

"That's true," admitted Bella. "But why the compliments?"

"Oh, I just wanted to let him know how much I appreciate what he does."

"Guys," interjected Michael. "I am sitting here, you know," and he laughed. "But Andrew, like Bella, I'd like to know what gives. Are you trying to get rid of me?"

"Far from it but I have to face reality."

"Oh?" said Bella and Michael almost in unison, staring at him.

"And what reality is that?" asked Bella.

Andrew paused and collected his thoughts. He and Angela had had several conversations about her taking over in the kitchen and both were aware that the time she was likely to take over from Michael was already on the horizon. "Look Drew," Angela had said, "Michael is a good cook, actually he's great, but there's no way that he's going to want to continue doing that for years to come."

"Why do you say that, Angela?"

"Get real Drew!" she had exclaimed. "That man is way too intelligent to be a short-order cook. All you have to do is look at him to see that, so….well, it's inevitable that he's going to go back to whatever he was doing before he came here. By the way, what did he do?"

"Bella said that he used to be a college professor."

Angela just looked at Andrew before saying, "I rest my case!"

As the latest conversation with Angela resounded in his brain, Andrew said, "The reality is that Michael here will probably want to go back into teaching. It may not be today or even tomorrow, but certainly soon. Let's face it guys, there's no way that Michael should be working in that kitchen when he has so much more to offer." He turned to Michael, "So, what's on your mind Michael? I mean, with regard to going back into education?"

Michael sighed. Although he and Bella had discussed things several times, those conversations had between them and he was uncertain whether he wanted them aired. He had known that he would have to address this question with Andrew eventually but evidently, that time had come, albeit earlier than he had expected. He glanced at Bella and, after receiving an encouraging nod, he said, "Bella and I have talked about this occasionally and ….uh….well, we are starting to make plans."

"Oh?" said Andrew. "Do you mind sharing those plans with me?" The last remark was made with some asperity, almost as though he assumed that it was his right to be fully informed of everything they did and even what they talked about.

Bella flushed with annoyance but Michael, unperturbed, said, "I'm not sure that our plans are really any concern of yours unless, of course, they impact the diner. Having said that, Bella and I aren't excluding you but tentative plans are just that, possibilities to be explored and hopefully realized in due course."

Andrew blinked. Michael evidently was not quite the passive pushover that he had assumed him to be, something he should have known if Bella wanted him in her life. Trying to save face, Andrew laughed and said, "I stand, no, I sit corrected. Obviously your plans are precisely that…I was just curious about what you both might be thinking, you know, your long-term plans."

Michael and Bella looked at each other and shrugged. After Bella raised a questioning eyebrow, to which Michael nodded, she started to tell Andrew what she had discussed at some length with him.

Andrew listened carefully to his sister but occasionally shooting the odd glance at Michael, almost as if to monitor his reaction to what Bella was saying. When Bella finished, he sat back and stared up at the ceiling, noting with some irritation that it was starting to show signs of needing repainting. Eventually he said, "Well, I can certainly see your point and that you seem to have a number of interdependent facets to your lives. Trouble is, like you, I'm not sure what has to be addressed first." He turned to Michael and said, "Okay professor, what do you think? As an economist, you must be very familiar with interdependency and how multiple things have to come into alignment before one can take action or bring things to a conclusion."

Michael, diplomatically ignoring the slight snarky note in Andrew's comments, merely nodded and said, "You are right, several things are interdependent. Bella and I cannot get married until I am divorced but even if I were divorced, I don't feel we should get married until I have at least a more certain future."

"What does *that* mean?" asked Andrew.

"There is a certain reality to the fact that this town is slowly dying and just how long this diner can survive with rising costs and a falling clientele is a serious problem. So, to be blunt, I have to be sure that I have a career independent of *The Second Street Café* before we can give serious thought to getting married." He stopped and collected his thoughts. "However, one cannot just announce that you are going back into education. It involves a whole lot of things, notably a suitable position being available, applications to be made, references provided and reviewed, college transcripts furnished, *Curriculum Vitae* written and so forth. As you have probably surmised, *inter alia*, when I left home, I also walked away from Hathaway College in Pittsburgh. Both events were cataclysmic and it's a toss-up which might have a greater long-term consequence or determine what I can, or cannot do." He paused and sipped some coffee. "So as you say, to a greater or lesser degree, everything is interconnected. The question I am facing is which needs to be tackled first…and that is something Bella and I have to work on."

Andrew grunted and nodded. As far as he could tell, nothing was likely to happen in the immediate future but certainly changes were on their way and all of them had to start making preparations. Fate, however, decided otherwise and precipitated a cascade of events.

Linda sat in the private office of Brandon Martindale, Attorney at Law, the man Victor recommended and with whom he had arranged a meeting for her. Now that she was here, Linda was having second thoughts, not about the divorce but as to whether she could afford to even talk to, let alone retain, this particular lawyer. To say the least, the office of the large legal practice Myers, Guttmann, Trimble, Lawson and Martindale, was palatial, with thick pile carpeting, lots of glass windows that overlooked the city, smartly dressed young people that walked purposefully around the extensive suite and more mahogany furniture that she had ever seen before. Brandon Martindale was adorned in what looked like an Armani suit, a custom-made shirt and a very expensive silk tie. He was suave, urbane and immaculately coiffured and manicured.

"Mrs. Woodman," said Brandon with a very pleasant smile. "What brings you to see me?" He was, of course, very well aware of why she was there but he had to play the part. A few days previously, he had been briefed by the firm's managing partner who apparently had received a call from Victor Bascombe who, personally and through Bennet's, was one of the largest clients of the firm. In essence, Brandon had been instructed to do everything possible to help Mrs. Linda Woodman but there should be no mention of costs. All legal fees would be settled by Mr. Bascombe privately and without informing the lady.

"I want to start divorce proceedings against my husband."

"I see," murmured Brandon. "Why don't you tell me the circumstances surrounding this case?"

After Linda had outlined what had happened with Michael, Brandon leaned back in his leather chair, glanced quickly through the notes he had made during Linda's exposition and then said, "Well, it does look as though there is a strong case against your husband." He hesitated and then added, "I have to ask you this but is there any chance of reconciliation?"

"No. I have heard nothing from him in months and months, and we have all moved on with our lives."

"All? I take it you have children?"

"Yes, two, Damion and Rebecca."

"I see. I take it that they are both of school age."

Brandon made a few more notes and then asked for more details of the children. He wanted to know their ages, where they went to school as well as details of Linda's financial circumstances immediately after Michael had left and what those circumstances were like now.

"Mrs. Woodman, I take it that there has been no physical or verbal abuse within the marriage and no…er…extra-marital affairs? Can I also assume that there are no hidden assets or large outstanding debts?"

"No, nothing like that."

"Good. Well, it looks as though we have a relatively simple case of abandonment. Will you be requiring alimony payments?"

"No."

"Good. Then, hopefully, all we have to be concerned with is child support."

"Mr. Martindale, could Michael ask me for alimony? My new business, you know the coffee shop, *The Café on Main*, is starting to do quite well, so my personal finances are improving. I should hate to have to pay him any alimony if my income is greater than his."

"Do you know what his circumstances might be?"

"No. I have no idea."

"I see. Well, this is something that I shall address with his lawyer if he contests the divorce. Otherwise, it is likely that the judge will grant the divorce and require your soon-to-be ex-husband to pay the legal costs as well as child support."

"We've managed quite well without child support up to now, so…."

"Child support will be decided upon by the judge, as will legal costs, but in all likelihood, child support will be required. As for alimony, well that should be settled relatively easily with his lawyer when he identifies that individual."

"I see. So, what happens now?"

"We will serve him with divorce papers and then let matters take their course."

"Do I have to pay anything now?"

"No. We'll worry about that when everything is settled." Brandon paused, stood up and held out his hand. "It was a great pleasure to meet you. Just leave everything to me. Ah….divorce papers will be served on Michael Woodman within the next few days and let us hope that everything will proceed smoothly. As soon as we hear anything, I shall be back in touch with you."

When Linda got back to the coffee shop, she quickly rang Victor.

"Did everything go well with him, this man I recommended?"

"Oh yes. He took lots of notes, patted my hand and said he'd take care of everything. He's a nice man and certainly reassured me that everything should go smoothly. He even said that Michael will probably have to pay legal costs, which was something that I was worried about because I'm sure that his services will not come cheap, at least not based on the appearance of that law office."

"Since he said that Michael will have to bear the costs, then that's what is likely to be the case," commented Victor reassuringly. "Now, on to more pleasant matters, when am I going to see you again? Tonight?"

Michael sat in his recliner and idly flipped through the newspaper. Eventually he scrunched it up and sighed.

"What's bothering you, Michael?" asked Bella.

"I'm trying to get my head around what to do first. I suppose I can open a dialogue with that college in Hood and see whether they have any interest in me. If they do, then there's the question of how I approach Hathaway."

"Well it seems to me that you could call Hood State College, make an appointment and simply go and talk to them. As for Hathaway College, why not telephone the Dean or whoever he is and talk to him? The worst that can happen is that Hood has no interest in you and Hathaway refuses to cooperate. I suppose you'll also have to get in touch with your wife and possibly even go up to see her. But if Hathaway College does agree to be helpful, then you could combine seeing Linda and going to Hathaway in one trip up to Pittsburgh."

"Funnily enough, that's what I've been thinking. If Angela can take over for a few days, then I can get in touch with both Hood State College and Hathaway, and at least get that matter sorted. The divorce and talking to Linda might be a little more difficult, and certainly more awkward."

"You never know, Michael, it might not be as bad as you think. I'll call Angela and set things up with her. If she can start immediately, then not only will that free you up to get started on all this but it will certainly make things easier for you at the diner in the interim. We might as well let her get her feet wet as soon as we can so that if everything works out the way we want, then she'll be in place to take over completely."

"That sounds like a plan….good idea. I'll start making calls tomorrow. Let's hope that you are right and that things are not as bad or difficult as I think they might be."

Rebecca tapped on the door to Damion's room and walked in. Damion looked up and slammed down the cover of his lap-top, asking, "What do you want?"

Rebecca smiled knowingly and said, "I suppose you're looking at porn sites again, aren't you?"

"No…and what's it to you anyway?"

"Nothing," said Rebecca, trying to avoid getting into yet another altercation with her brother. "Look, I wanted to talk to you about mom, you know, her getting married again. What do you think about it?"

"Not much, I suppose. Dad's long gone and I don't think he's coming back, so why shouldn't she find someone else? Besides, what we think probably doesn't matter to her anyway."

"Do you miss him?" asked Rebecca.

"Dad? No, not really. I dunno but he never seemed to take much interest in us when he was around, so what's to miss? Besides, he's probably shacked up with someone else anyway."

"He is? How do you know?"

"That's what men do when they leave their wives and family. Lots of guys at school told me that's what their fathers did."

"Yeah, you're probably right. Say, what do you think of mom's friend Victor?"

"He seems okay. I gather that he's rich, so that's a good thing, isn't it?" said Damion.

"What do you mean?"

"Well, if he's rich then he'll be able to pay for college and even buy us cars. I'll be old enough to drive soon and if Victor does get me a car, I'll be able to drive both of us around."

"You will?" exclaimed Rebecca.

"Of course I will. If you keep going to those pharma parties, then someone will have to get you home afterwards."

"What pharma parties?" asked Rebecca innocently.

"Oh get real!" snapped Damion. "I know all about those parties where everyone brings whatever pills they find at home, throws them all into a big bowl and everyone grabs some to swallow."

"We don't do that, at least not too often," said Rebecca quietly. "Besides, what harm does it do?"

"Sure" said Damion, almost in a shout. "You have no idea what you are taking but I suppose it's your life. Anyway, once I get a car, I'll at least be able to bring you home afterwards."

"Thanks a lot," snarled Rebecca. Of course Damion was right about the parties she sometimes went to but at least he didn't know, or pretended not to know, what also went on after everyone got together and popped lots of pills. She was a bit worried about getting pregnant but then, she surmised, Damion probably did much the same sort of thing, and probably worse. After a moment's silence, she said, "How do you know he's rich?"

"If Victor owns Bennet's, then he's got to be rich. Anyone who has a chauffeur-driven car and can eat at fancy restaurants all the time has got to be rich. But he's seems alright, so I really don't care."

"Yeah, you're probably right."

"About what?" asked Damion.

"Right about him being rich and also about him buying us cars and paying for college. Isn't that what step-fathers do?"

"Probably. Anyway, he seems to be nice and mom likes him, so what do we care? As long as we're alright and he leaves us alone, then it's okay with me."

"Okay," said Rebecca. "I suppose we'll just go along with whatever mom decides. As you say, at least Victor seems to be nice and being rich will be good for us." She looked at Damion and added, "Okay then, get back to your porn site. Hey, don't you get bored with looking at them all the time?"

"I don't look at them all the time and no, I don't get bored. What do you look at online when mom's not watching? I'll bet you look at stuff too."

"No I don't" said Rebecca but her suddenly reddened face gave the lie to that claim. She didn't exactly look at porn sites, well not too often, but she certainly liked to look at all those hunks photographed on beaches and exercising in gyms. Besides what she did was her affair and, brother or not, Damion had no right to tell her what to do. Talk about the kettle calling the pot black!

She turned on her heel and went back to her own room. Mom would be home soon and either they'd eat here or perhaps Victor would take them all out to eat. Suddenly she smiled; already she had accepted that Victor was a part of their lives and, if nothing else, he could be counted on to take them out to nice restaurants or even to his home to eat meals prepared by his housekeeper. Anything was better than the stuff their father used to serve up and even mom's cooking was getting to be very boring, and the company was probably better too. At least Victor didn't even bother trying to talk to them about school-work or their friends the way dad did while feigning interest, something he failed miserably at.

She thought about Damion getting a car. It would be cool and if he got one, then in a couple of years' time, she'd get one too and that would be *really* cool. For a moment she wondered about going to college but dismissed the thought. There was plenty of time to think about that. For now, homework was calling.

Michael was on the phone talking to the Dean of Arts and Sciences at Hood State College when the FedEx man knocked on the door. Interrupting the call, Michael opened the door, and accepted the proffered package after signing for it. As he went back to his phone call, he noted that the package came from a law firm in Pittsburgh.

Eventually the call was ended, and Michael promised to submit an application. Although nothing was concrete, the dean had implied that he could possibly be appointed as an associate professor, at an appropriate salary, and would get tenure after a probationary year at the college. Feeling pleased at what he had heard, Michael tore open the package and was both surprised and somewhat pleased that it contained divorce papers. He supposed he'd have to get a lawyer but at least things were now moving forward on at least two fronts. The good thing was that Linda had initiated things, which in turn gave him an excuse to talk to her.

Then mentally, Michael stopped dead in his tracks. Just how had Linda or her lawyer found him? He had been meticulous in not leaving any trace of his travels, had driven a non-descript car and never used a credit card, yet they had found him here in this small backwater town in Arkansas. Obviously Linda had hired a private investigator and somehow that person had found him, but how? Thinking things over, Michael quickly went online and looked at the website for Myers, Guttmann, Trimble, Lawson and Martindale in Pittsburgh, PA. As he suspected, Linda was using a very prestigious law firm and her lawyer was a named partner in that firm. Although he knew almost nothing about private investigators, Michael had read enough crime novels to know that the services of a PI were not cheap, so how was she paying for everything? When they were together, he and Linda never had a lot of spare cash and after he left, Michael surmised that finances would have been tight until she had managed to find a job. But could she have found something so well-paid? That was unlikely. While it was just possible that she had won the lottery, the chances of that happening were even less likely than being struck by lightning. So if she could not afford a PI or a very prestigious law firm on her own, just *who* was paying the bills? Had Linda hooked up with someone, someone obviously rich, that was paying for finding his whereabouts as well as for the divorce? This was a likely scenario but who could it be and he wondered how Linda had met him. Either way, it simplified the divorce.

After shutting down the computer, Michael returned to the question of how Linda's PI had found him. Then it struck him, perhaps the PI or someone associated with the law firm had contacts with one or more credit bureaux and learned that he had purchased a new car. Obviously they had traced him through the credit application but that raised the question of why they had been looking for him in the first place. Michael suddenly felt a cold shiver travel down his spine. If they could find him in semi-rural Arkansas, what else might they have learned? Checking credit reports was presumably relatively straight-forward these days and that was something which, along with a background check, was a matter of routine with almost any job application. Was it possible that someone other than a PI hired by his wife or her lawyer was taking an interest in him? Well, he now had a heads-up that he was on someone's radar and realized that he had to be doubly careful in what he did when indulging in his arcane hobby.

Now that he had been served with divorce papers, Michael knew that he would have to contact Linda either directly or through her lawyer. Since Bella had been through a divorce, he decided he would ask her advice on what he should do. If he did manage to talk to Linda directly, it was always possible that they would have an amicable interaction and hopefully get things settled quickly. Michael knew that Bella was very astute and might wonder how Linda and her lawyer had managed to find him here in Southampton. If the question did come up, he decided that he would admit to ignorance but suggest that since he and Linda had a joint bank account and credit card at one time, it was likely that she had learned about him buying a car through a credit bureau. Hopefully Bella would accept that explanation at face value and leave it.

The next item on the agenda was for him to talk to the dean at Hathaway. That conversation might be difficult but he felt he was on a roll. What was even more pleasing was the thought that if things went well with Linda and Hathaway College, then he could drive up to Pittsburgh and indulge in his "hobby" both on the way there and coming back. He felt a small tumescence in his groin and smiled at the thought. It had been far too long since he had killed anyone and the need was growing. He still had the gun hidden away and using it depersonalized what he intended to do. Nevertheless, he felt a nagging concern over the fact that a PI had located him and the thought that other eyes might be on him was very worrying.

CHAPTER 20

It had been at least two weeks since Steve Wellington had closed down the serial killer search and Randy was back sifting through routine paperwork, as was Ryan. Nothing held his attention and Randy was young enough to want something to happen in the same way that bored teenagers stare at their laptops and cell-phones waiting for messages from cyberspace. Sighing, he re-immersed himself in the closely-spaced text of a long and poorly-written report on the export trade in spare parts taken from stolen vehicles in chop-shops. This was something that happened all over the country but the topic held almost zero interest for Randy. Just then, his phone rang and, after picking it up., he heard a vaguely familiar voice saying, "Hi Randy, It's Matt."

"Er…Matt?" asked Randy tentatively.

"Yeah, Matt Downey…."

"Oh Matt," exclaimed Randy. "I'm sorry, my mind is in a complete fog from reading a report on the export of stolen car parts"

"I understand," sympathized Matt. "I read that same report a couple of days ago and it is really hard going."

"Tell me about it," said Randy. "Anyway, you called me."

"Yes I did. Do you remember I told you about a Sheriff's Deputy by the name of Jack Ormsted…he's in Southampton, Arkansas?"

"Yes, yes I do. Didn't he debunk the whole question of Michael Woodman being a serial killer….basically he laughed it off as nonsense."

"That's the fellow. Anyway, he called me this morning."

"He did? Why?"

"Apparently, he'd stopped by *The Second Street Café* yesterday and got chatting to the owner and head server, Bella Summerfield."

"Go on," encouraged Randy, wondering where this conversation was going.

"It seems that Michael wasn't back in the kitchen cooking, the job having been temporarily taken over by the fiancée of Bella's brother, Andrew."

"Yes?" muttered Randy, already feeling that he was about to get an extended dissertation on who did what to whom in Southampton, Arkansas.

"Anyway, according to Jack Ormsted, our friend Michael is looking for ways to go back into academia and has been applying for a professorship at some college or other. Not only that," said Matt somewhat breathlessly, "It seems that he and Bella are going to get married as soon as he can divorce his wife."

"Okay," said Randy cautiously. "And this affects us how?"

"It seems that Michael Woodman will be driving up to Pittsburgh and back quite soon to sort things out with his wife and with that college where he used to teach. Not only that, if he does get a teaching job, then he'll be driving to-and-fro every day from Southampton, in other words, he'll be on the road for several days."

Randy was silent for a few seconds, digesting what he had just heard. As he thought about things, the speaker squawked and he heard Matt asking, "Are you still there, Randy?"

"Yes I am…sorry, I was just thinking about what you told me. By the way, how is it that Ormsted heard so much from this woman?"

"Apparently Bella can be a bit of a Chatty Cathy and was all excited about getting married again, and to a college professor at that."

"Hey, I hope he didn't say anything to her about our interest in Woodman?"

"No. He's far too experienced and sensible to do anything like that."

"Good. I hope he didn't."

"Of course, it may all be nothing but…well…I thought that you might be interested."

"Yes I am. Like you, I have no idea what it means but I'm definitely interested. Look Matt, let me think about this and get back to you. As you say, it may all be nothing but I'm not sure. Anyway, thank you letting me know and we'll stay in touch."

After he hung up, Randy signaled to Ryan and said, "Something's come up and I want to run it past you and Steve."

Seeing the two men standing at the doorway to his office, SAC Steve Wellington waved them in with "What's up guys?"

Steve listened carefully as Randy outlined his conversation with Special Agent Matt Downey and then said, "And your point is?"

"If Michael Woodman does drive up to Pittsburgh, it'll give him an almost ideal opportunity to kill someone. In fact, two people, one on the way up and another on his return journey."

"That's assuming he's our killer." Steve paused and thought. "Look, we really don't have any real evidence that this Michael Woodman *is* our killer." He looked hard at Randy and said, "I know what you're thinking. You want to follow him up and back and try to catch him in the act. Right?"

Randy nodded.

"Randy, I appreciate your enthusiasm but it's too great a risk. If Woodman spots you following him, then we may be opening ourselves up to charges of harassment. After that fiasco with Arthur C. Doyle, we just can't risk it."

"But what if he does kill someone?" said Randy.

"I hate to say it but we're not those characters in that TV series *Person of Interest* and we certainly don't have a super-computer giving us information on whom the next target is going to be. Sorry to dampen your enthusiasm but we can't risk doing anything right now and, to be honest, I'm sure that you've got enough on your plate for the moment without going off around the country in search of murders that may or may not happen. Besides, we really don't know when he's likely to drive up to Pittsburgh, do we?"

"But what happens if he does kill someone?"

"Then we just have to wait until the local or state police contact us. We simply cannot interfere in police investigations until and unless they call us in. Bank robberies and kidnapping - yes but murders are another matter. Besides, if this guy does want to divorce his wife and get whatever he needs from Hathaway College or wherever it is that he used to teach, then it is wholly reasonable and very logical for him to drive up there and take care of things. At this stage it doesn't make sense to follow him, because I can't see any crime in his wanting to talk to his estranged wife or former employer."

Disappointed, Randy nodded and got to his feet, ready to return to his desk. Steve, seeing his crest-fallen look, added, "I understand you taking an interest in what might or could happen, Randy. However, until something actually does happen, all I can suggest you do is to hold a watching brief until something shakes and bakes. If this guy is the killer, then we at least have some idea of where to start, okay?"

Randy nodded again. Maybe he *was* too close to this purported serial killer. Nevertheless, his gut instinct was that Michael Woodman would kill again, and would do so on his trip northward. He resolved to closely watch news items on the internet for the next few weeks just in case Michael Woodman did strike again. He also decided he would map out possible routes that Woodman could take on his drive to Pittsburgh. That at least would give him some indication of where the man might strike again.

After Randy looked at a map, he realized with a sinking feeling that Michael Woodman could drive to Pittsburgh using several different routes even if he stayed only on the interstates. If he used back or minor roads, then he had myriad travel routes. He sighed. This would not be easy and he wished that he had been given permission to follow the man.

Dr. Henry Richardson, Dean of the School of Arts and Sciences at Hathaway College, sat in his office staring morosely at the budget sheets spread out on his desk. He had a budget review meeting with the College President, the Provost and the Board of Trustees that afternoon and he was not looking forward to it. Enrollment was up but faculty publications and extra-mural funding were both significantly down from previous years while costs and overheads were rising inexorably. Still worse was the announcement by his most productive faculty member in terms of grants and publications that she had been recruited to a prestigious Ivy League college and would be leaving at the end of the semester. Adding to his depression was the large number of faculty that had come down with the flu', a condition that had invaded his own home with both of his children and his wife lying in bed sick. It had not helped his mood that the drive in that morning had been long and tortuous as he navigated his way through streets still covered in ice and snow from the recent winter storms.

Richardson was muttering imprecations to himself when his phone rang and his secretary, a lady with a distressingly cheery voice, announced that a Dr. Michael Woodman wanted to speak to him. He was about to tell her to say that he was unavailable but amended that decision by asking her to tell Michael that he, Dr. Richardson, was tied up in a meeting and would call him back in 30 or so minutes.

Dean Richardson leaned back in his chair, asking himself what Michael wanted. Various scenarios played through his head, most of them not good. Technically Michael Woodman was still a faculty member of the College because he had not resigned. Might Michael Woodman claim that he had had some sort of mental breakdown and now that he was restored to health, would he demand to be re-instated and want to resume his duties? That would be difficult because Richardson had recruited a junior faculty member to replace him, thereby saving salary but eliminating the need for Dr. Woodman. What if Woodman wanted to claim that he had been on sabbatical leave and insisted that the sabbatical be combined with accumulated vacation time and sick leave and be used to account for the time spent away from Hathaway College? Was it possible that Woodman would demand to be paid for unused vacation time and sick leave? That alone would make a large dent in the already strained budget, which was not something that Dean Richardson wanted to announce at that afternoon's budget review meeting.

Although he had never been close to Michael, Henry Richardson had never had any trouble from the man, in fact he could not remember the last time they had spoken, and if they had talked about anything, it would have been at least a year or more ago and inconsequential at best. Richardson also had a sinking feeling that if the discussion with Woodman did not go well, then there might be the specter of legal action, again not something that he wished to bring to the attention of the President, Provost and Trustees. Eventually he picked up the phone and asked his secretary to call Woodman back. "Might as well get it over with," he muttered. "No point in getting agitated until I know what the fellow wants."

After being connected and the usual exchange of meaningless pleasantries was over, Michael asked whether he could come by the College and collect his notes, files and lap-top. Richardson blinked and asked, "You want to come and get your teaching materials? Is that all?"

"Yes, Henry, that's all."

"Really? Are you thinking of going back into academia or even coming back here to Hathaway College?"

"Yes…and no," said Michael simply.

"I'm not sure I understand," said Richardson hesitantly.

"I am going to apply for a position at Hood State College and I shall need my notes etc. By the way, can I rely on you for a good recommendation?"

Stunned, Richardson almost dropped the telephone receiver. What he had just heard was not what he had expected or feared, and he wasn't quite sure how to respond. After a beat or two, he said, "Of course I should be delighted to give you a very positive endorsement at…where is it?….Hood College. As for your notes and so forth, of course we'll make every arrangement for you to collect your things – that is not a problem, not at all."

"Good, thank you," said Michael. He hesitated before saying, "I assume that you got someone in to replace me – is he doing well?"

"Yes, he's Anthony Moorhead, a graduate of Yale and doing very well here. Obviously he's new to academia but he seems to be fitting in quite well. Thank you for asking."

"I'm pleased to hear it." Michael hesitated again before adding, "I'm sorry for all the confusion and chaos that my abrupt departure might have caused. Anyway, that is water under the bridge, as they say. I think it would be best all round if I simply pack up my things and apply to Hood. I'm sure that a strong recommendation from you would carry a lot of weight."

Dean Richardson was so relieved that he almost blurted out that the College owed Michael for unused vacation time and sick leave but decided against opening that particular can of worms. Eventually he said that he'd ask the President to also put in a good word for Michael and assured him that all of Michael's notes and so forth would be boxed up and be available to him whenever he chose to visit Hathaway College and collect them.

When the conversation was finally over, both parties were relieved and pleased that things had worked out so well between them. At least Michael had now made another vital arrangement. Although he was aware that he was probably owed for unused vacation time and sick leave, Michael decided that it was best to leave that matter in abeyance. The extra income might have been useful but by forgoing it, the good will he accrued would more than balance what he might lose monetarily. At least he was now fairly assured of being appointed to Hood State College and equally important, at least to him, was that he could drive up to Pittsburgh both to see Linda, collect his clothes and to get his lecture notes and teaching materials from Hathaway College. Not only that, through careful planning he would be able to quieten that demanding voice in his head insisting that he commit one or two more murders. Yes, life was looking good and he was satisfied. Bella would also be pleased to hear that his plans were going ahead. Although she had said very little, Michael was aware that she was secretly delighted that he was going back into teaching and that they could get married once he was divorced.

When Michael and Bella were able to get settled in for the evening at home, he told her of recent developments. "So Bella, it looks as though I might have things sorted out with both Hathaway and Hood but that still leaves Linda."

"What are you going to do about her?"

"I suppose I'll have to call her and see how the land lies."

"That's going to be awkward, to say the least," said Bella. "What are you going to say to her?"

"I just don't know. Have you got any ideas?"

After a moment or two, he continued, "Well it's obvious that our marriage is over and that she wants a divorce, at least I got served with papers."

"How did she find you?"

"I just don't know. These things always come out sooner or later. It's probably because they ran a credit check when I was financing the car and since we had a joint checking account, it might have shown up on a credit report that she got."

"Oh yes, that's probably what happened," agreed Bella. She really didn't care how it had happened but at least now the ball was moving and one day Michael would be divorced.

The next day Michael reached Linda by phone. They chatted for a few minutes and then Michael said, "Well, I got the divorce papers."

"Yes?" said Linda. "I hope that you are not going to fight it, or are you?"

"No. I'll have to get a lawyer and no doubt he'll talk to your lawyer. As the divorce will be uncontested, hopefully it will all get sorted out without too much fuss."

Linda smiled cynically. How typical of Michael to be so cavalier about what was a major event in both their lives! Still, his attitude about their marriage had been made very clear to her when he left home without a word to anyone. She paused for thought before saying, "So, where do we go from here?"

"What I'd like to do is drive up to Pittsburgh and get my clothes and any personal items from the house."

"Yes?"

"I've had a word with Dean Richardson at Hathaway and he's agreed to let me get all my stuff from the College. So what I was thinking is that I'd combine both of these things in a single trip. Is that alright with you?"

"Yes, that's not a problem. I assume that you don't want to see Damion and Rebecca." She waited with interest for what Michael would say to that. Frankly she did not expect him to want to see their children since he had made no effort to contact them since he had left. It was probably unrealistic of her to expect any fatherly concern over the children and she was not disappointed.

"No, I don't think that would achieve anything. It's probably best if I just swing round during the day while they are at school and just load up the car."

"Okay. When are you thinking of coming here? I want to be sure that I'm home when you get here."

"I'll let you know but it'll probably be in a few days…less than a week. As soon as I have things arranged, I shall call you or send you a text message. I assume, by the way, that you are working now?"

"Of course I am. You left us nothing to live on so of course I had to get a job. How else do you think we could eat or pay the bills?"

Hearing the growing anger in her voice, Michael quickly terminated the conversation. The last thing he wanted was to get Linda angry. He had been on the receiving end of that anger far too many times in the past and there was little need to aggravate the situation, particularly as he was going to meet with her face-to-face in a few days and a divorce was about to happen.

After hanging up, Michael knew he had to find a lawyer to deal with the divorce and he hoped that it would not cost too much. At least if Linda was working, and presumably making a good salary if she could afford an expensive lawyer and a private investigator, then she was unlikely to ask for alimony or child support although he knew the latter would be decided by the judge. Again he wondered how Linda could afford to pay for a very white collar lawyer and a partner in a prestigious law firm at that. It was possible that she had landed a well-paid job but, cynically, he decided that she had somehow hooked up with a wealthy man, not that it was any concern of his. If he was honest, he wished her the very best and decided to leave it at that. At least if the man cared enough about her and presumably wanted to marry her, then he would probably take care of any and all bills, and encourage her not to even think about alimony or child support…. at least he hoped so. He would not even address that question when he met up with Linda. That might stir up the hornet's nest and all he wanted to do was get his belongings and get out.

Snuggled together in bed after making love, Linda and Victor hugged each other before Linda said, "I got a telephone call from Michael."

"You did?" asked Victor. "What did he want?"

"Well, he got the divorce papers and, well, he said he agreed and asked whether he could come and collect his clothes and things from the house."

"Did he ask how you found him? You know, where to serve the divorce papers?"

"No, actually he didn't."

"That's odd. I wonder why not?"

"Why is it odd?" asked Linda.

"Based on what you've told me, Michael is a pretty smart fellow. He's an economist and if nothing else, he understands money and finance."

"So?"

"He's got to know that a private investigator was involved in finding him, and that costs money. He's also aware that your legal expenses will be costly in one way or another, either for you or for him. So, Linda, your Michael will be wondering how you can afford to do all this."

"Oh! I hadn't thought of that."

"I think that he's probably wondering whether you won the lottery, got some unexpected inheritance or…" and Victor stopped. Did he even want to get into the fact that Linda was hooked up with a very rich lover?

"Or what…that I've got involved with someone who's rich?"

"That possibility must surely have crossed his mind," Victor fell silent again. "Well, no matter what he thinks, we'll have to be prepared for any and all eventualities."

"How do we do that?" wailed Linda. "Also, what if he finds out about the coffee shop? Surely he'll want to know how that came about."

"That's always possible. Look, I have been thinking about this for some time, actually ever since we started this divorce business. Let's leave it alone for the moment and we'll make plans over what to do when, and if, Michael decides to come to Pittsburgh. Okay?"

"Great," said Linda, and promptly slid on top of him.

The next day Victor called Vince into his office and told him that Michael Woodman would be coming to Pittsburgh quite shortly.

"Do you want me to run interference?"

"No, Vincent. He's still married to Linda Woodman and, as far as I know, there was no acrimony in that relationship. He just simply upped and left. Apparently there was no physical abuse and no untoward verbal abuse, at least none that I know of, so stopping Michael meeting with his wife or collecting his clothes from the house is really unwarranted."

"I see," said Vincent. "So how do you want me to play this?"

"The situation is rather tricky. Mrs. Woodman knows nothing about the FBI suspicions of her husband and the last thing I want to do is bring it to her attention. There is no direct evidence that he is a serial killer and because it is all circumstantial. I don't want to be the messenger that brings bad news, especially if it all turns out to be a big mistake."

"I see," said Vincent. "What do you want me to do here?"

"I think the best thing is for you to be available should Mrs. Woodman need any help….you know, in case of trouble. As I said, she has no inkling of what Michael may or may not have done and whereas I should like for you to be at the house when Michael shows up, that would only alarm Linda and it would also tip Michael off that he is being watched." Victor thought for a moment before saying, "I'll give Mrs. Woodman your direct number and that of your cell-phone and tell her to call you if any problems arise. No doubt she'll assure me that Michael won't cause any trouble and tell me not to worry. I'll just tell her that I'm behaving like a wet hen."

"Right then, I'll make sure that I'm available when her husband turns up at the house. Hopefully we'll get some advance notice but I should be able to get over there pretty quickly if something does happen."

"Excellent, Vincent! Thank you."

Vincent nodded and returned to his own office, wondering yet again what might be the relationship between the CEO of Bennet's and this Mrs. Linda Woodman. Judging by his concern for her, there was likely some sort of romantic interaction but it was nothing to do with him. From the little he had seen of the lady, it seemed that she was a nice person and, clearly, Mr. Bascombe liked her a lot, if not more than that. Still, it was none of his business what went on in the personal life of his boss unless it affected his safety or Bennet's. As he ruminated, Vincent again wondered about that odd feeling he got whenever the name of Michael Woodman came up. Putting that feeling aside, he decided to call Randy and give him a heads-up on what Michael Woodman might be doing within a week or so. If the FBI still thought that Michael Woodman was *the* serial killer, surely they would want to know about his planned drive up to Pittsburgh. He doubted that they would be able to follow him but being aware of the man's intended travel plans might be useful for them, particularly the fact that they would take place quite soon.

While it was still in his mind, Vincent called Randy and told what he had learned. Randy sighed and said, "Yeah, I heard something very similar from a local cop down there. It was all a bit circuitous how I heard but, nevertheless, we can't do anything."

"Why not?"

"We've been told that it's all too circumstantial and there's no real proof that Woodman is the serial killer. The net result is that we've been told to stand down on this."

"That's a shame but I know how these things can be. It's happened to me many times while I was still on the force. The good thing is that if he is your killer, he'll eventually screw up and you'll get him. Nobody ever has that good a run of luck."

"I hope so, Vince, I truly hope so. But all we can do for the moment is watch and wait, and keep our fingers crossed. Anyway, thanks for keeping us in the loop. If anything else develops, let me know. We'll do the same with you."

'Sure you will,' thought Vincent cynically. 'Everyone knows the FBI is notorious for keeping things close to the vest and as for sharing with a civilian? Forget it.'

CHAPTER 21

Michael stared at the Rand McNally atlas and reviewed the possible routes from Southampton, AK to Pittsburgh, PA. It looked to be a distance of about 1000 miles, give or take. Unaccustomed as he was to driving, that meant it would be a 2-3 day drive plus a possible additional overnight stop somewhere close to or even in Pittsburgh. That additional stop would give him an early start to the day that he had to meet up with Linda and collect his things from Hathaway College, and possibly give him a head-start on the long return journey. He decided that he would take a more northern route going up and a southeastern route coming back. That way he could kill someone in Missouri, perhaps near to St. Louis or in Southern Illinois on the way to Pittsburgh and perhaps someone else in Kentucky or Tennessee on the way back. If nothing else, having victims in widely separated states would confuse the police and make detection that much more difficult.

Packing for the trip was relatively easy; a few changes of underwear and socks, some jeans and slacks, a spare pair of shoes, shirts and sweaters and his toiletries. His loaded revolver was packed securely in the bottom of his roll-on together with three pairs of heavy gauge household rubber gloves and some large potatoes taken from the kitchen. The rubber gloves would protect his hands and wrists from gunshot residue and the potatoes would be crude but effective silencers. Although it was unlikely that anyone would stop him after the killing, he did not want there to be any trace of GSR on his hands and the rubber gloves should prevent that. As always, he would dispose of the gloves and potato on the road miles from the killing site whereas the filed interior of the gun barrel should complicate identification of the weapon he used. Now all he had to do was decide what sort of victim he should select on each occasion. Then he paused. Would it be more sensible to slip a plastic bag over the victim's head and while they were struggling to remove it, he could then shoot them? Few people expected someone to sneak up behind and try to suffocate them for no reason, and even fewer would expect an assailant to shoot them as they were trying to tear off the plastic bag. Yes, that looked like a solid plan although Michael was aware that even the best of plans could go awry.

Despite having bought a relatively new car, Michael had not opted for the installation of a GPS system because it saved hundreds if not thousands of dollars on the price. Not only that, he belatedly realized that the absence of a GPS system would make tracking his movements almost impossible. He made a mental note to not only turn off his cell-phone but also remove the battery until he reached Pittsburgh, again to prevent anyone being able to track him during the drive. If he was ever challenged over why he had switched off the phone and removed the battery, he'd simply say it was to save power because he had forgotten to pack the charger. Not only that, it was a cheap disposable phone and who would want to call him anyway?

After he had arranged everything to his satisfaction and mapped out his route, he picked up the telephone and told Linda that he expected to be in Pittsburgh in about three days, and promised to call her on the day that he would go to the house. Then he put in a call to Dean Richardson's secretary to inform her of when he would come by for his lecture notes and other things from the College. Satisfied, he called it a night and went to bed with Bella. He would leave early in the morning, just after Bella left for the diner. That way he could make a final check of everything before leaving.

That day, Bella, Angela and Andrew sat down for a coffee mid-afternoon. The lunch crowd had come and gone, and now they had a little time to relax and chat before they had to fire up again for dinner customers.

"So Angela, how are things going?" asked Bella.

"It's a bit hectic at times but I'm coping," was the response. "It's a pity that I didn't watch what Michael was doing more closely. He developed a lot of time-saving techniques that I wished I had asked about. Still, I can talk to him when he gets back. When is he coming back from Pittsburgh?"

"It'll all take about a week, so I'm afraid you might just have to hang in there for a while. I'm surprised that he didn't show you more when you first started to take over."

"Oh he did but I just didn't listen closely. It's not his fault, not at all," Angela said. "I suppose it's just like everything else; you have your own ways of doing things and perish the thought that you listen to anyone else."

Both Bella and Andrew laughed. They remembered how frazzled Michael had been when he first started in the kitchen.

"Don't worry," Andrew said. "It just takes time. After a while, Michael could take one look at who was coming in the door and know what they wanted before they even sat down. Not only that, I'm sure that he also knew what customers would want depending upon the day of the week. The nice thing about this diner, and Southampton in general, is that people here are really predictable."

"Yeah, I suppose so but doesn't that get boring for you?"

"Yes and no," said Bella. "To be honest, I'm getting too old for surprises and I've begun to appreciate stability and routine in my life." She sighed and continued, "Back when I was married, life seemed to be one continuous upheaval as we went from one crisis to the next. Frankly it got old very quickly."

"Do you miss the excitement?" asked Angela.

"Hell no," said Bella. "It was fun but that was when I was much younger. Now I am grateful to have some stability, as I said, and nothing will give me more pleasure than to have Michael back teaching college and me playing the devoted faculty wife."

"What about *The Second Street Café*?" asked Andrew. "Are you giving up on us?"

"Of course not," said Bella. "This diner is ours and is part of all our lives. The good thing is that Angela is about to become one of the family, as is Michael, and as long as we all work together, then the future looks great."

There was silence and Angela and Andrew looked at each other. Bella, catching the look, asked, "Hey, what's going on? Is something worrying you two?"

After some hesitation, Andrew said, "Yes and No." Bella looked at him questioningly, "Okay, what's the 'yes' and what's the 'no'?"

Again another look passed between Andrew and Angela, this time more intense. Again Bella, seeing the unspoken communication, asked, "Guys, what gives? This is not like you two at all…tell me what's going on."

The silence deepened as Andrew drained his coffee mug and then got up to refill it. It was clear that he was uncomfortable about something and that made Bella all the more anxious. "For crying out loud Drew, what is bothering you?" she asked. "I'm sure that it's nothing too bad, or is it?" She looked at her brother and added, "Look, stop shooting glances at Angela and tell me what's going on."

Again Andrew looked at Angela but this time he spoke, "Bella, we're worried….worried about a number of things."

"Go on," said Bella quietly.

"This town is dying. People are getting older, industry and a lot of businesses have closed down and have you seen how few young people live here now? What worries us is how long this town and *The Second Street Café* in particular can survive. Is the fact that Michael is looking to get back into teaching your way of taking out insurance against what you think might be the collapse and forced closure of this place?"

"Ouch," said Bella. "Obviously I'm concerned about what is happening here in Southampton but I would never, repeat never, abandon you, Angela or this diner and ride off into the sunset without a backward glance." She paused for breath before continuing. "Actually, I really don't think this town is dead and gone, far from it. You've both heard the rumors that Toyota or Kia, or someone, is planning to build a factory outside of town and, let's face it, Sam's Club wouldn't be opening a big retail warehouse here if they thought the place is dying. Oh I grant you that things could slow down for a while and in which case, we'll just scale back a bit but in the long term, I think Southampton and *The Second Street Café* will be just fine."

Bella got up and refilled her mug before adding, "No, things are going to be fine. As for Michael, I think going back into teaching is the right thing for him to do but it certainly won't stop me being here. After all, mom and dad bequeathed this place to us and I'm not going to give up on it without a fight." Then she looked narrowly at Andrew and Angela and said, "But there's something else that's bothering you, isn't there? What is it?"

Again looks passed between her brother and his fiancée but both remained stubbornly silent.

"Look guys," snapped Bella. "What on earth is going on with you two? Are you splitting up or something?"

"No, of course not," snapped Andrew in reply. "We've never been happier."

"But there's something, isn't there? What is it? There's nothing you can say to me that will upset me, so what gives?"

Andrew looked at Angela again and, after getting a slight nod from her, he said, "It's something we heard the other day."

"Oh? What was that?"

Angela, with some hesitation, said, "You know my cousin Cindy…over in Andover?"

"Of course," said Bella. "She's a nice young lady. What about her?"

"It seems that she was in a restaurant having lunch with one of her friends and…." and Angela hesitated.

"So she was having lunch. So what?" asked Bella.

"Well, you know Jack Olmsted, that Sheriff's Deputy who comes in here every so often?"

"Of course I do. He comes in here every week or so. What about him?"

"When Cindy was having lunch, Jack sat down in a booth with another cop in the booth behind her and they got chatting, you know the way police do when they are off duty, taking a break or whatever."

"So?"

"The two men were talking quietly but Cindy has super-sensitive hearing and she could hear what they were saying…obviously Jack didn't know that Cindy and I are related otherwise he might not have said what he did."

Bella was getting irritated. Pulling information out of Angela was like pulling teeth. Calming herself, she asked, "So what's the big mystery?"

"Evidently the FBI thinks that Michael could be a serial killer that they've been looking for."

"What?" cried Bella and then burst out laughing. "That's ridiculous. Michael is the sweetest, kindest, most gentle man I've ever known. What a hoot....Michael a serial killer!" and she laughed again. "What nonsense. For crying out loud – he's a college professor and college professors just don't do things like that!"

"But just what do you know about him?" asked Andrew gravely.

"I know enough," snapped Bella. "We've been together every day for months now and if he's a serial killer, then I'll eat my hat."

"But you don't wear hats," protested Angela.

"That was a figure of speech, Angela. No, sorry guys, I just don't believe it." She paused for breath and then asked, "Was Jack serious or was he just sharing something with another cop? You know, telling him something that was ridiculous....that sort of thing?"

"I really don't know because I wasn't there," admitted Angela. "I'll ask Cindy what precisely was said but obviously it's not something that she can talk about to Jack Olmsted. Actually she really doesn't know him at all, except by sight. She shouldn't have been eavesdropping in the first place, so talking to him might be difficult, if not embarrassing."

"I can see that," said Bella thoughtfully. "Look, I'll just ask Jack about it the next time he comes in and that'll settle the matter. Of course I won't say that Cindy overheard him. No point in causing trouble for her. Anyway, this is all rubbish, so let's change the subject before anyone says anything that we'll later regret."

By mutual consent, the conversation moved on to other matters. Andrew and Angela, relieved that they had told Bella what they had heard, were only too happy to talk about football, the high school team prospects and things that were happening in Southampton.

Later that evening, after Bella had gone to bed, she thought about the conversation with Andrew and Angela. In her mind, what Jack Olmsted had said was plainly ridiculous but just what had prompted the FBI to even take an interest in Michael, let alone suspect that he could be a serial killer? When Michael got back from his trip, they'd talk about it and have a good laugh together. Professor Michael Woodman a serial killer? What nonsense.

As she turned over to fall asleep, a stray thought burrowed into her mind. As Drew had asked, what *did* she really know about the man? After all, he had just dropped everything and left wife, children, home and a job without explanation. Was it possible that he could be a cold-blooded killer? Surely not, please, surely not and Bella offered up a silent prayer before drifting into sleep.

The next morning, after a restless sleep filled with dark and ominous dreams, an exhausted Bella dragged herself out of bed to shower and get ready for work. She still could not believe what she had heard the previous day but vowed not to revisit the topic with Andrew or Angela. Hopefully Jack Olmsted would come into the diner in the next day or two and she would take the time to raise the matter with him, if only to reassure herself that it really was all nonsense. The last thing she needed was to harbor any suspicions over Michael and the best way to resolve her niggling worries was to talk to Jack.

As is often the case, that day Jack Olmsted decided to stop by and have a coffee and slice of pie at the diner. He parked himself at the counter and was busy sipping his coffee and devouring the pie when Bella stopped to face him across the counter. Fortunately the breakfast crowd had all departed and the diner was empty except for Jack, Bella and Angela in the kitchen. Andrew had taken off to go the bank and get some additional supplies so Bella and the Deputy Sheriff could talk undisturbed.

"Hey Jack," said Bella hesitantly. "I've been hearing something a bit strange."

"Oh?" said Jack, antennae up and attentive.

"It seems that you interrupted an FBI agent while on a stake-out." Jack remained silent; he did not like where this conversation might be going.

"Apparently," continued Bella. "You spotted someone staking out *The Second Street Café* and when you checked into what was going on, you found out that the man was a Special Agent and was part of a FBI operation."

"Just where did you hear all this?" asked Jack quietly.

"Oh these things always get out," said Bella blithely.

"Not from me, they don't" snapped Jack, wondering just who had leaked this particular item of information and made a silent vow to ream them out.

"So, is it true?"

Jack Olmsted was caught in a dilemma. Obviously Bella had heard about something that should have been very confidential but Jack was astute enough to know that the best way to stifle a rumor was to address it at once and lay out the facts as he knew them.

"Well some of it is," admitted Jack. After swearing Bella to secrecy, he went on to elaborate on what he had learned from Matt Downey and then assured Bella that he thought it was ridiculous. "After all," he said. "I know the man and I can't see him killing anyone. I know that anything and everything is possible, but Michael? Forget it!"

"Where did this whole business start, you know, suspecting Michael of being a serial killer?"

"I gather it originated out of the Kansas City FBI Field Office."

"Kansas City? Why on earth would they have any interest in Michael? He's never mentioned going there, so what on earth is that all about?"

"Hey, it beats me," sighed Jack. "I'm just a simple country cop and who knows why the FBI does what it does? I'm sure that they are great at solving bank robberies and kidnappings as well as rounding up drug dealers, but murders? I have no idea what those people in their Ivory Tower think or do." He sighed again and held out his mug for a refill.

Although he could not believe that Michael Woodman was a serial killer, he was a good enough police officer to know he had to inform Matt Downey of the proposed travels of Michael Woodman. This was not something that he would ever mention to Bella, or to anyone else for that matter, but Jack knew he would never forgive himself if Michael did turn out to be the hunted serial killer and did kill someone on his trip up to Pittsburgh. It was, to his mind, all highly unlikely but he had known of stranger things that had happened in the past and as a former military policeman, he knew that it was always sensible to cover your ass, the Army's beloved motto of CYA.

Bella, satisfied that even Jack Olmsted thought the FBI's suspicions regarding Michael were nonsense, felt relieved. She would tell Andrew and Angela what she had heard and then, hopefully, things would get back to normal in the diner. The last thing any of them wanted or needed was an atmosphere of suspicion. She was irritated that she had told Michael not to call her until he got to Pittsburgh. It would have given him a good laugh to hear about all this and probably lighten his mood regarding his meeting with Linda. Well, she couldn't do anything about that now. She knew that the disposable cell phone he had purchased had very limited capabilities and probably a short battery life as well as a limited number of pre-purchased hours. 'Once he gets that job at Hood State College, then he'll have to get a proper cell-phone, especially if he has to make that trek every day' she decided. Realizing that she had got lost in her thoughts, Bella snapped back into focus and thanked Jack for being so open and honest with her. When he reached for his wallet to pay for the coffee and pie, she waived his money away, "Don't worry about it Jack. This one's on us.... thank you."

Jack nodded, seated his hat back on his head and then leaned over to shake Bella's hand. "Great coffee and that pie was delicious. It seems that Angela does even better with pastry than Michael – must be that feminine touch. Okay, back to tackle the world of crime that spilling over in Southampton. Thanks again and I'll be back soon. Hey, I wonder how Angela does with cherry pie."

After Jack Olmsted had gone back on duty, Bella was able to tell Angela what she had heard and then, when Andrew returned from running errands, she brought him up to date also. Satisfied that the ridiculous notion of Michael being a serial killer had been settled, the three of them got started on making preparations for lunch and *The Second Street Café* got back into the swing of the daily routine.

Later that night, Bella was tired and lay in bed waiting for sleep to overtake her. She missed the comforting presence of Michael beside her but was enjoying the thought that he was taking care of things so that they could marry and he could resume his rightful place back in the academic community. Life was good and she drifted off to sleep. Then suddenly Bella awoke with a start, shivering slightly and lay there wondering what had crashed in on her rest. Then it struck her. Why was the FBI interested in Michael? They did not waste their time chasing phantoms, so why Michael? As she had said to Andrew, Angela and even Jack Olmsted, she was unable to think of a less likely person to be a serial killer than Michael, so why were the FBI interested in him? It did not make sense but something must have aroused their interest. What was it? Abandoning his wife and children and abruptly leaving that college might be reprehensible but it wasn't a crime; people did it all the time and the FBI never went looking for them unless something else was involved. So what was it?

She lay there, wide awake and feeling slightly sick. Andrew had implied that she really did not know that much about him, which was true. Did Michael harbor some deep, dark secret that he was keeping from her? Could he really be a killer, wreaking havoc across the Mid-West? She desperately wanted to call Michael just to hear his voice and have him reassure her that it was all nonsense and, for the second time that time, Bella regretted telling Michael not to call her until he got to Pittsburgh. Now wide awake, Bella got out of bed and slipped on her dressing gown. Slowly she went down to the kitchen and made herself a cup of tea before sitting down in the still dark living room to think. It was too cold to sit out on the porch and because she really did not drink and certainly didn't smoke, she did not have the usual props that people reply on when they needed to think.

Sick with worry and uncertainty, Bella stared unseeing at the blank television and tried to make sense of it all. Her Michael was kind, gentle, hard-working and reliable but he *had* abandoned everything back in Pittsburgh, almost on a whim. Being in love blinded Bella to what that all meant or, indeed, what it said about Michael Woodman. If he could cold-bloodedly just walk away from everything, what else was he capable of? Could he kill people? Was he some sort of psychopathic thrill seeker that enjoyed killing people for no good reason? What sort of man was he? Aloud she cried, "Michael, where are you? Why has all this come out when you are away from home and why now? I need you here to tell me that everything is alright, that there is nothing to any of these accusations and that I should not concern myself with such nonsense."

Bella fell silent and then she thought about Michael being out of touch with her by cell-phone and also that he had refused to have a GPS system in his SUV. She asked herself, 'Was that all a plan, a deliberate means of preventing anyone tracking his movements? Where were you before you came here to Southampton? What did you do for all those weeks and months between Pittsburgh and here? What were you doing? Is any of this possible?'

Suddenly Bella burst into tears. How could she have been that naïve, trusting and stupid? Had her pleasure in finding a warm, caring and passionate lover blinded her to reality? Now she knew how little old ladies and widows could be robbed of their life savings by clever, charming and unscrupulous con men who took everything in exchange for a few kind words, fake sympathy and feigned interest. Even astute and sensible people could be taken in by people who knew the right words, the appropriate buttons to push and possessed an uncanny ability to play on the emotional needs of others to steal from them. Was this what had happened to her? Had she believed and trusted Michael more than he ever deserved? Exhausted by the emotional turmoil, Bella suddenly crashed and fell asleep in her armchair.

Michael lay on his bed, tired from the long drive but still elated from his success with his latest victim. It had been easy, almost too easy, this time. The motel he had found was small and slightly off the beaten track, and the manager had been only too pleased to have a guest that paid in cash with no questions asked on either side. After a quick meal in a small roadside restaurant, he had headed towards the nearest Interstate and headed east until he saw a promising off-ramp. Driving through the quiet countryside, he spotted a diner beside the road and pulled into the parking lot just as three men climbed out of a large SUV. Two of them went inside while the third leaned against the side of the vehicle smoking a cigarette.

Michael walked over and called out, "Excuse me, do you have a set of jumper cables? I think I've got a flat battery."

"Sure thing, Bud. I've got a set in the back," and the man flicked away his cigarette and remotely opened the lift gate. As he leaned in to dig for the jumper cables, Michael quickly inserted the gun barrel into the pre-cut recess in the potato and fired almost point-blank into the left side of the man's back. There was a muffled whump and the man splayed forward, dead.

Nodding in satisfaction, Michael returned to his vehicle and drove back towards the exit and the welcoming road. He did not see the man coming out of the diner onto the porch. Even if he had seen the man, he would have known that he was already too far from the diner to be properly identified. Once on the road, Michael wound down the passenger window and tossed out the mutilated potato which quickly buried itself into the snow nestled at the bottom of a ditch. After he had pulled onto the Interstate, heading back to his motel, he rolled off the rubber gloves and tossed them out of the window several miles apart, first making sure that they were turned inside-out so that snow, rain and the elements would wash off his fingerprints. As he drove, he wiped the steering wheel and door handle with a sanitary wipe to remove any contact transfer of GSR. He would do the same with the exterior door handles once he got back to the motel. Although any GSR transfer was unlikely, additional precautions were always sensible and he sighed with satisfaction, the inner beast was stilled.

Michael, safely back in his motel room, lay on the bed and thought about the shooting and decided that it had all gone well. Then he sat up with a start. He had the spent cartridge ejected from the gun hit the inside of the SUV and it had spun off somewhere. He had quickly looked for it but since he couldn't see it, he simply climbed into his car and drove away. Of course, unbeknownst to him, if he had spent time looking for that cartridge, then he would have been seen by the man who came out of the diner just as he was leaving the parking lot. Unaware of his lucky escape, Michael thought about the spent cartridge. A good CSI would be able to identify the gun that fired it from markings on the rim and firing plate but then Michael realized that he had not loaded that cartridge into the magazine. If it was found and any fingerprints were on it, they would be those of the gun's real owner, and he was long dead, whoever he was. He relaxed again. There was no way that the actual round could be identified and neither it nor the spent cartridge could be traced back to him. He smiled in satisfaction and got ready for bed. He had a long drive ahead of him the next day.

As Ralph Westin came out of the diner and stood on the porch, allowing his eyes to adjust to the darkness, he noted the vehicle leaving the parking lot and, seeing that the driver had his lights off, he immediately wondered whether he would get a ticket for driving without lights. Shrugging, he walked over to the SUV and seeing the open lift gate, he called out, "Hey Hank, what are you doing back there, man? The waitress wants to take your order."

As he got closer, he could smell cordite and see the dead man's body lying half in and half out of the back of the vehicle. With a muttered, "Oh shit," he quickly called 911. As a veteran of the Iraqi war, he was all too familiar with the smell of gunfire and the appearance of a dead body. Within a few minutes, a patrolling Deputy arrived and he, after checking the scene, immediately called for back-up. After that, the parking lot was soon a mass of blinking lights as the watch commander, homicide detectives, crime scene investigators and myriad curious police officers pulled in to inspect the crime scene.

"Okay then," said the lead detective to Ralph. "Tell me again what happened here."

Quickly Ralph Westin told the detective how the three of them had pulled into the diner for dinner. Hank, his friend and the owner of the vehicle, had stayed outside to finish his smoke while he and his co-worker had gone inside to get something to eat.

"Why did you stop here?" asked the detective.

"We're renovating that farm house up the road and as it was getting late, we decided to stop in and get something to eat before going home."

"Do you often do that?"

"Yes, pretty much every day. The weather delayed things for us and we've been trying to get caught up so we work pretty late most afternoons," said Ralph.

"I see. Okay, did you see anything suspicious before you went into the diner or when you came back out to get your friend?"

"Not really, no." Then he paused and added, "I did see a dark SUV pulling out of the lot here. He didn't have his lights on and I remember thinking that he'd get a ticket if he wasn't careful."

"It was a male driver? Did you see him?"

"Not really – I just assumed that he was a man."

"I see. Did you catch the license plate?"

"No. It was dark and he was already turning out of the lot."

"Which way was he headed?"

"Towards the Interstate."

"I see," said the detective. Quickly he called in a BOLO for a dark SUV heading toward the Interstate but since at least 30 or 40 minutes had elapsed since the vehicle had been sighted, he knew that setting up the BOLO was a forlorn gesture. The killer was long gone. He turned to Ralph and said, "Okay, let's go through your story once more…you know, just in case I missed something."

By this time, Ralph's co-worker, seeing all the lights, had joined his friend and both of them were subjected to the same cross-questioning by the persistent homicide detective. With a sinking feeling, the men knew that they were going to be here for hours and, annoyingly, they had no means of getting home because Hank and his vehicle were now part of a crime scene. Without even seeking permission, they both called their wives to let them know what was going on and warning them that it would be some time before they could get home. Worse, their wives would have to come and get them from the diner, something that caused some annoyance with the two women who had already settled in for the evening.

Later the following morning, the chief of detectives discussed the case with his homicide detectives and he was not happy.

"What do you mean, there's nothing?"

"The two friends and workmates obviously had nothing to do with the killing. One was inside the diner and the other swabbed clean for GSR and neither had a motive to kill the victim, the same goes for their wives. The wife of the victim is about to go into labor and in fact spent the evening with her mother who's visiting to help out with the baby that's due any day now. So, no, there's nothing to point at friends or relatives. Apparently the victim, Hank Dawkins, is or rather was a really nice man, liked by everyone and his wife is devastated by what has happened to him. Mr. Dawkins is….was…a solid family man, devoted to his wife and young daughter and apparently was delighted that they were about to have a son. A solid, church-going man, hard-working, reliable and his only indulgences appear to be the odd cigarette and going for an occasional drink with his buddies after work."

"Did you hear of any enemies or signs of drug use, heavy drinking or gambling debts?"

"Nothing. The guy was a model husband, father and all-round good guy. Not even a speeding ticket."

"So why did someone shoot him?" asked the lieutenant. "There has to be a reason, even if it doesn't make sense to us."

"LT, that's the way it is. As I said, we've got nothing except for that vague sighting of a vehicle leaving the parking lot by the one witness, Ralph Westin. By the time that came out, the perp, if he was driving the vehicle, was long gone."

"Well, keep digging, will you? I can't see a random killing happening here. There must be something that we're missing. Things like this just don't happen."

After the detectives left his office and went back to work, the lieutenant scratched his head in irritation. Something nagged at his subconscious but he couldn't pin it down. Then he sat up straight and shouted for his homicide detectives, "Hey you two, get back in here."

After they had retraced their steps to his office, the lieutenant said, "Look, I want you to check with the State Police. I vaguely remember hearing of a random and unexplained killing a number of months ago, possibly late last year. I have a sense that it might have happened not too far from here but I could be wrong on that. Anyway, if my memory serves me right, the perp used a weird method of killing the victim but I don't recall the details. The State Police will have it all on file and they'll be able to say whether the two murders could be related in some way. I don't see it myself but they have much better resources than us, so you never know. One of you check with the State but both of you keep digging just in case there is something out there that we've missed so far. Keep me informed of progress, will you?"

Soon after the detectives had left the lieutenant's office, they got a call from the CSI unit and they hurriedly retraced their steps.

The lieutenant looked up and seeing them, asked "Something come up?"

"Yeah. Apparently the CSI team did another thorough search around that vehicle early this morning when it got light and one of them found a spent cartridge buried in piled-up leaves and trash some yards away. They recovered a partial print but they couldn't match it to anything on the FBI's Integrated Automated Fingerprint Identification System, you know IAFIS. We were pretty happy at first but it looks like that might be a dead end."

"Not necessarily," said the lieutenant. "I remember when I was on the course at Quantico a few months back, I remember them saying that they had a number of data bases that not everyone can access. Tell you what, get the CSI guys to send that partial print up to the FBI Laboratory, if they haven't done so already, and request a special review of it. It is possible that they may come up with something."

Eddie Parker was a bright, energetic and very talented young man that worked in the FBI Laboratory at Quantico. Thin, bespectacled and far from being fit and physically active, Eddie compensated for his lack of physical strength by working diligently at his chosen profession, aided by a meticulous approach to everything he did and an excellent, almost encyclopedic memory. When the partial print came in, Eddie was on call for IAFIS that morning and ran the print through the data base and, like the originating police CSI, he found no matches. Then he remembered something vaguely familiar about that particular print. Eddie, like many pathologists who look at clinical slides every day, had the ability to remember odd details and would file them away in his internal memory bank. He sat back in his chair for a few seconds and searched his memory for the elusive data that he needed. Then it came to him. Quickly he went to the data file for unsolved murders and there it was, a fingerprint had been found on a spent cartridge at another murder site. He reviewed the notations and was surprised to find that the fingerprint belonged to a man that was already dead, a Clyde Wilkins. Unless a colossal mistake had been made, just how had a dead man's finger print turned up on spent cartridges at murder scenes after that person had died? It was obvious then that whoever had committed these two murders had taken the gun from this Clyde Wilkins and simply used up the ammunition that Wilkins had loaded into his weapon. There was no other explanation.

Eddie went back to the notes on the first fingerprint submission and seeing that it had come in from the FBI Field Office in Kansas City, he looked up the number and called them. After a few minutes' delay, he got through to Steve Wellington.

After brief introductions, Eddie said, "Look Senior Special Agent Wellington…"

"Call me Steve," said Wellington as he focused on what his caller had to say.

"Okay, Steve," said Eddie hesitantly. "Some months ago we got an unidentified partial print which was eventually ascribed to one Clyde Wilkins, a person who apparently was already dead when that spent cartridge was recovered."

"Oh?" said Steve. "I remember that case, in fact we think it's part of an ongoing investigation. What's your interest in that particular fingerprint and why did you contact me about it?"

CHAPTER 22

After his conversation with Eddie Parker was over, Steve Wellington sat back, deep in thought. In common with law enforcement officers around the world, he disliked and distrusted coincidences and spent cartridges being found at two different crime scenes and each carrying a partial fingerprint that matched to a dead man was beyond coincidence. It simply was not possible unless the killer had used the same gun, one that he had taken from the slain Clyde Wilkins. Clearly, the unknown killer had suddenly started up again after being inactive for weeks and possibly months. Since the same gun had been used in both shootings, the same *perp* was involved but where had the man been for all this time? His behavior was not that of the usual psychopathic killer, so why had he stopped for so long and why did he start up again now? Was it just coincidence that this latest killing was within driving distance of an earlier killing, even if the MO used in each murder was different? Unlikely – and the logical conclusion was that geography played some part in the killings.

On a hunch, he pulled out a road atlas and looked at both murder sites and their proximities to towns and interstates. The interstates made sense and then it struck him: both murders were about 1-2 days' drive from Pittsburgh although both were also reasonably close to Kansas City. On the other hand, there was no reason to think that the killer had any association with KC but Randy's work did suggest a possible link, in fact a strong connection, with Pittsburgh. Not only that, the latest killing occurred about one day's drive from Southampton, Arkansas. Randy had suggested that the killer was living in Southampton with someone, a woman called

Bella Summerfield, part owner of the diner where he worked. Could this living arrangement have restricted his movements such that he could not slip away unnoticed and kill anyone? This was a likely scenario. Then the opportunity arose for him to leave town and that allowed him to go back to killing people. Was that it? He obviously had the means, now he had the opportunity.

Steve got up from his desk and grabbed another cup of coffee before sitting back down to review everything one more time. He did not like what seemed to be taking shape but the leap of logic was hard to deny. Eventually he made his decision and called Randy and Ryan into his office.

After they were seated, Steve quickly related what he had heard from Eddie Parker and sat back to watch the reaction. Randy looked both surprised and satisfied, almost smug, whereas Ryan just looked from Steve to Randy and back, his face unreadable. Eventually Steve looked at Randy and broke the silence to say, "So, what do you think?"

Randy shrugged. He resisted the urge to say, "I told you so" and simply said, "The evidence, such as it is, suggests that Michael Woodman is likely involved, doesn't it?"

Steve nodded, appreciating the unspoken comment that he knew Randy would have liked to make. His earlier decision not to continue watching Woodman was sound at the time but, hindsight being what it was, he was aware that now it was a mistake even though there was no way anyone could have predicted that Woodman would leave town so soon.

"Okay," he said eventually. "If Woodman is the killer, and that is still a big "if", then he's struck again while we weren't looking. We now know that he's taken this opportunity to leave town and drive up to Pittsburgh but there is no real proof that it's him. The trouble is, geography and the use of the same weapon, does logically point the finger at him although it's still circumstantial." He paused and looked at his two agents. Neither said anything but Steve could imagine what they were thinking. "In the absence of any other leads," he continued. "I think we have little option but to follow up on this. So here's what I propose we do. Both of you take your personal vehicles and get up to Pittsburgh as fast as you can. We know where he's going, so you can watch what he does almost every minute of the day. By the way, get rid of your suits and ties and dress casually so that it's not obvious you are FBI. Switch off when following him, just as you were taught to do at Quantico. On the road, keep at least one car between your vehicle and Woodman's SUV and switch off with each other every few miles just in case he is observant enough to spot the same vehicle following him. I know most people are oblivious to what's going on around them when they are driving but, careful as he is, he might just make you.

He looked at Randy and Ryan carefully and added, "Right then, go home, pack your bags and get on the road. I imagine he'll stay for at least a day in Pittsburgh sorting everything out but time may still be of the essence because he might take off back to Southampton that day."

"Should we try to stay at the same motel that Woodman does on the return journey?" asked Randy.

"Yes but book in separately and at least 30 minutes apart. Also, use your personal credit cards – we don't want to alert the management that you are Federal agents. That sort of thing can get out all too easily and could alert Woodman to what might be going on. If he goes out for a meal, at least one of you go in there too but the other has to stay outside keeping watch. You two can sort out between yourselves who does what but you cannot lose sight of him at any time. Any questions?"

When Randy and Ryan shook their heads, Steve nodded and said, "Okay, get going and good luck. You never know, we might even catch him in the act on his return journey. Take care of yourselves and don't take any chances. Don't forget that this guy might be a killer."

Just as the two young men got up to leave his office, Steve added, "Hey, don't forget to take binoculars and cameras and also have baseball hats, plain lens spectacles and sunglasses with you. If you wear sunglasses, make sure that they are plain ones, not those Secret Service-type aviators. As I'm sure you know, spectacles, sun glasses and hats all help to disguise you when you're driving." Realizing that he sounded just like an anxious mother on her child's first day at school, he added somewhat lamely, "You might also want to take a quick look at the Bureau surveillance manual when you've got some downtime, you know, to refresh your memories."

After Randy and Ryan had left, Steve sat back and muttered, "This might be too big an assignment for newbies like those two. Maybe I should have sent two more experienced agents on this." Then he thought some more before muttering, "Those two are good agents and it wouldn't be fair to send someone else after all the work they've put in. Ah well, it's too late now. Hopefully it'll all work out…it had better because I hate to think what Washington will think if I've sent two of my people on yet another fool's errand. Ah man. Maybe I should have gone with them but if things don't work out, explaining what I was doing with them would only make things look worse." Finally he said quietly but fervently, "Guys, don't let me down. Just get your man and please don't get hurt yourselves." He wondered for a moment whether he should alert the Pittsburgh Field Office but decided against it. His guys should be in and out within 24 hours and he didn't want the local agents to get involved; that might turn the whole thing into a circus and almost guarantee that Michael Woodman could slip away. On the other hand, Steve was aware that he was going against protocol and if it came out that he had two of his people on another Field Office's turf, then he could get into trouble, especially if the operation did not go as planned. So, Steve Wellington took a chance and fervently hoped that everything would work out successfully.

It took less than two hours for Randy and Ryan to get their things together and be on the road. They drove safely but as fast as they could up to Pittsburgh, almost miraculously missing any highway patrols on the drive. As they sat down for a food and bathroom break at a gas station diner just off the Interstate, they went online to sort out small hotels, one close to the Woodman house where Randy would stay and other near to Hathaway College where Ryan would position himself. Later, after booking in and unpacking, the two agents met up for dinner at a restaurant mid-way between the two hotels and planned their strategy. Sorting out what needed to be done and who did what was relatively simple. Because Randy was the lead on this particular operation, he had what appeared to be the easier assignments although both men knew that the task ahead of them was likely to be difficult and demand all of their attention. In addition to the risk that yet another victim could lose their life, failure in this particular action could spell ruin for their careers. They agreed that each man would have an early breakfast at or near their respective hotels and then Randy would station himself near the Woodman home while Ryan would park close to Hathaway College, with both men staying in constant cell-phone contact throughout the day.

If Michael Woodman visited his former home first and then went to lunch, then Randy would follow him into the restaurant and Ryan would hurry over and station himself outside ready to follow Michael to Hathaway College, or wherever else he was going. Randy would then catch up with Ryan and they would change car positions as and when needed. If the suspect went to the college first, then their roles would be reversed. Although both men knew that even the most careful planning did not always cover every contingency, their arrangements looked sound and manageable. The next day when, and if, Michael Woodman appeared at either location, they would be ready. They both hoped that they had not missed the man because Michael had got to Pittsburgh a day or so ahead of them. It was not likely but, as they were well aware, anything could happen. If they missed him, then they would have to report back to Steve Wellington and hope that no-one else died because Michael Woodman had driven up to Pittsburgh and completed his errands faster than they had anticipated.

After a very disturbed night, Bella dragged herself around *The Second Street Café* in a fog, taking care of customers efficiently but with a distracted air that several of the regulars picked up on. "Hey Bella," said Sid, a steady customer who always stopped in for breakfast before going off to a small local factory. "What's going on, girl? You're not your usual bright and cheery self. Is anything wrong?"

Barely able to stem back her tears, Bella shook her head and said quietly, "No, Sid, I'm fine. Just thinking about some things, that's all."

"Don't seem like it, Bella. If I can do anything to help, you need only ask."

"Thanks Sid but I'm okay," she assured him but wishing that her anguish over Michael could simply be wiped away by the kind words and concern of Sid. After posting the latest orders on the rack for Angela to deal with in the kitchen, Bella's thoughts returned to Michael. 'Was it all a lie? Could Michael really be the cold, calculating killer that the FBI thought he was? That surely could not be her Michael? Not the man that she cuddled up against at night, the man who liked to hug her and whom she loved to hug in return, the reliable and friendly cook who took pleasure in preparing food for the customers and who always had a smile and friendly greeting for everyone that came in? It cannot be true! But what if it is? What would she do then? How would she be able to look anyone in the eye again? Drew and Angela had already expressed concern, a concern she had ridiculed, but what if they were right? What would her customers think? Would they stop coming into the diner? Would they start to worry that their food might have been poisoned by Michael?"

Scenario after scenario played through her mind. Belatedly, Bella realized that if it ever came out that Michael was suspected of being a killer, regardless of his guilt or innocence, then not only her reputation would be ruined but it might spell the ruination of *The Second Street Café*. All the hard work of her parents as well as the efforts of Andrew and her in keeping the diner open could be lost almost in a heart-beat. Fervently, she offered up another silent prayer but the drops of acid imparted by doubt and suspicion had already started their destructive action. Sadly Bella realized that things might never be the same again with Michael. People often say, *"There's no smoke without a fire"* and even if they don't say it, that's what they would be thinking and that included Andrew, Angela and herself. Again tears welled up, tears of regret, sadness and self-pity.

Then suddenly anger washed over her. How could Michael have done this? Waltzing into their place of business, their livelihood, and do this to them? What right did he have to bring his malign influence to bear on all their lives? How dare he?

Snapping herself upright, Bella vowed to dismiss everything from her mind. If all these suspicions proved to be groundless, which she fervently hoped and prayed would be the case, then *no harm, no foul.* If the unthinkable did prove to be true, then she would deal with it when the time came. She had been through worse in the past and, no doubt, she would face other challenges in the future. She was a strong, self-reliant, grown woman, and nothing and nobody was going to defeat her. She was ready to face any and all challenges, and that was that.

Just then her two favorite army veterans came in, talking to each other, their words interspersed with quiet laughter. "Bob, Sam," said Bella with a smile. "It's great to see you so cheerful this morning. Come on in and sit yourselves down. I'll get you some coffee and menus."

Surprised, the old cronies looked at each other and then at Bella. They knew her usually to be polite and somewhat friendly, but this was something different. Neither said anything but both of them, in the cynical way of old soldiers, immediately jumped to the conclusion that she had got laid the previous night….and good for her. Their only regret was it hadn't been one of them who had graced Bella's bed.

Michael stretched and slowly got out of bed. The long drive, even if spread out over two days, together with sleeping in strange beds for three nights now had all taken their toll on him. He felt stiff and weary, and slightly sleep-fogged. A hot shower and some breakfast would help but it would be another tiring day for him. The drive over to Hathaway College through morning traffic was not a pleasant prospect but it had to be done. However, he knew that going over to the house and meeting up with Linda to collect his things would be far more stressful.

As he soaped himself and let the hot water run over his body in the shower, Michael tried to think what he could say to Linda. Undoubtedly she would be furious with him, understandably so if he were honest, and he wondered just how hostile his reception would be. He hoped that Linda had boxed up his clothes and his few personal childhood mementoes; then it would only be a matter of minutes to load up everything and be on his way. On the other hand, if she had done nothing, which was quite possible, then he might be there for much longer, prolonging the agony for both of them.

Once again he wondered what had prompted her to file for divorce and, for that matter, how she would be able to pay for it all. That was not his problem but he did speculate about the likely new man in her life, especially if it was him who pushed for the divorce. Was he rich or simply someone who was sympathetic and took an interest in Linda? It did not matter much either way and he was pleased that she had met someone because that alone made things a lot easier for everyone. Almost as an afterthought, he wondered how Damion and Rebecca viewed this new man but then smiled at the cynical thought that as long as the man bought lots of gadgets and let them do what they wanted, they would be happy with him whoever he was.

Finishing up breakfast and signaling for the check, Michael quickly called Dean Richardson's secretary to let her know that he'd be there about mid-morning to collect his things. Then he called Linda. As he expected, the conversation was short and terse but it was agreed that he'd come to the house in the early afternoon. When Linda hung up, she wondered whether she could call Vincent but decided against it. She had known the man for 20 years so what did she have to be afraid of?

Ryan Whitcombe parked close to Hathaway College and watched the students turning into the campus in a steady stream on their way to class whereas only a few vehicles went the other way. Then he spotted the approach of Michael's SUV and promptly called Randy to let him know that their quarry had almost arrived at the college.

"Okay," said Randy. "That's good. I'm at the house and in position. Nobody seems to be home so I imagine Michael Woodman is only going to get here around lunchtime or early afternoon. Anyway, when Woodman has finished there, just follow him and see where he goes next…hopefully he'll head this way. By the way, what does he look like?"

"Pretty ordinary….much like a college professor."

"That doesn't tell me much. What else can you tell me?"

"He looks to be about medium height and maybe 170 pounds or so. It looks as though he got sandy brown hair and he's wearing sunglasses but no hat. As I say, he's very ordinary looking and certainly doesn't look like a killer to me."

"So how many killers have you seen?" asked Randy.

"None I grant you but he certainly looks pretty ordinary to me."

"Sounds like half the drug dealers and con men in the country," commented Randy but he knew what his partner meant.

About 90 minutes later, Randy's intercom squawked and Ryan told him that Michael Woodman was just pulling out of the college grounds. He affirmed that he would wait until the SUV was a couple of car lengths ahead of him, and then pull out and follow him.

"Okay," said Randy. "Sounds good to me. I'll keep watch here."

Michael pulled slowly out of the college grounds and drove away, keeping up with traffic and appearing to be in no particular hurry. After two or three cars had passed his vehicle, Ryan started to pull out and accelerate to keep up with Woodman. Just then, there was an almighty crunch; a female co-ed, late for class but busy texting, slammed into the back of his vehicle. Instinctively, Ryan braked hard and sat waiting for the girl to stop texting and get out of her car.

As luck would have it, a campus security officer had just turned out of the college grounds and seeing the Hathaway College parking sticker on the student's car, he quickly did a U-turn and pulled up in front of Ryan's car. This action by the rent-a-cop security officer effectively blocked him in and the furious Ryan could only watch helplessly as Michael Woodman disappeared off into the distance. Quickly he tried to call Randy as the overweight, self-important wanna-be cop climbed out of his vehicle and rapped on the driver-side window, waving for Ryan to lower it. Ignoring him, Ryan tried to give his partner the bad news, infuriating the security guard and causing him to undo the flap on his side-arm and start pounding on the window.

The very unhappy Ryan signaled "okay" to the guard and fished into his pocket for his leather ID wallet, accidently revealing his holstered gun. This resulted in the security guard immediately pulling out his own weapon and backing up a few paces, gun pointed at Ryan. During all this, the co-ed was shedding copious tears but still continued to text her friends, oblivious to the drama unfolding right in front of her.

After climbing out of his car, Ryan eventually calmed the security guard down by showing him his badge but Michael Woodman was long gone. Fortunately the damage to his car was minor enough for him to be able to drive but the guard's car blocking his path and he had to wait another 30 or 40 minutes before the police arrived. The patrol police officer had started to take statements when the wanna-be cop informed him that the man involved in collision was an FBI agent.

After carefully checking Ryan's ID, the patrol officer wanted to know what Ryan had been doing there outside the college and why someone from Kansas City was here in Pittsburgh. He was not happy to hear that Ryan was on a confidential assignment but he was sufficiently astute and experienced to know that interfering with an active FBI investigation was not a good idea. After noting down Ryan's particulars, he signaled the college security guard to move his car back and waved Ryan on his way. If nothing else, it was amusing that an operation of one of the much-vaunted FBI had been screwed up by a college student.

Turning his attention back to the crying student, he handed her a ticket for dangerous driving, whereupon she immediately copped an attitude and started screaming about police brutality. Losing patience, the patrol officer snapped at her that she had just interrupted an undercover FBI operation and that she was lucky that he didn't arrest her for interfering with a criminal investigation. At which point, the student exclaimed, "I did? Oh how exciting!" and, ticket firmly clenched between her teeth, she immediately started texting her friends, tears and anguish forgotten.

Bemused by what was going on but deciding he needed to get back to work, the security guard got back in his cruiser, put his vehicle in reverse and, without looking, crunched straight back into a car exiting the campus. The police officer, barely able to contain his laughter, pulled out his pad and walked over to the latest car wreck. Already he could see the reaction of his buddies in the bar when he told them about this at their regular relaxation in a bar at the end of their shift. Not only was a Fed rear-ended by a ditzy student but an idiot of a campus guard had held the agent up while in pursuit of a suspect and then managed to back straight into what appeared to be the car of a senior college administrator. The police officer's only regret was that he had not video-taped it all because he wasn't sure that he could adequately describe the total farce. Then, as he noted down the particulars of this latest incident, he wondered what that FBI agent had really been doing there outside the college. Shrugging, he decided that it was none of his affair but he would still mention it to his duty sergeant, just in case.

After losing at least an hour and having no idea where Michael Woodman had gone, Ryan managed to get through to Randy to fill him in what had happened. Listening to Ryan's recitation of events, Randy sighed heavily and said, "Are you kidding me? You got rear-ended by a college student, held-up by a security guard and had to pacify a police officer regarding what you were doing outside Hathaway College." He paused and then asked, "You didn't tell him anything, or did you?"

"No, of course not. Give me a break, will you? This has been a bad morning and I have yet to contact my insurance company. Anyway, any sign of Woodman?"

"Not yet, no. Hopefully he's on his way here although I imagine he's stopped for lunch somewhere as it's getting near that time. I shudder to think that Woodman might have gone to the house yesterday and has taken off back home.

"Anyway, on your way over here, grab me a burger and fries…. and some coffee, will you? Let me know when you've got them and are getting close to the Woodman house. I'll drive around the corner and meet you to get the food and you can take up my position." Randy paused, and then added, "And don't get rear-ended this time."

"Oh screw you," muttered Ryan but did as he was asked.

It was not long before Ryan was positioned a couple of hundred yards down and across the road from the Woodman House. Another 30 minutes passed and he saw Randy re-park his car about the same distance from the house but facing towards him. Now both men had the house covered and regardless of which direction Michael

Woodman took, one or other would be able to tail him. The question they both were asking was where Woodman was likely to go after visiting the house. Would he head back to wherever he had stayed the previous night or would he start the return journey? Hopefully it would be the former so that both agents could fill their tanks before the long drive back to Arkansas.

Collecting his laptop, notes and other items from Hathaway College had been quick and painless because the Dean's secretary had everything packed up and ready for him. Michael did not see the Dean and suspected, correctly, that he was avoiding him, possibly because of unpaid salary and sick leave. As far as Michael was concerned, the loss of a few hundred dollars was more than compensated by the absence of hassle and the promise of a strong recommendation.

Upon leaving the college, he headed back to his motel to unload his vehicle. Reloading the next morning would take a few minutes but at least his vehicle would not look like a mini-moving van when he went to the house. Additionally, going back to the hotel and unloading would use up some time which, together with refilling his tank and having lunch, would put him on schedule to meet up with Linda. Then he thought about things. Did he really want to get his clothes and the pitifully small number of items that reminded him of his childhood? Deciding, Michael resolved to go back to his hotel and because it was not yet noon, he could check out and save an additional night's room charge. That would save him about $100, money that he could ill afford.

It was a matter of only a few minutes to settle his bill and Michael was on his way back to Southampton. He would call Linda while on the road. As he drove, Michael thought about where he would stay for the night and, based on what he could tell from the map, it might help him decide where he should look for his next victim. It also occurred to him that because he had left Pittsburgh earlier than planned, he would get back to sharing a bed with Bella at least a half to a full day sooner than expected, and that was a definite bonus.

As he drove Southeast on I79 and headed towards I40, Michael called Linda. "Look, I've been thinking," he said. "It's a bit pointless stopping by and getting my clothes. They are less than fashionable and the last time I looked, they were showing signs of wear and tear."

"Oh?" said Linda.

"Yes. Look, it would be better all-round if you simply box them up and donate them. The tax write-off might help."

"Possibly," said Linda before adding, "So you are not coming here. I can understand that but don't you even want to see our children?"

"Is there any point?" asked Michael laconically. "We were never that close and by now, I doubt that they even care about me now."

"No, I don't think they do since you've been gone from their lives for so long." She paused before saying, "Okay, go back to wherever it is you came from and, frankly, good riddance. Just tell your lawyer to get in touch with mine and we'll call it quits. Goodbye Michael, and enjoy the rest of your miserable life." With that, Linda shut down her cell-phone. Was that how marriages usually ended? Twenty years gone just like that? Well, it was Michael's decision and, if she was honest, it was all for the best. Now she and the children could get on with their lives.

Outside in the street, Randy and Ryan watched for the approach of Michael in his SUV. The hours inched by and Randy started to feel nervous. Logic indicated that they hadn't missed him, so where was he? The man had collected his things from Hathaway College that morning but where had he gone after that? Had he left everything at his hotel and was now getting lunch before heading over to his former home? It was already three o'clock, so where was he? With a sinking feeling, Randy realized that it was possible that Michael might have taken off back to Southampton that morning and simply not bothered to go to the house. By any measure, this operation had now become a disaster. He was reluctant to abandon his watch but when he saw Linda leave the house, he realized that it was unlikely that Michael was due here any time soon, if at all. He signaled to Ryan and pointed for him to follow Linda while he remained on watch at the house.

After talking things over with Ryan by phone, Randy in his heart of hearts knew that they had lost Michael Woodman. With great reluctance, he called Steve and told him of the no-show situation. Then Randy told him about Ryan being rear-ended and how he had been unable to follow Michael. Steve listened intently and, like Randy, muttered, "You have to be kidding me," but thinking, 'This is a disaster.' He really had no idea what his agents should do. They could stay on watch for a few more hours, possibly overnight or they could head back home. With a sinking feeling, Steve knew that their quarry had escaped and it was all over. He told Randy to hold on for a little while longer just in case Michael turned up but that possibility looked increasingly unlikely.

After hanging up, Steve cursed loudly. How had the man the man escaped again? The rearing ending of Ryan had given the man a window of an hour or more and rather than go to the house, he could have just taken off again back to Southampton. A quick look at the map told him that there were several routes back to Arkansas from Pittsburgh and given the several hours' lead Michael had, the odds of finding him again were almost vanishingly small. He toyed with and then dismissed the thought of putting out a BOLO on the man. He could be anywhere and multi-state alerts like that had a nasty habit of back-firing. No, all he could do was to tell his agents to hang on for a few more hours just in case and then head back in the morning.

With a sick feeling, Steve made notes on what he had heard and the instructions he had given his agents. What was it about this man Michael Woodman? He had all the skills of Harry Houdini and the Scarlet Pimpernel wrapped into one. Sadly it bore in upon him that the actions he had taken might unleash a shit-storm because he had gone against protocol. Washington would not be pleased when it all came out. He sighed loudly and then proceeded to write a report on everything that had happened since he had first heard about Michael Woodman. It would take a lot of time and effort to compile the report but he knew he was going to need it, and possibly quite soon.

CHAPTER 23

Police officer Daniel Roberts had finished his shift and given his after-action report to the duty sergeant, Lionel Baxter. After hearing about the two car wrecks and allowing his laughter subside, Lionel went in to see his lieutenant and informed him of the covert FBI operation involving a Special Agent out of Kansas City. The lieutenant was as surprised as his sergeant and Officer Roberts about this operation and he promptly reported it to his captain, Walter Thomas. Capt. Thomas, after listening carefully to what was said to him, thought for a moment and then called his friend and golfing buddy Milton Rothman over at the FBI Pittsburgh Field Office.

When he got through and the two men had exchanged their habitual joshing, Thomas then said, "Hey Milt, what's this I hear about a covert FBI operation over at Hathaway College?"

"What are you talking about, Walt? We don't have any operations going on over there. That place is scarcely a hot bed of anything criminal apart from some kids smoking weed, and that's so common nowadays it's hardly worth worrying about."

"I didn't think so," said Walt Thomas. "So what was someone from Kansas City doing there?"

"Did you say Kansas City? Hmm, I have no idea what that's all about but I'll look into it. Usually agents from one field office will inform the local office of what's going on and commonly liaise with the locals, so this is very much out of the ordinary." He paused and then asked, "What was the name of that agent? He *was* an FBI agent, wasn't he?"

"The patrol officer Daniel Roberts who talked to the guy is pretty experienced and no fake badge would fool him. No, this was the genuine article."

"Okay, thanks, I'll look into it and get back to you once I know what's going on. It might be nothing but when a field office ignores protocol, then something's up and I want to know what."

"Thanks Milt. Now you've got my curiosity all stirred up. If there's something going on in my city, I want to know about it."

"No problem. Hey, are we up for a round on Saturday?"

"Sure thing, buddy, I'll look forward to it. Besides I want to get back that $100 you took off me last week," and he laughed.

After hanging up, Walt Roberts thought about the conversation. Although Milt was a good guy and a friend, he was still FBI and the FBI always kept things tightly wrapped, rarely sharing anything unless they absolutely had to and this situation probably did not fall into the category of needing to be shared. Whereas what he had heard might amount to nothing, he decided to take it on up the ladder to the precinct commander. If whatever it was could possibly involve the Pittsburgh Police Department, then it was up to the senior brass to deal with it…that sort of thing was well above his pay grade.

Lunch finished, Michael had a quick look at the map and tried to decide where he would stop for the night. There were lots of choices, some promising and others less so, and in the end, he decided to keep driving until he started to feel tired and find somewhere to stay with lots of off-shoots from the interstate where he could kill someone. Then it occurred to him that he had not spoken to Bella in several days so he called her. Admittedly he had had several things on his mind but neglecting to talk to Bella would not be easily forgiven by her. Before leaving the diner, he bought a mobile charger for the phone just in case anyone asks why the phone was switched off. Bella would be one person who might ask about that. To avoid any awkward questions, he paid cash, as he had with most of the motels on the drive up.

After she picked up, Michael, "Hey Bella, it's me."

"Michael, where have you been? I thought that you would call me when you got to Pittsburgh."

"My phone went dead. Anyway, I've now got a recharger for the car so I'm calling you on my way back home."

"You're coming home?"

"Yes, absolutely."

"Did everything go well? Did you have any problems?"

"No, surprisingly I didn't. I went to Hathaway College this morning to collect my lecture notes, lap-top and things…"

"What about….er…your clothes and other things from home? How did that go?" interrupted Bella, anxious to hear how the meeting went with the soon-to-be ex-wife.

"I didn't bother."

"What? You just left them? Why on earth did you do that?"

"Well, I got to thinking. Most of my clothes were getting a bit seedy and, to be honest, I really did not want to confront Linda. At this stage, being served with divorce papers and all, there is not a whole lot to say to each other. Besides, I have started a new life with you. So, in answer to your question, one of the important things to do when starting a new life is to get rid of the old stuff."

"But what about things from your childhood, you know, keepsakes and that sort of thing?" asked a perplexed Bella.

"All gone. They were all part of my old life and that is definitely over. My life is now with you and I really don't want to be reminded of the past. It wasn't that great anyway, so…"

"Oh Michael, that is wonderful. Did you say that you are on your way home?"

"Yes, and with luck I should be there late afternoon or early evening tomorrow. It's a long drive but I am really looking forward to being back with you. It's been too long since we were together and I miss you."

Bella and Michael chatted a little longer and then she said, "A funny thing happened a couple of days ago, Michael."

"Really? What was that? Nothing serious, I hope."

"That depends on what you call serious," said Bella and then went on to tell him about the conversation that Cindy had overheard and the subsequent conversation that she had had with Jack Olmsted. "It's all nonsense of course but I do wonder what the FBI was thinking when they suspected you of being a serial killer."

Although Michael felt a chill running down his spine, he made light of Jack Olmsted's comments. "Me? A serial killer? What nonsense. Was he serious in what he said? I know Jack and he always struck me as someone who was pretty sane and sensible. Surely there's been some sort of mistake."

"That's what I said…I told him that it was ridiculous. I cannot imagine anyone less likely to be a killer than you."

"Neither can I," agreed Michael. "Given half a chance people will always think the worst but this is surely above and beyond what anyone would do. It's ridiculous."

"Yes, that's true but why would anyone, let alone the FBI, think such a thing?"

"I have no idea but I really don't like it. I don't even own a gun, so how could I kill anyone?" said Michael fervently but thinking, 'So I was right, people are looking into me and trying to follow my movements. I'm sure that I didn't leave any real clues anywhere but someone somehow has been connecting the dots. Well whatever is going on, the first thing I'm going to do is get rid of that gun, the potatoes and everything else. The good thing is that I bought that charger and can explain why my phone was switched off.'

"Neither do I," said Bella. "I really want you back home and for you to clear your name."

Michael hesitated for a moment before saying, "That really is not a good idea, Bella. As I always tell my students, you cannot prove a negative; consequently, I can't prove I'm not a serial killer and clear my name. No, the best thing is to ignore it all and sooner or later, preferably sooner, everyone will forget about these ridiculous allegations and we can get on with our lives together."

"I suppose you're right," said Bella hesitantly. Michael's words reassured her and the thought that he was openly admitting that his life was to be with her from now on was wonderful news. Thankfully she could ridicule all these stupid allegations, especially if he could get a teaching position at Hood State College. Quickly she added, "How did things go at Hathaway College? You didn't say."

Although he was about to say that she had interrupted him, Michael said, "Oh they were great. The Dean and probably the College President will write good references for me and as I've got all my teaching notes, I'm hoping that I can start there soon without having to do a whole lot of work before I can get started. The important thing is that I may be on my way to making a new career, one I'll share with you."

"Oh that's so wonderful," said Bella fervently. "I'm so glad." She paused and then said, "I simply can't wait for you to come home. You'll have warm and very welcoming arms waiting for you. So, drive carefully my darling…we've got our whole lives ahead of us."

"That we have," said Michael. "This whole nonsense will go away, I promise."

"I hope so," said Bella. "I really hope so."

Michael plugged his phone in to recharge it and drove carefully for about 70 miles. On his way through Kentucky, he spotted a bridge up ahead. The traffic was light and when Michael pulled over, he grabbed the gun, the box of ammunition, potatoes and rubber gloves, stuffed them all into a plastic bag in which he punched a couple of holes and, as he crossed the bridge, he tossed everything into the river, making sure that there was no passing traffic before he did so. As he resumed his drive, Michael carefully thought about whether there might be anything incriminating left in his car. There was nothing he could think of but he would thoroughly check the car and everything in it as well as clean it when he stopped for the night. He was disappointed that he would have to put his hobby on hold indefinitely but better that than run the risk of being caught. Even the thought of being arrested let alone being put on trial filled him with horror. He would rather kill himself than be put through that.

As he drove, Michael thought about what he had said to Bella. He really was starting a new life and that was a sort of catharsis. He felt sad that his marriage to Linda had ended the way it had and felt a small twinge of guilt over his children. When had things gone so wrong with Damion and Rebecca? He realized that he and Linda should never have married. They were both nice people but if he was honest, he would have to admit that they were really a poor match for each other. That, however, was something that he could not do anything about now, if he ever could. Then he started to think about his killing spree. Why had he done it? The killing spree, while it lasted, had given him some sort of visceral pleasure but he really could not explain it. The psychiatrists probably could give him an explanation but that was something he could never discuss with anyone.

The more pressing considerations for him, however, were the who, the why and the how anyone would suspect that he was the killer. Both the who and the why were important but the how was critical. He assumed that someone very smart at the FBI had been assigned to investigate the killings or had somehow stumbled across them while looking into something else. The reason for the FBI to look into unsolved serial killings was obvious once they had appeared on their radar, so to speak. It really did not matter who was leading the investigation; the essential point was that someone was looking into them. But just how had they connected the dots and decided that he, Michael Woodman, might possibly be the killer? Michael turned the matter over in his mind but could not reach a conclusion; he then decided that he would let his sub-conscious mind deal with it. He had several hundred miles of almost mindless driving ahead of him and that should provide sufficient time and opportunity for something to rise to the surface to account for what seemed to be happening.

The vehicle ate up the miles and Michael wondered again whether he could give up killing people. As long as the FBI or anyone else might be watching him, he could never kill again. That was a bit of a disappointment, but reality had to be respected. He was aware that fear of imprisonment probably deterred more people from criminal acts than any spiritual or religious beliefs. By the time he found a motel, ate dinner and then settled in for the night, Michael realized that he was very tired. "Just as well that I don't dare go out again," he muttered. "I might have got careless and that would have been disastrous."

As he lay in bed, he started to wonder again what had clued the FBI into his activities. There had been no real evidence left behind and no rationale for the killings so the fact that someone had honed in on him was astonishing. How had they done it and what had steered them in his direction? He reasoned that any evidence connecting him to the killings was all circumstantial but connecting the dots must have been the work of one or more very smart people. Because the murders had been randomly committed in different states, at varying intervals and always some distance from any large towns or cities, it was a mystery that he might have been identified. He could understand how the FBI might have been called in, probably by State Police trying to deal with random and inexplicable murders but how had the FBI identified him? He had been so careful not to leave anything behind. There had been no obvious connection between his victims; they were just there and that was that. Not even he could explain why he had picked them out. One day he might discover a rationale for his actions and choice of victims but for now, he would just go sleep. As he had said to Bella, he was starting a new life and everything had to be left behind.

It was late and both Randy and Ryan were tired. Their backs ached, their rear-ends were sore and they were decidedly hungry. Taking intermittent bathroom breaks and alternating with each other for coffee runs had been tedious and wearing on them. Finally Randy admitted defeat and called Steve Wellington at home.

"Sorry boss, Michael Woodman was a no-show. Mrs. Woodman went off to that coffee shop of hers for the rest of the afternoon and then returned home, presumably after it closed. Later, a limousine collected her and she joined someone for dinner at a very up-scale restaurant. She's just returned home and now the lights have gone out. It looks as though she's in for the night. We could hang on here in case Woodman shows up but, to be honest, that doesn't look very likely."

"No, don't bother," sighed Steve. "That man had only two things to do in Pittsburgh. We know he went to Hathaway College this morning and he either stopped by the house yesterday or he just skipped meeting his wife altogether. As you might say, Randy, it's a bust." He paused and then said, "Okay, call it a night and you might as well head on back here in the morning. By the way, both of you start thinking about your reports on the way; it's a long drive so you'll be able to compose and polish them as you go. After the local police identified Ryan because of his being rear-ended, I'm sure that there's going to be a major fall-out because of you two being in Pittsburgh without anyone, notably me, informing the local field office that you were there." Steve sighed deeply. "Ah man, what a fucking disaster. Of course, the way things have been going with this case, it's always possible that Woodman might go over to the house tomorrow but I wouldn't count on it." He paused for a moment and then said, "No, just get back here and let's hope that something turns up down the road."

Steve hesitated again and then added, "I should think that by now the Pittsburgh Field Office are well aware that you two were up there. I haven't heard anything yet but I have a nasty feeling that I'm going to hear about it very soon. This could turn into a nasty mess, so take care what you put into your reports. Come to think of it, I suggest that you and Ryan make a start on them tonight before you go to bed. Oh, by the way, don't either of you even think about getting a speeding ticket….I've got enough to worry about as it is." Steve sighed again as he thought about what might be about to descend on him.

When she got home from the coffee shop, Linda called Victor and told him that not only didn't Michael show up but he had told her to donate all his clothes and other things. In effect, he wanted nothing from the house.

"That's interesting," said Victor. "So he's thinking of something along the lines of out with the old, in with the new, is he?"

"That's what it looks like," agreed Linda. "I didn't really want to see him but it's sad that he didn't want to see the children. He's a pretty heartless individual if he can do that. Abandoning his clothes I can understand but to reject his own flesh and blood, that's something else, isn't it?"

"People are strange," said Victor but thinking, 'Your Michael is a whole lot stranger than most. If he's a serial killer, not bothering with his children is the least of his mental problems. He's one sick SOB and no mistake.' Victor then went on, "Well I suppose we can celebrate that it seems Michael is gone from your life, can't we? Can I take you out to dinner tonight? Perhaps the kids might want to come too if they're not otherwise engaged?"

"Actually they're with their friends but yes, a celebratory dinner would be delightful."

"Great. I'll send the car for you a little later."

Seated in the restaurant and sipping pre-dinner drinks, Victor asked, "How is *The Café on Main* doing?"

"Actually it's doing very well. Business seems to be booming and that new line of pastries has been a great hit. They are selling so well, I might have to find an additional supplier." Linda paused and then added, "Is there a reason for asking or are you just making polite conversation?"

"Both actually," said Victor. "Obviously as a businessman, I want the investment to pay off and the Café to be a huge success but there is always the question of Michael."

"Michael?"

"Your divorce is on track now and, cynical man that I am, I wonder whether he knows anything about *The Café on Main*. If he does, there is always a risk that he might sue for alimony…I'm sure your attorney mentioned this possibility."

"Yes he did but said it was something that he and Michael's lawyer would address if it even came up….he said I shouldn't worry about it. Child support might be something else as the judge would decide that. Frankly I don't want it but that may not be my decision to make."

"Probably not," agreed Victor. "From what I gather, Michael collected his lecture notes and other things from Hathaway College…."

"How did you find that out?" asked Linda.

"One of my people checked up on it…nothing terribly difficult, I assure you. Anyway, if Michael collected his notes and lecture outlines from the college, then it is reasonable to assume that he is thinking of going back into teaching but not at Hathaway, I gather. I have no idea where he might be thinking of going but I'm sure it will come out one day. The important thing is that if he does go back to teaching, then he should have a decent income and any claims to alimony will not be a problem."

"That's a relief…I should hate to think that all our hard work and your trust and backing of me could be in jeopardy. That would be terribly unfair…actually downright wrong if you ask me."

"I doubt that it would have come to that," said Victor. "But it is always better to avoid conflict if at all possible. Anyway, it is not over by any means but the end, meaning your divorce, is in sight. How do you feel about it?"

"It is very strange. Twenty years of marriage and a life together will be gone with just the bang of a judge's gavel," replied Linda. "I have two children and a house out of the marriage but everything else seems to have gone up in smoke. As I say, it is all very strange…. and hard to grasp. I suppose everyone must go through this sort of inner turmoil. It seems to be all such a pity."

"Do you regret initiating the divorce? Would you want Michael back, I mean?"

"No, that ship has sailed. Even if I had wanted him back, which I don't, it is hard to imagine him even wanting to come back. Nobody walks away from a marriage after all those years without really, you know *really* wanting, to go off on their own. As I say, it was all a bit of a shock but if I'm honest, it was probably a long time coming and not only didn't I see it approaching, I probably never even saw the straws in the wind."

The regret in Linda's voice was obvious but Victor was not sure whether it was for the break-up of the marriage, for missing of the signs of the impending disaster or simply the wasted years. Whatever the source of her unhappiness and regrets, Victor was undecided how best to address them. "I'm told that this sort of thing, you know, confused feelings, is very common but the sensible thing is to accept life for what it is and move on. Anyway, all being well, you will be a single woman again in only a matter of months, if not sooner. Not only that, you're becoming, no, you've become, a successful business woman in your own right….and that is marvelous. My only question is, will you still want to marry me once all the dust has settled?"

Linda looked at Victor and smiled warmly, "Silly man, of course I will. Even Damion and Rebecca seem to like you and that in itself is almost a miracle."

"Am I that hard to like or get along with?" said Victor in mock horror.

"No, of course you aren't. It's just that those two, like all teenagers, don't seem to like anyone over the age of 25 and neither of us has seen the age of 25 for more years than I care to think."

The pair of them laughed companionably and then clinked their wine glasses together in a silent toast. Their future looked assured, and very rosy at that.

Bella went into *The Second Street Café* the following morning in a much better frame of mind than for the past few days. Just talking to Michael had been a major relief and, she decided, all those accusations did indeed appear to be a load of old rubbish, as Michael would say. She was annoyed with herself for letting doubts cloud her judgement; she *knew* Michael and it was both sad and foolish to have let unfounded gossip get in the way of her relationship with him. Cindy, Andrew and Angela loved to gossip and talk about their customers and everyone they knew. Their attitude was understandable if reprehensible but Jack Olmsted…well, he should have known better. It was incredible that he had been gossiping about someone that was under investigation in a public place. She was almost of a mind to file a complaint and then thought better of it. Even acknowledging that a Sheriff's Deputy put credence in an obviously foolish rumor could have long-term repercussions. No, it was best to say nothing and, however difficult it might be, she still had to treat Jack the same as always. If he ever mentioned the subject again, she'd just laugh and josh him for being so naïve. As Michael said, let it slide and the rumors would die on their own.

She called out cheerily to Angela in the kitchen and smiled warmly at Andrew as he sat checking the accounts for the diner. It was a chore to balance the books each and every day but at least they had never been audited because of his meticulous attention to detail. As she walked past him, Bella said, "Hey I got a call from Michael yesterday."

"Really?" said Andrew. "Did everything go well up there in Pittsburgh?"

"He said they did. He got all his teaching materials from the college and both the dean and the college president said they would write good references for him, which is really a blessing. I'm sure their positive endorsements of him and his ability will go a long way with Hood State College."

"Excellent…I'm glad to hear it. Ah…how did things go with his wife?"

"Actually, they didn't"

"What does that mean?" asked Andrew.

"Apparently, upon reflection, Michael decided that he really didn't want his clothes and things. As he said to me, we're starting a new life together so why carry over any of the old stuff?"

"That's interesting…and probably a healthy attitude," said Andrew. "I take it that he didn't actually meet up with her then."

"No, he decided not to, if only to avoid any risk of a confrontation. As you know, Michael is pretty laid-back and, for him, an in-your-face attitude just doesn't fit."

"Hmm…that sounds very sensible of him. I obviously don't know all the ins and outs of his marriage but I've always heard that keeping the two parties as far apart as possible is always a sound position to take, as we both know."

Before Bella could respond to Andrew, and basically to agree with him, Bob and Sam walked in and Bella greeted them with a warm smile, "Hi guys, I suppose you want coffee and the usual, right?"

"Right on, girl," said Bob. "As for the coffee, we need lots of it….strong and black like always."

"You got it!" said Bella, and hurried to put their order in and collect mugs for them together with the coffee carafe.

After Bella moved away to attend to another customer who had come in, Bob leaned towards Sam and said quietly, "You know, this is the second time in almost as many days that I get the feeling she's been laid….and good luck to her."

"Well I hope not," said Sam. "Her Michael's off up North somewhere and I hate to think that someone else might be taking care of her."

"Nah, not our Bella. No, I'm sure that she's just happy about something. Maybe he's coming back today and she's looking forward to a fond and passionate reunion."

"I expect you're right," said Sam. "At least I hope you're right. That Michael's a good guy and I wouldn't want to see him get hurt."

"Neither would I," said Bob. "Hey, I heard something about him…"

"You mean that he's applying to go to some college or other? You know, going back to be a professor again."

Swallowing the gossip that he was about to share with his friend, Bob erred on the side of caution and said, "Yeah, that's what I heard. It would be great for both of them if he does. I always said that he was a bit too smart to be a cook."

"You're right but he could cook a real good omelet and his hash browns were always great. Still, Angela is doing pretty good in the kitchen and she's getting better by the day."

"Yes, she's doing real good and being as attractive as she is, that's a plus, isn't it? Andrew seems to have won the lottery with that one, didn't he?"

After that, the two men chatted on about other things until their food arrived.

Bleary-eyed and dropping with fatigue, Randy and Ryan made their way into Steve's office. Without a word, they handed over their reports and Steve thanked them. Then he held out copies of his own report to the two men, saying, "Guys, you look like shit. Read this and let me know what you think but I suggest that you go home and get some rest. We can discuss everything later this afternoon once you've got some shut-eye and had showers and things. Okay?"

Mutely, both men nodded and went home, too tired to even think but they knew that they'd have to go through Steve's report carefully before they met up again later. Although exhausted, they were aware that the shit already had or was about to hit the fan over their trip up to Pittsburgh. The actions of a stupid co-ed were going to have a ripple effect - the only question was how serious that would be.

Vincent and Madge were idling over their late afternoon coffees and pastries at *The Café on Main*. It had taken longer to free up some time to get to the place than Vincent would have liked, but he was a busy man. Anyway, they had now got here and it was worth the effort.

Marge looked at Vincent and said, "This was such a treat Vince, thank you."

"It was my pleasure and I'm glad that you suggested coming here. It was everything you said, and more. I'll tell you one thing though, I couldn't do this too often."

"Why not?"

"I feel as though I've put on 10 pounds just looking at those pastries, let alone eating them. No dinner for me tonight Madge, my waistline can't take it."

Madge laughed. "I'm so glad that you approve of this place."

"That I do," said Vincent.

As their coffee cups were refilled by the server, Madge suddenly asked, "Hey Vince, did anything come of that…er…matter that Mr. Bascombe asked you to look into for him? You know what I'm talking about, don't you?"

"Yes I do. As for coming to anything, the answer's no. Whatever was potentially a problem seems to have either been settled or gone away on its own, thank goodness."

"Oh that's great. I hate the thought of Mr. Bascombe having any problems like that, although I really don't know what those problems might be."

"As I said, that's all died down and I can get back to doing my regular job. Hey, what about another pastry? I can feel my blood sugar dropping," and he laughed but thought, 'I should give Randy a call and find out what, if anything, developed with regard to Michael Woodman. Probably nothing but I want to be able to close this chapter.'

After each almost gobbled down a chocolate éclair, Madge suddenly asked, "Vince, are you happy with what you are doing? You know, being Head of Security at Bennet's? Is it really satisfying or what you want?"

Vincent looked steadily at his wife as he pondered her question. Eventually he said, "Well, it's not the same as being on the force, nowhere near. On the other hand, I am very well paid and have nowhere near the same level of stress, and certainly none of the danger. Am I satisfied? That's a good question. Most men, and women for that matter, when they retire face an emptiness, almost as though they no longer have any direction in their lives...which they probably don't."

"Go on," encouraged Madge.

"We've both seen far too many retired men wasting their lives playing golf or wandering aimlessly around supermarkets as their wives do the shopping or they sit around watching TV all day and drive their wives crazy. At least we've been spared that because I am very busy at Bennet's and I really do an important job. Basically, I have learned to make the best of things and, to be honest, I am truly grateful that I landed this job. As I said, our financial situation is better than it has ever been before and, if I'm honest, I have nothing to complain about." He smiled at his wife and said, "I am delighted the way things have worked out, As for being satisfying, every so often something comes up that requires me to do some detective work and that keeps things interesting. What life will be like when I retire from Bennet's is another matter but, hopefully, that is a long way off and at least we now know what retirement is all about and we are prepared. Now, do we just call it a day here or are we going to have one more pastry?"

As Madge looked at him in mock horror, Vincent added, "Don't look at me that way, I know you want another one too." To which Madge laughed and nodded in agreement. Just one more did sound good and to hell with the calories...she'd work them off in the gym tomorrow.

CHAPTER 24

A chastened Steve Wellington returned to Kansas City from being summoned to The FBI Headquarters in Washington, D.C. Having to explain, and justify, his recent actions with regard to the putative serial killer Michael Woodman had been a very unpleasant experience. Fortunately the complaint from the Pittsburgh Field Office had not risen to the Director or Assistant Director level but it had risen high enough on the totem pole for Headquarters to send a Lear Jet to bring him to D.C.

"So SAC Stephen Wellington," said the very senior Charles Willoughby. "You are telling me that you decided to ignore protocol and send two of your agents chasing after someone based only on suspicions?"

"Yes but our suspicions were…" said Steve.

"Your suspicions are just that, suspicions. They are not proof and circumstantial evidence along with innuendo and supposition cannot and will not permit indictment of a man who is innocent until proved guilty. This is one of the cornerstones of our Constitution and our Legal System. You would agree?"

Steve nodded mutely.

"Now I do understand your enthusiasm to catch a serial killer, if indeed this Michael Woodman fellow is that killer, but the protocols we have in place are there for a reason. Ignoring them not only causes problems within the Bureau but in this particular instance, your actions resulted in a great deal of embarrassment with the Pittsburgh police force." Charles Willoughby paused and then tapped the two piles of reports on his desk. "After carefully reading your report and those of your two agents Cunningham and Whitcombe, I can see that a great deal of effort went into the efforts to identify this serial killer. But there really is no proof and whereas none of us like coincidence, a good defense attorney would claim that this was such a case and argue for, and probably succeed in, having any and all charges dismissed. That we cannot have. And then we have this report from the Pittsburgh Field Office," and he tapped the smaller pile of reports on his desk. "And we also have here a summary of the very embarrassing conversations between our people and senior officers in the Pittsburgh Police Force. Not only are our people in Pittsburgh upset but also the local law enforcement officers are displeased, to put it mildly, that agents from a Field Office in another state felt that they could operate like cowboys in their city."

A very unhappy Steve started to explain what had happened and why he took the actions he did when Willoughby peremptorily held up a well-manicured hand to say, "SAC Wellington, you have had a blemish-free record to date and you are, well you were, on a fast track to move up here. I can understand the persuasive factors that might have induced you to do what you did in authorizing those two agents to follow the alleged suspect up to Pittsburgh and then tail him back to Southampton, Arkansas. The underlying assumption being that they might have caught him in the act or at least garnered enough incontrovertible evidence that Woodman is the killer to lead to arrest and conviction. However, merely because certain actions look to be a good idea, there is no need to pursue them, particularly when they jeopardize your career. The net result of all this is that Woodman might have learned of your interest in him, or may well do so shortly. At the very least, if he was the killer, then he would likely cease his activity for months if not years. At worst, Woodman, with the aid of an aggressive and greedy attorney, could well sue the Bureau for defamation of character. That action would cause even more embarrassment for us and we need to discourage anything like from happening."

"Do you mean I should apologize to Woodman for suspecting him of being a serial killer?" asked Steve in horror.

"No, of course not. That would only encourage him to sue us." Willoughby paused again and then said, "No, from now on, you will do nothing, and I repeat *do nothing*, with regard to this Dr. Michael Woodman. You will either safely and discreetly archive or destroy all your files and notes on the man together with those of Cunningham and Whitcombe. Unless Woodman should be caught in the act of killing someone with an axe in front of your building and be seen to do so by at least a dozen unimpeachable witnesses such as priests, nuns, officers of the court and the like, he is now a strictly hands-off person. He is untouchable from this day forth." Willoughby then stared hard at Steve before adding, "You will convey these instructions to Cunningham and Whitcombe. If any of you even thinks of undertaking any future cowboy actions like those we have just seen, your futures collectively and individually will become severely and permanently compromised. In fact, it is possible for your positions to be eliminated. Do I make myself clear?"

A stunned Steve could only say quietly, "Yes sir, I completely understand. This will never happen again, I can assure you."

"Good. I do not want to have to discuss this matter or anything like it again."

Willoughby nodded at Steve and then pressed a bell to alert one of his assistants that his visitor needed to be escorted from the building. After Steve had left, Willoughby looked at all the files on his desk and sighed. The case against Michael Woodman *was* persuasive, in fact very persuasive, but the fall-out from the action of the Kansas City people had tainted the case beyond acceptability. Yet another criminal, and a nasty one at that, would likely go free because of the unwise and precipitate actions of his agents. For a moment, he rued the passing of the old days when the FBI could almost do whatever it wanted without recourse or recrimination but those days were long gone, and perhaps for the best. Then he smiled; it would have been a major achievement if those KC people had been able to apprehend a serial killer but that didn't happen and probably never would. With another sigh, he stacked the reports together and then started to work on another project.

As he lamented to his wife later that day, "My job is no different from that of a filing clerk. Whatever happened to all that fun and excitement of chasing and catching criminals?"

"Oh I'm sure things aren't that bad," his wife assured him, earning her an undeserved glower from his husband together with a nasty grunt.

The next morning, Steve called Randy and Ryan into his office and conveyed to them in no uncertain terms what he had been told in Washington.

"But what about the evidence?" protested Randy.

"That is all circumstantial," said Steve and before Randy or Ryan could say anything further, he held up a hand and said very firmly, "This matter is officially closed as of now. You will securely archive everything to do with Michael Woodman and you will not, and I repeat, you will not, take any further action with regard to him." He stared at his two junior agents and said softly but menacingly, "We have been warned about this. Disobeying direct orders from Washington will result in our being sent to Alaska or somewhere equally inhospitable or even dismissal from the Bureau. I am sure that none of us want that to happen. So you are officially being told as of this moment to stand down on this matter of Michael Woodman."

Seeing the disappointed looks on their faces, Steve added, "Whatever our personal thoughts and opinions might be, we have received strict instructions and we *will not* disobey them. Understood?"

Randy and Ryan nodded and then Steve said, "You will need to contact that special agent down in Arkansas…"

"You mean Matt Downey?" asked Randy helpfully.

"Yes him. Not only that, you will tell Downey to tell that local Sheriff's Deputy…"

"Jack Olmsted?" asked Ryan.

"Yes him," snapped Steve. "And also tell that fellow Vince Dodson from that department store in Pittsburgh that what we have been dealing with was a serious case of misidentification. You can be apologetic, even grovel if you have to, but you must impress on everyone that this case is closed. If you have to, invent another suspect but don't give him a name or identify him in any way, and tell everyone that you are desperately sorry to have caused them any difficulties or to have wasted their time and efforts. As far as anyone is concerned, whether or not Michael Woodman is a serial killer is moot. It is over….do you understand?"

"Yes sir," said Randy and Ryan in unison. Neither man was stupid enough to go against orders from on high. The only thing that they were not looking forward to was telling Matt Downey, and by extension Jack Olmsted, that they had made a mistake. Telling that to Vince Dodson was even less inviting because the man had had too many years under the belt in a senior position in the world's largest police force to be fooled by anything either of them could say. Randy was even less enthralled by the thought of having to tell his father that the investigation of the murder at his bar had all been a bust. Both men sighed and went back to their cubicles, dreading the conversations that they would have to have with Downey, Olmsted and Vince.

Vincent sat across the desk from Victor Bascombe and after dealing with the routine affairs of Bennet's, he said, "I heard from Randy in Kansas City."

"The FBI man?" asked Victor.

"Yes, that's the man."

"And what did he have to say?"

"Apparently it was all a case of mistaken identity," said Vincent flatly.

"Mistaken identity? Are they saying that they got it all wrong about Michael Woodman? Really? And you believe them?"

"Well that's what they said. As far as they are concerned, it was all a mistake and they have no further interest in Michael Woodman, none at all."

"Good heavens," said Vincent. He paused for thought and then said, "Well then, no matter what we might think, Michael Woodman is off the hook." He paused again before adding, "That's a good thing really because I dreaded the thought of having to tell Linda that her husband of twenty-some years might be a serial killer. That would have caused her, and the children, unbelievable trauma. Probably so much so that she would never be able to hold her head up again. Perhaps it's all for the best because I doubt that she would even consider marrying me or anyone else for that matter if her husband was arrested as a serial killer. So, Vincent, no matter what we might think or what the FBI thought in the past, it is over and probably for the best."

"It's not for me to say, Mr. Bascombe, but I tend to agree with you. The book is now officially closed. I hope, really hope, that if Woodman was or is a killer, then he mends his ways and calls an end to his activities."

"He's sensible enough…I can scarcely say that he's sane…but certainly he's sensible enough to avoid any suspicion now or in the future." Victor sighed and added, "As you say, it's all over….and thank goodness. At least now Linda can get on with her life and never have to even address what her husband was or might be as a person." He paused again and muttered, almost to himself, "It's funny how things work out, isn't it? Michael Woodman, the serial killer that never was."

Jack Olmsted slid onto a bar stool facing Bella across the counter and asked for coffee and a slice of pie. As he washed down the last mouthful of pie with a swallow of coffee and also checked that no-one was in hearing distance of him, he suddenly said quietly, "Hey Bella, you remember that matter we talked about a while back?"

Bella nodded, and said equally quietly, "Yes. What about it?"

Jack, making sure that he avoided any hint of cynicism or irony in his voice, said, "Apparently the FBI thinks that it was all a matter of misidentification. As far as they are concerned, Michael Woodman had nothing to do any of those murders and they have no further interest in him whatsoever. As they told me, he's no longer a suspect or even a person of interest. Apologies all round although no-one would ever admit that they even had any suspicions of him."

"Really!" said Bella dryly.

"Yup," said Jack. "Case closed, sealed and disposed of. Sorry if I caused you any alarm but…" and Jack paused for a moment or two. "These things happen sometimes and probably more often than anyone would like. Again, I can only apologize if I caused any problems for you."

"Don't worry about it, Jack. You were just doing your job and no real harm was done. As I say, this stupid mistake didn't become a matter of local gossip because that would really have caused problems for everyone. I'm sure Michael will be pleased to hear this but while he didn't laugh about it, he thought that it was all a big mistake. So, matter closed. I hope that you'll still keep coming in here?"

"Of course Bella, wouldn't miss it. By the way, where is Michael these days?"

"Oh they've offered him a senior position at Hood State College and he's busy getting lectures and courses prepared. He starts soon but has a lot to do in preparation for the new semester."

"That's great. We'll miss him here but going back to being a professor makes sense."

"Not only that," said Bella. "Once his divorce is finalized, we'll be getting married."

"That's great, Bella, I wish you every success and happiness."

"Thank you, Jack. I know you mean it."

"Of course I do. Hey, will you still continue on here or will you think of moving to Hood?"

"Not for now. Perhaps in a year or two, you know, once things have settled down and Michael is comfortable there. But, you know, I really don't want to leave Southampton. It's been my home now for so many years that leaving would be difficult. Besides, *The Second Street Café* is so much a part of all our lives that I just can't think of leaving."

"That's good. We don't want to lose you here."

After a few more pleasantries, Jack Olmsted went back on patrol, relieved that his apologies had been accepted. In his heart, he really didn't believe that Michael Woodman was wholly innocent but that was not something he could or would do anything about. If nothing else, he knew when bucking the system could only cause trouble and this was a situation in which no-one would win if he did or said anything. He was a simple Deputy Sheriff and that was good enough for him.

It was with great excitement that Bella told Michael about her conversation with Jack Olmsted. "He was so embarrassed about it and even apologized."

"I told you it was all nonsense, didn't I?" said Michael laconically.

"Yes you did, and I never believed a word of it anyway. So, with that business behind us, let's hope that everything works out with Hood State College…and with your divorce too."

"Yes, let's hope that everything works out. Then we can get married and move on with our lives together…and the sooner the better."

Hey boss," said Randy, poised in the doorway of Steve's office. "Guess what? There's been another inexplicable murder…you know the type…no suspects, no motive, no evidence, nothing."

"I don't want to know," said Steve flatly.

"Apparently the killer used a potato silencer but he also filed the inside of the gun barrel so that they couldn't get any identification marks on the slug other than that it was a .38."

"Don't tell me, no cartridge or anything else was left behind and no-one saw a thing. Yes?"

"You got it. It was committed somewhere up in Illinois and, guess what, it happened about the time Michael Woodman could have gone that way on his trip up to Pittsburgh."

"That's a big "could have" isn't it? Sorry Randy, but no matter what we might think, not only will we pass on this, you had better not even think of talking to the police up there or to anyone else about this case or Michael Woodman. Got it? Unless you really want to get send to Guam or the Aleutian Islands, just file it away as an interesting tid-bit of information and forget it…and that is an order."

A few days later, Randy was visiting his parents for the weekend. Big Jim had arranged for a relief manager, so the three of them could enjoy a quiet dinner. After eating, the table cleared and the dishes washed, dried and put away, Randy and Big Jim sat out on the porch, sipping brandies and puffing on cigars.

After chatting idly for some minutes, Big Jim eventually asked, "Did anything come of that murder investigation?"

"Yes, I mean no," said Randy.

"So which is it, yes or no?" asked Big Jim mildly.

"No. Nothing came of it."

"I see," said his father but the irony in his voice was obvious.

"Oh we had a suspect but…" and Randy hesitated, trying to find the right words. "Well, it turned out to be a case of misidentification and…er…we were told to drop it. I really cannot talk about it."

"Misidentification? You were told to drop it?" and Big Jim barked a short laugh.

"What's so funny?" asked Randy testily.

"Randy, I was a police officer for as many years as you have been alive and when someone says it was misidentification and that he has been told to drop the case, I know what that means."

"And what does it mean?" asked Randy.

"When police officers, the FBI or anyone else is told to drop something, then I suspect, no I can *smell*, a cover-up."

"But dad…"

"No Randy, I understand, I really do. Cases get dropped for a variety of reasons but usually for political reasons or because the perpetrator has money, power or influence. You've been muzzled and I understand that." He took a long drag on his cigar and sipped some more brandy before continuing, "Well son, welcome to the real world. I understand and respect that you cannot talk about it but I suspect you know who the killer was but cannot do anything about it. These things happen and will continue to do so as long as people have enough money and influence to pervert the course of justice."

Randy stayed silent.

"As I said, welcome to the real world. This sort of thing will happen again and again. Regardless of what you think, my advice to you is to follow orders. Doing anything else will only damage your career and, in the end, solve nothing. Sooner or later, it will come out and you will be vindicated but that's off there in the future. Do your job and leave it alone. Okay?"

Randy nodded but said nothing.

Big Jim looked fondly at his son before saying, "I know it galls you but that's the way things are. Life is unfair, unjust and often cruel. There is nothing we can do about that. Now, to change the subject, who do you fancy for the NCAA?"

Michael Woodman sat behind his desk at Hood State College and reflected about things. The letters of recommendation from the dean and president at Hathaway College had not only landed him a job but he been appointed a full professor with a salary to match. His career was firmly back on track and he actually enjoyed teaching again. As he relaxed, he burst out laughing. People said that the perfect murder has never been committed but here he was, the one person who had committed not one, but several perfect murders. Of course, he could never kill again but that urge had been subsiding for some time. It was over. Soon, he and Bella would be married and this new phase of his life would be underway. As his laughter slowly quietened, there was a heavy pounding on his office door.